FRECKLED VENOM

COPPERHEAD STRIKES

JULIETTE DOUGLAS

BEARHEAD PUBLISHING

- BhP -

Brandenburg, Kentucky

BEARHEAD PUBLISHING

- BhP -

Brandenburg, Kentucky
www.bearheadpublishing.com

Freckled Venom
Copperhead Strikes
by Juliette Douglas

Copyright © 2013 Juliette Douglas
ALL RIGHTS RESERVED

Cover Photography by J.C. Leacock Photography

Cover Design & Layout by Bearhead Publishing
First Printing - November 2013
ISBN: 978-1-937508-23-4
1 2 3 4 5

Disclaimer

This book is a work of fiction. The characters, names, places, and incidents are used fictitiously and are a product of the author's imagination. Any resemblance of actual persons, living or dead is entirely coincidental.

NO PART OF THIS BOOK MAY BE REPRODUCED IN ANY FORM, BY PHOTOCOPYING OR BY ANY ELECTRONIC OR MECHANICAL MEANS, INCLUDING INFORMATION STORAGE OR RETRIEVAL SYSTEMS, WITHOUT PERMISSION IN WRITING FROM THE COPYRIGHT OWNER/AUTHOR

Proudly Printed in the United States of America.

ACKNOWLEDGMENTS

The author would like to thank the following:

Once again, the trusty, artsy, fartsy, creative duo of Drechsel & Drechsel of Bearhead Publishing have out done themselves. Making pages that sat in my computer for five and a half years, come to life. Enabling others to enjoy the tall tales that percolate around in this goofy boat washer's mind.

Rodney Bleidt, and Mary Ann Douglas, who continue to encourage me to pursue this new adventure in my life.

Jack Phelps, thanking you again for the wonderful title. Apparently a hit with readers.

My daughter, Suzi. My son, Ben, his lovely wife Liz and now their own little blue ribbon prize, Will. Your support and love means so much to me.

The folks who continue to surround Froggy Flats Farm. Jake, Jondra, Collin, John Case and Jared Shadowen.

My basketball buddies: Barb and Dick Page, and Sandra Lovett Cope. Many thanks for being the 'best-est' neighbors ever.

J C Leacock, photographer extraordinaire, whose photos continue to grace the covers of these books. Thank you.

And of course the folks whose boats I've washed over the years...without your continued support, none of this would have been possible. Thank you from the bottom of my heart.

Now...I'm ready for basketball season...bring on the HOOPS!

Go Marshals and Lady Marshals, Murray State Racers and UK Wildcats! (And from one of the trusty, artsy, fartsy Drechsels, that being Mary, don't forget UL Cardinals :)

DEDICATION

This book is dedicated to my grandparents

Harry and Lucetta Douglas

Who could really spin a yarn or two in their day.

CHAPTER ONE

Winter 1879

Rawley Lovett held the door open for his feisty deputy, Lacy Watson. Lacy slipped into the warmth of Stewart's Saloon followed closely by the marshal. Not surprisingly, the nasty weather outside had kept everyone home this dreary night.

Mike Stewart, barkeep and owner of Stewart's Saloon, looked up as the pair walked over to the bar. "Well, young lady, it sure is good to have you back," he said smiling. "What'll it be, coffee or a sarsaparilly?"

Surprised by Mike's reaction of her returning to White River, Lacy frowned. Two weeks ago, the marshal had touched raw feelings Christmas night, shredding what few intact nerves she still had further into pieces with his barbed words. The impact earlier of celebrating Christmas, in a family-like atmosphere that day, had also made stringy nerves even rawer with memories she had stuffed down so deep she thought they would never resurface, but they had. So Lacy disappeared, slinking away under the cover of darkness in the wee hours of a brutally cold morning following Christmas.

Rawley had followed. Her trail led him back to the cabin where the two of them had previously caught up with the Dillard Brothers, ending in two brother's deaths and one's capture. He'd convinced her to return to White River and so…here she stood, back in the same saloon she'd entered last fall, when once again following her prey had brought her back to the town she'd disappeared from over nine years ago. *I seem to be going around in circles here lately,* she thought.

Lacy's frown focused on Rawley, he just grinned. Turning to Mike again, she shrugged, finally answering his question, "Just water."

"Water, it is," he said, smiling even wider as he poured her a glass.

Mike's mind traveled back to the time when this copperhead had first graced his saloon. That soft husky voice of hers sure had him fooled into thinking a young boy stood on the other side of his bar asking for water. He'd never figured on the kid being wounded, he'd found that out later. The wound had festered causing a fever and blood poisoning. But even that hadn't stopped her from pouncing on Rawley, landing him flat on his back. It took a lot to land Rawley Lovett flat on his back, as big as he was. But, Lacy sure as hell did. *And White River hain't never been the same since*, he mused, chuckling to himself.

"Uh…you…Rawley?" he asked the marshal, almost as an after thought.

"Coffee," the marshal replied.

"Coming right up," Mike said. After sitting a cup of steaming coffee in front of the marshal, he rested his thick arms on the bar. His bulky frame leaned over hands wrapping around his own cup. "Never run into a female who could bust up them barroom brawls like you can, Missy," his eyebrows waggled at the red-head. "Hain't that right, Rawley?"

The marshal replied, "Uh-huh," watching Lacy's expression.

Lacy just rolled her eyes while she exhaled noisily. "Just doing my job, Mike," she replied. She proceeded to stare at the monstrosity that first caught her attention months ago still hanging on the wall behind the barkeep while she sipped her water. The painting hanging behind Mike was of a nude female, filmy gauze covered her body as she lay on a chaise. But, it still revealed the naked body underneath, leaving nothing to one's imagination. Done in colors of mostly white and various shades of blue, curly brown hair adorned the woman's head framing a cherubic face. The only vivid colors were her rosy cheeks and a big, bright red apple as she bit into it. Lacy sighed inwardly, *Men,* she thought.

"Yeah? Well...hain't had no more trouble, neither. Say, ya know, them old timers, is talking, what with the winter we been having, gonna be a rough spring. They say the river will be way out ta've its banks. Saying, gonna be a hot, dry summer, too."

"I swear Mike, you hear more drivel within these walls," Rawley sighed. "Anything else I should know about, besides the weather forecast?"

Mike puckered up his face. He looked at the hole still in his ceiling Lacy had put there with his scatter-gun last fall, putting an end to the brawl that had busted out in his saloon that night. Mike thought for a moment, and then said, "Naw...naw. Not that I can recollect, right now."

The marshal nodded. "Thanks for the coffee and the water," he said turning and leading the way across the floor and out the door, his deputy on his heels.

Stopping in front of Ezra's store, the outside coal oil lamp lit the words as Lacy and Rawley read a poster in the store's window announcing the Winter Dance coming up Saturday.

*Annual Winter Dance,
Saturday, 7PM, Crescent Hotel, music by:
White River String Dusters.*

"Hum...those boys are pretty good, wanna go?" Rawley asked.

"Who? Me?" Lacy thumbed at herself.

The marshal grinned at her response. "Sure, why not?"

FRECKLED VENOM
COPPERHEAD STRIKES

He watched those lips lock up tighter then the Denver Mint, once again, giving her customary silent no.

"You sure? Meet a lot of nice folks there that you haven't already met. Doc and Liv always come. It'd be good for you to socialize some away from the job."

Again, Lacy just shook her head no, and began walking back towards the warm office. She jammed her hands deeply into the pockets of her coat. She'd never been to a dance before. *I wouldn't know the first thing about what I'm supposed to do.* Sure, her mama had taught her some dance steps, back in happier times. How to curtsey, and things like that, but Lacy had never danced in a man's arms before. *Nah....I'll just tell Rawley I'll cover his shift that night, so he could go to the dance.* She thought.

Tilting his head he watched the freckled vixen shy away from him and continue across the street toward the office. That cute as a speckled pup copperhead had slammed into his world four months ago and the life he might've called normal back then had totally disappeared. 'Course falling in love with the petite spitfire didn't help matters none either. He sighed heavily beginning to follow his redhead.

She stopped just inside Rawley's office and now hers, too. Lacy once again looked around the familiar log walled surroundings. Pot-bellied stove for warmth and the always perking pot of coffee. Desk remained in the same place, in front of Rawley's quarters now. File cabinets pressed against a wall next to the door to his room, and a hallway that led to a back door and her quarters. A timepiece hung on the wall where it always did, next to the door leading into the cell block. A chain and lock was still on the gun rack, loaded with rifles for emergencies. A peg underneath held the keys to the cell block. A slab of wood held more pegs for coats, rigs and hats, to the left of the gun rack.

Just as suddenly as the familiar surrounding gave her a feeling of warmth, harsh memories of a whole other time pushed them away. Lacy recalled the awful night she showed up in this very office, the night her mother committed suicide. Changing the life she'd known forever, that one horrible night had been added to other unspeakable nights she had endured when she was a little girl and still resided at Carrigan Ranch.

Vern Edwards had been the marshal for White River at that time. She showed him the letter her mother had written. The letter incriminated her grandfather of atrocities. But when Vern couldn't convince Lacy to stay and press charges against her grandfather, he retrieved some supplies from Ezra's General Store and boxes and boxes of cartridges for the Sharps rifle he gave her along with powder and shot for her cap and ball Navy Colt pistol. With those items jammed into her saddle bags she left town. *Never to return*, she thought. *But here I am, deputy in the town of White River. A place I thought I'd never see again.* She sighed deeply.

After she'd left Vern that night, she had shoved the horrific memories into the dark recesses of her mind where daylight could never reach. Vern had suggested that she change her name, so her grandfather couldn't track her down. Prompting Lacy Watson to be born. After that, with her new name, Lacy Watson became a bounty hunter.

The reward money she did receive was puny at best and most times nothing at all. On those rare occasions when she did receive money, she would treat herself to a real knife and fork dinner and maybe a sit down in a real bathtub for a change in a room that had a nice soft bed and real sheets...clean...real sheets.

Lacy sighed inwardly. Those had been tough times for her.

Rawley, not paying attention after speaking to Doc outside, who had been on his way to Mike's for his nightcap, bumped into Lacy's backside as he entered the office. That jerked her out of her memories. Lacy threw a dirty look over her shoulder. Walking to the pegs she hung up her gear, and then silently went to her room.

FRECKLED VENOM
COPPERHEAD STRIKES

What the hell did I do, now? He thought, as fingers scratched dark stubble, watching Lacy go to her room. He finally hung his gear up, too.

CHAPTER TWO

    The chair gave its customary squeak as Lacy swiveled it around when Rawley came out of his quarters. "My, my, don't you clean up nice," she said, as her eyes trailed appreciatively from his glistening black hair, Wyoming summer sky eyes and down his long, trim body, stopping at his boots. Even they were shiny.

    Looking back up, she saw that his string tie remained crooked. She stood and reaching up, straightened it. Her hands continued working his collar down flatter, smoothing the material of his coat across his wide shoulders. She stopped abruptly, a flush beginning to travel across tawny freckles, as she realized that her hands were getting a little too familiar with the lawman. She quickly shied off, wiping hands down the sides of her britches in embarrassment. "Sorry, I didn't mean to do that."

    "Oh, I don't know, it felt kinda natural to me. Since you're sending me off to the dance…," Rawley paused, teasing her, "Unchaperoned."

    Lacy plunked herself back down in the chair, it squeaking in response. *Gotta get some oil for this damn chair,* she thought. Papers crackled as her fingers shuffled them around, as she announced, "You can take care of yourself, you're a big boy."

    "Still, I might need some protection," he returned. Sitting on the edge of the desk, he leaned in closer toward her. "Never know, I might get attacked," he said, teasing Lacy some more.

She caught a whiff of his tantalizing scent, and that nice smelly stuff he always bought at Ezra's. It sent her heart to tickling against her ribs. Lacy tried breathing out of her mouth to cut off that wonderful masculine scent. It didn't work. The scent still surrounded her senses. Rolling her eyes to hopefully hide her nose whiffing up that nice smelly stuff, she retorted, "Pffttt, you'd love every minute of it!"

Rawley grinned. "There's still time for you to get ready, and go with me, Sunshine," he added softly.

"Nah…you go ahead, enjoy turning all those female's heads. *Now why did I go and say something stupid like that,* she wondered. Clearing her throat, she added, "Besides, I wouldn't want to ruin *all* your fun," she said. Then shaking a finger in his face, she warned, "But, you'd better come back all in one piece. I don't feel like getting promoted over your stupidity."

"Awww, now…you think I'd do something like that to you?"

"Uh-huh," she said, knowingly. She shoved Rawley off the desk, giving him a dismissive wave of her hand. "Go on, Miss Liv is probably waiting on that first dance with you. Well, go on," she said, tossing a pencil at his chest.

"Okay boss," Rawley said, eliciting a big grin as he scooted out the door. Rolling his shoulders back, he adjusted the coat across his wide shoulders. His fingers pulled the sleeves down as he continued walking toward the hotel. He smiled to himself. Lacy had been warming up a little more each day since returning from the cabin this last time. He'd been finding out that she had a sense of humor, too.

Conversation seemed to flow easier for her, the more comfortable she became around him. As Liv had said, "Give her time." Even so, it would be hard dancing with someone else, and not the little copperhead he loved.

Being the marshal for a small community and the outlying area like White River, Wyoming had its advantages. Meals on a regular basis, boy, did he enjoy that. Liv's mouth watering cookies, he really enjoyed that. And folks he could have real conversations with, instead of talking to scraggly cows or his horse all the time.

Before this, Rawley Lovett had pretty much been a drifter, following the cattle drives, taking odd jobs, doing a little bounty hunting and just drifting until he came upon Sam Luebker hunkered down trading lead with some men he'd been after.

The rest became history. Sam took him under his wing as his deputy. When Vern Edwards passed away, Sam recommended him for this job and Rawley took it. For the first time in a long while, he had a place to call home, instead of the stars for his ceiling and wide open expanses for walls. He now had a roof attached to log walls, and that suited him just fine.

*   *   *

Lacy couldn't concentrate on the paperwork. The only noise in the office was her fingers drumming on the desk and the slow *tick-tocking* of the timepiece hanging on the wall. Burnt coffee eyes kept glancing at the clock, its hands moving way too slow. She couldn't help but wonder who Rawley could be dancing with.

She'd seen how the single women ogled the handsome and eligible marshal. Lacy had also noticed, how Rawley continued being friendly and polite, but not teasing or flirting with them, like he seemed to do with her. *Aw… we're just business partners, in a way. I work for him.* He treated her school days teacher, Miss Olivia Johnston, the same way, constantly teasing and flirting with her all the time, too.

Tossing the pencil across the desk, Lacy gave up speculating. Shoving arms into the sleeves of her coat, she went to make rounds.

The brisk, cold air fanned her cheeks, helping to clear

the cackling in her head. Lacy welcomed the change of temperature as she walked through the quiet town, checking doors.

Throngs of two and four seated sleighs lined both sides of the street closer to the hotel. A few fancy Surreys, buggies and buckboards added to the congestion. Horses and mules stood quietly, with the occasional blowing and shaking of harness, ringing in the winter stillness like sleigh bells. Puffs of grey fog rose above nostrils.

Strains of fiddles produced a catchy tune mingled with the sound of a bass thrumming along hitting the deeper notes. Lacy could pick out the tenor resonance of a banjo adding its voice to the music reaching her ears.

Turning the knob on the door, she pushed it open. Peeking her head around, Lacy looked inside Stewart's, only a few patrons' for Mike tonight. They'd all be streaming in after the dance. She threw a wave at Joe Jenkins, tending bar while Mike called the dances. The latch connected with a solid click as she closed the door. She moved to the edge of the walk. Lacy leaned against a post, jamming hands deep into the pockets of her overgrown coat. She stood, watching and listening. Nothing reached her ears except a few dog barks and the soft strains of music coming from the hotel. Gazing down the empty thoroughfare, the scent of wood smoke teased her nose. It layered itself halfway above the street, about porch roof high, creating a low grey ceiling. *Not a breath of wind, to whisk it away, cleansing the air,* Lacy noted. She straightened, her boot heels creating a light cadence across the scarred wooden planks as she moved toward the hotel.

Standing in the street, she faced the front of the hotel. Lacy gazed at the backdrop of dancing silhouettes from the hotel's windows. She decided to go around to the side and have a closer look see.

Peeking in the windows, she watched couples swirling around the floor. Lacy sighed wistfully. Groups of four or five stood together, the tinkle of their laughter reached through the closed windows. Lively music played as she spied the crusty town's doctor and her old school teacher Miss Olivia Johnston sitting, heads together, conversing. Lacy spotted Rawley, holding a glass of punch, plastered against the door jamb as if he were trying to keep it from collapsing. A gaggle of pretty women had him boxed in. "Serves him right," she muttered.

Rawley had been wondering how he might be able to untangle himself from the women who surrounded him. Trying to catch Liv's eye wasn't working; she was too busy listening to Doc. Rawley's eyes kept skirting over the heads of the women in front of him, seeking someone to rescue him. *Yeah....*he thought. *I need to be rescued.* Rawley had never given it much thought in the past, but these women just didn't interest him anymore, only that freckle faced copperhead did.

Continuing to rove his eyes around the room, he did a double take as light from the room highlighted a face with two huge black dots for eyes peering in the window. Rawley smiled, recognizing who the face belonged to. Handing the punch to one lady, he began pushing himself through. "Excuse me, ladies, excuse me."

Reaching the cold air, he took in a big breath, sticking a finger in the collar of his shirt. He tugged, trying to loosen it. Those women were suffocating him.

Coming around the corner of the building, his steps slowed as he continued to observe Lacy, hunched over peering into the window. Rawley took several steps closer. His warm caramel voice interrupted the muted sounds from within the hotel. "Find anything interesting in there?" He said.

She jumped, whirling. Lacy lifted her coat and pulled her weapon just as fast. A hand slammed the hammer down, the cylinder rolled, stopping under the nipple with a slight metallic click. Suddenly she recognized the tall man standing in the shadows. Her breath caught in her throat.

Recognizing the metallic click, Rawley quickly threw up his hands in surrender, saying, "Whoa, there, Sunshine, it's just me," continuing to hold up his hands.

"Dad Gummit, Lovett," she hissed. "You keep sneaking up on me like that, one of these days, I'm gonna blow a hole clear through you! Damn it! Don't do that to me," Lacy tersely said as she eased the hammer back down, slamming the pistol back in the leather. She gulped in more air trying to calm her sloshing insides.

"Little touchy there. Huh…Sunshine?"

Jamming hands deep into the pockets of her coat, she remained miffed at the marshal for sneaking up on her. "Old habits die hard," Lacy finally answered. "What are you doing out *here*?"

"What are *you* doing out here?" Rawley countered. Lacy sent a blistering look through the dark. "The way I heard it, you're not supposed to answer a question with a question. Besides, I asked first," she retorted.

"I saw your face in the window, came out to investigate," he said.

"Or…, you needed a reason to escape?" Lacy answered dryly.

"Yeah…alright," he grudgingly admitted. "So why *were* you peeking in?"

"I'm just curious as to which one of those women had caught your fancy, that's all," she inquired.

"*Ahhh*," Rawley thought. "Well, there is one…," he began then allowed his voice to trail off.

Turning back to peer in the window, Lacy asked, "Which one?"

"She couldn't come tonight, pulled shift so someone else could come to the dance," Rawley said, as he continued to watch Lacy's back for a reaction.

Knowing full well the meaning behind his words, Lacy rose slowly. Edging away from the window, she continued to back up, "Umm," she said, waving an arm behind her. "I'll, uh…I'll just go finish my rounds. See ya in the morning," she said hurriedly, beginning to walk faster, putting more distance between her and the lawman. *I asked for that*, she thought. *You bird-brain!*

"Lacy," he called out, stopping her in her tracks. Slowly, she turned back towards him. There remained a lot he wanted to say to his deputy. Instead, something else came out, "See ya in the morning," he said.

Lacy gave that half nod that was so characteristic of her.

Rawley smiled at the wordless nod. He watched as she meandered down the street. Turning, he went back into the dance.

* * *

Lacy had been fidgeting for the last hour and a half; the dance had been over two hours ago. *Where the hell is Rawley!* Hearing the latch open, Lacy got busy working on the paperwork she should have finished way before now.

Stepping in, Rawley shook himself like a wet dog, dispersing the cold, one hand hidden behind his back.

Lacy looked at the timepiece on the wall. "Pffftt! Took you long enough, where have you been? The dance was over two hours ago!"

"I think I'm old enough to not have a curfew, Sunshine," he replied.

"Pffftt," came her answer.

Seems Lacy is jealous and testy about it, too, he thought. He kept his voice light, teasing his deputy, saying, "Oh, I walked someone home, and decided to stay awhile."

Lacy's eyes became shrewd. Waving papers in his face, she spouted off, "Didn't Sam ever tell you how to write up reports? It's a wonder you haven't been reprimanded by the Mayor and council!" Color blazed across freckled cheeks.

"Where's your log book?" She demanded, shuffling papers around on the big desk, looking for it.

"Now, you just hold on a minute, Sunshine. Sam always wrote up those reports," Rawley retorted. Then, something dawned on him, he asked, "How'd you know to write those up?"

FRECKLED VENOM
COPPERHEAD STRIKES

"Because I had better handwriting than he did, so he made me write those reports! Here, this is what you wrote, and this is how they should be done," she told him, handing the marshal a revised copy. "See, you nitwit! Tomorrow, you go to the store and get a log book and while you're there, get some oil for this damn chair. Start running this office like you should!"

"I see."

"I hope you do," she said, the chair squeaking as she rose. *I swear sometimes Rawley Lovett ain't got the brains of a grasshopper.* She sighed inwardly. Pouring herself another cup of coffee, she took her seat again, the chair squeaking.

We're making progress, Lacy's jealous, good. Taking the hand from behind his back, he placed a covered plate in front of Lacy. "Liv sent that to you," he said, giving his lop-sided smile as a truce.

Mouth dropping in very un-deputy like pose, she sat and continued to stare.

"That's who I took home tonight and decided to visit awhile."

"Well...why didn't you just say so in the first place? Mr. Wise Apple!" She retorted.

Rawley cocked a brow when she came out with, *Mr. Wise Apple.*

The chair squeaked as she reached behind her. Retrieving a fork from the table, Lacy spun back around. The chair squeaked again. She dug into the pie, "Ummm, apple."

Rawley's lips curved up, then. He tightened them, erasing the smile, but it didn't hide the twinkle in his eyes. Life sure wasn't dull with his deputy around.

Taking his string tie off, he undid the collar button and poured a cup of coffee. Next, he sat in the chair beside the desk. He slouched and stretched long legs while he continued to watch Lacy dig into Liv's pie. "Since you're so good at those reports, I'll just let you do them," he said.

Wagging the fork in his direction, she tucked the delicacy into freckled cheeks reminiscent of a chipmunk before saying, "Oh, no you don't," Lacy said. She swallowed the mouthful of pie. "One of these days, I might not be here. You're gonna learn to do them yourself," she said, sticking another fork full of Liv's dessert in her mouth. Lacy gave him a wide-eyed stare.

"Nah, you're the best man...er...woman for the job. You do 'em," he said, grinning as he caught Lacy's dirty look thrown his way.

Gathering the leftover juices from the plate on her finger, her tongue licked them. She felt eyes watching her. Lacy glanced over. Rawley's eyes were, well...somehow different as he continued to study her, making her feel uncomfortable. "Umm, it's late, I'm going to bed," she said abruptly. Rising, the chair squeaked again. Leaving the empty plate and fork on the desk, she scurried down the hallway, boot heels echoing against the wood planks. Her door opened, then whispered close.

Watching Lacy lick the juices off her finger, gave him a desire he hadn't felt in a long time. He heaved in a deep breath tamping down those feelings. Rawley knew Lacy felt something had been happening between them, but he also knew she wasn't sure at the moment what it could be. Living a solitary bounty hunter's life had kinda cut into any social skills she might have learned or picked up. But, Lacy would figure it out eventually, *if I last that long,* he thought wryly. And when she was ready for love, he'd be there.

CHAPTER THREE

Spring 1879

The old timers were right. The snow melt and the spring rains turned a gently flowing river into a raging, roaring torrent, taking trees, cutting new sides into the banks and demolishing the bridge over what had once been a peaceful scene. As one old timer stated; 'Hell of a spring!'

* * *

Justin Carrigan's ego had become larger than his ranch. He knew the dark recesses and trails of the political platitude in state government, which he used to his advantage. Sharp dark brown eyes with gold flecks surrounded the pupils set in a deeply lined pock-marked face that was also worn by the harsh Wyoming elements. Thick fluffy sideburns framed his cynical facade with hair that had turned the color of cotton. An over long white mustache drooped across the corners of thin lips. A lean, but muscular frame for his age filled his clothing with ease. Glad that the bitching cold weather had finally ended, as his bones had complained all winter with the temperatures, he hitched up his buggy, driven by one of his green cross-bred studs. Carrigan decided to see what was going on in town for a change. Check out the gossip he'd heard. The town marshal had hired a female for his deputy. He wanted to see this for himself. *Any female thinking they could do a man's job, well...somebody had to be a damn crazy fool. The marshal for offering it or the girl taking the job,* he thought.

Thinking back, something he didn't do very often, he recalled Vern had been worthless as a marshal. He hadn't even bothered to follow up on the circulars he'd had printed over nine years ago, when his granddaughter ran away. She stole a thousand dollars from him, too, along with his most promising filly. He didn't care about the girl. He just wanted his money and the filly back. Justin Carrigan had been happy when the old marshal finally died.

His bones told him, that girl child was dead now, had to be…not one word had ever been heard from anyone about her in nine years. *Well...good riddance! Women weren't good for nothing, 'cept cooking and breeding purposes, like them mares he had,* he thought as he laid the whip across the rump of the bay. Startled, it jumped and began pulling the buggy away from Carrigan Ranch.

CHAPTER FOUR

Sitting on the second step, back resting against the porch post, Lacy's freckles were tilted toward the warm rays of sun. Spring had finally arrived.

Standing behind her, Rawley noted how the sun picked up the coppery glints in her hair. The effect made it look almost on fire. "Better go get your hat, Sunshine, otherwise you're going to have even more freckles," Rawley teased.

"Shut-up, Lovett."

Rawley grinned. He liked it when Lacy bantered back with him. Hearing the dull thud of shod hooves on the finally dry street, he looked up.

Something told Lacy to open her eyes, and then stand. Doing so, all the color drained from her face. Lacy gasped, realizing that the man in the carriage was her grandfather. Even after all these years, she still recognized the face that had become burned into her memory by pure hatred. Lacy stood glued to the steps, her mind unable to make her feet move. *My luck just ran out,* her mind tumbled over itself.

She watched the scene, which at first glance seemed to play out in slow motion as her grandfather drove toward them. Slowly, she dragged one foot up the step then the other. Lacy felt as if she was wading through molasses. It seemed ages before she finally stood alongside the marshal, her back to the street. Her insides felt like she'd just eaten a strip of barbed wire, it slicing and chewing her gut into shreds.

Tawny freckles popping out like polka dots on colorless cloth prompted Rawley to ask, "What?"

Lacy nodded over her shoulder, her voice barely a whisper, "Justin Carrigan."

After watching the buggy roll closer, he, too, recognized the man sitting on the seat. Rawley cut another glance down at Lacy, looking as if she had seen a ghost swinging from a hangman's noose.

Her eyes pleaded with him, as fingers became talons, wrapped around his arm in a death grip, pinching his skin. She whispered, "I'm not ready to face him yet. Please?" Forcing legs that seemed weighted down with balls and chains, she dragged herself into the office, closing the door softly. Lacy leaned against it, her heart thundering against her ribs like a thousand head of cattle stampeding across the plains, making it hard to breathe. She gulped air into her starved lungs.

When she had recovered a little, her body moved, hugging the wall, as if she were in a fire-fight. The thick logs, the only protection against flying lead. She slid next to the window, out of view of her grandfather, but where she could still watch him. *Why...oh, why did I ever stay in this town?* She asked herself. Her heart and stomach tumbled like rocks in a barrel down a steep hill, taking her breath along with it. Memories of her grandfather suddenly invaded her mind. She gagged.

Rawley adjusted his pose as Carrigan drove by. Anger, at what the old man had done to Lacy, turned fun loving eyes into blue ice, mimicking a deeply frozen mountain lake in the dead of winter. They continued to follow the buggy as Carrigan pulled to a stop some twenty feet away. Rawley kept the man under surveillance as he lighted down, dropping the tie-down weight for the big bay. Carrigan then walked along the street stopping in front of the lawman. He squinted up, saying, "Morning Marshal."

"Morning Carrigan," Rawley drawled.

FRECKLED VENOM
COPPERHEAD STRIKES

Placing one booted foot on the first step, Carrigan's eyes became hard and cynical, as he said, "Heard you'd got yourself a new deputy, heard, too, you hired a female."

Eyes remained sheets of blue ice, but he spoke softly, that softness hiding his true feelings. "You heard right, Carrigan."

One eye squinted almost shut. "What'd you go and do a damn fool thing like that for? Ain't you got no brains, boy?" The gravelly timbre in his voice carried a mocking tone.

Rawley's hand clenched and unclenched, his fist itching to slug the bastard across Wyoming, but instead, he answered calmly, "She's good at what she does, worked for an old friend of mine."

His mouth twisted, curling upwards into a snarl, reminiscent of a mountain lion. "You still ain't got no brains, boy," Carrigan said.

Rawley straightened up from the post. He gave the man a steely glare as he barely managed to hang on to his temper. He remained silent.

Noting the silence, Justin Carrigan continued to push. "Where's this new deputy of yours? I want to meet her," he said.

"You're just itching to start something, ain't cha, Carrigan?"

"Nah, just wanna see this new little filly, hear tell, she's been staying with you, too. It's not wise to mix business with pleasure, could get you in big trouble, you know, marshal." Carrigan's eyes gloated with his threat.

Rawley took one step closer. Still towering over Carrigan, his move forced the man back so he could focus on the marshal's face. It reminded Rawley of a turtle stretching its neck over the shell.

Holding on to his temper, he answered calmly, "My deputy is busy right now and not available for you to meet her. Come back another day."

A groan forced its way through her lips when Lacy

heard this exchange. She couldn't permit Rawley to carry on, covering for her against her grandfather. *Hell, I've faced worse criminals and survived.* Sucking in a deep breath, she opened the door.

Suddenly Lacy arrived at Rawley's side, her hand resting lightly on his arm.

Casting a quick glance down, his eyes questioned. His deputy shot him a no with a slight shake of coppery curls.

Using that soft husky tone of hers, she spoke, "Marshal, this man bothering you?"

Lacy's almost black eyes then zeroed in on her grandfather. They seemed to spray merciless doses of noxious toxin into his face, like the exposed fangs of a copperhead spurting venom.

Confusion traveled across Carrigan's face in waves. He continued to stare at the copper headed girl with the dark vile eyes.

"No," replied Rawley. "He was just moving on, weren't you, Carrigan." He said, trying to stall off what he knew was bound to happen, knowing Lacy's temper.

A sudden smile appeared, never reaching his eyes. "Well now, you gotcha self a right purity little filly, there, marshal. What's your name, sweetie?" Carrigan asked.

The tension rolling off of Lacy in waves, continued. Rawley felt her stiffen up even more when she heard the word, *sweetie*. He realized now why she had slapped him, when he had addressed her as such walking back from Liv's Christmas festivities.

Lacy planted a booted foot down on the next step. When the old man had said *sweetie* her mind clicked in another word alongside it. *Bastard.*

Her other boot slid next to the first one. Suddenly both hands rammed into Carrigan's chest pushing him back. Carrigan taken by surprised uttered, "What the hell?"

Stepping closer still, Lacy smashed the heels of her hands into him again.

FRECKLED VENOM
COPPERHEAD STRIKES

Close-set shiny eyes, reminiscent of a snapping turtle stared at his shirt, still feeling the quick punches, then those eyes resettled on the red-head. Confusion wrinkled his forehead, not sure what to do with this physical onslaught from a female.

Venom dripped from her words. "You don't know, old man?" Freckled hands shoved him further into the street. Lacy followed crowding into his air space.

Carrigan stepped back.

Following him again, she crowded him further, her face stopping only inches from his. Striking again, Lacy asked, "You don't remember; old man? Take a good look, a really good look!"

Slow recognition finally flitted across Justin Carrigan's own dark eyes. "Lacy? Lacy, is it really you? You've come home to me, finally, sweetie?" He reached for her.

She dodged his hand, countered by thrusting him further into the street, her tone going softer, more deadly. "Yeah...old man, I finally came home, but not to let you continue where you left off," she hissed again.

"Lacy, I...I thought you were dead," Carrigan said, reaching for her again.

Quick as a geyser bursting from the ground, Lacy's fist erupted. Her knuckles cracked when they made contact with his jaw. The angry force sent Carrigan sprawling in the dirt, his hat flying. Puffs of dust resembling brown flour rose around him, and then settled back down across his clothes.

The momentum of her attack sent Lacy crashing against the steps. Rawley quickly lifted her setting the copperhead back on her feet. Lacy struggled against his grip, but he held on. "Lacy...," he began. She hissed like a mad cat, "Stay away from me, Lovett!" she said, jerking her arm from his grasp.

Hastily covering the short distance, she placed her hands on her knees, leaning closer to the man she hated so much, Lacy spoke soft, lethal. "Surprised, old man, that I'm still alive? Did I make your day, today?"

Carrigan blinked in surprise at his granddaughter.

Rawley remained where he stood next to the steps. His height enabled him to gaze across the gathering crowd.

Pushing open the swinging doors to Mike's place, Rooster crowed, "Hey, Mike! Sumsing's going on between Ole Man Carrigan and that girl deputy down the street!" Chairs scraped and boots thundered through swinging doors, sliding to a stop at the edge of the scared planks. Mike shoved his way between his patrons. He stood wiping hands on the apron around his barrel middle. He too, had eyes transfixed on the copperhead. Seeing the gathering crowd, his eyes searched for Rawley and found him not far behind Lacy, one big palm resting on the butt of his pistol. Mike gave a sigh of relief.

Maddie, who ran the restaurant in town, was drug to the window by one of her girls. She stared at the scene in the street. Jerking the door open, she muttered, "Chust, what 'cha think ye gain' tae do, lass?" Stopping at the edge of the walk, Maddie placed hands on her generous hips. Everyone crowded onto the porch behind her. Their eyes wide, they gazed at the two in the street.

Increasing noise from the street had Luke moving away from his bellows. Standing in the door of his livery, he was surprised at the crowd gathering. His height, his shortcoming, Luke whirled, and headed toward the loft, Picking up his scatter gun on the way, he flipped it open, and saw it still loaded. A flicking motion of his wrist snapped it shut with a click.

Sharp blue eyes caught Luke's appearance in his hay loft. He waved his scatter gun at Rawley, then afterwords rested it in his arms. Luke stood waiting and thinking, *been a long time since this town's seen a shoot-out. Last one...Vern had still been alive.* He continued watching the drama unfold on the street below.

Rawley's calm appearance and penetrating eyes belied the internal turmoil and quickened pulse hidden beneath that facade. Eyes still the color of pristine Wyoming skies roamed the faces of his town. His mind traveled back in time to another War, which tore this country apart several years ago. Blue against grey, of blood fighting blood, it all seemed to be repeating itself in his street. But instead of a nation divided, it had become a war between two people, but blood nonetheless, Carrigan against Carrigan.

"What in tarnation is going on, Rawley?" Doc asked, his heels thumping across wooden planks. Coming to a stop behind the marshal, he looked down at him.

Dragging himself back to the present, Rawley folded his arms as he continued to watch the events unfolding in the street. "Lacy and her grandfather," he stated simply.

"You not gonna stop it?"

A massive shrug sent muscles rippling beneath the fabric of his grey shirt. Rawley said, "You know how hard-headed she is, Doc. But, she can also handle herself pretty well. This is something she needs to do, work out the anger, bitterness and hatred she's been harboring all these years against this man," he finished. While his mind added, *so she can be free, a slave no more to the memories.*

Tugging on his ear, Doc said, "I sure hope you're right, but maybe I'd better hang around." Sticking the match stick back in his mouth, Doc moved into the shade of the porch, leaning back against the building.

"Suit yourself, Doc."

Lacy fixed toxic eyes on her grandfather as if she were wearing blinders. Anger and hatred mingled with her sweat akin to venom from a copperhead's fangs, shot out of her pores.

Justin Carrigan rubbed his stinging jaw. He didn't recognize this woman standing over him. This wasn't the little girl he used to visit at night, who'd cowered and pleaded with him.

"Lacy, what's come over you?" he asked while he rose. Dust flew when his hand brushed his britches and coat off, and then straightened his holster back into its rightful position.

"You didn't used to act like this before?"

Burnt coffee eyes concentrated following every split-second movement her grandfather made. Her peripheral vision took in his hands while her eyes remained on his face. "I grew up, old man, way before I should have, thanks to you."

His voice, icy as a mountain stream in winter, ordered, "Get your things, girl. You're coming home with me."

Abrasive laughter filled the air, and then ended as quickly as it had erupted. Lacy placed her feet in a wider stance. Folding her arms, she asked, "Why? So you can rape me over and over again like you did my mother! Beating her senseless, when she stood up to you?" Saying the words she hadn't allowed herself to think or say for all those years, she continued to confront him. "So you can come to my room, raping me over and over again, like you did when I was a little girl?" She harshly ejected the words she hadn't allowed herself to speak until now.

Rawley's ears picked up the low mummer that whispered through the bystanders, rising like an incoming tide that splashed against the town's buildings.

Doc bit clear through his matchstick. Angrily tossing both pieces aside, he marched to the edge of the walk, standing behind Rawley. "That rotten sum-bitch," he muttered.

Maddie collapsed against a porch post, tears springing from green eyes. Her girls rushed to keep the woman from falling due to the shock.

Mike yanked his apron off, tearing the strings that kept it tied to his ample girth. Storming into his saloon, he came back out a few moments later with his sawed off scatter gun. Resuming his post with his patrons, he announced, "Boys, ya'll make sure ta toast me at ma hanging, 'cause I sure ain't letting that sum-bitch leave this town alive!"

"I'm warning you, girl," Carrigan said, beginning to back up. "I'm warning you, I won't hold with you telling lies about me!"

"Lies?" Her voice screeched resembling two branches

scraping against each other in a storm. "Lies? What's the matter, old man?" She asked, waving her arm at the gathering bystanders. "You afraid of what these good people would think of you, when they finally find out about the dirty little secrets you've been keeping behind closed doors," she shouted.

"Shut up! Shut up, you little bitch! I'll make sure you never see a penny!" Carrigan threatened.

Lacy's laugh, hard and abrasive, echoed against the buildings eerily. Keeping an eye on her grandfather, she watched him continue to retreat. Her body and voice followed him, "Go ahead. I'm ashamed to even carry the name Carrigan," she yelled.

His eyes drifted over the gathering crowd. Rawley could hear the collective intake of breath that whispered through the stand of spectators as the knowledge finally sunk in. Lacy Watson had suddenly become the long ago missing Lacy Carrigan.

The yellow specks surrounding Justin's pupils brightened within the brown of his eyes. These glared from under a thick cotton overhang. *The whole damn town is finding out about my personal business,* his brain buzzed. Beady eyes surveyed a crowd that seemed to grow by the second.

"Marshal," Carrigan shouted, changing tactics. "Arrest her, she's ah horse thief! And she stole a thousand dollars from me, too!"

Lacy watched nothing except his eyes; they remained wild looking. His hair seemed to puff out with his anger, like a cotton boll when the wind hit it. His eyes kept darting all over, taking in the crowd. She knew when they settled down the old man just might try to kill her.

Making sure her voice carried, Lacy yelled, "A horse thief? A thousand dollars, old man? That was my pay, for services rendered. Pack of lies, old man? Let's see how well this one sets with you! You know why my mother killed herself? Do you, old man?" Lacy became aware that his eyes had settled down now, completely focusing on her. "She killed herself, because...," She paused before she dropped the bombshell. "She carried your bastard child!"

Stunned, Justin Carrigan just stood there, his mouth moving silently. A few moments later, that same mouth twisted, curling into a snarl. "Why you lying little sack of sh...," He stopped himself before he finished; his eyes darted around. The crowd still there and growing, he wasn't going to allow this little trollop to ruin his reputation. Gazing around again, he straightened his shoulders. *I'm still a powerful man in this territory,* he told himself. *Having ties all the way to the Governor's office.*

Narrowing eyes at his granddaughter, Carrigan spoke quietly. "Your mother didn't tell you the truth, I never touched her," he lied.

Lacy tilted her head, as her eyes met his in a steady gaze. "Oh?" she inquired. "Then how do you explain all those bruises she always carried around?"

Carrigan became belligerent as he barked. "Your mother was clumsy. Always falling or running into something."

Folding her arms as she took that wide stance again, Lacy spoke with a deadly calm, confronting him, "You're not a very good liar, Carrigan. You're a bully and a tyrant. Not only that, you're a coward. Picking on a defenseless woman and child, something you couldn't get away with, with men. Mother was beautiful until you made her ugly with your constant beatings. Many a day I saw her face as black as your heart is," she said.

Lacy dropped one arm, the other bent tucking a thumb into her gun belt near her pistol. She moved her weight to the balls of her feet, as her gut instructed her to do.

"You're poison, you know that?" Lacy continued, "Just deep, down, rotten poison. Poisoning and killing anything you touch," she said, still watching her grandfather. "Mama told me before she died that she was carrying your bastard child, Carrigan," she lied.

FRECKLED VENOM
COPPERHEAD STRIKES

So what if the information came in the form of a letter after her mother had died. He didn't know that.

Lacy shouted, "There must be a God somewhere, as I was never that lucky." Her eyes never left the face of the bastard who remained her grandfather in name only.

Justin Carrigan lost his composure after hearing his granddaughter's words. "Shut up, just shut up! Or I'll kill you, I'll kill you for spreading those lies," Carrigan threatened, flicking his coat behind the butt of his gun.

A piercing shrill laugh escaped her throat, then abruptly cut off, when she said, "Old man, you can't kill me." Walking toward him, she continued to taunt her grandfather, "I've come to haunt you the rest of your days. No one wanted to cross you back then – afraid of what you might do to them. Well…I'm here…and after a long absence, ready to do something no one else would. Put you in your place for once. You're finally gonna pay for the destruction and death you caused," Lacy's soft voice threatened.

Face blanching white as his cotton sideburns. He remembered another copper-headed female, his drunken son's wife, Marie. Carrigan realized then, that woman had come back, reincarnated in his granddaughter. And that revelation scared the hell out of him, more then any ghost story or grizzly he'd ever run across.

Lacy walked to within a few feet of Justin Carrigan. Her tightly controlled anger had her appearing taller than her five feet two inches. Rolling her tongue around behind her teeth, she suddenly spat. Her venom sailed through the air landing neatly between his dusty boots.

Carrigan stared at the teardrop shaped wet splotch gracing the dirt. Glancing up at his granddaughter, he chewed the words out, "You bitch! You ranting, raving, stupid bitch! Just like your mother!"

Teeth clicked hard against each other hearing his words, Lacy spoke through a thin white line, "That's right, old man, a bitch I am. The bitch you turned me into."

The marshal took several steps closer. "Lacy," he warned, "Don't do something you'll regret later!"

Without relinquishing the glare aimed at her grandfather, she yelled back, "You stay outta this, Lovett! This ain't your fight!"

Lacy's temper had gone to the next level, Rawley knew, cold, calculating and calm, a deadly combination with her.

He stepped further into the street, placing himself between grandfather and granddaughter. Facing the man, he said, "Go home Carrigan, its over." His hand rested lightly on the butt of his weapon.

Furious at Lovett stepping between her and her grandfather, Lacy angrily rushed the marshal, yelling, "Outta my way! Lovett!" She tackled the big lawman, her small frame not making much of a dent.

Wrapping a huge arm around the squirming female, and pinning her tightly against him, he hissed, "Damn it, Lacy! This ain't the time or place! Now simmer down!"

"This is my problem, Lovett! Let me go!" Kicking his shins with her boot heels, she wrestled with the grip he had on her.

Rawley had placed himself in a precarious position, and Carrigan knew that. A feral smile spread across Carrigan's face, lurking just beneath the surface of his thick mustache. While Rawley had his hands full with a feisty wildcat, Carrigan could draw, killing Lacy, or the marshal or both of them. And the marshal wouldn't be able to stop it, his hands full. Lacy's anger fueling the blood in her veins to white hot, made it difficult to hold her back.

Steely blue eyes never left Carrigan's face, dissecting each display of emotion on it while he held a squirming copperhead. "That's enough, Sunshine! You'll get us both killed," he spoke harshly out the corner of his mouth.

Lacy suddenly stilled, his words finally sinking in. She wrenched her body loose from Rawley's grip. Her boots touched the ground, and she moved off to his left. The back of her hand swiped across her dry mouth as she breathed heavily. Sucking in more air for her starved lungs, Lacy moved her weight to the balls of her feet, again anticipating, relying on what her gut told her.

The marshal finally breathed a sigh of relief as Lacy moved off to his left. He turned his attention back to Justin Carrigan. "Go home, Carrigan. It's over."

"Like hell it is! I'll have your badge before this is all over. You'll be sweeping that jailhouse floor soon, I'll make sure of that," Carrigan threatened as he climbed into his rig. Still standing, he turned back to stare at the woman who had been his granddaughter. Suddenly his face twisted into something not human, becoming a grotesque creature out of a fairy tale.

Carrigan's hand disappeared. Her reflexes kicked into high gear. Pulling her weapon, she dropped and rolled, moments before her grandfather's bullet hit the dirt, raising dust, where she had just been standing.

Holding the pistol in two hands, her thumb quickly cocked back the hammer. She aimed, finger steadily pulling the trigger, a *thwack* sounded accompanied by flames spitting out of the muzzle. A pea-size piece of lead hit the old man in the shoulder, surprising Carrigan as he flipped out of the buggy. Lacy blinked against the grey haze and acidic smell of spent gunpowder as it burnt her eyes and nose.

Hitting the dirt, too, Rawley pulled his weapon, and glanced back at Lacy. She hadn't been hit. *Yet,* he thought.

Horses reared, accompanied by shrill whinnying that echoed against the buildings from the sharp retorts. The bay took off. The horse continued pulling, sidestepping the tie down weight attached to its bridle. Rounding the corner at a high speed, the buggy flipped dragging the bay down with it. Shrill whinnying accompanied the accident. Struggling against the harness and overturned buggy, the horse became frantic, its screams bouncing off buildings. Finally breaking a shaft in its struggles, the bay scrambled up, running, and still dragging the tie-down weight with the broken buggy in its wake, finally disappearing from view.

Lacy was oblivious to the noise and mayhem encroaching on the town. Instead, the whole scene replayed itself in slow motion in her mind. Lacy saw the flames exiting the muzzle of her pistol. The velocity of the ball, spiraling, sailing through the air, and hitting Carrigan. Slowly spinning him around, and forcing him out of the buggy.

The dust, which had billowed around him in a thin cloud as Carrigan landed in the street, just started to clear. Now Lacy watched him slowly rise. His body wobbled, legs staggering, as he tried to remain upright.

Lacy realized she had replayed this scene too many times in her head over the last nine years. It now carried an ethereal feel to it. As she continued to lie there, her calm demeanor belied the turmoil within. Her heart thundered against her ribs like a damn buffalo stampede. The stench of her fear, sweat dribbled down the base of her neck, behind one ear, and coursed downward between her breasts. Her palms were also wet with the anticipation that the worse was yet to come. She kept a watchful eye on her grandfather.

White hairs from his mustache danced as spittle flew when he spoke. "I'll get you yet, bitch!" He yelled.

Then Lacy's watchful eye caught the shaking hand of her grandfather as the muzzle of the weapon rose and he aimed it on her. Lacy rolled. Dust, dirt and pebbles flying as her elbows, knees and boots dug into the street, pushing her along.

Carrigan fired. A puff of dust flew as his second bullet bit the street beside her, again.

Rawley and Lacy fired in unison. Flames accompanied the sound of the duel blast that ricocheted off the buildings. Their pea-sized pieces of lead lifted Carrigan off his feet, sending the old man flying back to land with a heavy thud in the hard packed street. Dust billowing, and then settling down quietly like a shroud covering the body of Justin Carrigan. A dead quiet permeated the scene, not one soul breathed or moved.

It only took a few seconds for the scene to reach a climax, but to Lacy it felt like a lifetime. Quietly drawing in air, the pistol drooped in her hand, its muzzle resting in the dust. Laying her head on her forearm, she felt the beginnings of tears stinging the backs of her eyes.

Long strides quickly took him to his deputy's side. Kneeling, he touched a shoulder, followed by his hand pulling her up, setting her on her knees. "Lacy, you okay?" He asked softly.

Giving that wordless half nod, Lacy continued to stare at the gun she held in her hands. Gulping at air and blinking furiously, she tried to keep the tears from running down her cheeks.

Rawley left Lacy, walking over to the body of Justin Carrigan. The marshal knelt and stared at the man's shirt. Two holes oozed blood in Carrigan's chest, only inches apart. Another blood stain came from his left shoulder. His gaze wandered back over to the small figure, still kneeling in the street.

A thick fog seemed to roll in enveloping the scene, Lacy's eyes glazed over presenting tunnel vision within burnt coffee eyes. Climbing to her feet, Lacy slowly came to stand next to her grandfather, seeing nothing, but the face she had hated for so long. Tears spilled over, tracking along freckled cheeks dripping off her chin and sprinkling the dirt with moisture.

"I hope you rot in hell! You sick bastard," she whispered hoarsely. Slowly, her gaze found fingers still wrapped around the grip of the weapon that killed her mother and now her grandfather. Raising it, Lacy cocked her head, staring at the pistol as if it had become some foreign object. Dropping it suddenly the same way one would a hot poker, it landed in the dirt with a dull thud, next to Rawley's boot.

His eyes filled with pain as he observed the stiff posture of Lacy. Killing her grandfather only opened old wounds, cutting through the scar tissue turning them into raw flesh again. Rawley followed her slow trance-like walk taking her toward the stable.

Mike's hands came together in a slap, beginning a single cadence, and then picking up the beat. Others followed the cadence, it slowly becoming a low roar.

Lacy didn't hear a thing.

Luke stood at the entrance to his livery, silently watching the lonely figure trudge into his stable. Still in a trance-like state, Lacy fumbled with Fancy's bridle. Luke removed it from her hands. *The girl ain't in no shape to saddle her harse.* He did it for her. Standing aside, he watched her vault into the seat. Kicking the grey's ribs, Lacy Carrigan tore out of his business.

Doc placed his hand on Rawley's shoulder, easing himself down on one creaky knee. "Humph, she's a good shot, but then, so are you," he said.

"Yeah," Rawley sighed, "Too, good, sometimes." Helping Doc stand again, he issued orders, "Clay, get some men together, take Carrigan to the parlor." Turning, he spoke to the man closest to him, "Rooster, you need to ride out to Carrigan Ranch and inform Adam," he paused a moment before continuing, "Tell him what happened, if he's got any questions, tell him to come see me."

Hearing hooves beating a fast tattoo on hard packed earth, both Doc and Rawley faced the sound, their eyes tracking a girl astride the big grey, riding hard heading for the river.

Rawley made a move to go after her, when the toe of his boot kicked something, sending it skittering. Looking down he saw Lacy's pistol.

Doc touched his arm, "Not now, son, give her a little time, that wasn't some fugitive she just sank two bullets into, it was her blood kin, no matter how much she hated him."

CHAPTER FIVE

Walking out of his tack and bunk room, Luke stopped alongside Rawley, watching him saddle his mount. "The li'l gal ain't in very good shape, Rawley," Luke said.

His hands stilled. Rawley looked over his shoulder at the wiry bow-legged stable owner, "I know, Luke," he said. Throwing the stirrup over the horn, he tightened the cinch some more.

"I ain't had no kinfolk for a long time, but I knowed, if I was in them boots of hers, I'd ah kilt the sum-bitch ah long time afore this. Pushing up daisies is 'bout all he was good fer." Luke voiced quietly, "Hain't never liked the man, Rawley." He gave a slight shrug, his hands holding a strip of leather harness, "But he was a customer. Tweren't like that when he first came here," Luke said, his fingers running across the holes punched in the leather. "But then his wife died…after that…he seemed tetched…" he took a finger and tapped his skull, "like he had a loose connection up here."

Taking the bridle, Rawley led the bay out of the stall, stopping by Luke. Looking at the little bandy-rooster, he sighed, mumbling "I know Luke, I know."

"You gonna go check on her? Make sure she's awright?"

Swinging easily into the saddle, Rawley looked down at the stable master. Weight as heavy as Luke's anvil seemed to set on his shoulder's collapsing his lungs. He inhaled deeply, trying to restore air back into his lungs. "Yeah, Luke, I'll make sure she's okay," he said, touching the bay's sides with his heels. Ducking his head, he trotted out of the stable. Following the rider to the door, Luke stood watching the marshal ride off down the street. "Take care of that li'l gal, Rawley. I kinda got attached ta her," he said to the air. Turning, his gimpy hobble took him back into the tack room.

CHAPTER SIX

Rawley continued to sit on the rise, gazing at the lone figure, standing on the shore, skipping rocks across the water. Lacy had her own way of dealing with upsetting incidents, her anger, clamming up, and now, standing on the riverbank skipping stones.

The marshal looked down at his hands holding his reins. Pursing his lips, he blew hard, expelling the hot air that seemed to be clogging his lungs. Her pistol, stuck into the waistband of his britches, was a sharp reminder of what had occurred in town. It had been over an hour since he and Lacy shot and killed her grandfather, not seconds ago as he felt. It was self defense, but Rawley did not like the way the incident had gone down.

Carrigan wasn't satisfied to leave town and just let it be. No, he had to fire on his granddaughter. Lacy's first shot had been to the old man's shoulder. She hadn't set out to kill him, no matter how much she hated the man.

Carrigan, firing off that second round, forced Rawley to step into the fray, trying to keep that feisty copperhead he loved, from being killed. They never would know who fired the killing shot as both he and Lacy wore Navy Colts. Maybe it was for the best, if they never found out. *God! How he hated gun play! No one ever won.*

Clucking at his bay moved him down next to Fancy. He

dismounted, patting the mare on her neck. She butted him in the shoulder, acknowledging his presence.

Boots crunched across the pebble strewn riverbank. Rawley stopped a few feet from Lacy. She continued skipping stones across the water's surface, "Lacy, I'm..." he began. Whirling on him, tears coursing in little rivers down her cheeks, dripping off her chin, she threw out a question. "You know why I didn't go to the dance with you?" She quickly spun back around, sending another rock skipping across the water with vengeance. Lacy answered her own question, "Because...I can't dance!" She cried.

Bending, her eyes continued to fill and overflow with more tears, making it hard to search for more flat rocks. Finally picking up a handful, she resumed sending them angrily across the rippling surface.

Rawley's eyes followed the splish-splash as stones skittered across the water. Hearing Lacy begin to speak, he tilted his head as he listened to the war-torn emotional voice. "That old man took a little girl's dreams away, took her childhood away, making her into a woman, way before her time. He took that little girl's hopes of just wanting to...to grow up normal. Anticipating her first dance, her first real party dress, her first beau, her first kiss," Lacy said, continuing to flip stones into the river.

"That old man took all those dreams away from a little girl. All she wanted to do was ride those horses like the wind. Find a man who would love her as much as she loved him. Be married in a fine white dress, with imported lace and satin. To come to her husband's bed that night, whole and pure, not soiled, not tarnished. All those dreams, that little girl had are gone," she faltered, then the war-torn voice painfully squeezed out a final word, "Forever."

Rawley's brow furrowed while he'd listened, the pain evident in his eyes. Someone else, that's how Lacy saw and defined her childhood, this was how she had survived, by detaching herself from the memories, the pain, the hurt, and the grief.

"Lacy…" he began again.

Spinning toward him, Lacy's eyes picked out her pistol sticking in his belly behind his belt. Ripping it from the waistband, she stuck the muzzle under his nose.

Rawley stared down the blue-steel of the barrel, gazing into a dirty tear-streaked face, eyes red, and filled with so much pain.

Waggling the weapon poking at his nose, Lacy said, "See this? This gun is what my mama used to kill herself!"

Rawley peeled the pistol from Lacy's fingers, tucking it out of sight behind his back. Lacy was so engrossed in her grief and pain she didn't even notice the gun went missing.

Her eyes clouded over, dredging up more memories from deep within her soul. "My mama was smart, had spunk," she said, spinning away from him again. Picking up more rocks, she sent those across the water. "That old man, he hated his son for some reason, always using vicious, cutting talk. Finally the only way his son could deal with the old man was to turn to drink, making him even more yella. Not able to stand up to the old man, not able to protect his wife and daughter."

Lacy inhaled deeply, her bitter voice resuming, "The little girl's mama stood up to the old man, but, the old man would beat her so bad, the little girl didn't recognize her. The little girl tried to stand up to him, too, but he started…he started, the first time, holding a knife in her throat, to silence her, while he…he, then the little girl's mama killed herself. The little girl found her, holding her mama's bloody head in her lap," she said, sending another stone viciously across the water. "A little girl cried her life away that night. Later, she found and read the letter her mama left her."

Lacy stumbled over to Lovett, her fingers clawed into his shirt like a cat. She tried the virtually impossible task of shaking him.

"Her mama wanted her to live! That little girl's mama told her to run away, so she wouldn't die, like her mama! So she did! She ran...ran far...far away!" Lacy cried, trying to shake the big lawman again. "I wanted to live!" Fists pummeling into his chest, "Don't you see! Mama wanted me to live! She wanted me to live!"

Rawley calmed Lacy's fists by pulling her against him. She sagged with emotion into his body. Her gut wrenching sobs filling the air.

"Sunshine, it's over now, all over." His thick caramel baritone, quiet and soothing, bathed her. His fingers gently tangled themselves into her copper rope, smoothing it down her back. "It's all over now, all over," he said, trying to reassure her.

Straightening, Lacy suddenly pushed herself away from Rawley. Retreating further, she heaved in a ragged breath, wiping her face with the sleeve of her shirt.

"Go! Leave me be," she ordered him. Red rimmed eyes tried to glare at him through the pain and tears. Stumbling away, she crumpled to her knees, curling into a little ball at the water's edge.

Hearing her gut wrenching sobs piercing the air again, Rawley moved toward her. Squatting down, he placed a gentle hand on her shoulder. "Lacy, let me help..."

"No!" Picking up a handful of stones, she angrily threw them at his chest. "Leave me be! Go on!" Seeing Lovett not moving, she picked up another handful, and tossed the pebbles at him. "Git! Git! Leave me be," she yelled, her eyes full of the grief racking her body.

Rawley stood, his heart aching for what this woman was going through. Too stubborn and proud to allow someone to share that grief, to hold her, help ease her through the pain. Lacy had shut down those emotions for so long, now with what had happened today, it cascaded out of her, like the flood they'd had that spring, torrents of water, washing, cleansing her soul. He walked away.

Mounting slowly – *at least I have her gun* – he glanced across at Fancy, his eyes touching on the empty scabbard.

Good, she'd left that buffalo gun in the office. Even though she had said she wanted to live, no telling what she'd might do as distressed as she was. Gazing one more time at the small balled up figure on the bank crying out her heart and soul, he headed toward town.

CHAPTER SEVEN

Kneeling on the bank gazing over the peaceful scene of the flowing river, Lacy listened to the quiet burble as the water eddied around boulders. Ears picked out the repeated cries of quail and evening doves, their calls echoing each other in the brush. A deep calm had replaced the turmoil she had lived with for over nine years. Her heart and soul had been emptied.

A nudge pushed Lacy forward. Dimples appeared when the corners of her mouth curved upward in a long forgotten smile. Reaching back, she patted Fancy's jaw. "I know, it's getting to be your suppertime," Lacy said. Fancy nudged Lacy again, nibbling her shirt. She spoke softly, "I guess I made up for not crying all those years, in one afternoon, huh, Girl?" Washing her tear-streaked face in the river, its icy waters feeling good on her hot face, Lacy rose. Continuing to watch the sunset, she told Fancy, "Guess we'd better get you home, get you some supper." Taking the reins, Lacy stuck a boot in the stirrup, and then hesitated, she'd said *home*, a word she thought she'd never say, ever again. "C' mon Fancy, let's go home!"

Slowing Fancy to a plodding walk, she rode into the outskirts of the town, which just a few short moments ago she had called home. A hesitation begin mingling with nerves still raw, realizing she may have burnt her bridges with the little community by killing Justin Carrigan. Sighing inwardly, she

FRECKLED VENOM
COPPERHEAD STRIKES

considered. *I may still have to move on; the town may not want me here anymore.* A deep sadness began filling her soul, realizing that she didn't want to leave. Gently tugging on Fancy's reins, Lacy halted her forward movement.

Red-rimmed eyes swept the town's landscape in the dusky twilight. Her mind retrieved the memories from seven months before, when, wounded, she had rode into a town she'd run away from nine years earlier. Tears suddenly filled dark eyes and a hand angrily brushed them aside. *If I have to move on, well...I'll just move on,* she told herself, dreading that conversation with Rawley. Squaring her shoulders, she urged Fancy into her impatient clip-clop toward her supper.

CHAPTER EIGHT

Rawley had been on pins and needles, since leaving Lacy doubled over with grief on the river bank.

That crazy copperhead had become more precious to him. Since he figured out he'd fallen in love with her, and especially after what had happened out on the street today. He felt empty, lost when he wasn't near her. But he realized he still had to keep his distance, allowing Lacy the space she required. His patience was beginning to grow really, really thin.

As she opened the door, Lacy noted Rawley's attempt to jump out of his skin when she entered. A frown pulled on her face as she moved toward the coffee pot, pouring herself a cup. She stood sipping, eyes staring at the cracks in the scarred plank floor.

She couldn't bear to look at the man she had emptied her soul out to. She didn't want to hear the words she just knew were on their way. *Pack your gear, get out of town.*

Rawley straightened, sending a little thank you to the heavens above through the ceiling. He picked up his cup and refilled it, too. Sitting on the desk top, he took note of Lacy's appearance, quietly standing in front of the pot-bellied stove, staring at the floor. Her face resembled rice powder, the freckles like beacons again. The dark circles, resembling bruises, were back, her eyes red rimmed, face swollen from crying. She had expelled the grief she'd held onto all those years. Other then that, she looked fine physically. Emotionally, that might be another thing altogether.

Moving toward the chair next to the desk, Lacy thought sitting might help stir the air that had become thick with emotion. Taking her perch, she forced more of the stale brew through a half-closed throat, while she waited for Rawley to say something; he always did. *Jabber-mouth,* she thought, not too nicely. Instead, Lacy focused on a tiny spider crawling up the wall toward the ceiling.

"Lacy...," Rawley began. "I'm sorry about what happened today." Seeing her about to speak, he held up his hand. The motion made her close her mouth; she waited. "I should've stepped in a lot quicker, try to get your grandfather out of town sooner; then, maybe none of this would've happened," he said.

Brown dots grew wide with surprise. *He's not firing me! Taking the blame himself for what happened today!*

Briskly shaking her head, Lacy willed her brain to find the words she needed.

"No, no, none of this is your fault. It's mine. It had to happen some day. It just...just came quicker than I thought." Her ragged intake of breath seemed to scorch her already emotional state further. "You were right. I needed to face that old man. Take my fears head on, not allowing them to control me any longer," she whispered.

Sitting the cup down, she rose, moving to stand in front of the marshal, tucking fingers into her back pockets. She tried to swallow that damned pebble that showed up out of nowhere. Dark coffee eyes filled to the brim with tears again, as she focused on his sky blue ones.

Lacy spoke in a husky whisper, "You're a good man, Rawley Lovett and… and I thank you for that," she said as the tears began to dribble down her face. Raising her chin upward, she looked at the ceiling, spying the cobwebs draped amongst the beams. She hoped the tears would stay in her eyeballs. It didn't work. They still slid down her cheeks.

"You have high standards, I…I'll never be equal to

that. I am who I am, been this way far too long, I can't change now," she added quietly. Looking down at her boots, she watched the tears sprinkle the dusty leather with wet splotches. She thought she had cried herself out, didn't know she any tears left, but here they were, dribbling down her cheeks, dripping onto her boots. Lacy heaved in another shuddering breath.

Rawley smiled, his heart tugging with each teardrop. "Sunshine, your past is what made you the strong willed independent woman you are today. You're temperamental, irascible, with a head that's as hard as granite, but that makes me," he stopped suddenly, the word love almost slid off the tip of his tongue. "Like you even more," he said instead.

Pulling a hand out of her back pocket, he held it up and tapped a finger. "You have more courage and spirit in this little finger, then most folks I've known, men or women. The past has made you what you are today and I wouldn't change a smidgen of it."

His hands moved to cup that cute as a speckled pup face and make her look at him.

Lacy did, but only for a moment. Closing her eyes, she snuggled a cheek into his cool, calloused hand, allowing his touch to soothe her jangled nerves.

Thumbs wiped away her tears. His soft gesture had Lacy re-opening her eyes. Tired and emotionally drained, they gazed into blue ones that still mirrored a summer sky. The smile broadened as he asked, "There is one thing you could do for me?"

A questioning look slid across tawny freckles.

Tilting his head, he gave her his lop-sided grin. "Smile more, show off those cute dimples. You know, I've never heard you laugh either; it would be nice to hear that. Oh, and one more thing, will you have supper with me tonight?"

Lacy shied away from him then, her hands wiping the leftover moisture from the freckles. Shaking her head, she said, "I don't think I can face those people out there, after what I did today."

Rising and stepping toward her, Rawley pulled his redhead into his arms.

The warmth of his body flowed through Lacy like warm honey pouring over flapjacks, soothing her.

At first he felt the hesitation, her stiffness, then, her body relaxing, melting into him as her arms slowly edged around his back.

He savored the closeness. The scent of lavender soap lightly washed over him mingled with her ever present *Perfume of Fancy*. He smiled. After a few moments, Rawley gently pushed her back. Steady blue eyes searched emotionally drained dark ones.

"Sunshine, I think you're gonna be pleasantly surprised by the reaction from the folks in this town," he said. Remembering the applause his little copperhead received after the death of Justin Carrigan. "So…," he began, tucking a loose copper tendril behind her ear. "So, why don't you wash up, change your shirt," his eyes trailed down to her muddy knees, "And your britches, and then we'll go to Maddie's."

Lacy hesitated.

"You are hungry, aren't you?"

Her soft throaty voice whispered back, "I don't know if I am or not."

He smiled once again, "You will be once you get a whiff of Maddie's cooking. Now go on."

Lacy took off her gun belt and after hanging it up, her hand continued to linger on the empty leather holster, remembering what she had done to her grandfather. Then without another word, she turned going toward her quarters.

CHAPTER NINE

Rawley pushed open the door to the *Blue Bird Cafe*, beckoning Lacy to enter first. Stepping over the threshold, she stopped suddenly. The marshal bumped into her backside. Burnt coffee eyes swept over the diners in Madeline Campbell's *Blue Bird Café* as their chatter ceased. Pewter utensils pinging against earthenware grew quiet. More then several pairs of eyes focused on the redhead.

However, Lacy did not catalog their faces into her memory bank as she had the first time she'd walked into Maddie's establishment several months ago. But more with a curiosity than anything, she waited for their reaction on the death she caused of Justin Carrigan.

Maddie placed two plates in front of a couple. Turning she gazed fondly at the marshal and his deputy. Slowly she brought her hands together and began clapping. Other patrons put down their forks and knives and followed suit.

A slow flush began climbing from the V of Lacy's shirt, rising, changing colorless skin to cinnamon red, and spreading quickly across tawny freckles.

Whirling, Lacy ran smack-dab into the large frame of the marshal, blocking her escape. Dark dots rose, stopping at smiling Wyoming skies.

Speaking in that soothing caramel baritone, Rawley told her, "This is what I tried to tell you when I said you'd be pleasantly surprised by the reaction of this town." Tilting his head, he looked into the girl's stunned face.

Turning slowly, Lacy took a few tentative steps further into the *Blue Bird Café*. Rawley gently prodded his deputy from behind, forcing her to move inside so he could stand beside her. Lacy's eyes skittered across the now familiar décor.

Robin's egg blue and white carried the theme throughout the small diner. White bead board graced the lower half of the walls, above that, robin's egg blue highlighted the white shelves holding teapots and other nick-knacks. Checkered tablecloths on each of the eight to ten tables, along with curtains in the windows completed the warm inviting atmosphere.

Maddie, a robust woman with frizzy brown hair, threaded with silver, and smiling green eyes, began shushing the diners. Her Cheshire cat grin filled ruddy cherubic cheeks as Maddie beckoned energetically, urging the pair further inside. Meeting them half-way, she enveloped the marshal in a huge hug. Turning, she opened her arms again for Lacy.

Lacy faltered, cutting a swift look at Rawley.

He gave her a nod.

Maddie's fingers coaxed Lacy into her warm embrace, smelling of roasted meat, fragrant onions and cinnamon. Whispering in the deputy's ear she said, "Proud of ye, lassie. Aye…ya, that took ah lotta nerve fer ye tae do that." Releasing the girl, Maddie stepped back as a fond gaze enfolded the pair, "Laddie, suppers on da house tae night," she announced.

Later, digging into their pie, both were interrupted by a stern tweedy voice.

"Marshal Lovett, I'd like a word with you?"

Glancing up as one, they noticed a severe woman dressed in black, standing stiffly at their table. "Yes, Miz Dawson, how may I help you?" Rawley asked politely as he rose, wiping his mouth with the napkin.

The first thing entering Lacy's mind: *this woman could be trouble,* as coffee colored eyes continued to take stock of the woman who appeared almost as tall as Rawley.

Beginning with the woman's scuffed and worn high-top button shoes, peeking from under a dusty hem, Lacy continued her journey, eyes taking in frayed pleats that had been taken in and released too many times. Long talon like fingers gripped the bone handle of a shiny black parasol, the tip impatiently tapping the floor, in time with a pointed toe. Lacy continued to take in the woman's appearance, traveling upwards and stopping at her dour expression. Small eyes were set in a steep angular face, cheek bones sticking out like knots on a log, and a long nose dripped over a lip-less mouth above a sharp chin. Lacy blinked, thinking not too nice thoughts.

Cutting another piece of Maddie's pie with her fork, she poked that into her mouth. Apples, cinnamon and sugar mingled, making her mouth water when the flavors hit her tongue. Her eyes rose once again taking in the last remaining bit of attire the woman wore; her hat.

Chewing, Lacy gasped, forcing a sliver of pie to dive down the wrong pipe, cutting off her wind. The chair scraped back from the table. Lacy placed her head between her knees, and giving a hale and hearty cough, brought up the offending particle. She wheezed in air as she sat up, glancing at Rawley who'd thrown a cock-eyed look in her direction. Lacy shrugged, picked up her cup and swallowed back a slug of coffee.

Cautiously, Lacy resumed looking, no, not looking, but ogling in amazement at the monstrosity that sat on the pewter colored hair of this woman. Eyeballing the arrangement, that in most circles folks would call a hat, Lacy saw black netting, resembling an oversized bird's nest, resting on a smidgeon of black felt. Inside that nest a crow or raven had taken up squatter's rights, in attack mode, dusty wings spread, mutely squawking as if protecting its young. Its beak and glassy yellow eyes dipped low over the front of the hat, threatening anyone, if they came too close.

"Marshal, that incident out in the street today...," Miz Dawson began.

FRECKLED VENOM
COPPERHEAD STRIKES

Ooh, bother, thought Lacy, *here it comes.*

"Was totally uncalled for, why if my late husband were still alive, he and the town council would never have," she continued, giving Lacy a dirty look, "allowed you to hire a...a female gunslinger!" Miz Dawson finished by sticking her long nose in the air resembling the beak of that dead bird.

"That's true, M'am. However, I laid down certain conditions, in writing, that the council agreed with, and continue to support my decisions. Including hiring a female gunslinger as you put it."

Narrowing eyes at the old bat, Maddie warned, "Widder Dawson? Ye be ah poking ye nose in where it don't belong!" Placing one hand on her hip and the other on Lacy's shoulder, she announced, "Ye be getching yer knickers in a twist ober nuthin'!"

Pushing herself away from the table, Lacy stood, facing the widow, and presented the woman with one of her best blistering looks. "M'am, I've been hired to help protect this town and the surrounding territory. I have a mean and nasty reputation," Lacy lied. "You can ask Marshal Lovett here, how mean and nasty I can get." She moved closer to the widow. Threatening eyes bored into the woman's unpleasant face. "If it takes being a gunslinger to maintain law and order, then, a gunslinger I am."

"Why you insolent little...! Marshal, you should be ashamed of yourself, allowing this...this, little tart, to...to even work for you," the old bat said. Flouncing off, the tip of her black parasol tapped the floor in perfect rhythm with her shoes as she hurriedly moved toward the door, opening and slamming it shut, fluttering the curtains.

Laughter erupted in the room.

Watching the woman leave, Lacy turned her attention back to the marshal. Placing palms flat on the table, she leaned across into his face, hissing, "Who...the hell...is that?"

"Oh...that's just Miz Birdy Dawson," Rawley replied. "Her bark is worse then her bite."

Taking her seat again, Lacy went, "Pffttt! More like the wicked witch of the west, if you ask me! Instead of a parasol, all she needs is a broom!"

A deep baritone laugh rumbled from a broad chest.

"And did you see that monstrosity she's wearing on her head?" Lacy exclaimed, leaning across the table whispering, eyes round as saucers, "She's gotta be half crazy wearing a dead bird in her hair!"

He laughed, again, watching his fiery redhead talk in amazement about her first encounter with Miz Birdy Dawson. He took note of the color returning to a face that held a million freckles.

Sashaying back over to their table, Maddie announced, "Aye, Lassie, me thinks ye put the ol' battleaxe, in her place fer once!"

Dimples peeked at the marshal as she leaned back. "Maybe that will keep her mind off of...," Lacy became somber, pain wavering in burnt coffee eyes. "Of what happened today. I'm really tired, can we go?"

CHAPTER TEN

Sending Lacy in to get some rest. Rawley headed toward Stewart's. Doc usually visited Mike's about this time for his nightcap. Carrying his drink over to Doc's table, the usual mummer of voices and laughter flowed around him, his ears tuned to pick up any discord as Rawley sat down next to Doc.

"How's Lacy doing?"

The marshal allowed his gaze to wander over Mike's patrons. He listened to the rustle of shuffled cards, coins sliding across wooden tables and bottles tapping glasses, tinkling as amber liquid splashed. His nose tickled with the scents of cigars and rolled cigarettes, smoke billowing above each table, creating a light fog, along with the light, sweet smell of whiskey. Recognizing all the customers, Rawley brought his eyes back to Doc, answering, "She just met Miz Birdy Dawson for the first time."

Doc let loose with a loud snort, "How'd that come out?"

Rawley shrugged. "You know Miz Birdy Dawson, Doc. Flapping her wings and beak as usual. Didn't like the fact I'd hired me a female gunslinger, as she put it."

Doc rephrased his question, "So…besides meeting Birdy Dawson for the first time, how is Lacy really doing?" He asked.

"On the outside, seems fine, inside, don't know yet.

"Tell her you love her, yet?"

"No, and I'm not going to, either…yet. Like Liv said, Lacy has to do things in her own time frame. If and whenever she figures out she loves me, then I'll tell her, and only God knows when that 'll happen," he exhaled noisily.

"Son, one of these days, you're gonna run out of patience with that girl."

Cocking an eyebrow in Doc's direction, Rawley grinned, "Do' no 'bout that, but, she sure as hell keeps me on my toes," he grudgingly admitted.

"Son, if and whenever you marry that catamount, you're gonna be in for the ride of your life!"

"Fraid so, Doc."

* * *

Hanging up his rig, Rawley went to check on Lacy. Since he'd known her, she hadn't had nightmares, but he didn't know if today would set them off. Opening her door, he peeked his head around the edge, then walked in and stood by her bunk. She wasn't curled up in the ball, sleeping like she did in the past. That copper hair, now loose, streamed across the pillow; her face was calm and relaxed, and her hands weren't clinched into fists, either. Lacy slept peacefully.

Rawley read all of this as a good sign. Maybe now she could move on, making a new future for herself. He hoped she would allow him to become a part of that future. Kissing her softly on the forehead, he quietly tip-toed out the door.

CHAPTER ELEVEN

Stocking feet trudged silently down the hallway into the main office, as she still braided her hair. Lacy glanced up at the clock, *eleven AM!* "Why didn't you wake me?" Lacy asked. Pouring herself a cup of coffee, she moved to the chair next to the desk, and proceeded to sit cross legged in it.

Rawley looked over at his deputy. He didn't know how that girl could squeeze herself into those tight positions, but she always did. He answered, "Thought you might need to sleep in, what with all that happened yesterday."

Resting the points of her elbows on her knees, as her hands wrapped around the cup, she sipped the coffee. Lacy said seriously, "We need to talk, man to man."

Blue began to twinkle within black framed lashes. "I'll talk if it's between a man and woman."

Lacy shot him a dirty look, scoffing, "Pffttt! You and your technicalities!" She retorted. Then aiming a square look at Rawley she told him, "You need to fire me."

"Fire you? For what?"

Taking another sip, she swallowed saying, "I didn't do my job yesterday. I let that old man goad me into shooting him. I know better, I shouldn't have done that."

"Sunshine, you goaded him, he didn't goad you," Rawley stated softly.

Lacy's eyes quickly sent sparks flying across the short

space, "I did not!"

The chair gave its customary squeak as Rawley leaned back, his eyes thinking as he asked, "How much do you remember about yesterday?" Doc had told him about how folks would sometimes have short-term memory loss after some kind of trauma. Lacy just might be going through the same thing. "What do you remember," he asked softly, prodding her.

Lacy gave her customary shrug, "Just that my grandfather came to town and now he's dead."

"Do you remember what you said to him?"

Another shrug. "Not really. What's all this got to do with firing me?" She demanded.

The marshal replied, "Because if the truth be told, you were the one who goaded him into firing first and..."

"All the more reason for you to fire me," she butted in.

The girl can really try my patience, he sighed inwardly.

"Most folks would say it was self defense, you're lucky your aim and mine was better. You recollect going to the river? What you said to me there?" Rawley continued to ask the questions.

Lacy nodded.

Okay. It's just the events with her grandfather that Lacy blocked out of her memory, Rawley figured.

"You still need to fire me," Lacy said piping up. "Miz Dawson is right, you know, I'm gonna ruin your reputation, if you keep me on."

"Since when do you let what other people think bother you, specially, with someone like Miz Birdy Dawson."

"I don't, but, she's right. I don't need to be sleeping here either, it doesn't look right," she said, then paused looking at him. "For you anyway." She rose pouring more coffee for the both of them. Looking around the office, Lacy added, "Guess I'll have to see if Miss Liv has room for one more," Lacy added.

Rawley gave another exasperating sigh. "Sunshine, we

haven't done anything wrong, you have your quarters and I have mine," he said with his brain thinking otherwise, how much he'd love to move Lacy into his bed. He sighed deeply. *And that ain't gonna happen anytime soon.* Giving Lacy another long look, he added, "And you will still be my deputy."

"Yeah…well…the Mayor and Council may think different, once Miz Birdy Dawson gets a hold of them," Lacy retorted.

"The Mayor and Council already knew about you. I told them you worked for Sam, same as me. They know better then to buck me on my choices for deputies. Besides Mike, Maddie, and Liv are on the council, that's a majority of the vote. So, enough talk about me firing you, you're staying. Nuff said! You hear me?"

Lacy rolled her eyes and exhaled a "Pfftt," into the air for her answer.

CHAPTER TWELVE

Rawley came outside, from his office, stopping alongside a twosome. He patted Fancy's neck asking, "How was the fishing today?"

"Miffer Rawwee, wook," young Cotton said, trying to lift the trout. Lacy helped by holding out a nice string of fish threaded on a branch. "Better get cleaning, Miss Liv is expecting them for dinner," she said to Rawley.

Hands going up in the air, Rawley backed off quickly, "Oh...no! You caught 'em, you clean 'em."

Leaning down to Cotton she asked the little boy, "Who caught these fish, Cotton?"

"Me!" The little boy chirped.

Cocking her brow at the lawman, she gestured with the trout, "See! I don't want Cotton cleaning them, he's too young to be wielding a knife," she said. Waggling the limb loaded with fish again, Lacy challenged Rawley, "Aw, c' mon Lovett, it ain't gonna kill you to clean a little ol' mess of fish."

Taking the branch, Rawley groused, "You'll pay for this, Sunshine!"

"Take it out of my next payday!" Lacy shouted as she trotted off to take Cotton back to Miss Liv's.

Cleaning the trout out back of the office, Rawley soon had more company then he wanted. Furry felines entwined themselves around his legs, all talking at once. He kicked out

FRECKLED VENOM
COPPERHEAD STRIKES

his foot, "Git! Git! Go on now, scat!" He threw a handful of fish heads and guts away from him. The cats scampered toward the pungent delight.

Lacy observed the predicament she had placed the marshal in. Sticking fingers in her britches hip pockets, she smiled to herself, saying to him, "Well…well, looks like our marshal got himself caught right smack dab in the middle of a cat house!"

Giving Lacy a dirty look, Rawley wiped his sweaty face on his sleeve. "Ya know I'm gonna stink for a week, after this," he said.

Lacy rocked back and forth on her heels, thinking, *Oh, this is fun.* "Nah…I've got water heating so's you can get all that fish stink off, though, these ladies won't love you as much," she teased. Turning, she stepped back into the office.

The marshal, gazing at the retreating back of his deputy, had to smile.

* * *

The days were becoming more summer like, this late spring day. Summer was almost here.

School had let out for the day. Lacy's eyes roamed over the community's children, her mind clicking a physical description of each child into her memory bank. There were eight girls and six boys. Little pinafore dresses in browns and dark blues, mostly, seemed to be the color of the day for the girls. Dark stockings ended in high top button shoes encasing small feet. Multicolored shirts graced the backs of the boys, dark to light colored pants, some with patches on the knees and elbows, held up with suspenders. Billy, the tallest of the youngsters, threw a wave as he ran by. Heading, Lacy knew, to eat his fill of Liv's mouthwatering cookies.

The others dawdled, whispering amongst themselves, pushing at each other as kids will do. Finally one brave little boy straightened his shoulders and walked closer to the steps. After digging in the dirt with the toe of his shoe, he looked up and asked, "Mister Rawley, when we gonna start playing checkers again?"

"Soon, I'll get the board set up out here and we'll start playing again, okay?"

A big smile creased the little boy's face as he whirled around, jumping, fists pumping the air with glee. The kids cried in unison, "Yippee!" The boys ran off in different directions while the girls walked slowly up the street, heads together chattering like magpies.

One little boy dragged behind the others, his shoe kicking a pebble along raising puffs of dust as he slowly trudged down the street.

Rawley called out to him, "Thad? Where's Chad?"

Thad walked over and stated, "He got in trouble. He has to do my 'n his chores for a week!"

"What'd he do?"

"Lied 'bout his homework," Thad replied.

"Well son, you tell him, I said not to do that anymore, you hear?"

"Yes…sir," Thad replied running off to join the others.

Lacy's eyes followed the boy running after the others. She glanced up at Rawley, questioning, "Thad and Chad?"

Rawley smiled, looking down as he answered, "Yeah, first set of twins Doc delivered in White River."

"Ahh. Why, you're just a regular Pied Piper of Hamlin ain't cha, 'cept it's the Pied Piper of White River!" Lacy teased the big lawman.

"Who?"

Getting up, she jumped the steps, heading across the street toward the stable. Turning, Lacy replied. "The Pied Piper of Hamlin," she called back.

"Who's that?"

Continuing to back up, Lacy's lips curved upward forming deep dimples in freckled cheeks as she replied, "Ask Miss Liv!"

Sometimes Lacy could come up with the damn dis' lit-

FRECKLED VENOM
COPPERHEAD STRIKES

tle snippets of conversation. Resettling his hat, Rawley stepped off the walk, heading toward Mike's, to see what kind of gossip he had to share. *Hopefully, its better then the Pied Piper of what-ever,* he sighed.

CHAPTER THIRTEEN

Summer 1879

Striped to the waist, Carson Beckett knelt at the river's edge washing a week's load of dust and grime off. What he really wanted was a hot bath and a full glass of rye to wash the thick dust out of his mouth, water just wasn't cutting it anymore.

Glancing around at the stark emptiness of the plains surrounding the river, he knew that wasn't to be found on this bare turf way out here.

Wells Fargo boys had gotten him out of prison early, to work a special undercover mission as he had done in the past for them. If he accomplished what they wanted him to do, with his old partner Lacy Watson, his sentence would be commuted. Wiping his neck again with the wet bandana, the cool water felt good against his hot skin.

It had taken some time, but Beckett finally trailed Lacy Watson to White River, Wyoming. From word he'd heard along the trail, she had become the deputy marshal for a little spit-in-the-dust town by the name of White River.

Several, it seemed long years ago, they had worked undercover missions together, helping out the Pinkerton and Wells Fargo boys, in tricky situations.

Carson knew Lacy wouldn't give him the time of day,

if he walked up to her on the street. Hell, she'd just find some way to throw him in jail. Their last meeting hadn't ended on good terms. Knowing that, he began to formulate some sort of plan in his head, however weak it might be.

According to the questions he'd been asking in other towns, White River probably didn't have much in their cracker box bank, no railroad nearby, a few big spreads, mostly small homesteads. Not his kind of pickings, robbing a bank. Carson Beckett liked flashier gigs with gambling and women, lots of beautiful women. But it had got him in trouble, big trouble this last time.

His horse slowly clipped-clopped through the mid-morning warmth, sun catching dust motes sailing languidly through the atmosphere. Pockets of gnats hung in the warm air, clustering here and there.

Carson Beckett saw a clean, quiet town, with not much traffic for the middle of the week. Gazing around, he took in the faded whitewashed clapboard buildings, log building housing the marshal's office and jail, and the brick bank. His eyes noted the two-story hotel looking newer then the rest of the structures. He sighed wistfully, thinking of a hot bath and a long glass of rye. His hazel eyes found the nondescript saloon. By the looks of it, he wouldn't make much money gambling there. He liked bright lights, fine women and good smooth rye. He doubted he would find all that here. Nope, all he'd find was just a redhead, who sometimes could be loaded with as much venom as three copperheads.

Carson reined up in front of Ezra's General Store and nonchalantly dismounted. His eyes lazily roamed the town's landscape, resting for a few seconds on the marshal's office, thinking of a redhead as he did so.

Dragging hazel eyes away from the log building across the street, Beckett climbed the steps. Boot heels thumped across the planks slowing as he turned the handle and pushed open the door. He listened as a bell above his head dinged at his entrance.

At the jingle, Ezra turned from his chores, seeing the stranger in his store. Taking his position behind the counter, he placed both palms down on the well worn top, asking, "Yes suh? What kin I do for ya?"

The store didn't have all the trappings of a big city establishment, but was adequate, Beckett noted. The tantalizing scent of fresh store ground coffee enveloped him. He sniffed appreciatively, remembering how his partner Lacy Watson could make a good cup of coffee. He picked up other aromas, too. The slight odor of coal oil, new leather, the scent of store bought clothes, shipped in from back east. He caught the tangy sweet fragrance of smoked tobacco and fresh sawdust used to sweep the floor each day.

Beckett continued to glance around. He spied a large combination table/shelf unit that held various bolts of colorful, textured and drab material. A yard stick was nailed into the top of the table along one side for measuring. Spools of ribbons, all widths and colors were tucked into shelves on one end like books, colors reflecting their shiny outside as if one were looking through a kaleidoscope. On top of that end of the table, more colorful spools were threaded on a narrow rod set on braces. His eyes continued to roam. The stairs to his right traveled to a loft area that offered women, men and children's ready made clothing. Shelves set into the exterior wall held pants, shirts and other sundry items. Realizing he was spending too much time looking, Beckett continued his trek to the counter, asking, "That coffee I smell…that fresh ground?"

A little under six feet, Ezra Shemwell had well defined muscles under his spotless white shirt from lifting fifty to one hundred pound grain sacks over the years. Now, that he'd let that girl deputy talk him into hiring a saddle-tramp some months back, by the name of Cody Brown, that had taken a lot of the load off of him. He had to admit the boy was working out just fine. This morning Brown was delivering a load of lumber out to Joe Jenkins' place. "Yea-up. Jus' finished grinding, how much ya need?"

"Oh, a pound...and do you have any feed oats?"

"Yep...how much ya need?"

"Oh, I guess two pounds ought to do it."

"That ain't much fer yure harse."

"I don't have much further to go until I reach my destination." A thought suddenly occurred. "Uh...do you have about two dozen washers also?"

Ezra threw the stranger a cock-eyed look. "You want two dozen washers, too?"

Beckett answered, "Uh...huh. Now, what do I owe you?" He asked, reaching into his pocket for the money.

Raising salt and pepper eyebrows, Ezra slid a small pad of paper closer. Taking the pencil out from behind his ear, he began writing. "Let's see...that's two cents a washer...times twenty-four...that's forty-eight cents and a dollar for the oats...and two bits for the coffee...comes to dollar and seventy-three cents," he said.

"Fine," Beckett said.

Ezra went about his business filling the man's order, and in a short while he handed one leather sack, a small bag of coffee and one muslin filled sack of oats to the stranger.

Throwing two coins on the counter top, they skittered until Ezra's hand stopped their momentum, Becket said, "Thanks, keep the change." Taking the three sacks, he strode back the way he'd come.

After scratching his head in puzzlement, Ezra put the money in his cash box while staring at the back of the fancy dressed stranger with a funny accent going out his door. Shaking his head, he returned to his chores.

After riding through town, Carson Beckett cut a back track to the alley, behind all the structures on that side of the street, following it until he came to the only brick building in town, the bank. Reining up behind this building, he slipped off the leather seat. After glancing around, he walked toward the barred back window. Becket peeked inside, sharp hazel eyes scoping out the interior.

Besides the window he looked in, another barred window divided the wall to his left. A large desk centered the room. The grey head of someone sitting at the desk rose above the chair back. Two chairs were placed in front of the desk, both empty. Behind them, sat the big bank safe, and through an open doorway he could see into the main lobby of the bank. Not another soul could be seen in the red brick building except the man in the chair and a teller standing at his post in the lobby. Beckett tied off the sorrel to one of the bars on the window. He heard a buckboard rattling by, stopping him in his tracks. His ears became aware that the sound came from the street in front of the bank, not the alley. Beckett let the air escape that he didn't realize he'd been holding.

Walking toward the lone door in the expanse of brick, his hand reached out touching the door handle, turning it. The door was locked. "Damn it," Beckett whispered. *Now, what!* He sighed inwardly. Bending down, he squinted one eye shut while the other stared into the hole for the key. Picking locks wasn't his best trait. Beckett straightened his lanky six foot frame back to its full height. He'd always left that up to his partner, Lacy Watson. Sighing, he walked to the corner of the building and peeked around the brick, down a short alley that ended on the main street.

Standing back, Beckett dug his bandana out of a pocket. Taking his hat off, he wiped the moisture from the inside band, thinking. Replacing the hat, he methodically folded the handkerchief into a neat little square before sticking it back into his pocket.

Carson sighed again. Going in the front door did not suit him. Thoughts running a muck through his brain, he realized this situation was definitely not going according to his plan. Peeking around the corner again, Beckett squared his shoulders and began walking toward the street.

Coming to the edge of the brick wall, Beckett stopped and leaned against it. Shade from the big oak brought welcome relief from the persistent sun. His head peeked around the front corner, observing the door to the bank and taking in the walk further down. *No one on this side,* his eyes noted. They continued to scan the other side of the street. *Just a few folks out and about,* he thought. Then, his eyes looked up and down the main thoroughfare of the small hamlet of White River. His eyes landed on the sign above the saloon. Beckett sighed wistfully again, thinking of that nice tall rye. His tongue sneaked out wetting his lips, imagining how the amber liquid would smell and the taste rinsing his throat clear of the dust. He exhaled noisily.

Boots took a few steps forward and then landed on the scarred planked walkway. They continued toward the bank's doorway, stopping suddenly when the door opened, surprising Beckett.

"Thanks Bill," a female voice called out. Olivia's skirts swished through the rest of the doorway, her hand closing the door with a soft click. Turning, she ran into the stranger, "Ooh…excuse me, sir," she said. Becket stepped to the side, bowing slightly. Two fingers brushed the brim of his grey felt hat in acknowledgment. "No harm done, Ma'am," he said, flashing a generous smile.

Olivia nodded. Stepping off the walk, she continued on down the street. She slowed at one point, turning, and looked once more at the stranger, thinking, *now who is that?* Nodding once again at the nicely dressed man, Olivia continued toward home.

Carson Beckett heaved a huge sigh as he thought. *Now, that is one fine specimen of a female.* As he watched the woman walk down the street, he considered, *Too bad I won't be around long enough to get to know her.*

He turned his attention back to the bank. Stepping closer to the door, Beckett peeked in and saw only the teller. Opening the door softly, he walked in shutting it behind him. His hand turned the deadbolt, locking the door, while his other hand flipped the open sign to the closed position, pulling down the two shades on the double doors.

Watching the stranger, Bill's brow wrinkled. "What 'da think you're doing, mister?" Bill demanded. "It ain't closing time yet!"

The stranger crossed over toward the teller, "I have some business I need to transact with you and the bank president," the stranger said smoothly, looking at the teller's magnified buggy eyes blinking at him like a barn owl through the bottom of two whiskey bottles.

"Frank?" Bill squeaked. "Frank…you better come quick," he screeched, seeing the pistol level at his chest. "Frank…I mean it! Get yore butt out here!"

Tearing his eyes away from the paperwork he had been trying to concentrate on, Frank Toomey looked up. A square built man, with tightly trimmed salt and pepper mustache that graced the space between his mouth and nose, Frank had opened the one and only bank in White River nineteen years ago. The backing of some eastern investors, and a few western ones, had helped to bring about the bank's existence. Justin Carrigan, being one of those western investors, had placed a lot of his own money into the bank. Frank didn't care how much money Carrigan had to invest, he'd still never liked the man. Frank put up with the sour, mean-tempered jackal because he had to. The bank had thrived, though not on back east standards, but, good for out here.

"Can't you take care of it yourself, Bill? That's what I pay you for, you idiot!" Frank groused.

A gun nodded at the teller. Eyes bulging further, Bill gulped, "Uh…no. You need to get out here, Frank. I mean it, Frank! Get yore butt, out here!"

Noting a different timbre, urgency in his easily flappable bank teller, Frank rose. Walking into the lobby of his establishment, he realized why the sudden insistence he'd heard in Bill's voice. The stranger's hand pointed a cannon at Bill's maroon vest. At least to Frank Toomey, it looked like a cannon, but then, all guns looked like cannons to Frank.

The stranger gave his winning smile, saying, "I need to

transact some business with you two."

Frank spluttered, "Like hell! You intend to rob us, you idiot!"

Beckett tilted his head. "That's true. But it's just a temporary withdrawal," he said.

Frank's face became redder by the second, turning more purple then red. "Like hell!" He repeated. "This bank ain't never been robbed before..."

Bill remained silent, barn owl eyes blinking rapidly, darting glances from one man to the other.

"Well, then," Beckett interrupted. "Let me be the first to congratulate you on such a finely run institution," he smiled. "Now..." He gestured with his pistol, directed the question toward the teller, "How about you finding a sack and filling it from your cash drawer?"

Bill swallowed, his adams apple bobbed like a cork on water as he nodded. His hand reached under the shelf where not only the extra sacks lay, but also a pistol. His hand moved to wrap fingers around the grip.

Spying the slight movement, Beckett warned him. "No sir, I wouldn't try that, just the bag is all you'll need," his foreign lilt said.

Bill released the pistol, laying it back down and reached for a sack instead. Pulling it out and opening it, he cleaned out his cash drawer, putting the cash in the sack. A shaking hand held it out to the stranger.

Retrieving the sack, Beckett said, "Thank you, gentlemen. I must say it has been a pleasure doing business with you." The pistol gestured for the two men to move into Frank's office. Both Frank and Bill stumbled over each others' feet to get through the door first. Beckett closed the door behind them, locking it. He quickly ran to the back door. Turning the key, he heard the tumblers roll then stop with a slight click. His hand opened the door.

Stepping out, he first went to his gear bag, pulling out the muslin sack of oats. He thrust the bills inside of that, and returned the sack to his gear bag. Next, he moved to his saddlebags, pulling out the leather pouch, switched the washers for the bills in the *First National Bank* bag, re-stuffing that into his saddlebag.

Dropping the leather sack, he grabbed his mount's reins. Leather creaked as he settled into the saddle. Nudging his sorrel out of the alley, Carson Beckett moseyed back the way he'd come. No sense in stirring up suspicion, he'd get caught soon enough. *I hope,* he thought.

Bill heaved in air, as a shaking hand pulled out his handkerchief, mopping his shiny top as he collapsed into a chair. Frank paced to and fro in his office, fist smacking into his hand every few seconds. His face had a bluish cast to it. The veins in his forehead and neck, pulsing at a rapid rate, seemed ready to explode any minute.

"We've got to get a hold of Rawley," Frank muttered under his breath.

Bill looked up, still blinking owlish eyes at Frank.

Stopping by the door, Frank rammed a thick shoulder into it. "Well…get over here and help me! You mealy mouthed rat!" Frank growled in frustration. Both men crunched shoulders into the door, neither physically fit to accomplish that feat. They couldn't climb out the windows either, bars prevented that.

Bill finally took a chair and using the legs, he tentatively first poked them through the bars. After several tries, he smashed the window. Tinkling as it broke, shards of glass sprinkled across the floor and ground outside. Bill heaved the chair aside, sending it clattering against the desk. Both Bill and Frank began hollering through the broken window.

Mike sweeping his walk, heard yelling coming from up the street. Resting the broom against the wall, he headed toward the sound. Stopping in front of the bank, Mike listened. The yelling came from the side of the building. Stepping around the corner, he saw shards of glass littering the dirt under the window. Continuing on, he became surprised to find

FRECKLED VENOM
COPPERHEAD STRIKES

Frank Toomey and Bill Wilson yelling their fool heads off through a broken window in the alley.

Giving both a disgusted look, Mike asked, "Here now, what 'r you two idiots screeching yure fool heads off for?"

Four eyes bulged, faces pressed against the bars. "The bank, it's been robbed! Get Rawley!"

Disbelief washed over Mike's face. "What? The bank's been robbed?"

"That's just what I said, you moron!" Frank's purple-red face spluttered, "Get the marshal! Damn it, Mike, move!"

It took Mike awhile to find Rawley and Lacy eating dinner at Maddie's. Rushing in, he sat down, trying to catch his breath. "Rawley…," Mike said heaving in air. "Rawley, the bank's been robbed!"

"What?" Two voices cried in unison.

"That's right, we've been robbed."

"When? Anyone hurt? I didn't hear any shots being fired," Rawley asked, Dropping his napkin, he hurriedly rose, pacing quickly out the door.

Lacy sprinted to keep up with his long strides.

Mike trotted keeping pace with Rawley. "I heard all this yelling, turns out Frank and Bill are holed up in Frank's office. That's all I know," he said.

The threesome arrived to find the shade pulled down and the sign saying closed. He tried the knob, it was locked. Rawley backed off and kicked the door, it gave some. Raising his leg, he gave another powerful kick. The door splintered, along with the windows shattering under the impact. The door now hung on its loosened hinges. He leveled his shoulder against it while his hands lifted the handle. Rawley pushed it open the rest of the way. The bottom edge of the door scraped against the plank flooring with a raspy sound. His boots crunched glass underfoot as Rawley entered calling out, "Frank? Bill?"

"In here, Rawley," came the muffled reply.

Moving toward Frank's office door, his fingers turned

the key in the lock. Rawley heard the tumblers roll, unlocking the solid fir door. He opened it, and surveyed the scene, safe still closed, a chair upturned by the desk, glass shards on the floor beneath the barred window. "You two okay?" He asked. Both nodded.

The marshal asked, "What happened?"

Two sets of bug-eyes just stared at the marshal, finally answering in unison. "We were robbed!"

"You recognize him? How much did he take? Describe the clothes he wore, horse he rode?" Pausing, Rawley waited on an answer from the two men, "Well, answer me!"

"We don't know who!" Frank spluttered, face a now deep purple. "Damn it, Rawley! No mask, fancy dresser, spoke with a foreign accent. After he took the money, he locked us up in my office."

Lacy had seen the back entrance open, stepping outside, she found the leather pouch. Her fingers toying with the bag, she knelt studying the boot marks and shod hoof prints. Following them she stopped under the big oak. A "Pffttt," escaped her lips, blowing copper feathers off her forehead. *No telling which way he went,* she thought. Looking up and down the street, Lacy saw the tracks mingling with many others in the dirt. Turning she began her backtrack down the alley, when she decided to take one more look. Going back to the big oak, she allowed her eyes to veer to her right. Walking over, she squatted next to the steps of the walk in front of Lydia's Millinery and Ladies Apparel Shoppe. Looking over her shoulder, Lacy's eyes picked up the tracks from between the alley. Following them once again, she could discern the tracks led northwest out of town. Standing quickly, Lacy ran back through the busted front doors of the bank.

"Didn't you hear me," Frank yelled. "I said he locked us up in my office, we didn't see which way he went!"

Tossing the leather pouch at Rawley, she said breathlessly, "He's heading northwest!" Lacy backed out of the office. Picking up speed, she ran to the stable, quickly slipping a bridle on Fancy. She grabbed a handful of mane and flung herself on the horse, bareback.

Rawley shoved the pouch into Frank's belly, "Gotta go," he said, rushing out the door, leaving Mike, Frank and Bill blinking in his wake.

Muscular legs pounded the street, Rawley slowing for only a second as the big grey flew by him, prompting a fleeting thought, *Damn kid!* His legs picked up their pace again as he made his way towards the Livery.

Mike, taking Frank's and Bill's arms, steered them across the street. "Those two will get yure money back, Frank. C' mon, you need a drink," Then, seeing the veins still rat-a-tat-tatting on his skull and throat, along with the red face," he added, "on second thought, maybe several," and he led the way to his place.

Carson Beckett sat on a little knoll, overlooking the road coming from town, waiting. Finally, he spied a trail of dust heading in his direction. *Well, that didn't take long,* he thought as he turned his horse, beginning a leisurely trot. He'd give them a chase in a little bit.

Lacy spotted the man and horse up ahead, and urged Fancy into her racing stride. Carson looked back. Seeing the gap closing, he clucked and kicked his mount harder.

Thirty yards, twenty, ten, five, Fancy matched pace alongside the rider. She prepared to jump the man next to her. *A little more*, her mind said, urging Fancy with pressure from her legs. Hands dropped the reins as both of her arms stretched, reaching for the man's shoulders. She made her move. Hands digging into his coat, she hung on. Lacy's muscular legs pushed her away from Fancy, her body shoving both her and the man off their horses in the process. The man twisted, placing Lacy under him as they hit the ground. The man's full weight landed on her, causing an *uff* to escape, accompanied by a rush of wind exiting her lungs.

Beckett scrambled off, running, sliding down the bank, disturbing rocks and dust that lifted in a haze following him.

Fancy slowed, whirled back, doing as she had been trained to do, cornering the man against a rock outcropping from the washed out bank.

Still lying where she'd tumbled off the horses, Lacy laid there blinking. She forced herself to breathe, trying to get the wind back into her lungs.

Noticing Lacy lying in the middle of the road had Rawley's heart jumping into his throat. In one fluid motion, he leapt off the bay. His boots, landing next to Lacy's prone body, produced puffs of yellow-brown dust. Noticing that she wasn't unconscious, his hands reached for her.

Two big paws suddenly grabbed the front of her shirt, yanking her up with such force, that her feet left the ground.

Rawley sat her back on her feet.

Lacy coughed as the air revitalized her lungs.

"Damn it, Lacy! What the hell were you trying to do? Get yourself killed? You damn fool!"

Her breath caught in her throat as she looked up at the marshal, prompting her air supply to be cut off, once again. She continued to marvel at Rawley's strength, *I'd forgotten how strong he can be.* Lacy blinked. Out of the blue she realized this man could suck the wind right out of her, and without him sitting on her, squishing her lungs, either!

Immediately, Lacy needed more air. Quickly bending over, she hid those thoughts from perceptive blue eyes, while her hands gripped her knees. She resumed coughing and gasping for air. Finally, she looked up. "I've done that before, never got hurt then," Lacy wheezed.

"You fool! You could've broke a leg, or worse, taking a risk like that!"

Lacy just stared at Rawley, as if marbles were clacking around in his head instead of brains. She continued gulping more air. Lacy squeaked, "Your hammerhead never would have caught up, that nag is only good for short distances!" She stopped, hauling in more wind for her starved lungs. "Fancy's built for the long haul," she said, taking another deep breath as

FRECKLED VENOM
COPPERHEAD STRIKES

she straightened, and then headed for the bank.

Rawley reached out, grabbing the first thing he could, that long copper rope, yanking her back to him. "Oh, no, you don't!"

"Oww! That hurt!" She said, as her elbow rammed into his muscular gut. Lacy's hands tried to wrestle her braid from his hand.

Releasing the copper rope, his other hand shoved Lacy toward his horse. "Git up there, you go get his harse," he growled, pushing her again.

Burnt coffee eyes were beginning to snap as Lacy gave him a look that should have singed his eyebrows.

He saw *that* look and knew what it meant. "I mean it, Sunshine. Afore you make me turn you over my knee and warm yure britches real good. Now, move it!" Rawley ordered her.

Furious at Rawley Lovett, Lacy opened her mouth to start a retort then changed her mind, snapping it shut, instead. She mounted his bay. Her legs too short for Rawley's long stirrups, she clamped her legs tight around the horse's ribs, and rode after the man's sorrel.

Rawley, shaking his head and watching Lacy go after the other horse, muttered, "Damn fool girl!"

Turning his attention toward the big grey, he saw she was giving the absconder fits. A swirling cloud of dust hung in the air over horse and man, as his legs kept dancing a little jig, dodging Fancy's powerful hooves. Her big head pushed at his chest, as she continued to snort into his face. He yelled and flailed his arms as he tried to protect himself.

Fancy's scared the living daylights out of the poor fella. Rawley grinned as he slid down the embankment, dislodging stones and dirt, leaving another plume of dust to follow mingling with the one Fancy and the man continued stirring into the air.

"Fancy," he said, coming alongside and patting her neck. "Good girl." Taking hold of her bridle and pulling, Rawley said, "Back, girl, back." Then, pulling his weapon, he stepped in front of the horse, his gun wiggling at the man. "Throw your pistol over here, two fingers."

"You keep that monster away from me, if I give you my gun, you understand?"

Rawley grinned his answer. "Aw, Fancy wouldn't hurt you. She just doesn't like people robbing her bank."

"Her bank? My ass!" Beckett returned grouchily, tossing his pistol at the marshal's boots. He hadn't expected this!

Tucking the man's weapon into his britches, Rawley gestured for him to begin moving up the slope.

Pulling the man's sorrel, Lacy began to hand the reins over. Seeing the man's face, her mouth dropped as did the reins, going bug-eyed at who stood in front of her.

The man gave a silly grin at Lacy's response.

"What the hell," she spluttered sliding off Rawley's horse. Turning, she picked up Fancy's reins and flung herself back on the grey. Then she just sat staring down at her old partner, Carson Beckett.

Rawley didn't know what was going on, but something sure as hell was. Swinging himself into the leather, Rawley directed his question at the two staring at each other. "You two know each other?"

Lacy's eyes never left Beckett as he, too, mounted. "You could say that."

Rawley leaned on his saddle horn. *The girl had more folks coming out of her past than bugs out of the woodwork.*

Still scrutinizing Beckett's face, her dark eyes dissected him. "Where's the money, Carson?"

Beckett took his time answering, his eyes focusing on the puffs of clouds sailing across the blue sky, instead of on dark eyes that had to be full of venom just about now. "Must have dropped it," he said in his lilting accent.

"Dropped it, my ass," she said testily, sliding off Fancy once again. She moved toward his horse. Her hands began digging through his saddle bags. Beckett turned in the saddle, the leather creaking as he watched the redhead rummage through his stuff.

Her hand felt something different, grabbing hold, she pulled it out. Turning it over, Lacy saw the words, *First National Bank*. She smiled.

Beckett tamped down a grin.

Opening the bag, Lacy stuck her hand in. Feeling cool metal coins, she pulled out a handful. Her smile disappeared into disbelief at what she found in her hand.

Giving Beckett a disgusted look, she said, "Aww…c' mon now…Beckett…the old washers in the money bag trick? That…Is…So…Old! Couldn't you come up with something better then, that?"

Tilting his head, Carson Beckett gazed fondly at the redhead. Copper feathers fluttered from a soft breeze surrounding a petite face smothered in freckles. Remembering a past that seemed to have flown by, with only the memories of a woman he'd fallen in love with, to keep him warm all those nights, he noted, *Lacy is still beautiful*. The young ingénue he'd met a long time ago had been an insecure, frightened kid back then; now, that image had vanished. The soft delicate edges becoming harder, Lacy had grown up.

He shrugged, saying with the soft lilt still in his voice, "You were the one who taught me that trick, *Cherie*."

Lacy rolled her eyes at his comment, and then focused them shrewdly on the wily Canadian. "Alright, Beckett, where'd you stash it this time?" She demanded, looking up at her old partner.

Beckett's mouth twitched, eyebrows rose as shoulders and hands gestured in a, 'I don't know,' expression.

"Damn you, Beckett," Lacy groused. Grabbing his gear bag, she pulled the string loose. Fingers opening the mouth wider, she upended the bag, the contents spilling across the road.

"Hey! That's my stuff you're treating so rudely."

Lacy gave him a smug look as she knelt next to the contents.

Sifting through the items, she picked up the oat feed bag and glanced up at Beckett. As she stood, her fingers dug a small pocketknife out of her back pocket. A sly smile tweaked the corners of her mouth, revealing shallow dimples in freckled cheeks. She proceeded to pull the blade out of its casing with her teeth. Lacy brandished the blade at Beckett giving him one last chance to fess up. Copper eyebrows rose when he remained silent. She slit the sack open, spilling the contents. Satisfaction slid across those freckles as the bills fell out with the oats. "Dropped it, huh?"

"Now, look what you have done, *Cherie*. You've ruined my poor horse's supper," he admonished her.

"Marshal, I'd like you to meet Carson Beckett. A silk tongued, handsome, intelligent, slippery, wily, double dealing, dirty rotten Canuck. Beckett, this is Marshal Rawley Lovett," Lacy said.

Acknowledging the marshal with a touch of two fingers to the brim of his grey felt hat, Carson Beckett turned his attention back to Lacy. "And you, my dear, Miss Watson, still haven't lost that sharp tongue of yours," he said giving her the smile that made women swoon over him.

Lacy tilted her head, allowing the dimples to show again. "Thought you were going to be out of circulation for a while?"

"Got out on my astute, good behavior," the lilt replied.

"Pfffttt, you? Good behavior? Tsk! Tsk! Leads me to think less highly of our judicial system," she replied. Picking up the bills scattered across the dirt, she stuffed them back inside the *First National Bank* bag. Lacy tossed it to Rawley. She then busied herself picking up all of Carson's belongings, replacing them in his gear bag, and hanging that back on his saddle horn. Giving him one last shrewd look, she walked over to Fancy, picking up the reins again. She flung herself back up on the grey and clucked her into motion. Lacy trotted out ahead of the men.

Rawley and Carson glanced at each other.

FRECKLED VENOM
COPPERHEAD STRIKES

Carson rolled his eyes.

Rawley grinned. So, he wasn't the only one Lacy pulled that venom-packed temper with, *Fang...you're dead,* he thought. His smile grew wider. *Nope! Life sure wasn't dull with Lacy around.*

CHAPTER FOURTEEN

Listening to Beckett and Lacy talking in low tones, their laughter leaking from the cell block, made a little green-eyed monster rise from within, giving fuel to unexpected anger, startling Rawley.

Calling out, Lacy said, "I'll bring you something to eat later." She closed the door behind her; then, stopped short, her smile fading quickly when she glimpsed Rawley's look.

The marshal moved to within a few feet of her. From that distance he still towered over the redhead, his jaw hard, lips in a tight line. Rawley's Wyoming blue eyes sent shards of flint her way.

Lacy blinked, and then returned the glare with one of her own. She folded her arms and stood her ground, waiting for him to say something; he always did. *Jabber-mouth,* she thought, not too nicely.

His anger dissipated as quickly as it had risen. Rawley moved to his desk. Sitting on a corner, he crossed his arms across his chest, as he asked, "What do you know about this Beckett?"

Relaxing some, when the flint disappeared from his eyes, Lacy gave her customary shrug. She moved, standing in front of the marshal, her fingers tucking themselves into back pockets. Her eyes resting on his, she answered, "Worked undercover with him a few times."

"Pinkerton's? Wells Fargo?"
Lacy nodded.
"What happened after that?"

She moved to rest her fanny on the edge of the desk next to him. "I don't know. I'd heard rumors the assignment he was working went bust. I guess he became the fall guy. Got five years, I'd heard," she said, her hands resting on the edge of the desk.

"I see," Rawley replied. "But why rob our bank?" He asked. "Though," speaking out loud, thinking. "We don't have much in it, but, by his clothes, you would think, he would have picked a big city?"

"I know," Lacy agreed. Her hand rubbed her forehead. "Robbing small banks is piddle squat to him, he likes flashier…" her voice trailed off, sudden realization hitting her. Moving quickly, Lacy flung open the door to the cell block, yelling at their prisoner, "Carson Beckett! You dirty rotten scoundrel, you'd better fess up! Robbing banks is not your style, you'd better fess up!" Color high in her cheeks, attesting to her volatile anger, Lacy planted fists on narrow hips, as she waited on Beckett to answer.

Following his copperhead into the cell block, Rawley thought, *I'm not about to miss this!*

Beckett watched the lawman enter on the heels of Lacy, and then rest his large frame against the bars of the opposite cell, with his bright blue eyes tinted with just a tad of merriment as he relaxed behind Lacy. Beckett noticed the thick arms as they crossed over a broad chest, sleeves of his cotton shirt rolled up exposing muscular forearms while a long dark encased leg bent its knee, and then pressed a booted sole against the bars.

At the same time, perceptive eyes took in Beckett's appearance. A stature of medium build, about six feet, dressed in a grey tweedy looking suit, with black piping accenting the edges of the coat. Curly sandy brown hair, framed a rectangular face with a deep clef in the chin. Hazel eyes above a nondescript nose, smiled with mischief at Lacy, now, too.

Beckett came to stand next to the bars, leaning against them. "*Mon Cherie,* if I had tried to contact you, you would just have thrown the letter away."

Lacy raised her voice saying, "I would not!"

Beckett waggled a finger in her face. "Ahh, Lacy," pronouncing her name *Lay cee.* "You know, it is not so."

"But, why our little po-dunk bank," she pressed.

Holding up his hands, palms open, he said, "I had to get your attention."

"My attention? You side-winding little pipsqueak! You didn't have to rob our bank, just to get my attention! You dumb-cluck! You could 've just asked for me? You didn't have to rob our bank," she said repeating herself.

"No, *Cherie,* you would not have given me the time of day. You forget, we did not part friends, eh?"

Rawley chuckled.

Lacy spun on him, bristling like a porcupine ready to throw its quills into his chest. "What's so funny?" She threatened.

The marshal raised his hands, fending off her anger. He also shook his head.

Lacy whirled back on Beckett, her eyes hot. "Why are you really here?" She asked. "You didn't get out just on good behavior, what's going on?"A thought suddenly exploded in her brain. "No. They let you out to go undercover again, didn't they? And they want us to work together again, don't they?"

Beckett looked over Lacy's head to the lawman. "See, marshal, our little Lacy, she's an intelligent one, no?"

Rawley moved alongside his deputy, looking down at her. He felt the anger rippling through the air around Lacy. He then looked back at Beckett, grinning. "That she is."

Her eyes bounced from one man to the other while her anger festered. Growling like a bear at the two men, she said, "*Our* Lacy? I belong to no one! You men are all alike, you think you've got to own a woman! Well, I've got news for both of you, you don't own me, and never will." Angry boot heels chewed up the wood planks as she marched out. She stopped and whirled back. Her fists struck her narrow hips as Lacy hissed at the two men like a mad cat, "Like I've said before, the only thing men are good for is target practice!" Her hand grabbed the edge of the cell block door, angrily flinging it shut as she exited, rattling the jamb.

Carson's face lit with mirth at Lacy's display of defiance. "A real pistol, that one, eh?"

Rawley couldn't keep the smile hidden either as he watched Lacy leave. "Yeah, she is that," he agreed. Turning his attention back to Beckett, he became serious. "All right, now that she's gone, how about telling me the real story?"

Leaning against the bars with his arms crossed, Carson began filling the marshal in. "I was framed on that last job. Let my guard down, getting myself into big trouble. The Wells Fargo boys found out where I was, said if I found Lacy Watson and we did this job together, they'd commute my sentence. So here I am."

"Lacy said you must've been framed," Rawley said, thinking as his eyes narrowed shrewdly at Beckett. "I'm going to have to check all this out, you know?"

Beckett nodded. "Just wire the boys in Cheyenne. Tell them, too, I've found Lacy. We'll get started as soon as we can," he said.

"I can't do that," Rawley replied.

"Why?"

"You've worked with her before, you know you can't tell her what to do, or had you forgotten that part?"

"I was hoping her disposition might have changed, even just a tiny bit," Beckett said sheepishly.

"I don't know what she was like then, but since I've known her, she's hard headed, stubborn, hot tempered, daring and a whole lotta other words, it'd take a month to say," Rawley finished, shaking his head.

Beckett's hazel eyes roamed the marshal's face, thinking, *he loves her*. He spoke quietly looking for verification of his thoughts, asking, "You love her, don't you?"

His head jerked up as Rawley cut the man in the cell a hard look. "That's my personal business," he said.

Carson moved to the bunk, sat and leaned against the wall. Hands laced behind his head, he gazed steadily at the lawman. "I fell in love with her once, too," he began. "Still do…love her, I mean. But not as a man loves the woman he'll marry. Now more like a deep friendship. The little sister I never had. A long time ago, I had asked her to marry me. I could offer her things, money, travel, my love. She turned me down flat. After she left, I realized she could never love me back. Sure, I could offer her things, things she might have wanted, but not the things she needed," Carson said.

Sitting up, he walked back to the marshal. Arms slid through the bars, elbows resting on the cross pieces, hazel eyes squinted at the man on the other side.

"The things she needed most of all, I could never give her," he said. Carson paused a moment, his mind retrieving the memories. Then he continued, saying, "A home, a real home, with kids underfoot and laughter. Lacy needs a lot of laughter. But, most of all, I wasn't the kind of man who could understand her and all of her persnickety ways," he stopped then, saying, "I get the feeling you understand her a lot better then I ever did."

Beckett's eyes canvassed the marshal's face. "I tried to change her to fit my way of life, but, I couldn't. That's why we didn't end on good terms. It bothered me enough that I let my guard down, why I got caught. So, if you love her, like I think you do, hold on to her, and take good care of her for me, will you?"

"That's an awful lot of words, for a con man, but then, con men are good with words," Rawley said, giving Beckett a contemptuous look. He walked out of the block, closing the door.

Combing his hair back in frustration, he thought, *Surely*

I can't be that transparent. A total stranger had voiced the same thoughts he'd had bringing Lacy back down from the mountain after she'd run away at Christmas. Why in the hell, hadn't she noticed it! Fetching his hat, Rawley headed for Ezra's where the telegraph office resided inside his store. He thought some more, *maybe she had, or maybe she hadn't. The way she's always clamming up and flattening her features, I can't tell.* Sending off the telegram, he'd get an answer in a few days.

* * *

Sitting in the rocker, brushing her hair, Lacy heard a soft knock on the door. "It's open," she said. Lacy stood as Rawley came in her quarters.

The marshal couldn't take his eyes off of his deputy, looking all soft and delicate, wearing that pretty pink and white gown. A far cry from the way she normally appeared. Rawley felt that damn desire clamping down on his gut spreading south. His longing to tell the redhead he loved her, to make love to her…but, Lacy had to make the first move. If he did, he'd just frighten her, and then he'd be back to square one again. Rawley put a lock and chain on his feelings for the moment.

Seeing his hesitation, Lacy stepped closer, asking, "What?"

That soft throaty voice of hers made his stomach wring even tighter. The lock and chain threatened to break. Dragging his eyes away from the redhead, he flicked them at the telegram, "Uh…I got a reply from the telegram I sent on Beckett," he said handing her the slip of paper.

Taking it, she read, *Confirmed. Carson Becket working special mission. Know whereabouts, Lacy Watson, please advise.*

Rawley hesitated again, before finally saying, "I'm gonna let him go tomorrow. If you want to go with him, I'll make sure your job is waiting for you, when you get back."

"I don't understand. You want me to go help Carson?" Lacy asked as confusion traveled across puckered up freckles.

"I just thought you might like to go, is all"

Still confused Lacy asked, "Why? I already have a job, I don't need another one."

"Lacy, you know I can't keep you from doing whatever you want. You're too independent for that," he replied. "If you want to go…go."

"You really don't care what I do, do you?" She asked. Just a little miffed that he hadn't tried harder to persuade her to stay.

Exhaling heavily, Rawley closed the few feet separating them. Soft lavender teased his nose. Taking his hand, he laid it alongside her neck. His thumb lightly caressed a thousand freckles. He spoke softly, "Sunshine, I care more then you know, but, that's a decision you'll have to make," he said brushing her lips softly with his. Rawley then turned. Walking out, he quietly closed the door.

Leaving Lacy standing, stunned.

* * *

Shaking hands the next morning outside the marshal's office, the two men reached an unspoken truce, about the woman they both loved. Rawley observed his redhead and the Canadian, as if watching a theatrical act in a big city. Lips moving mutely, their hands gesturing and smiles lighting faces like footlights at the front of a stage. He watched as Beckett brushed a kiss along Lacy's cheek. She smiled at him, and then reached up, wrapped her arms around his neck, and returned the kiss.

Resting against a weathered post on the edge of the walk, summer sky eyes turned just a tad bit frosty watching Lacy's display of affection for Beckett. Lips drew themselves into a tight white line. This was the only exhibition of emotion in Rawley's otherwise laid back persona.

Slipping into his saddle once again, Beckett leaned

down one more time to say something. Rawley noted that the words brought a quick smile to his copperhead's face.

Touching two fingers to the brim of his grey felt hat, Carson smiled at Lacy. He then looked up and gave a slight nod toward the marshal.

Tucking one thumb in a back pocket, Rawley returned the gesture.

Carson Beckett then headed out of town. Lacy's eyes followed him. He stopped one more time, turning in the saddle and gave the girl a salute. Lacy returned with a big wave and continued to follow him with her eyes, until he vanished out of sight.

Jamming hands in her hip pockets, she slowly walked toward Rawley and then began to climb the steps.

Watching his redhead come closer, he straightened. The other thumb found his other hip pocket and tucked itself inside. Rawley inquired, "That a see ya later wave, or good-bye?"

Her gaze drifted toward the dusty haze left by Beckett. Then refocusing and turning, Lacy took another step up. Tilting her head, she gazed at the marshal. A faint smile curved into freckled cheeks bringing out two dimples lighting a face with burnt coffee eyes. She finally said, "That was good-bye."

Rawley nodded.

"Umm…I was thinking to ride out to the ranch," Lacy said. "I want see Luis about something. You want to go with me?"

Surprised that she wanted to ride out to Carrigan Ranch and at the invite, he agreed.

* * *

Quietly riding alongside each other, Rawley had a question burning a hole in his gut. Finally he asked, "Do you love him?"

"Love who?"

"Beckett."

Pulling up Fancy, Lacy smiled slightly, looking across

the expansive vista. A multitude of soft purples, greens and golden prairie grasses were waving in the slight breeze. Mountains broke into the distant landscape, their peaks towering at the edge of the plains. The hardwoods, decked out in their bright green summer finery in the lower elevations, melted into the darker blue-green of spruce, pine and fir, dotting the mountainous panorama.

Lacy spoke with a quiet calm. "Carson Beckett is a charming, handsome rogue. When I first met him, I didn't like him. But, we had an assignment to work together. Carson has the personality that kind of grows on you. For the first time in a long time, I laughed, over silly stupid things he'd say. Carson made me feel like a woman too," Lacy said cutting a shy glance in Rawley's direction. "No, he didn't bed me, though, I know he wanted to. I also knew that he loved me, but I knew I couldn't return his love." Heaving a big sigh, she admitted, "I may never be able to love anyone." Then glancing at her hands, she said, "And that scares me, and I may never get over being afraid, either. But, well, back to your question, do I love Carson Beckett?" Shaking her head, she told him, "No. I never have and never will." She smiled quietly.

Watching sun-ripened copper curls whisper against a million freckles in the breeze, his stomach clenched. He wanted to make love to her right now, right here; surrounded by rich smelling earth and sun warmed grasses. But as Lacy had just said, she may never get over being afraid. Knowing that, he didn't want to take the risk of losing her when he'd just found her. Rawley silently expelled the breath he'd been holding, tamping down his feelings.

Lacy revealed a little more of her past with each passing day, giving him more of an answer than he'd expected. This last string of words she'd put together showed him that she was warming up to him, prompting her to become more comfortable with speech. She'd come a long way since that day he'd found her on the river bank, loaded with fever and blood poisoning. *We're making progress,* he thought.

CHAPTER FIFTEEN

Looking around at what she once called home, Lacy felt odd. Long ago memories kept invading her mind. Rawley, watching her closely, noticed that the veil had dropped down again.

Visibly, she shook herself trying to rid her brain of the memories, dark feelings that hadn't dissipated with the passage of time. Lacy rode Fancy into the barn, calling out, "Luis? Luis…you here?"

Lacy's nose tingled at the ripe barn scents wafting across her face in the warm interior. The sweet smell of hay and oats, the sharp odor of manure and well-oiled leather, along with a deep horsey aroma permeated the air. Slight rustlings were heard scurrying through old hay.

Hopping down, she began stripping Fancy of her gear. Rawley asked as he took the saddle from Lacy, "What are you planning on doing?"

She threw him a look, answering smugly, "You'll see."

He cocked a brow at the redhead, settling the saddle on a stall partition.

Lacy called out again, "Luis, you here?" Receiving no answer she proceeded to walk over to the riding gear, her hands running lightly over the smooth well-oiled surfaces of the dark leather.

Hearing footsteps, both visitors turned toward the

sound.

"May I help you, Señor?" The man addressed the marshal.

Rawley nodded toward Lacy.

The small muscular-framed man turned, facing the girl. Questions flickered across a time worn face, as weathered as old saddle leather, then slow recognition.

"Niña? Iss it really you?" He asked, holding out his arms. Lacy went into them. Luis pushed her back, proudly gazing at the young woman his little protégé had become.

Seventeen years ago, Luis Garcia and his wife, Maria had come to work for Justin Carrigan. Maria in the house and he, Luis as a horse trainer for the exquisite cross-blue bloods Justin Carrigan wanted to raise, sell and race.

It had been a happy home in the beginning, but then storm clouds seem to rise from the horizon and remained to this day, shrouding the ranch in their darkness.

Justin Carrigan became a hard taskmaster with a volatile temper. One learned quickly not to cross him, if one wanted to see tomorrow. Luis and Maria both knew what went on in the house at all hours of the day and night. But, remained quiet, keeping their thoughts to themselves.

Adam Carrigan, no longer able to control his drinking, became a shell of a man. Marie, Adam's wife, tried to maintain some sort of normalcy for the little redhead. She did what she could. Then darkness descended. Both Luis and Maria felt something had snapped in Justin's brain, causing a ruthless, evil personality to explode.

Only Luis and Maria attended the burial of Marie Carrigan, along with a few ranch hands, adding one body to the other already in the family plot, Emily Carrigan, Justin's wife. The little one, Lacy, had disappeared.

Now Justin Carrigan lay in the family plot next to his wife. The storm clouds, a little less threatening, allowed just the tiniest bit of sunshine to break through with the return of this red-head.

"Ahh, little one, you have grown to a beautiful woman!" Luis looked over his shoulder at the marshal, "Eh, Señor?"

Rawley nodded.

Luis asked, "Little one, you back to stay? Here at the ranch, ride the horses again?"

She shook her head, "No. I want to see if Fancy still has the speed she had when she was younger. I want you to help me train her again. We're entering the Fourth of July race this year," Lacy announced, cutting a fleeting look at Rawley, knowing he'd balk at the idea.

A chiseled jaw ground down hard hearing her plans. "Now...you just hold on a minute, Sunshine!" Rawley said sternly. He walked over to stand in front of her. "That's a rough race; it's not the same as running in circles. That's a man's race!" Realizing he'd slipped up. "Uh...it's a tough race even for men, no girl has ever ridden...uh...'er...woman...rode in it." Knowing he'd dug a deep hole, he cast his eyes toward the barn's rafters, staring at the strings of dusty cobwebs dripping from the beams.

Speaking around the smile that threatened to bust out, Lacy gave her old trainer a smug look, "Well...guess there's always a first time, right...Luis?" She said. "How about we show the marshal, a few things, huh...Señor?"

Picking out a saddle for Fancy, Lacy walked back to the big grey, throwing the little thing on her back.

Rawley walked over. "What the hell is that?"

Seeing Lacy's withering look, Luis spoke matter factually, "A saddle, Señor."

"Like hell," Rawley groused. "That ain't no saddle, that's nuthin' but a pimple!" He spun around addressing the little Mexican. "How do you expect to stay on that little thing? Why...there's nuthin' there, to hold you in!" referring to the lack of a more pronounced pommel and cantle, like the saddles Rawley was familiar with. How'd you expect to stay on that?" He repeated.

"That's the idea, light, the horse move smoother, increasing speed. Though, it help, you got good rider, and if horse loves to run and this one..." Luis said patting the big grey's neck. "She love to run."

Two dimples graced freckled cheeks as Lacy smiled, listening to the conversation of the two men while cinching the saddle tight around Fancy's girth.

Rawley just exhaled noisily.

The three walked out of the barn, Fancy between them. As they neared the track, Fancy's eyes became more alert, her ears perked up, she blew loudly, shaking her head, making the bit jingle. Her legs danced with excitement.

Barely able to hang on to the bridle, Lacy yelped, "Luis, look! She remembers! You remember this don't you, Fancy girl!" She crooned to the grey.

Leading Fancy onto the track, Lacy turned to Rawley, saying, "Boot me up."

"Huh?"

"Boot me up, please?"

Realizing now what she wanted, Rawley complied by cupping his hands. As soon as Lacy placed her foot there, he lifted the light weight of his deputy.

Settling her seat, Lacy stuck her boots in the irons. "I'm going to limber her up a bit," Lacy said clucking Fancy into a lope.

Rawley, still skeptical at Lacy's attempt to ride the big grey in the Fourth of July race, resettled his hat, bringing the brim down lower against the sun's glare on the dirt track. He squinted, his eyes following the girl, so easily riding the grey.

Seeing the marshal's look, Luis took his arm and steered him off the track. "Señor, if things had not turned out as they did, the little one would be training and riding these exceptional animals. She has the gift, you see, you wait and see," Luis said.

Cocking his brow at the man, Rawley answered with more skepticism, "If you say so, Luis, if you say so."

FRECKLED VENOM
COPPERHEAD STRIKES

    Luis grinned at the marshal's reaction. The man was in for a big surprise, a really big surprise.
    Lacy loped past them and then turned Fancy back. "She's chomping at the bit, Luis," she said with a big smile. The combination of wind and excitement made Lacy's face bloom with color overshadowing tawny freckles.
    Arms resting on the fence, his hands laced together in front of him, Rawley knew now that Lacy was in her element riding the mare. A woman of many talents, despite a past that had plagued her for so many years, the girl continued to amaze him. Rawley watched Lacy line Fancy up with the pole. The mare's hooves continued dancing in the dirt with impatience, stirring miniature dust devils.
    "Ready when you are," she called out, hunching over the neck of her friend, fingers entwining themselves in the black and grey mane. Lacy waited for the shot to ring out.
    "Señor, will you do the honors?" Luis asked, gesturing, at Rawley's pistol.
    Looking down, Rawley pulled his weapon. Raising it in the air, he pulled the trigger. Flames burst out of the muzzle, accompanying the loud retort, which reverberated against the clear warm air.
    Luis hit the button on the watch simultaneously.
    Fancy bolted, taking off around the track. Lacy moved in rhythm with the mare. Four hooves pummeled the dirt, reminding Rawley of a storm with distant thunder.

    *   *   *

    Continuing to stand at the window in the house, Adam Carrigan observed the activity happening at the track. Deciding he'd waited long enough, nine and a half years was long enough not to see or speak to his daughter.

    *   *   *

    Horse and rider flew by. Luis clicked the button, stopping the clock. Glancing at the time, he gave a whoop and began dancing a little jig.

Rawley laughed.

Luis stopped. "The little one, she can ride, no? Señor?"

"Yeah, Amigo, the little one can ride," Rawley admitted slapping Luis's back.

"You let her ride the race now, Señor?" Luis asked.

"Well...that's up to Lacy, I don't make her decisions for her," Rawley replied.

"The little one, she strong headed, like a donkey...eh?" Luis said voicing Rawley's thoughts.

Rawley grinned, "That's putting it mildly, my friend."

Both men faced the excited rider coming up. With color fanning that freckled face, and eyes shining like dark obsidian, Lacy asked, "Well, how'd she do?" Sliding her feet out of the stirrups, she let them dangle down the horse's heaving ribs. She patted Fancy's wet neck.

"Little one, age has caught up with this one," Luis stated sadly.

Lacy's face fell a mile.

Rawley ducked his head so he wouldn't give Luis's secret away.

"This one," Luis began, rubbing Fancy's nose. "She only ten seconds off her best time!" He shouted.

Lacy looked as if she hadn't heard right, then it dawned on her. Squealing, she flung herself off the horse into Rawley's arms, taking him by surprise. Squeezing his neck hard, she plastered a hard kiss on his cheek. Leaning back, her arms resting lightly on his shoulders, she smiled into his eyes, exposing rare glimpses of dimples in a cute as a speckled pup face.

Taken aback at Lacy's display of emotion, Rawley just stood there blinking with his arms wrapped around this firebrand. The soft curve of her breasts pressed against his chest, legs wrapped tightly around his waist, made his stomach flip. The sensation continued crawling toward his knees.

Realizing what she had just done, Lacy slowly extracted herself from the marshal's body, stirring more emotions within her own inner core. Unaware of the strong impact it made on him, she shied away suddenly, wiping sweaty palms on her britches. "I'm sorry, guess I got too excited."

The moment disappeared. *Damn,* he thought, wishing the moment had stayed just a bit longer. He said instead, "Don't be sorry, I kind of enjoyed that." Rawley gave the rider one of his lopsided grins.

Nibbling on her bottom lip, Lacy just nodded, leading Fancy back toward the barn.

* * *

Luis proudly showed Rawley all the records he'd kept on the Carrigan stock.

I need to get a grip, she thought. *Throwing myself at Rawley like I'm some kind of hussy, he's my Boss for heaven's sake!* Once again her mind told her one thing, her heart another. She chose to ignore the heart part.

Reading over Luis's shoulder, Rawley watched as he wrote down Fancy's time. "Moonlit Fancy?" He asked directing the question over his shoulder at Lacy.

When Rawley said the grey's full name, her hand hesitated over Fancy's coat. Lacy wandered over, her boots pausing several feet from the two men. Her hands continued to twist the towel into a tight rope, try as she might to gain some kind of control over her unexpected emotions.

She nodded as she said, "Uh-huh. I used to come out at night and watch her when she was little. One night the moon hit her just right, so I named her Moonlit Fancy," Lacy hesitated, mentally shaking herself as more memories invaded her mind. "Then she became my birthday present," she said.

Rawley caught the veil dropping down again in Lacy's eyes with the words *birthday present.*

Her eyes quickly darted down, hopefully hiding those memories from Rawley's penetrating gaze. Her boot began digging a trench in the dirt floor, then stopped. Lacy turned, hurrying back to rub the grey down.

A shadow graced the door, causing chatter from both Luis and Rawley to cease as they recognized the one standing there.

Hearing the quiet all of a sudden, Lacy glanced back at the men. The direction of their eyes told her someone stood in the doorway. Stepping away from Fancy, her eyes came to rest on the man she had neither seen nor spoken to in over nine years.

Wordlessly, Lacy walked over to her gear. Picking up the blanket and saddle, she began putting the tack back on Fancy. Reaching under, her hand grabbed the cinch, trying to fasten it. But her hands trembled so hard, she couldn't seem to get the band attached to the buckle. A big palm was suddenly there, taking over. Rawley had placed himself between Adam Carrigan and Lacy. Not knowing exactly what Lacy's reaction would be. At least this time she had left her pistol in the office.

Footsteps moved closer, crunching the hay strewn dirt. A quiet voice spoke, "Lacy? I'd like a word with you, please?"

Her hands kept fiddling with the saddle blanket, tugging here, smoothing there.

"Please? I'd like to speak with you," the voice pleaded.

Moving around Rawley, Lacy took Fancy's reins and walked toward her father and *escape.*

Stopping alongside her father, Lacy looked up, speaking softly, "You said it all, over nine years ago, by not doing anything. There's nothing left to say," she said. Continuing outside, she mounted the big grey.

Placing his body near Adam Carrigan, Rawley waited.

"Lacy, wait," her father cried, quickly taking hold of Fancy's bridle. The horse's head jerked at the sudden movement. "Wait! I really want to talk to you. I have things I need to say."

Her eyes spewed venom. Lacy gazed into what once had been a handsome face. Now, blood-shot brown eyes were the main focus, accompanied by lined pale yellow skin. Too much grey shot through dull brown hair for his age. Clothes which once fit a muscular body, hung haphazardly on an emancipated frame.

"I...I wanted to say I'm sorry. I should've done something years ago, but, I didn't, I'm sorry. I hope that one day you can find it in your heart to forgive me," her father said. His hand dropped from the bridle at his daughter's silence.

A hard freckled face replied, "A little late for that now, isn't it, Mr. Carrigan? If you weren't so yella in the first place, your wife would still be alive and your daughter wouldn't have run away. No, Mr. Carrigan, it's a little late to be making amends now," Lacy said as a boot slid out of the stirrup. Quick as one might snap their fingers, the sole of her boot punched Carrigan's chest. He gasped, landing on his backside in the dirt.

She stared at her father for a moment before saying, "That's where you belong, in the dirt with the hogs, you bastard!" Lacy banged heels into Fancy's ribs, making the horse bolt.

He slowly pushed himself up, staggering as he did so. His shoulder's slumping, he watched his daughter riding out of his life once again. Adam Carrigan turned and headed for the one thing that seemed to console him, and relieve him of his constant misery.

The barn remained thick with the fumes of emotions. If someone were to light a match, it would have exploded.

Eyes sparking with anger, Rawley turned to Luis, asking, "Where's he going now?"

Luis sighed resignedly, "Where he always goes, Señor, the bottom of a bottle."

"He has a ranch to run! A daughter, he could have back if he worked at it!"

"Señor Carrigan, he have good men to run the ranch for him. The little one...," Luis sighed, shaking his head. "It may be too late for that. Only the Father above knows."

These Carrigan men had pushed him to his limits. First the old man and now Adam. Knowing it wasn't any of his business, Rawley strode purposely to the huge log home. He was going to straighten out Lacy's father, even if he had to take the man into Doc to patch up afterwords.

* * *

Lacy slowed when she saw the family plot. She sat staring at the three graves from Fancy's back. One still so new the grass hadn't taken hold in the dirt, yet. Slipping out of the saddle, she dropped Fancy's reins and slowly made her way toward the only one she cared about. Her eyes caressed the marker. *Marie Carrigan, Beloved wife and mother, 1828 – 1869.*

A bitter laugh escaped her throat, surprising Lacy. She whispered violently to the stiff breeze blowing the red-gold curls framing her face. "Beloved wife? Ha! You bastard! You didn't love mama and me. No! The only thing you loved was your whiskey!" Lacy let fly with a wad of spit, emphasizing her words. Somehow, someway, it landed on Justin Carrigan's marker.

Kneeling by her mother's marker, Lacy rested a hand on the sun-warmed stone. "I'm home, mama. I did what you told me to in your letter…it was hard, mama. So very hard, but, I…I survived, like you said I would," she said. Her finger traced the name carved into the pebbly stone. Dark coffee colored eyes suddenly filled with moisture and spilled over on freckled cheeks, dripping off her chin onto her britches. "I guess you already know…I killed the bastard…I…mama? I miss you…so much…I…," her voice choked.

Lacy rose quickly and ran to Fancy. Wiping her face with the sleeve of her shirt, she picked up the reins. Hurriedly mounting, she headed for the river, the memories still too painful, even after all these years.

CHAPTER SIXTEEN

Slamming the door hard enough to rattle windows, Rawley stood in the rich, dark interior of the Carrigan home.

Hearing the door slam, a pretty dark-haired, hourglass figure of a woman came running from the back of the house. Stopping in front of him, Maria questioned the marshal, "Señor?"

"Where is he, Maria?"

Black eyes big in her pretty face, she swiftly glanced toward the study. "There, Señor. What…?"

"Maria, I'm gonna close those doors," Rawley said with his finger pointing, and his voice low with anger. "Don't come in, no matter what you hear. You understand me?"

"Si, Señor." Round eyes followed the big marshal as he entered the room, watched as he closed the doors, then she ran to get Luis.

* * *

Adam Carrigan slouched in a big leather chair. Glass cocked crazily in one hand, liquid threatened to spill any moment. The other hand held on to the neck of a corked bottle, resting in his lap.

Rawley narrowed blue eyes that had turned to steel chips at the man who remained Lacy's father. The room, carrying the light sweet smell of whiskey, was stuffy and overly warm due to the fire in the hearth. The only light in the darkened room, heavy drapes had been pulled across large windows shutting out the summer sun. Strolling closer, Rawley continued to send a demonic gaze toward Adam.

Carrigan squinted bleary eyes up at the marshal. "Well…now, marshal, you still here?"

"You and I have a little business to take care of."

Slurring, "Well, I jus' ah l'il bussy right now, come back 'nother day." He moved the glass toward his lips for another sip.

Stepping forward, Rawley swatted the glass out of his hand with such force that it smashed in the fireplace, igniting more flames. "That get your attention, Carrigan," the marshal growled.

"Why, marshal, ya din'na haft tae do that?" Adam said. He struggled out of the chair, a hand hanging on to the corked bottle. He weaved toward the sideboard for another glass. Finding one, he turned, and leaned against the piece of furniture, his body continuing to totter. He tried to steady himself, by placing his feet in a wide stance while he pulled the cork out with his teeth. A hand gestured at the marshal. Speaking around the cork in his mouth, he asked, "Wanna one?" Receiving no response, Adam shrugged, replying, "Sush…yourself." As he splashed the amber liquid into the glass, it slipped through his fingers, shattering when it hit the floor. "Oh, damn," Carrigan slurred reaching behind him for another glass.

Rawley took the bottle out of his hand. Turning, he threw that into the fireplace, where it exploded. The sweet smell of sour mash rose into the thick heavy air.

The sound of the bottle shattering caught Carrigan's attention. He squinted blearily at the hearth, and then dragged his eyes away from the fire, trying to focus on the big man glaring angrily at him. "Aww now…you din'na haft tae do that," Adam slurred.

"You've had enough, Carrigan," Rawley said as two big hands grabbed Carrigan's shirt, pulling him within inches.

FRECKLED VENOM
COPPERHEAD STRIKES

Rawley recoiled at the awful stench of soured booze emitting from Carrigan's gapping mouth.

Adam's eyes blinked as he tried to focus on the marshal.

"When you gonna find some guts in that yella belly of yours and face up to the facts! Huh, Carrigan! Your daughter has, now it's your turn," the marshal said, shoving the man away. Rawley watched him tumble to the floor. He made no attempt to help Carrigan.

Adam just laid there staring at the lawman. Finally, he moved using a chair to pull himself up, Carrigan stood swaying. "You like my daughter, marshal? She warm your bed nice at night?"

Flashes of angry red and yellow sparks appeared to fly in front of his eyes. Rawley backhanded Carrigan, hurling him into the big leather chair. It flipped, landing on its back, sliding across the wood floor from the marshal's impact.

Carrigan twisted against the leather, trying to right himself. He gasped as two hands dragged him up, slapping him once, and then again. Adam's knees sagged, as blood oozed from his cut lip. Rawley wasn't through. He continued to hold the soppy weak excuse for a man, upright.

The anger in his voice came out like cold steel in zero degree weather. He gritted between clenched teeth, "That's your father talking, I'll let that one ride, for now," he said. "I respect and admire your daughter, which is more than I can say for either you or your father. You're a stupid fool! Life is hard. Instead of running and hiding in a bottle, face up to it! You need to get a grip, Carrigan. Your daughter has had a hell of a hard life! Something she should've never experienced! But she survived, and in some ways, is a better *man* then you'll ever be."

"You have a ranch to run, and a daughter you need to mend fences with! I had hoped if I knocked some sense into that soggy brain of yours, you just might become a father to her," Rawley said shoving him. Carrigan fell against the toppled chair, arms and legs sprawled like a rag doll. Bleary eyes blinked. Trying to focus again, he just stared at the lawman.

"I can see I was wrong. Lacy is right, it's too late to make amends now," the marshal said.

Rawley walked out of the room, surprised when he opened the door to find Luis and Maria standing there, listening. "He's alright, I didn't kill him, though I should have," Rawley threw the words over his shoulder as he exited the house.

* * *

When she became upset, Lacy had taken to going to the river, skipping rocks across the surface. Something about the flow of water, skipping the flat stones, counting the times each one jumped, seemed to calm her.

Lacy thought, *I need to bring the boys out here for a day of fishing and rock skipping, yeah, that would be fun.* After the race, before school started again, she decided.

* * *

The marshal sat astride his bay, watching the lone figure skipping stones into the river. Calm now, Rawley wouldn't blame Lacy if she never wanted another thing to do with her father. It would serve Adam Carrigan right. He didn't know how Luis and Maria continued working for the man.

Turning his horse, Rawley went back to town. Lacy would come when she was ready.

CHAPTER SEVENTEEN

Lacy remained quiet the next few days. Rawley had learned the hard way, to leave her alone, let her come around in her own time frame. She'd never been a chatter-box; at least since he'd known her, so used she was to keeping a tight grip on her mouth all those years. He knew it wasn't easy for her to talk about her personal side, feelings and what-not. Even though Lacy continued being kind of stringy with words, at least now, it wasn't always a one-sided conversation, either.

* * *

Finishing up supper one evening at Maddie's, Lacy broached the subject of the race. "Umm, do you know the area where the race is run, the direction, uh, the course they take?"

"Yeah...why?"

"I want to learn it, take Fancy over it enough, so that's she familiar with it too. Could you show it to me?"

"You're still serious about this race, aren't you?"

Fiddling with her napkin, Lacy nodded.

"Nuthin' I say will get you to change your mind?"

Eyes still downcast, she shook her head no.

"I supposed that if a vote were taken, you and Fancy would vote yes?" He grinned across the table at his redhead, "So I'd be out voted, right?"

Tilting her head, burnt coffee eyes peeked at him from

under red-gold lashes, allowing the dimples to sneak through for her answer.

A black brow cocked. "I see. Alright, we'll go out there tomorrow," Rawley finally agreed.

CHAPTER EIGHTEEN

Turning in his saddle, the leather creaked. They were on the southeast side of town. His finger gestured while Rawley said, "That telegraph pole is the start and finish." Giving Lacy a long look, he noticed how her eyes, surrounded by those freckles, had brightened, her cheeks carrying a dusting of pink from the excitement. He'd seen that same look when they'd tested Fancy back at the ranch. He knew in his heart, this was her first love, racing Fancy. Everything else played second and third fiddle, including him. "C' mon, Sunshine, I'll show you the rest of the course."

The bay and the grey loped, shoulder to shoulder, their riders sitting relaxed, hands easy on the reins as they rode through the open grasslands.

Rawley slowed, reining up in front of a grouping of boulders. There was one huge boulder surrounded by smaller ones that reminded everyone of a mother hen and her chicks. "When you come to Hens and Chickens," he said. "You circle and head for that stand of pines," he added pointing ahead.

Nearing the pines, Rawley pulled up. He pointed across at three downed trees. "That was part of the course until a big storm took down those trees, now we go through these pines."

"Is there any rule that says I can't go that way?" She asked, pointing over at the downed trees.

Resting his forearms on the saddle horn, Rawley

answered, "Well…no…but, it's not exactly safe…too many holes. The riders didn't want to ruin a good harse, so they just changed the course a little."

Riding over to the downed trees, she looked over the situation. Sliding out of the saddle, Lacy climbed on the first tree, there she sat calculating the distance between the first and second tree, *two lengths.* Hopping down, Lacy walked over to the second tree, and calculated again, *length and a half,* to the third tree. Each tree was only three, maybe four rails high. Fancy had cleared higher than that on occasion. Looking over the ground, she found most of the holes by the roots, the soil smoothing out, becoming firmer, further up the trunks. *We could do it,* she thought. *If Fancy jumps the trees, further away from the roots.* Lacy climbed back over the trees. She picked up Fancy's reins.

Rawley interrupted her thoughts by saying, "If you're thinking of trying it, Sunshine, don't. Too many holes, you could break Fancy's leg, I'd hate to see that happen to her."

Grabbing a handful of mane, Lacy vaulted easily into the saddle. "Okay…," she said.

Surprised, Rawley asked, "That's it? No argument? No fussing, ranting and raving?"

"Nope! Where to next?"

His eyes narrowed shrewdly at the redhead. Lacy had something up her sleeve Rawley knew. The girl could be a persnickety cuss and tight lipped as a locked trunk, *or the Denver Mint.* "Don't play innocent with me, Sunshine."

Lacy gave him a flat stare.

"You got something up your sleeve, I know you do. I'm warning you, you lose Fancy, I'd have to put up with you not talking to me again."

"Where to next," Lacy just asked.

Rawley gave up. She wasn't going to listen anyhow.

Leading the way through the pines, ducking low hanging branches, Rawley warned, "Be careful, when you come through here, some of the riders like to snap the branches back, knocking others off."

Lacy just shrugged.

Rolling eyes as he walked his mount to the edge of the stand, he pointed once again. "You cross the creek, head straight up that embankment, then you'll be on flat ground again," he said urging his horse forward, both traveling this part of the course. "Then circle north around the stand of pines we just came through and come back to Hens and Chickens. The final stretch is all grassland back to the pole," he finished and then waited to hear what Lacy would say next.

Nibbling on a corner of her bottom lip Lacy said. "Fancy could do it. How many are usually in the race?"

"Oh, ten to twelve, maybe more this year, you're causing quite a stir," he admitted. "Never been a girl…ah…woman enter the race before."

"Well, there's always a first time," she said heading back to Hens and Chickens. As they neared the rock formations that stuck up out of the prairie grasses like knots on a log, Lacy said, "Race you back to the pole?"

Rawley hesitated; he knew he was no match for his deputy.

Lacy answered his silence, "You win, I buy supper, if I win…"

"I buy supper," was his reply.

"Uh-huh. Well? You wan' a see what kind of stuffing your bay pony is made of, or not?" Lacy teased. "I'll even give you a ten yard head start."

Narrowing his eyes, he gauged the distance. "Make it twenty, and you got a deal."

Nibbling on that bottom lip again, Lacy sat thinking. Fancy hated having a horse in front of her, it always made her run harder. "Okay," she said. "Start whenever."

Lining up alongside Lacy and Fancy, Rawley then kicked the big bay.

Telescoping her gaze, Lacy squinted against the sunlight as the distance grew, five, ten yards. Leaning forward, a fist wrapped itself in the black and grey mane. She whispered to Fancy, "Let's show that silly marshal what' cha really got, girl!"

Taking off after the bay, Lacy held the reins light, moving as one with the mare, allowed Fancy the freedom she loved. It didn't take long. The grey's strides approached the pony's rump. Pulling alongside the bay, two horses raced nose to nose. Fancy kept pace with the bay for about three lengths, and then pulled away leaving the bay and the marshal in their dust. When that happened, Rawley just reined his horse up.

Lacy came back to him with a big smile on her face, dimples deep within that smile, her eyes shining like polished pecan shells. She said, "Told ya, Fancy was built for the long haul. We need to walk them so they don't stiffen up." She led the way back to Hens and Chickens.

Rawley just rolled his eyes, thinking, *Maybe Maddie will let me pay her a little each payday.* He exhaled noisily, resetting his hat more firmly on his head.

Throwing a look over her shoulder, Lacy cut the marshal a sly glance. *I'm ordering everything off the Blue Bird's menu tonight! Especially apple pie!*

CHAPTER NINETEEN

Standing in front of Lydia's Millinery and Ladies Apparel Shoppe, Lacy's eyes took in the dress hanging on a form in the window. *That's the one I want, but in a different color.* The dress in the window was made of a deep rose material, with a square neckline and capped sleeves. The neckline and sleeves were edged in a pretty white lace. Four large buttons, down the front of the bodice, ended at the waist, where a big bow was tied. The back of the bodice had corset like ribbon that criss-crossed for a slim, tight fitting look. A full skirt overlaid layers and layers of white petticoats peeking from under the material. A draped effect had been achieved by splitting the rose colored material at the waist under the bow, allowing a deep upside down V to emerge, exposing the layers of white petticoats in front. Widenned and curved across the back, it stopped about six inches above the petticoat hem. White lace accented the edges of the rose material.

Hands stuck deep into her front pockets, Lacy rocked back and forth on the balls of her feet. Her fingers touched the bills she had stuffed in one pocket, the money she'd been saving in secret, still there.

Lacy had wanted to visit this shop for a long time, but didn't want to ruin her hard-nosed reputation by becoming too…feminine, although she knew Rawley would appreciate it, if she did.

She "pfftted," copper bangs off her forehead. She wanted to surprise Rawley for the Fourth of July dance. Lacy had never bought a dress before. Her mama had always attended to those things in the past. Buying her first real dress had Lacy's insides tickling with anticipation.

Her hand reached out, turning the crystal and brass knob. She pushed open the door. Lacy stepped over the threshold, with the bell above dinging once and then again as she closed the door with a soft click. All those colorful hats and dresses dotting the interior of the shop had her gazing around in wonder. Walking over to a rack filled with pre-made dresses, skirts and blouses, her fingers caressed the different materials, enjoying the sensation of the cloth against her fingertips.

Lacy sighed wistfully, reminiscing her childhood, how a dress had made her feel back then, like a princess. She sighed again; she couldn't bring back those days, nor did she want to. But, she did want to feel like a lady for once, if that could be remotely possible.

"Yes…may I help…Oh, it's you," Lydia Marshall said without enthusiasm when she saw who happened to be standing in her shop.

Lacy half turned, throwing a glance in Lydia's direction. "Meaning…"

Taking a few steps, Lydia closed the gap between the two women. Dove grey eyes took in Lacy's manly attire. The sleeves rolled above the elbows exposing tan freckled arms dotted with tiny little hairs, glistening red-gold in the sunlight streaming through a side window. A light-weight green and cream checkered shirt was tucked into tan canvas britches. A pistol rested underneath her left arm, belt notched neatly around a small waist.

"Meaning…I'm surprised to see you in my shop. Ezra's clothing is more your style," Lydia said in a clipped northern accent.

A red-gold brow soared at the barb. Lacy kept quiet as she continued to roam around the shop, looking.

FRECKLED VENOM
COPPERHEAD STRIKES

Lydia Marshall had heard the rumors surrounding the female deputy. Lacy Carrigan provided new fodder for the gossip mill, always, packing that hardware, like a gunslinger. She couldn't for the life of her understand what Rawley Lovett saw in this little tart. A handsome man like Rawley, taking up with the likes of her, why...she even lived in the office with him! She could just imagine what went on behind closed doors at night. Lydia didn't care for the deputy or her ways, trying to be a man all the time. The sooner she could get her out of her shop, the better. After all, she, Lydia Marshall had a reputation to maintain.

"Is there something in particular you are looking for?" Lydia asked, removing the pincushion from her wrist, laying it on the counter.

Looking up from the dresses, Lacy stared at the black-haired dressmaker, whose hair was encased in a black netted snood, confining her shiny tresses.

A crisp white shirtwaist blouse accented the delicate creamy porcelain skin; a dark blue skirt finished the ensemble. Big round dove-grey eyes held a haughty look from under sculpted brows, above pretty nose over pouty lips. Lydia Marshall had the same petite frame as Lacy, only taller.

"You came from back east, didn't you?" Lacy asked, her fingers trailing along the clothes, nonchalantly.

"Yes," came the clipped answer, "From Philadelphia," Lydia said. She moved toward the deputy; her hand slapped Lacy's fingers away from the clothing. "Did you wash your hands before coming in here?" Lydia snapped. "I don't want your dirty paws leaving marks on my dresses, it's not polite."

Lacy's gaze quickly shifted to her hands. *Uh...well...no,* she thought. Coffee colored eyes narrowed, drawing the freckles in closer, "Didn't know that was a requirement to enter your shop," she replied.

Lydia sniffed, pouty mouth aimed at the ceiling.

Lacy pressed. "What brought you all the way out here? I'm sure your dresses would be more appreciated in Kansas

City or even Cheyenne," she said.

"My personal affairs are none of your business." *I'm not telling this hussy anything,* Lydia thought.

Shrugging, Lacy looked at the ceiling, *not a cobweb in sight.* "You make Olivia Johnston's and Miz Birdy Dawson's clothes don't you?" She asked, changing the subject.

"Look...if you are going to waste my time with idle chit-chat...," Lydia began, walking back to the counter. She picked up the pincushion and slid it back on her wrist. "I'm going to have to ask you to leave. I have work to do."

"I wouldn't call it idle chit-chat, I'm just curious, especially when I intend to throw some business your way," Lacy said. "I want to buy a dress."

Disbelief flew across Lydia Marshall's face. "You...a dress?" She exclaimed.

Walking over to the display window, Lacy pointed. "That one, I want that style but in a different color," she said, glancing over her shoulder at Lydia.

The dressmaker cleared her throat, "That's one of my more expensive creations," knowing the town deputy couldn't afford it. "That one is fifteen dollars," she said then adding too quickly, "And I need the money up front."

Fifteen dollars, one month's pay, Lacy thought. Throwing the woman a disgusted look, Lacy's hand dug into her pocket. Then, she changed her mind, pulling it back out. She asked instead, "You always treat you're first-time customers so rudely?" Knowing full well, Lydia Marshall had preconceived notions of her. *Probably from Lydia's daffy gossip mongers,* she thought, *Thank goodness, Liv doesn't fit into that category.* Folding one arm, an elbow rested on her wrist, as a finger began tapping her lips, Lacy gazed at the dress she wanted. *I want it, but I'll be damned if I buy a dress from this b..., woman,* she thought.

Turning slowly toward the dressmaker, Lacy said quietly, "You know...I think you are right. I will just take my business elsewhere..." she moved toward the door, reaching

FRECKLED VENOM
COPPERHEAD STRIKES

for the handle.

"Wait!" Lydia said. Her hand stretched, hoping to stop Lacy, emphasizing her words. "I'll make you a deal...to you, the dress is twelve dollars."

Leaving her hand on the knob, Lacy turned half-way around, "Twelve dollars? How nice of you Miss Marshall, to be so considerate," Lacy said in her own best clipped English adding a bit of sarcasm to her tone. She then bestowed the nastiest look she could muster on the woman. The one that would make a skunk roll over and play dead. "But I don't give rude people my business. Good day, Miss Marshall." She pulled the door open.

"Wait...I'll make it ten!" Lydia exclaimed. Wringing her hands now, she chewed on her lower lip. *I don't need to lose a possible customer. I don't care who she is.*

Pretending to be surprised, Lacy said, "Ten? Why...how generous of you to think of me, Miss Marshall."

Lydia gave a weak smile.

Closing the door, Lacy took a few steps toward the dressmaker. Re-tucking fingers into her back pockets, Lacy allowed her eyes to roam some more around the shop. Thinking as she asked, "How's business been lately?" Eyes cutting toward the dressmaker, she waited on a reaction.

"That's none of your concern," Lydia replied curtly.

Red-gold brows rose again, Lacy maintained a deadpan façade. "From what I hear...you're kind of expensive, more along back east prices..."

"I am not!" The dressmaker retorted.

"The only reason Olivia buys a dress from you now and again...she says ya haft tae eat," Lacy lied, throwing her own barb. *That one is probably gonna come back and bite me in the butt,* she thought.

"Why...you little tart! Get out of my shop!" Her finger pointed toward the door. "I mean it, get out of my shop!" Lydia shouted at the redhead, her porcelain face launching a dusting of bright pink.

Ignoring the woman, Lacy offered, "I could bring you more business, if you'd let me..." her voice trailed off. She looked around the colorful shop, and then brought her gaze back to the dressmaker. "Kinda like taking out an ad in the newspaper, but I'd be wearing the advertisement," she allowed her burnt coffee eyes to bore into the dressmaker.

"You? Advertise for me? Not on your life! You're no lady...you'd scare off any potential customers I could get!"

"Well...you see...that's just the point, I'm trying to make," Lacy said continuing her dead-pan look, rocking back and forth on her feet. *I'll get that dress yet,* she thought, watching Lydia's eyes become thoughtful. "I don't claim to be a lady, but, I could at least make a stab at it..." she said pointing to the dress in the window, "With one of your dresses."

Lydia threw a look at her latest creation, her mind tumbling with material cost and her time involved, doing the quick calculations in her head.

"You're a talented woman, Miss Marshall," Lacy began, "I'd be honored to wear one of your dresses," she said, laying the compliment on so thick, even flies couldn't resist swarming to the sweet syrup dripping over the edges of flapjacks.

Lydia nibbled on her bottom lip, thinking, as she threw her pert little nose in the air, and then rolled her dove grey eyes back down taking in Lacy's appearance. She sniffed saying, "Being a lady comes from the inside, going to school for it, the right and wrong way to be a lady, and then being exposed to culture, to...to practice what you have learned." She sniffed into the air, "Wearing a dress won't make you a lady," she said.

Throwing one red-gold brow up, Lacy sighed, "Awright, I guess I will take my business elsewhere," she said, moving toward the door. "I was just trying to help..." Lacy's hand turned the knob, halfway opening the door.

"Wait! I'll do it!"

A big grin graced freckled cheeks, forcing dimples to appear, and then she quickly erased them. Replacing the deadpan look, Lacy closed the door, and turned around to face Lydia, again.

"I'll need money for the material," the dressmaker said.

Lacy reached into her pocket.

Grey eyes hungrily watched a hand pull a wad of bills out of tan britches. Lydia's voice cracked when she said, "I need four dollars for the material." After receiving the bills, she cleared her throat. "Uhmm...you said you wanted a different color. Do you know what you want?"

Lacy's mind had her feet dancing a little jig, and her fist mentally punching the air. *Yes!*

CHAPTER TWENTY

Looking at the calendar, Lacy saw the Fourth of July was only eight days away and with the Fourth, came the big race. Her stomach took a nose dive toward her knees, leaving her breathless. She swallowed. *I know Fancy can win the race, but I've never done anything this public before,* she thought. Always in the past, she preferred to remain in the background, not drawing attention to herself, blending in with the crowd, observing. Many a time she'd followed her prey for days, observing, listening, learning their habits, before making her move.

Lacy poured more coffee for her and Rawley. Two heads turned when the office door opened.

Luis entered, lugging a big wooden box, followed by Maria, which he sat on the table. "Niña, I brought you something you can use for the race," Luis said. Taking a feed sack off, he dug, pulling out a pair of shinny boots.

Lacy gasped, "My old riding boots."

"Si', I thought you might like to have them, as good luck for the race," he said, handing them to her. "And this," dragging out the pimple that some folks called a saddle. "You'll need this," his hand patting the well-oiled leather. "Your father, he enter, too. He ride Blue Devil, same sire as Fancy, different dam. Your father, he want to show you, he the best, but, you little one, have the gift. Your father, he does not, you will win, because you have the gift," Luis stated quietly.

Lacy's mouth dropped open, stunned by Luis's

announcement that her father was to be racing against her. Abruptly, her knees became weak. Not able to remain standing, she sat down, heavily. "My father? But…why?"

Luis nodded at Rawley. "Señor Marshal, he may have little something to do with that."

Rawley took a sip of coffee before leaning back in the chair; it squeaked while he waited for the explosion from his redhead.

Lacy's head swiveled. "What'd you do? Bribe him to race against me?"

Shaking his head, "Nothing, like that, Sunshine. After you left that day, I just had a real good talk with your father. Didn't think he'd sober up long enough to enter a race, guess I was wrong." The chair squeaked as he sat forward again. Rawley picked up a pencil, twiddling it between his fingers. "This race is turning out to be a real humdinger, ain't it Luis?"

"Si', Señor."

CHAPTER TWENTY ONE

Fourth of July morning, dawned bright, hot, little to no wind. The old timers were right; so far it had been a hot, dry summer, something the homesteaders and ranchers didn't take well, the hot sun drying up their crops and grasslands. One lighting strike could set the whole territory up in flames. They'd kept their eyes peeled to the sky, watching and waiting, except for today.

* * *

Rawley tried to get Lacy to eat something, but to no avail.

The inner turmoil of racing against her father had her stomach so tied up in barbed wire she could barely hold any coffee down. Her gut threatened to upchuck at any moment. Lacy tried to hide the turmoil from Rawley. But, he knew.

* * *

Getting Fancy ready, Lacy knew the horse was excited. A bright gleam lit the mare's dark heartwood eyes. Her nostrils wide, she constantly bobbed her head, while impatient feet stirred the hay strewn stall. This was in her blood, to run like the wind. Whether chasing fugitives, or racing across open prairies, Fancy just liked to run.

Walking out of the barn, the mare between them, the trio stopped as a man came by, astride a wild eyed colt. Adam Carrigan, no match for the animal, dug his spurs into the colt's ribs trying to control the big mount. Distressing the animal further, it continued whirling and dancing with agitation, body covered in nervous foamy sweat.

Lacy knew the signs – this horse wasn't ready to race yet. She never agreed with the use of spurs. Watching her father dig them into the sides of the colt, drawing blood, made her even more nervous.

Calling out, her father said smugly, "I'll see you from the winner's circle, Lacy!" Carrigan tried to hold the big animal in check, causing the bit to dig into its tender mouth. Bloody froth slung from the bit as the horse tried to rid itself of the pain cutting into its mouth. Adam made the horse move forward, swatting him with a short whip. Hooves dug into the dirt with agitation, raising puffs of dust as it danced down the street.

Lacy's heart clawed its way up her throat, choking off her wind. Her voice squeaked as she told the big grey, "Fancy, that's the one you've got to beat."

She swallowed and then turned to speak to Rawley and Luis. Sandpaper gargle seemed to come out as she addressed the two men, "That horse is too high strung, too green; he's not ready to race yet, because of that, he could be trouble on the course."

Luis stated to Rawley, "See, I told you…the little one…she have the gift."

Rawley's stomach, already tied up in knots, clenched tighter. He didn't like the way this race was starting out, either. Too, he didn't like spurs, whips or a hard hand on the reins. More often than not, those actions ruined a good horse. He helped boot Lacy into the saddle.

Luis touched her leg. "Little one, remember what all I have taught you, you guide Fancy, hold her back, just a little, when she reach her stride, you let her have her head," he said patting the grey neck. "This one, she smart, she know what to do," he said, backing away. "God go with you, little one."

Staring into a face he had grown to love, freckles, temper and all, Rawley reached up. Taking a handful of shirt, he pulled Lacy to him. Her lips received a hard kiss from the marshal. Releasing her, his hand settled lightly on her thigh. "You be careful, Sunshine," he said. Then he nodded toward her father, "Watch out for him…he's a desperate man." Immediately, Rawley smiled, saying, "But…you'll do just fine, honey. Everything will be okay," he reassured her, retreating from the big grey.

Lacy bit down hard on that bottom lip, surprising her when she tasted blood. Reining the grey around, she trotted Fancy to the starting line.

The one street, thick with excitement, had become clogged with wagons, buggies, mules, horses and people. Carrying a carnival like atmosphere, the acidic scent and haze of spent firecrackers added to the drone of voices resembling a hive of busy bees. Olivia and Maddie had been in charge of the colorful bunting that hung from the edges of the porch roofs lining the street. The material fluttered every once in a while in the almost non-existent breeze.

Shop doors were thrown wide. Colorful booths of merchandise, placed at every available space along the street, offered baked goods for sale, including miniature versions of Maddie's fifteen-ton fruitcake, along with various other sundries that dotted the tables.

Homesteaders and ranchers from the outlying territory all co-mingled with an unaccustomed jovial presence. Selling or trading horses, mules, along with milk cows and good seed bulls, they set aside their differences for at least one day.

These folks also entered into contests of horseshoes, sack races, pie eating, wheelbarrow racing and watermelon seed spitting along with the all important – poker, drinking and eating, in that order, too.

At the opposite end of town by Luke's stable, the wooden dance floor had been constructed for the yearly Fourth of July dance. Torches stuck into the four corners to light the area later as darkness approached. Blue, red and white bunting, nailed to the edge of the platform, added a festive air.

Lacy felt Fancy's muscles bunching in anticipation under her legs. The mare's ears pricked forward, focused ahead. Both rider and mount calmly waited on the starting gun.

Out of the corner of her eye, Lacy saw her father having trouble. The horse, reared, and then kept whirling and butting the mounts closest to him. Voices raised in anger, the other riders yelled at Carrigan.

Venders bellowed, taking last minute bets. Others shouted encouragement for their favorite rider. The rapid *pop-pop-pop* of firecrackers going off back in town, accompanied by the delighted squeals of children, combined to upset the green colt even more.

Lacy didn't hear a thing, concentrating only on the line of horses. Ignoring the fracas further up the line, she hunched over Fancy's neck, whispering, "This is your time to shine, girl. You can do it, I know you can!" The mare flicked an ear toward the familiar soft husky voice.

The gun fired at that moment. Fancy bolted, causing Lacy to almost lose her seat. She quickly grabbed a handful of mane, leaning over the grey's neck. Then she relaxed. Picking up Fancy's rhythm, she continued to hold the big grey in check.

The roar of the crowd followed the riders, individuals waving hats and running a short distance after the horses. Lacy allowed the others to pull ahead, their trail leaving a plume of dust, covering both she and Fancy in its fine yellow-brown powder.

Her peripheral vision scanned the area on both sides of her. She had no idea where her father was, and didn't dare look back under her arms. She concentrated only on Fancy's movement forward. Lacy's eyes refocused between two upright ears, moving as one with the horse. Her mind blocked out all other sounds, absorbed in hearing only the steady drumbeat of Fancy's hooves hitting the ground resembling rolling thunder. Her breath matched that of the big grey, slow and steady. Her legs felt the powerful strides of the horse under her.

The pack clattered around Hens and Chickens, with spectators standing in their wagons. Other folks littered the ground waving arms holding hats. Bodies bounced up and down, urging their favorites on, their voices blending with the thunder shaking the ground.

Carrigan had gotten off to a bad start, bringing up the rear. Several riders were heading into the pines; Lacy still paced Fancy, five, six riders behind.

Reining up the bay, Rawley saw from his viewpoint, Lacy suddenly veer off to his left, heading toward the downed trees. He watched other riders follow, her father one of them.

He muttered, "Damn you, Sunshine, damn you." Holding his breath, he stared in disbelief as Fancy took the first tree in two strides, the second, and then the third. Smooth as honey dripping on buttered bread.

Lacy took the creek, the big grey climbing the embankment. Part of the pack came out of the stand of pines, on Fancy's heels, along with Carrigan, pushing the blue roan, smacking him constantly with his whip.

Bands of a black and grey mane assaulted Lacy's face causing tears to stream through dusty freckles. Rounding Hens and Chickens, she didn't hear or see the cheering crowd. Still not knowing where the rest of the field could be, she only knew they were strung out behind her, somewhere.

Lacy shouted, "This is it, girl, give it all you got!" Easing the reins, she felt Fancy stretch, her legs reaching for more ground. The grey's tail rose, black and grey streaks fanning out with her speed.

Suddenly, Lacy felt a presence beside her. Both horses were running neck and neck. Next thing she knew, Fancy was bumped, throwing her to her knees. The horse rolled. Lacy flew clear, somersaulting in the air before hitting the ground. A few moments later, Fancy stood and shook herself, making dust fly. She then took a few tentative steps, her sides heaving.

Recovering, Lacy ran to Fancy's side taking the bridle

and walking her a few feet. *Fancy is okay,* her eyes drifted toward the rump of the blue roan now out in front. *You bastard!* Her head swiveled back and saw the oncoming pack thundering, gaining on her. The saddle had slipped, instead of taking the time to straighten it, she un-cinched it, and tossed the leather aside. Lacy grabbed a handful of mane and flung her body back on the grey.

Time an essence; she banged her heels into the horse's ribs. She leaned over the neck of the grey, urging her faster.

Lacy let out even more on the reins, giving Fancy her head. "This is what you love girl…git 'em! Go git 'em!" She yelled. An ear twitched back at the voice, then pricked forward, the horse gaining speed. Long legs stretched, eating ground.

Instinctively, Lacy knew she no longer controlled the big grey. She was just along for the ride. The race belonged to Fancy now.

Rawley didn't know where in the hell Carrigan had come from, having eyes only for Lacy. But, he saw the bump, watched horse and rider tumble. His heart squished his throat closed. He banged the bay into motion, yelling, "You, son…of…a…bitch!"

He quickly pulled up the bay when he saw both Lacy and Fancy rising, *they're not hurt,* he thought, allowing a huge sigh of relief to escape. Rawley watched Lacy throw the saddle aside and mount again, urging Fancy to pick up her pace. *I'll take care of you later, ya yella bastard! You caused Lacy to lose this race! I'm gonna teach you a lesson, you'll never forget!* His mind whirred angrily.

Not expecting Lacy to catch her father at this late point in the race, he watched in amazement as the grey closed the gap. Nose to rump, nose to withers, nose to nose, pacing Carrigan's blue roan for a few lengths, and then she began to pull away, increasing the distance. Fancy slowly gained ground ahead of the roan by one length, two, finally three lengths, crossing the finish line first.

The crowd roared, closing in behind the big grey, following the pair. Lacy slowly reined up the horse, oblivious to the hands patting her and Fancy, and their congratulations bouncing off the buildings.

She searched the sea of faces for Rawley. Looking over her shoulder, Lacy found him on the outskirts of town, slowly riding in, carrying her saddle. Reining Fancy around they plowed through the crowd, folks finally allowing them to ride through.

Seeing his redhead separating the crowd like Moses parting the Red Sea, Rawley reined up the bay and waited for her. When Lacy came alongside, she took her shirtsleeve and wiped her dirt crusted face, saying hoarsely, "That bastard nearly killed us!" Then she gave that rare smile exposing two dimples within that dust. Patting Fancy's neck, she said, "But we did it, didn't we? We won!"

Rawley smiled. "That you did, Sunshine. That you did." Edging his horse closer, his hand snaked out. Reaching around the back of her neck, he pulled her to him.

"I'm proud of you, Sunshine," he said.

Lacy's eyes grew round as saucers, *uht-ooh...* she thought. Her insides began tumbling like rocks in a barrel rolling down a steep hill. She pinched that bottom lip between her teeth, realizing at that moment she needed his kiss and his reassurance that everything was still going to be okay.

He saw the venerability, the questions in her eyes as they searched his face. He allowed his lips to brush hers, his nose whiffed Lacy's favorite scent, *Perfume of Fancy* that she always wore. His mind smiled. And then Rawley deepened the kiss, tasting dust and salt.

Lacy did not shy away or resist him. *Progress...we're making progress,* he thought. Finally releasing her, he noticed a rosy hue flushing those dusty freckles. Rawley smiled again, saying, "You and Fancy make quite a pair."

Silence from Lacy, her eyes downcast, she nibbled on her bottom lip again.

FRECKLED VENOM
COPPERHEAD STRIKES

Nodding back toward town, he said, "You need to go collect your prize. I'll catch up with you later."

Lacy nodded silently as she reined Fancy around, trotting off.

Arms resting on the smaller saddle draped across in front of him, he watched Lacy head toward the dance platform, her hand reaching down, shaking the ones stretched up to her. Rawley grinned again as he caught her rare smile beginning to blossom amid that freckled face.

On the platform, Billy passed up Cotton to sit with her. Liv, her arms full of fresh cut flowers from her garden, handed them to Lacy. Mike, standing on the platform, his arms raised, snapped a crisp hundred dollar bill in the air, then he handed it to her, shaking Lacy's hand in the process.

Circling the bay around, Rawley went in search of Adam Carrigan. He had some serious business to take up with the man.

After delivering the saddle back to Luis, the marshal caught up with Carrigan in Mike's place, leaning against the bar, a bottle by his elbow already half empty. His big hand grabbed Adam's shoulder whirling him around, surprising the man.

Rawley drew back his fist, then sent it flying, giving Adam Carrigan a hard left upper cut. Bodies sitting in chairs sent them clattering. Boots scuffled, hurrying to get out of the way. One didn't cross Rawley Lovett when his temper emerged. Lacy's father reeled backwards, landing into a table. It flipped, crashing to the floor. He slithered on to the planked boards as if his bones had turned mush.

The marshal towered over Carrigan's body sprawled like a rag doll. His voice crackled with anger, "That's for bumping Lacy and Fancy, trying to throw the race. You bastard! You almost killed your daughter and a prize horse! From now on you stay away from them, or you'll have me to deal with," he threatened. "And I can make your life hell!" Rawley threw one last devilish look before walking to the bat-wing doors. Palms shoved them so hard they banged against the outside wall, rattling the big window.

Tending bar for Mike, Joe Jenkin's eyebrows soared at the news. Glancing over at Adam Carrigan as the man tried to stand, no one offered to help. Joe growled, "Git yore carcass outta here, Carrigan!"

Embarrassed, Adam slowly stood, his eyes taking in the silent crowd. He moved toward the bar. Joe picked up the half empty bottle and thrust it at the man, saying, "Now, git yore arse outta here!"

Carrigan cradled the bottle against his chest as he backed out the swinging doors. Turning, he fled.

* * *

Catching up with Lacy as she rode back to the stable, his hand took hold of Fancy's bridle. Rawley bent, looking at the grey's skinned knees, saying, "Better take care of those scrapes, Sunshine." Looking back up he saw Lacy nod in response. "You're both lucky you weren't killed."

A long look passed between the pair, each remembering the kiss they shared not long ago. Two sets of ears didn't register the din that surrounded them, hearing only their own hearts beating a fast tattoo within their bodies. Color climbed into a wind-burned, dusty freckled face, turning it even brighter; Lacy ducked her head. Finally Rawley broke the silence by asking, "What do you plan on doing with your winnings, Sunshine?"

At his question her face rose. Dark eyes cut a shy glance in Rawley's direction. "Oh, I do' no," she said. Looking down again, her hand patted Fancy's neck, then fingers tangled themselves in the black and grey mane, twisting the locks into miniature ropes. She added as an afterthought, "I just might buy me a dress, so you can take me to the dance tonight," she said, not revealing that she already had a dress hidden in her room. Boots quickly nudged Fancy into a trot.

Rawley stood alone, stunned. Pushing his hat back on

his head, he couldn't help but grin.

* * *

Luis finished bandaging Fancy's knees. Billy continued rubbing the grey down giving her sips of water, per Luis's instructions. Finally, Lacy had to sit down, before her legs collapsed or she passed out. All the excitement began to catch up with her. Besides, she was beginning to get stiff and sore as hell from the fall.

Luis sat next to her. "Niña, you ran a fine race today. Señor Marshal, he told me how you worked Fancy. Your father, he bump you good, you keep your head and won."

Lacy shook her head, shrugged a stiffening shoulder as she answered. "No, it wasn't me. I just gave Fancy her head. That last stretch, was all Fancy, I had nothing to do with it."

"Even so, you and Fancy…," he hesitated. "We need you, you come home now…?" Luis left the question hanging in the air.

"No, Luis. I'll never return to Carrigan Ranch. That part of my life is over," she said.

Slurred words reached their ears. "I lak ya ta…turn, Leeccy," a soppy voice said.

Two sets of eyes turned in the direction of the voice.

Tottering, he took a few steps toward them. Carrigan then wound his way toward a stall partition, and leaned against it, needing the support. "Ya rud ah fine race taday, effen butter…I…sss…pected," her father admitted. "I poud…ya," he wavered before he expressed his next word, "Aughtter…" Adam Carrigan hadn't said that word in over nine years, not realizing how the word came out. "Pease, Leeccy? Come…ome…ya belong," her father pleaded. "Come…family…gain." He swayed. Uncorking the bottle he held against his chest, he took a swig. He swiped at the dribbles running down his chin after, that motion almost costing him, his balance. "Pease…"

Swift as a cat stalking its prey, Lacy's anger pounced.

"Family? Why you bas...you almost killed Fancy and me!" Luis' hand touched her arm.

Lacy cut a sharp glance at the weathered face of her old friend. She slowly eased back down on the bale of hay. Pinching her bottom lip between her teeth, Lacy gave a slight nod at Luis as she sipped air.

Looking over at her father, he reminded her of other drunks she'd seen over the years. But Adam Carrigan had something else eating away at him besides the whiskey. A long ago question flitted through her brain. *Might as well get this over with...then I won't have to deal with him any longer,* she thought.

Walking over to her father, she saw that the years had not been kind to him, his body had been riddled with drink for too long, trying to drown those horrible memories. She knew all about those horrible memories; she'd lived with them, too.

A deep bruise began to show itself on his jaw. *Someone slugged him,* she wondered if Rawley did that.

"Do you miss her?" Lacy asked abruptly.

Adam Carrigan, shocked at the question, retreated, bumping into the stall partition.

Lacy followed. "Well, answer me! Do you miss her?"

Adam Carrigan balked at first. Then glancing down at the dirt, he whispered. "Yes."

Recoiling from the sour sickening stench from her father, Lacy stated simply, "I see, Mr. Carrigan."

Her father cut a whiskey-soaked glance at Lacy.

"Did you ever, truly love mama and me?" She asked.

Her father sagged against the partition. Slowly his legs slid out from under him until his butt rested in the hay strewn dirt. Adam sat looking up at his daughter, blinking watery eyes.

She didn't know if the moisture in his eyes came from the whiskey or her question. Cold steel wrapped around her heart, Lacy didn't care anymore. Her next words kept the long ago fence still standing. "Mr. Carrigan, thank you for your offer, but, it's not for me," she said stepping over his legs as she left the stable.

Luis helped his boss to stand. "The little one, she's a strong one, no? Señor?"

Carrigan glanced at Luis then wordlessly weaved away still clutching the bottle, causing Luis to sadly shake his head.

CHAPTER TWENTY TWO

In the office, Rawley paced to and fro. Why did it always seem women took three times longer to get ready for these things! Sticking a finger down his collar – darn thing made him feel like he was choking – he tugged on it.

Walking halfway down the hallway, he shouted. "Hurry up Sunshine! We're gonna be late!"

"Shut up, Lovett," came the muffled reply.

Rolling his eyes, Rawley walked back to his desk, sat on the edge and waited. His foot began an impatient jiggle. Looking down, he stopped it.

Lacy peered into the looking glass. Licking her fingers, she tried to straighten some flyaway curls. It wasn't working; she gave up. Taking the last flower, she tucked it along with the others at the side and a little to the back over her ear. She'd piled her hair on top of her head tonight, with a mass of curls still cascading down her back. Wild white daisies she'd found on the prairie adorned the copper tresses.

Rubbing her cheeks hard, then pinching them, she tried to bring more color to her face. Looking back at her reflection, she realized she didn't have to do that; she had enough color as it was, too much.

Lacy sighed and straightened. Moving away from the glass, she turned sideways, hands smoothing the dress, as she saw her reflection. Lifting the skirts, she looked at her new shoes. Lacy hoped she wouldn't make a fool of herself tonight. She'd worn boots for so long, she wasn't sure how she'd do in new shoes. Looking at her reflection one more time, she contemplated, *well, it'll just have to do. I hope Rawley likes it.* Glancing back in the looking glass, she made an observation. *The dress does make me feel like a lady, though.*

Opening her door, Lacy stepped into the hallway, fingers tugging on a sleeve, hands smoothing the lightweight cotton material of her skirt, perfect for the overly warm July night. She straightened the bow at the waist one more time as she walked toward Rawley. Her skirts rustled with all the petticoats underneath when she moved. Her new shoes, tap-tapping along the scarred plank flooring, lightly echoed in the hallway.

He stood. Rawley had to swallow his heart back into its rightful place, somewhere behind his deflated lungs. His eyes feasted on the transformation of his deputy as she walked toward him, dressed in the most beautiful gown he'd ever laid eyes on. The blue hued-forest green of the material accented her coloring. He swallowed more air.

He didn't care that Lacy was a fiery redhead with a volatile temper, or that she could be a persnickety little cuss most of the time, arguing with him at the drop of a hat, or that she could lock lips tighter than the Denver Mint, or that she had a million freckles. No. Because at that moment he stared at the most beautiful woman he'd ever come across. His lungs lost even more air.

The tap-tapping eased then stopped altogether. Lacy stood in front of the marshal and waited. He uttered not a sound, and that worried her. She tilted her head, "Is something wrong?" Her eyes skimming across his face, seeing his perplexed look, she asked, "You don't like it?" Still not a word from Rawley, Lacy groaned inwardly.

Skirts rustled and new shoes began a tap-tapping back down the hallway to her room.

Finding his voice, he called out, "Sunshine…" Then added, "Just where do you think you're going?"

"To change," she threw over her shoulder.

"Like hell! You come back here," he ordered.

"No! You don't like the dress, so I'm gonna change," she said.

"I didn't say that!"

Whirling, Lacy placed her hands on her hips and gave him *the* look. "Yes...You...Did! You didn't say one word about whether you thought it was pretty...or ugly! You said nuthin'! So I'm changing! You can go to the damn dance by yourself!" She whirled again, new shoes tap-tapping toward her quarters.

Rawley sighed inwardly, thinking, *females!* "Sunshine! You stop right there!"

Hearing that certain authoritative tone in Rawley's voice, the tap-tapping slowed, then stopped; she waited.

"You march yourself right back, here," he said sternly, a finger pointing at the floor in front of him.

The skirts rustled as she half turned, "Why?"

"Because I'm not through with you...just yet," he told her.

Lacy threw him a crooked look, as new shoes tap-tapped and skirts rustled their way back to the marshal. She stood patiently waiting on him to say something. *He always does, jabber-mouth,* she thought.

Rawley looked at that miffed, cute-as-a-speckled-pup face. He spoke in that smooth caramel baritone. "You took my breath away, Sunshine. That's why I didn't...couldn't, say anything," he told her truthfully.

Coffee colored eyes brightened, growing round as saucers, "Really? You really like the dress?"

"No."

Lacy's face fell a mile. She whirled to go back to her room.

Rawley caught her arm, and turned her back to him. A finger tilted her face upward. "I love you...uh...in the dress," he stumbled, realizing he'd just told her how he felt. "It's as beautiful as you are tonight." He tilted his head. *She didn't catch my slip,* he thought. His voice took on a teasing quality, "I always knew there was a lady in there, somewhere. I'm glad she finally decided to come out."

Lacy blushed.

Taking his finger, he motioned for her to turn around.

Lacy just stared.

Rawley motioned again, saying, "Turn around, let me see."

Whirling around for him, she asked, "Satisfied now?"

"Hummm…very much so… Sunshine."

"Please don't tease me anymore. I'm embarrassed enough already as it is. What with all the fuss after the race and everything," Lacy said softly.

Stepping closer, his finger gently lifted Lacy's face again as he said, "Don't be, Sunshine. You deserved to win the race. And you're lovely tonight. Just the way I pictured, you would look. I'm honored to escort you to the dance this evening," he said brushing a light kiss across her lips, catching Lacy by surprise.

That's the third time today, he's kissed me, she thought. *And I let him!*

Opening the door, Rawley offered his arm. Lacy hung back then slowly tucked her hand in the crook of his elbow. Covering her hand with his, Rawley squeezed it gently. At the gesture, Lacy's breath disappeared. They took a few steps. She hesitated on the edge of scarred walk. She had to swallow her heart back down as it seemed to be lodged in her throat. Swallowing again, the lump finally fell back into her stomach with a thud. She breathed deeply. The warm air still carried the light acidic scent of spent firecrackers. Strains of music and the dull din of voices reached her ears. The urge to turn around and go hide in her room became overwhelming, she glanced at the closed door over her shoulder.

"It's okay, Sunshine," he said softly. "It's just a dance."

Brown pools shyly grazed his face. "To you maybe…but, to me…" she hesitated. Her look continued to search his face, "To me, it's like learning to walk all over again," she said quietly.

"Baby steps...huh?" He grinned. "Well, you just hang on to me...we'll just go through those baby steps, together, Okay?" Rawley knew Lacy felt unbalanced, out of kilter in social situations. Wearing britches and toting a side-arm still remained her only comfort zone, except for Fancy. Tonight, though, she was willing to step out of her comfort zone, doing something she had never experienced in her life.

Lacy just nodded. Knowing she felt safe, reassured with him by her side.

* * *

The buzz of voices and strains of music became louder as they approached the dance platform. Mike's voice bellowed in rhythm with the beat of each song. He chanted out calls for the dancers to follow.

Walking across to the festivities, Rawley stated, "I get dibs on the first dance with you."

"You're going to have to get in line, there's three others ahead of you."

"Who? No one thought you would come tonight."

"Oh, there were a few," she said as her ankle took that moment to turn over, causing Lacy to almost fall. "Oww!"

Rawley caught her, asking, "You okay?"

Straightening, Lacy nodded. "It's just that I've worn boots for so long." Pulling her skirts up, she showed him her new shoes. "It'll take me a little while to get used to these higher heels," she disclosed.

Rawley gave a wide grin. She was trying. His little freckled tomboy was taking steps, becoming a lady. *At least for tonight, anyway,* he thought.

Throngs of townsfolk milled about. Boys teased girls, causing them to squeal and chase after the boys. Tables were set up for refreshments. Mike's special potion in one area had six deep waiting to drink the brew. Maddie had tables as well, for those not hardy enough to try Mike's swill. The dance floor, full, had dancers spilling out on the ground. Torches lit the area, resembling filtered sunlight that flickered here and there like fireflies across smiling faces.

Lacy spied Maddie's tables laden with food, punch, and cider, the Scotswoman laughing and bantering as she served.

"Food," Lacy whispered realizing she hadn't eaten all day. "I'm starving!" She left the marshal, standing where she dropped his arm.

"Maddie, you made all this food?" She asked. Reaching for a few choice morsels, Lacy stuffed them into her mouth. She closed her eyes as the delectable tastes hit her tongue. Opening them again, her eyes began searching the table for more goodies. Her fingers picked up a few more and stuffed her mouth with those, too. Poking the morsels into her cheeks, Lacy talked around the food, "I'm starving Maddie!" She explained. "May I have some cider, please?"

Looking up, Maddie's green eyes grew round in disbelief at the transformation of the red headed deputy. Prairie daisy's adorned copper curls piled atop Lacy's head tonight, red-gold waves continued cascading down the girl's back, finally free of their constant braid.

A lace-trimmed square neck bodice, with small capped sleeves, showed off a million freckles. Green eyes followed the four buttons down the front, taking in the huge, but stylish bow that opened the frock, exposing yards of ruffled white petticoats. A deep, forest blue green shade of the overlaying material only enhanced Lacy's coloring.

Her voice registered shock as she exclaimed, "Havers…lass! Iss it really you?" Coming around the table, Maddie took Lacy's arm, spinning her. "Aye…lass, it iss you," Maddie said delightedly. She gave an appraising glance at the young woman standing in front of her. Beckoning to Rawley, she said, "Laddie, ye wee lassie, she's sometin' tae night, 'eh?"

"Yes ma'am," he replied proudly.

Sneaking more morsels of food into her mouth, Lacy

replied as she chewed, "I haven't changed that much!"

"Ach no! Ye just being ah right purity young lassie, tae night. Ye may 'aps be turnin' many ah young laddie's heads this night, lass!"

Lacy swallowed the cider before replying, "I don't think so, Maddie." *This is embarrassing,* she thought, *just because I put on a dress.* Spying Billy standing all by himself on the other side of the dance platform, she saw her chance for escape. Sitting the glass back on the table, Lacy said too quickly, "I've got to go see Billy." Skirts rustled as she hurried toward the young man.

Two pairs of eyes watched the girl scurry toward the young man. "Och, laddie, ye got yer hands full tae night," Maddie cautioned Rawley. Sliding her arm into his, her hand patted his muscular upper limb.

Looking down, Rawley told her, "Maddie, I've had my hands full ever since I met her!"

Maddie laughed. "Aye, ye have at that, laddie," she said patting his arm again before going back to serving.

Moseying over to Doc and Liv, Rawley picked up Cotton, and the foursome watched the dancers on the platform. Boots and high-topped shoes had the wooden floor bouncing and echoing with their rhythm.

Doc motioned with a glass. "You try that pharmaceutical swill Mike made this year?" He asked, nodding toward the six foot deep crowd at the table.

Looking up, Rawley gazed at the men laughing and jostling each other, tasting Mike's latest recipe. "No…why?"

Giving a loud snort, Doc said, "If that don't clean yore pipes, nuthin' will," he coughed.

Rawley grinned. Mike could come up with some real doozies in his recipe department. He liked testing them on folks at events like this. He'd found out from experience, that some of those mixtures would flat out curl your nose hairs.

Shifting Cotton in his arms, Rawley let his gaze wander over to where Lacy stood with Billy.

FRECKLED VENOM
COPPERHEAD STRIKES

Sidling up to him, Liv spoke softly. "Our tomboy deputy turned out to be a beautiful young lady tonight, didn't she?"

Dragging eyes away from his redhead, Rawley looked down. "Did you know about this?" He asked.

Light grey eyes twinkled like morning dew. "Know about what?" She teased.

Giving his friend a squirrely look, Rawley said, "About the dress."

"Umm…maybe," she said as her eyes skated back toward the redhead. "She wanted to surprise you tonight. Lydia did a wonderful job on the dress, but Lacy picked out the style and color." Liv brought her eyes back to the tall lawman. "Well…what did you think…when you first saw her?" She asked.

His eyes drifted back to Lacy and Billy. "Uh…I…she took my breath away," he said.

Patting his arm, Liv replied, "Good…I knew it would."

Tilting his head, Rawley gave Liv a shrewd look. "Anything else you're keeping secret from me?"

"Nope!" She said, smiling.

Rawley cocked a black brow at her reply.

* * *

"Aren't you gonna ask Angela to dance?" Lacy asked.

The street urchin, Billy Atkins now lived with Olivia and Cotton-Top. Lacy had discovered the dead body of Clete Atkins one cold night, leaving Billy an orphan. The young man had flourished under the kindness of four adults.

Scuffing the dirt with the toe of his boot, Billy replied, "Nah…I don't know how to dance."

Lacy glanced at the new britches she'd bought Billy. They fit his long legs just right. He had long legs like Rawley, though not as nicely shaped as the lawman's. *Now, where did that come from?* She thought, tossing it quickly out of her head, she concentrated on Billy.

"If you want, I can show you something real simple?"

"You can?" He asked, his face lighting up.

Taking his hands, she told him, "Now…you hold Angela like this, now pretend I'm Angela; hold me like I just showed you."

Billy did.

Lacy nodded. "Okay, it's just a simple box step, one foot back, bring the other next to it, take a step to the side, other foot next, step forward, slide the back foot up, step to the side again, bring the other next to it, and do it all over again."

After a few tries, Billy had the hang of it.

"See nothing to it," Lacy said smiling. "Now, go ask Angela to dance."

Billy hesitated.

"Go on, before someone else beats you to it."

"Yes, Ma'am."

Dark eyes softened as she watched Billy find Angela. Taking her hand, he pulled her onto the platform. Lacy sighed wistfully, *Young love,* she thought.

Someone touched her shoulder. Lacy jumped. She was surprised to see Doc and not Rawley standing there. "You owe me a dance, young lady, for fixing that bullet hole, when you first got to town," he gruffly stated.

Lacy tilted her head. She smiled, exposing two dimples as she said, "I reckon, I do, Doc." Taking the arm he offered.

"Oops, sorry," she said after stepping on Doc's toes. "I've never danced before," Lacy admitted.

Doc just harrumphed. "Never thought I'd see you in a dress, young lady," he said instead.

She smiled into the time worn face. "Never thought I see you clean shaven, young man," Lacy teased.

"Humph," Doc said whirling her around again. Lacy threw back her head and laughed.

Finally, Rawley thought, watching his redhead with Doc. An honest-to-goodness real laugh had erupted at whatever she and Doc said to each other. His hands found their way into his trouser pockets. Rocking back and forth on his heels, he smiled.

Later, Lacy held Cotton, spinning the both of them around to the music, the little boy laughing with delight. She was glad the little cotton-top seemed to be recovering from his family's deaths. Watching as the tow-head threw his head back in glee, her mind retrieved the memories of her first encounter with the little boy. Even though legally his name remained Howard Clancy, Howie for short, he would always be Lacy's Cotton-Top.

Crawling under the porch that day coaxing the lone survivor of a family of five from his safe hiding place had torn at Lacy's heart. The deaths of the little boy's family had left him all alone in the world.

Tracking the Dillard Brothers for the large bounty had landed her right smack-dab in the town she'd run away from over nine years ago. Recovering from wounds inflicted by one of her prisoners placed Lacy in the gentle but constant infuriating presence of Rawley Lovett. If Rooster hadn't come in and told them about the murder of the Clancy family, she'd probably still be in jail after trying to throw a knee into the marshal's crotch during one of their squabbles. Lying to Rooster, she told him she was a federal marshal. Thank goodness, he actually believed her. He let her out. An angry Rawley followed her to the homestead. After the gruesome discoveries of the murders, finding the boy and another tangling of strong personalities, they formed a reluctant partnership. Together they tracked the Dillards putting an end to their sick rampages.

Her nose caught that nice smelly stuff Rawley liked to wear for special occasions, before she saw him.

"Mind if I cut in on all this fun?"

Stopping, Lacy's breath disappeared. She gazed at the dark haired handsome man, all decked out in his one, nice suit. Now her nose really whiffed up that nice smelly stuff, since he stood so close to her. *Lordy...I could stand here all night breathing him in.* She realized. Shaking herself mentally, she tossed the thoughts aside. At that moment Cotton grabbed her neck, making sure those thoughts were tossed for good. "No! Only Miff Wafy 'n me!" He exclaimed.

Taken back, Rawley asked softly, "How 'bout the three of us dance?"

Cotton peeked around at the marshal. "Like mama n' papa?"

"Yes, like your mama and papa," the marshal replied.

"Kay," the little boy agreed. His other arm stretched, wrapping itself around Rawley's neck.

An awkward moment presented itself as Rawley and Lacy tried several dance poses before finding the right one that included a little boy.

Not knowing what to do after that number ended, they continued to stand in silence, staring at one another. Cotton knew though. Putting pressure on the back of Rawley and Lacy's necks, he simply stated. "Now you, kissy face!" Little hands continued to apply pressure, bringing Lacy and Rawley's faces closer together.

Breaking out in a grin, Rawley asked, "Should we oblige the young man, Sunshine?" He watched as a blush began to rise covering Lacy's freckles.

Once again, Cotton piped up. "Mama n' papa did when done dance, you mama n' papa now, you kissy face!"

Lacy sucked in a breath at what Cotton just revealed; her dark eyes darted back at the marshal, and she waited.

Rawley leaned closer, enclosing her lips with his, lightly tasting his deputy. Lacy's knees almost buckled. Locking them so she wouldn't collapse, she allowed his tender touch to wash over her. She felt like a moth flying too close to the flame. Abruptly she stepped back, breaking the hold he had on her.

Rawley frowned, searching her eyes for an answer. The veil had dropped back down covering her emotions, confusing him. He sighed inwardly, *one step forward...three back.*

FRECKLED VENOM
COPPERHEAD STRIKES

"See! Nice, kissy face!" Cotton crowed gaily.

Taking the boy from Lacy, Rawley set him down. "This is my dance, son," he said, patting him on the rump. "Go see Miss Liv." Both watched the little tyke scamper to Doc and Liv.

Rawley turned to the woman, who stood before him, nervously twisting her hands, as she watched Cotton hop down the steps, then crawl into Liv's lap. Rawley gave a slight smile. With no pockets in the dress to hide her hands, they remained in plain view, attesting to her nervousness. "Miss Carrigan, may I have this dance?" He asked softly holding out his hand.

Her head swiveled toward the marshal; Lacy hesitated. Rawley was stirring too many emotions in her tonight. In fact, he'd been doing that all day. Emotions she'd never felt before and didn't know what to do with.

"Don't tell me you're gonna go all bashful on me, now, Sunshine?"

Licking suddenly dry lips, she whispered. "I don't know."

Gently taking her hand, Rawley pulled her into his embrace. He guided Lacy around the wooden platform. She gracefully and easily followed his steps. He asked, "Thought you said you couldn't dance?"

"I can't."

"Seems to me you're doing just fine."

"Mama taught me a few steps, before, before…"

Rawley cut in, "She taught you just fine."

Mike, announcing a breather for the band, gave Lacy the chance she needed to break out of the warm and comfortable, too comfortable embrace of this gentle man.

Swallowing, the marshal had her insides all in a tizzy tonight. She had known handsome men before, but not like the marshal, where he combined good looks with a fun gentle personality, able to read her like a book. He was scaring her again, the way he could make her feelings go all topsy-turvy, making her head spin.

Taking the glass of cider Rawley offered her, Lacy drank it all down, hoping the liquid would settle her stomach. It didn't. It landed in the bottom with a thud. She held out the glass for a refill; Maddie complied. Her legs suddenly felt weak. "I need to sit down," she whispered. Taking her elbow, Rawley led Lacy over to Doc's and Liv's table. She sank down gratefully, Rawley next to her.

Looking around, her fingers absentmindedly kept wiping at the droplets that formed on the outside of the glass. Lacy spotted Lydia Marshall, her head bent close to Cody Brown, listening. Then surprisingly, Cody took her hand and they walked over to Maddie's table. One red-gold brow shot up at the gesture. *Well, maybe Lydia will keep him in line, she's persnickety enough,* she thought.

Half hour later Mike bellowed. "Aw right gents, grab yore ladies! Time for a reel!" Doc and Liv hopped up, going to the floor.

Rawley gave Lacy a long look. His face carried the question. *Wan 'a dance?*

Noticing that, Lacy hesitated. "I don't know how."

Standing, he took her hand, pulling. "You don't have to, Mike's calling it, he tells you what to do," Rawley said.

Forgetting that she should have lifted her skirts to climb the steps, Lacy tripped landing on one knee. Whirling, Rawley's big palms circled a small waist, preventing her nose from meeting the step. Her hands gripped his arms. "Oh…" Lacy exclaimed. A rosy hue flared across a million freckles as she looked at Rawley. He just smiled into burnt coffee eyes. His look accompanied by his warm smile had Lacy's breath disappearing, once again.

"I forgot…" a small voice began, "been wearing britches for so long…I forgot how to climb steps in a dress," Lacy shyly explained.

Pulling her upright, reluctant to drop his hands from the trim waist, he tilted his head. "That's okay, Sunshine," He reassured her. "At least you didn't crack your nose on the steps and bleed all over that beautiful dress."

Straightening her shoulders, Lacy heaved in more air for her starved lungs. She didn't know how Rawley did it, but he always seemed to suck the wind right out of her.

Taking her hand, he led Lacy over to the two lines formed for the reel.

Liv motioned for Lacy to slide in next to her, in the ladies line, across from Rawley. Looking up and down the row, she spotted Lydia Marshall and Cody Brown and Angela across from Billy, along with Luis and Maria. She smiled.

Cotton pushed his way between the marshal and Doc, looking way up, "Me, thoo, me thoo!"

Rawley grinned, as he looked across at Lacy, she too smiled back at him, finally. A small tug wrapped around his heart as he continued to marvel at Lacy's transformation in the last ten months. That tug pulled a little harder.

Mike began chanting. "Aw right, gents bow to yore lady!"

Following Liv, Lacy skipped forward, swishing her skirts as Liv did, and curtsied to both her men.

Cotton, mimicking the big man next to him, bowed deeply, head almost touching the platform floor. They all skipped back to place and waited on the next call.

"Now do-si-do yore man, ladies. Forward and back, make those feet go clickity-clack, swing that li'l gal, men!"

Acting as one, Lacy and Rawley each took one of Cotton's hands, picking him up in the air, the threesome swinging round, to the delighted squeals of a happy tyke.

"And back we go, fall in, and promenade round the mountain. Men take that gal and sashay home, raise that bridge and follow through."

A threesome sashayed home. Rawley lifted Cotton, placing him on his shoulders, taking the boy's hands, pressed them into Lacy's, forming the bridge for others to pass under.

Lacy's eyes shining like obsidian into the little towhead's, her smile wide with dimples deep, laughing. It made Rawley catch his breath once again at the transformation she had made. From an angry, sour, temperamental female, to the beautiful smiling, laughing woman, dancing across from him.

Lacy caught his gaze, making her suck in air. The look he gave her was different, not the teasing look he normally gave her. Something else, something deeper. Confusion rattled her brain, causing her to pucker her brows. Her mouth suddenly went dry, like she'd been sucking on cotton. She ran her tongue over her lips, then catching the bottom one with her teeth, nibbled on it. Lacy darted her eyes away, back to the little boy's gleeful face.

Mike calling the next step, "Do-si-do, yure partner back, make those feet go clickity-clack, gents swing that li'l lady, one last time!"

This time Rawley swung Lacy. Cotton, with a death grip around Rawley's neck, squealed as the pair made a fast turn, causing the two adults to burst out laughing.

Everyone clapped, whistled and hooted when Mike finished. Mike flashed his big toothy grin.

Cotton leaned down and patted Rawley's cheek. The marshal rolled his eyes up, peering into the cute face. "Now, kissy face 'gan," chirped the towhead.

Rawley switched his eyes to Lacy. "What say you, Miss Carrigan? Shall we oblige the boy one more time?"

Chewing on her lip again, she rose on her toes and gave him a swift peck on the cheek, then backed away just as quick.

"Aw, now Sunshine, you can do better than that!" He said, taking her in his arms once more, covering her mouth with his, and prolonging what he had wanted to do all evening.

"Aw right, you two, cut it out! Folks is beginning to stare!" Doc butted in gruffly.

The marshal lifted his head, giving the crusty bachelor a dirty look. "Doc, you sure do know how to ruin a good thing," he said, releasing Lacy. She retreated quickly, fingers pressing against her burning lips.

FRECKLED VENOM
COPPERHEAD STRIKES

Liv stepped in, arms stretched to receive Cotton. "Time you were in bed, young man! Tomorrow is another day." The three waved goodbye as they wandered back to Liv's house.

Mike announced. "Last dance gents, take that li'l lady in yure arms, we'll do a nice waltz, to close out the evening!"

Lacy headed down the steps of the platform, when a hand grabbed hers, pulling her back to the floor. "No, I'm tired," she complained.

"One more, Sunshine, just one more," he requested pulling her into his arms again, savoring the moment. "Last one, Sunshine," Rawley whispered into her hair. Light lavender from the copper mass filled his senses. He breathed deeply.

Lacy just nodded. Closing her eyes, she rested her head on his chest, allowing herself the comfort of his embrace.

Later, the marshal and his deputy said goodbye to other folks on the way to their homes, stopping by Maddie's table for one more drink. Pouring each a large glass of cider, she offered up. "Ach, ye two, cut ah nice pitcher, out there. Aye ya, a real purity picture."

Scrutinizing Lacy's face, Maddie said, nodding at the girl. "Laddie, ye need tae be seeing the wee lass home, she's aboot done in."

Realizing that Maddie was right, Rawley took Lacy's arm. "C' mon Sunshine, you've had a really long day, let's go home," he said, throwing a wave to Maddie.

Maddie watched as the marshal draped his arm across Lacy's shoulders. The girl's arm slowly eased around the sturdy back of the lawman.

It was plain to everyone tonight. Rawley Lovett had fallen in love. The Scotswoman chuckled; lots of young ladies were heartbroken. They all saw he had eyes only for his deputy. In fact, everyone's eyes had been focused on the copperhead in disbelief tonight. They had been so used to seeing the girl in britches and toting a sidearm.

"Aye ya," she whispered, saying to the stars above.

"Aye ya, we'll be a having a wedding afore too long, if yon lassie ever figures out whether she loves 'im or not!"

* * *

Entering the office, Lacy broke away from the man who stirred such emotions in her tonight. Emotions she thought she would never, ever feel. She stared at the floor.

"Thank you for taking me to the dance, see you in the morning," she said easing down the hallway to her room.

"Lacy?"

She stopped. Glancing over her shoulder, she waited for his words.

"I'm glad you went, it was nice to see you laugh and smile."

Lacy just nodded, as she entered, and then closed the door, to her room.

Containing his feelings for Lacy was becoming harder to pull off, but he needed to be patient with her a little bit longer. Rawley knew Lacy was feeling something; she didn't pull away or argue with him tonight. Hopefully she'd figure it out soon, afore he did run out of patience. Pulling his string tie loose, he unbuttoned his collar. Rawley emitted a long noisy sigh as he entered his room; the door whispered close with a click.

* * *

After tucking in a sleepy tow-head, Liv had poured Doc his nightcap. Settling down next to him, she gave a happy sigh.

Doc cut her a sharp look. "What was that for?"

"Nothing, I'm just happy tonight," was her reply, sliding her arm into the crook of his elbow. She rested her head on his shoulder.

"Why, cause of those two love birds?"

"Rawley is, Lacy is not sure yet."

"How do ya know that?"

Lifting her head she gazed fondly at the crusty doctor. She smiled, saying, "Woman's intuition."

"We back to that again?"

"Uh-huh, you know you need to talk to the powers that be, and see if the town would buy a house for the marshal."

"What in tarnation for? You're on the council, you bring it up!"

Smiling once again, she answered, "I might just do that, the marshal's office isn't exactly the best place for a young couple to set up housekeeping."

"Sheesh, Liv," Doc said, sitting upright. "You got those two married off already?"

"It's coming, you wait and see."

"Harrumph," Doc said settling back. "It'll take Rawley all he's got to tame that one."

"Maybe, maybe not," she returned giving Doc a kiss on the cheek. "You better be going. I've got a big day tomorrow."

"Humph," Doc intoned.

* * *

Hanging up her dress, her hand caressed the material. It was her first one in many years. Taking out the pins holding her hair, Lacy stared into the looking glass as she began brushing the dark to coppery gold waves. Stopping, she looked at her reflection, her hands fingering the brush. Then her eyes settled on her lips, fingertips rose and touched them. She remembered how Rawley had kissed her tonight, how her knees had buckled and in front of all those people, too.

Lacy realized she had been falling under his spell; her heart said to go with it, her mind said to run. But, she didn't want to run anymore, she wanted to stay. Even if Rawley constantly made her gut twist like snarled barbed wire, Lacy wanted to stay.

Sitting in the rocker, she continued to brush her hair. Tomorrow she would have a good talk with the marshal. He was her boss, for heaven's sake! He shouldn't be kissing her in front of the whole town. Going to bed, Lacy was out before her head even hit the pillow.

CHAPTER TWENTY THREE

Strolling back toward the office after picking up the mail from Ezra's, Lacy sniffed at the faint remnants of yesterday's firecrackers. Circles of scorched earth dotted the main thoroughfare; with paper casings littering the street. Today breezes fanned the bunting hanging in front of businesses. Her ears plucked sounds out of the air of hammers pounding and the screeching of nails being pulled out of the dance floor as folks began dismantling it.

Walking through the open doorway, Lacy said, "Got some new circulars," then waved a letter in Rawley's face. "And you got a letter from," looking at it, "Denver."

"Denver?"

Giving him a wide eyed stare, Lacy handed Rawley the letter, then poured coffee, and curled up in her perch. Taking the circulars she began going through them.

"Says here Jack Drake, broke jail, they were supposed to hang him. His old buddies used enough dynamite to blow out a wall there," the marshal said.

"At a federal prison?"

Rawley shrugged. "That's what it says here."

Watching the muscles ripple under the cream colored shirt he wore today had Lacy sipping air. *Cut it out,* she told herself, *he's my boss.* She asked, "What are you going to do?"

"Nuthin', leased ways not yet."

"Well, from what I've heard about Jack Drake, it ain't pretty," Lacy finished.

Rawley nodded in agreement.

"Denver's not that far, well, it is and it isn't," said Lacy. "Think he might come here?"

"He might, since it was me n' Sam who put him behind bars, didn't get the rest of them, figured since their leader was gone, they'd disappear. Looks like I was wrong."

Lacy stood, going to the files, and pulling a drawer open, it protesting the sudden use. She asked, "You got any old information on him? Description? That sorta thing?"

"Yeah," he answered. Coming to stand alongside of her, he pulled open another drawer. Sifting through the files, he stopped and pulled one out, laid the file on top of the cabinet and opened it.

Standing on her toes, Lacy peered at the paperwork.

The two of them were only inches from each other.

The heat and light scent of lavender emitting off of Lacy this morning distracted him. The tension of wanting her, yet having to maintain his distance was driving him nuts.

"Lacy?"

Glancing up, she saw the same look he gave her on the dance floor last night. Retreating suddenly, she jammed hands in her hip pockets. "We need to talk."

"You bet we do," he replied gruffly.

"I mean about last night, you don't need to be kissing me in public! It's not right, you're my boss. I work for you."

"Sunshine, there's more going on here than just you working for me."

Lacy swallowed. "I know, and it's gotta stop," she said.

"Why?"

Her heart, beginning to bang against her ribs, cut into her air supply. Lacy inhaled deeply, saying, "Because…because it's not right, that's all."

"What's not right?" Rawley beginning to tease her now, trying to get Lacy to spit the words out that he longed to hear.

Sipping wind through her teeth, she repeated, "Because

it's not right," backing further away. One hand came out of that back pocket and flipped through the air. "You set tongues a-wagging all over town this morning, making me and you, both of us look like fools! Miz Dawson is having a field day with this. Why...I had looks and hushed whispers following me everywhere, and...."

"And, I didn't feel you resisting my attentions last night," Rawley butted in.

"I was doing it for Cotton!" She quickly retorted. "That little boy is finally happy again, and if he's replaced his mama and papa with us, well, that's just fine with me! I didn't want to disappoint him," Lacy said lamely.

Sticking thumbs in his own back pockets, he said, "You don't have to be afraid of love, Sunshine." *Here's hoping,* "It's just natural for men and women to fall in love, all part of God's plan," Rawley explained.

Lacy snorted very un-lady like. The marshal cocked a brow at the expression.

"I don't believe in God! If there's a God, then I wouldn't have turned out like I did," she said.

"Sunshine you would've been dead a long time ago, if God hadn't been there protecting you. The way you carry on, it's a wonder some relative hasn't come out of the woodwork, bush whacking you, shooting you in the back, leaving you for dead! You've been lucky, is all."

The two of them just stood glaring at each other, anger bouncing between two bodies, both waiting on the other to say something first.

Lacy wasn't gonna budge, Rawley knew, her lips locked up tighter than the Denver mint, again.

Moving to the edge of his desk, he sat. The heel of his hand rubbed his forehead. Dropping it, Rawley gave the redhead a steady look and then offered up. "Lacy, I know you're struggling with emotions you've not allowed yourself to feel before. I can understand that. But underneath all that bluff and bluster, you're warm and caring. It's okay to show those emotions now, you can feel safe here."

"*Damn it! He thinks he can tell me what I'm feeling? Like hell!*" Her mind said.

Color rising covered tawny freckles as burnt coffee eyes slithered into narrow lines. "Safe? What the hell do you know about being safe? As big a moose as you are! Who gave you the right to tell me what I'm feeling? You've got it all wrong, Lovett," she argued giving a dismissive wave of her arm. "You can kiss love goodbye where I'm concerned. I don't need love or a man to make me happy!" She spun ready to run to the sanctuary of her room when his words stopped her in mid-stride.

Rising abruptly, Rawley said angrily, "Damn you…Sunshine! The biggest mistake I ever made was following you to the river after you slugged me in Mike's place!"

Whirling, surprise flew across Lacy's freckled features. "I didn't slug you…"

"The second mistake," he interrupted. "Was not walking away when I should have, leaving you to molder and rot with your blood poisoning!"

Lacy spoke quietly. "I hate you," she said.

Rawley shrugged, wincing at her simple words. He walked to the door and spat in disgust. He watched the wetness land on the dusty boards.

Spinning on her toes, Lacy ran to her room.

The door slamming echoed up the hallway, reaching his ears.

Taking in a calming breath as he leaned against the open doorway, Rawley rested a big hand on the opposite door jamb. *Damn, that girl can push my buttons like no other.*

Rawley understood what had caused her outburst and his own anger at Lacy. The girl still refused to acknowledge her fear, that niggling fear, fear of allowing someone to get close to her, afraid of being hurt, like she had been all those years ago. Rawley reasoned with himself, *But, that's how one grew, learning to trust someone enough, to get beyond those fears.* Shaking his head, one of these days, if he didn't run out of patience, he might be able to break down those barriers. Rawley knew Lacy loved him, he'd seen it in her face on rare occasions. The way her face became so soft, allowing a sweet smile to peek through a million freckles. And those burnt coffee eyes shining with mischief. He also knew that she really hadn't recognized the emotion she exhibited on those rare occasions as love.

Lacy had been doing so well, too, coming out of her shell. The day of the race she remained strong keeping a cool head and still winning the race even after losing precious minutes being bumped and thrown by her father. And last night at the dance, even now the memory of her in that dress still took his breath away. He exhaled noisily, *taking two steps forward, three back, or more*, he thought. Sometimes she acted like a fox on the run, staying just ahead of her hunter; in this case, Rawley figured Lacy felt he was the hunter.

CHAPTER TWENTY FOUR

Lacy ripped the dress down, began tearing it up into shreds, grabbing her knife, cutting it into smaller strips. With tears flowing, she kept shredding. Her eyes flooding spilled over, dripping onto the dress. When it was in tatters, she finally stopped, collapsing in the rocker. Staring at the pile of material, she'd worn with pride last night, she wiped her cheeks with her hands, and grabbed some matches. Unscrewing the top to the coal oil lamp, laying the globe and wick aside, she gathered that and the pieces of material. Walking out her door, then through to the back, she threw the dress in the barrel and poured the coal oil on the frock. Dropping the glass base, it hit the ground with a dull thud. She struck several matches and watched as the dress caught fire. When it began burning, she ran as hands frustratingly swiped at her tears. Coming from between two buildings, Lacy ran quickly crossing the street, not bothering to check for traffic, to the stables. She was going to ride till she and Fancy could go no more.

Seeing Lacy go through the back door, carrying something, he waited a few moments, and then followed her. Stepping outside, Rawley saw the barrel in flames. He grabbed the bucket by the pump, filling it and quickly doused the flaming article. Reaching inside, he pulled out the dress Lacy had worn last night, now in tatters and burned. Dropping the garment he hurried around the side of the building, just in time to see Lacy tearing out of the stable, riding Fancy bareback, heading toward Hens and Chickens.

Sticking thumbs in back pockets, he pursed his lips and

blew frustratingly. Then, he tugged on his ear, mimicking Doc, and decided he'd wait awhile. She wasn't wearing her rig, didn't saddle Fancy, and took no gear with her. Lacy would be back, he decided. Rawley returned to his office.

CHAPTER TWENTY FIVE

Picking up the tension emitting from her rider, Fancy balked. It was different this time the horse knew. She kept throwing her head around, arguing with her rider, sidestepping, not wanting to take off as the girl wanted her to.

"Cut it out Fancy! We're going for a ride, a long ride, so just settle down!" Banging her heels into Fancy's ribs, and not gently, Lacy jerked the reins. She couldn't understand Fancy's resistance today. Usually the horse would be chomping at the bit with the prospect of a good run.

Heading Fancy toward the three downed trees, she took the route as they had in the Fourth of July race past Hens and Chickens. Coming upon the downed trees, Lacy's knees guided the horse toward the jump. Fancy didn't want to jump. The horse shied hard to the right, catching her rider off guard. Lacy sailed to the left, and her body flew over the first tree. She hit the ground with a thud, even though the thick grass softened the blow, somewhat. Her body continued to skid along, leaving a trail of flattened grasses and then stopped. She laid still.

* * *

Glancing at the timepiece on the wall next to the cell door, Rawley realized Lacy had been gone for quite a spell. Usually it only took a couple of hours for the copperhead to simmer down. Throwing away the match stick he'd been chewing on, he headed toward the stable. Saddling his bay, Rawley rode in the direction he'd last seen his redhead, Hens

FRECKLED VENOM
COPPERHEAD STRIKES

and Chickens.

Coming upon the stand of pines, he glanced to his left. There, he saw Fancy standing near the downed trees. Rawley made a beeline for the horse. Reining up the bay short caused the horse to whinny. Leaping out of the leather, he yelled at the big grey, "Fancy! Where is she?"

The horse looked up when she'd heard the bay whinny. Dark heartwood eyes followed him, and after a few seconds resumed filling her belly with tasty grass.

Hurrying over toward one of the trees, he saw Lacy lying in the grass between the two huge logs, not moving. Scrambling over the tree, Rawley knelt by the girl. Turning her over, he noticed one side of Lacy's face covered in dried blood and grass. Quickly checking her other body parts, he noted they looked okay. Rising, he ran and retrieved his canteen. Returning he sat down and pulled Lacy into his lap. Digging his bandana out of his back pocket, he unscrewed the cap pouring water on the piece of blue cloth. Gently, he began to clean her face and the scrape.

Lacy stirred, moaning.

"That's it, c' mon, Sunshine, wake-up," Rawley said as he continued to wipe Lacy's forehead and cheek.

Lacy moved some.

"That's my girl, c' mon wake up."

Lacy cracked her eyes open; they gazed into smiling Wyoming summer skies framed by black lashes. Her heart tickled her insides. Moaning again, she whispered, "Why?"

"Why what, Sunshine?"

Lacy swallowed. Her voice cracked with dryness when she asked, "Water…you got some water?"

Lifting her head and shoulders, he held the canteen up to Lacy's lips. She took several sips.

"Better now?" Rawley asked.

Swallowing once again, Lacy whispered in that soft throaty voice of hers. "Why? Why do you always have to follow me, pestering me?"

"I never know what kind of trouble you're gonna get yourself into," Rawley answered. "This time, it's a good thing I did come after you. Thought you could ride," he said teasing her.

His last comment had her squinting, the gesture made her cheek sting. "Fancy was giving me a hard time; don't know what was wrong with her."

Rawley glanced back at the horse, noting his bay munching contentedly next to the grey mare. He turned his attention again to his redhead. Wetting the bandana some more, he continued to wipe her face. "Maybe, she knew something you didn't," he finally said. He knew animals could easily pick up discord or tension when they were close to their owners. And Fancy and Lacy were sewn at the hip. Rawley thought, *Can't get any closer than that,* instead he kept that thought to himself.

Lacy didn't want to talk. Her head had begun to hurt; the side of her face stung like she'd burnt herself. But, that didn't keep her mind from whirring, thoughts tumbling over each other like rocks in a barrel heading down a steep hill.

She threw lame words. "I can take care of myself," she barked weakly.

"Uh-huh, seems like ever since I've known you, if I hadn't been there to patch you up, or dig you out of trouble, you'd be in a bigger mess."

Emotions seemed to slice her insides like barbed wire. Lacy struggled to sit up, trying to get away from this big moose. She had to go someplace quiet to untangle those emotions from the barbed wire. Figure things out.

Rawley pulled her back down, wrapping his arms around her. He held her tight.

Taking her elbow Lacy tried jabbing the marshal with it.

"Sunshine I've 'bout flat run out of patience with you," he gritted, holding her tighter.

"Let me go."

"No."

Squirming against muscular arms, she knew it was impossible to break the hold he had on her. Her heart just wasn't in it anymore to physically fight him.

She remembered the dance, how Rawley had held her in his arms and the way he'd kissed her. She bit back the tears that threatened, squishing her lids shut to keep the moisture from spreading.

Lacy didn't want to succumb to Rawley's spell, which became stronger with each passing day. She'd tried throwing mean words, making him mad, nothing worked. He just kept dogging her tail infuriating the hell out of her. Throwing her all out of kilter, he made her feel things she didn't want to. Then when she did, she didn't know what to do with these feelings.

Emotionally, she felt like a big locomotive that had just crashed into a granite wall. Never trusting anyone after her grandfather molested her forced Lacy to stay on the move. Bounty hunting soon became a means of simple existence, putting food in her belly and a little cash in her pocket. Staying on the move all the time she knew she could never form any sort of attachments. Only then did she feel safe.

Finally letting her guard down, Lacy allowed herself to become attached to Sam and Sally Luebker. When Sam had died in her arms from his heart going out on him, Lacy picked up where she had left off, resuming her solitary life as a bounty hunter. Then she found herself cast back into the lives of the folks in White River and especially a big moose by the name of Rawley Lovett.

Lacy wasn't going to give into what her heart told her to do. *It'd never work anyhow,* she told herself. Men only wanted women so they could control them, like her grandfather. She wasn't going to allow that to happen to her. But, here she was lying in this gentle man's embrace, and liking the comfort that it gave her, his warm arms making her feel safe. That thought just made her nerves jangle even harder.

Even though her eyes remained closed, Rawley could

feel Lacy's heart beating a little faster than a normal tattoo against his hand resting along her ribs. Long fingers picked the grass out of copper curls framing a freckled face. *Lacy...Lacy. How much longer am I gonna have to wait to hear you say three little words,* He thought as he hand brushed copper tresses from her face. He sighed heavily.

Hearing the exhale, Lacy opened her eyes and saw the blanket of stars covering the expanse of sky, surprising her.

Focusing on a strong, square jawed face that carried Cheyenne blood, Lacy asked, "Why...why did you come after me?"

Shifting a little, releasing the pressure on one long leg, he replied, "Because I care about you Sunshine," Rawley said. He continued softly, "I have feelings for you." He held back the words, *I love you,* that sat on the tip of his tongue. "Don't ask me why, as contentious, argumentative and bullheaded as you are, but I do. And I think you have feelings for me, too,"

She groaned inwardly hearing his words. *I know I do! You nitwit!* She thought. Suddenly it dawned on her, *I'm afraid! I'm afraid to fall in love.* Her eyes grew round at what she realized. Lacy quickly shut them, so perceptive blue ones couldn't read her mind. *I'm afraid of loving and then losing again, like I did mama and Sam.* The thought landed a hard punch to her gut, she groaned silently.

"You just aren't sure what they are yet, and when you do finally figure it out, I'll be here to listen."

Listening to the soft caramel baritone that seemed to drip like dew in the quiet night, she swallowed, thinking, *I can't. I'm not the woman this kindhearted man needs.* Lacy opened her eyes. She threw out words trying to dissuade him otherwise, "I'm not your type."

Rawley's mouth twitched. "No, you're not, but somehow, somewhere, you kind of started to grow on me."

She wanted to groan hearing his words. "I'm not normal," Lacy said instead, still trying to throw a wedge between them.

FRECKLED VENOM
COPPERHEAD STRIKES

Smiling again, her said, "Nope, but I wouldn't change a thing. You have a way of taking a dull, mundane day and making it brighter, not just for me, but, for a lot of other folks too," Rawley added

Watching eyes slide closed again, he asked, "You got a headache?"

Lacy gave a slight nod.

"Big one or little one?"

Lacy's head went one way then another.

"Think you can ride?"

Again a nod yes.

"Sunshine, don't think you're ever gonna be a chatterbox! Okay, let's get you back to Doc, so he can put some salve on that scrape."

* * *

Reading one of the new medical journals that had just arrived from Boston, Doc looked up as his door opened. Taking one glance at Lacy's disheveled appearance, one eye beginning to discolor, one freckled cheek scraped, grass sticking to her clothes and hair had Doc roaring, "Thunder boy! What the hell did you do to her now?"

Flinching at the roar, Lacy glanced at Rawley.

Rawley tapered eyes at what Doc insinuated. "I didn't do nuthin' Doc! She did this all by herself!"

"Uh-huh." Cocking a black and grey bushy brow, he said "Well…c' mon, young lady." Doc patted the exam table. "Hop up."

Tilting her head, Doc looked at the scrapes. "They're not deep, might have a discolored eye for a few days." Pouring some astringent on a cloth, he warned, "This might sting a little." He patted the scraped area.

Lacy's arm erupted at the pain, hitting Doc in the elbow.

"Here now, you cut that out! I've got to clean this so it don't get infected!"

Lacy, realizing what she had done, sat on her hands, burnt coffee eyes downcast.

"You try that again, young lady, I'm just liable to haul you off that table and warm yore britches good," Doc warned gruffly.

Rawley bit back the grin threatening to bust out.

"You hear me?" Doc asked.

Lacy nodded.

"Good. Now let's try this again. I told you it was gonna sting some," he said.

Lacy winced as he patted the area again

Finishing up with the salve, hazel eyes looked into Lacy's tired ones. "You got a headache?" Doc watched the red head nod. "Big one?"

A slight back and forth no.

"Little one?"

A nod yes.

"Humph. Awright, hop down, and go get some rest," Doc said; his eyes following Lacy as she opened the door. He noted her gate remained steady. Hearing light footsteps recede as she descended the stairs, they fell silent when they reached the street. Sharp hazel eyes settled back on Rawley. "Keep an eye on her, she ain't wobblin', but that don't mean she won't have a reaction later, any change come get me."

"Thanks Doc, and night."

"Night, son," Doc said softly, closing the door behind the lawman with a slight click.

Not spotting Lacy waiting for him, Rawley clattered down the steps and hurried back to the office.

Opening the door and walking inside, he saw Lacy already half-way down the hallway to her room. Rawley called out, "Lacy," stopping her.

She turned, eying him warily.

Grabbing a couple of matches from the holder on the desk, striking the tip of one against the plaster chinking, he lit the lamp hanging on the wall in the hallway.

FRECKLED VENOM
COPPERHEAD STRIKES

Blowing out the match before it burnt his fingers, Rawley took note of the hooded look that shrouded pretty features. He knew something had happened at the downed trees. It wasn't something physically, so it had to be with Lacy's emotions.

Walking toward his redhead, he took her arm. "You're going to sleep in my room tonight," he said.

"No," she replied, raising her arm trying to twist it out of his grasp. "I'll sleep in my quarters tonight," she argued.

At her resistance, he told Lacy, "Doc said to keep an eye on you, can't do that, you sleep back here."

He guided a reluctant redhead back to his quarters, forcing her to sit on the bed. He grabbed her pants leg and began pulling off a boot. Lacy swatted his hand. Rawley backed off. "Alright then, you do it," he said. While he waited, he lit the lamp in his room, then he turned. One boot, then two, thumped to the floor. He took the spare coverlet on the foot of his bed and covered Lacy.

Rawley blew out the lamp as he said. "I'll be right out here, if you need me."

Lacy didn't want to go to sleep. She had to think! The shock of realizing that she was afraid of falling in love had her scared witless. A small sob slipped out. She rolled over, burying her face in his pillow. His pleasant masculine scent filled her senses teasing them. She was even able to pick out that nice smelly stuff he wore for special occasions. Stuffing her face further into the pillow, Lacy muffled a groan. Her resistance to the handsome marshal was weakening, and she didn't know how to stop it. Except by slinking away under the cover of darkness again. But, she didn't want to run any more; she wanted to stay.

CHAPTER TWENTY SIX

Coming back across the street with a covered tray from Maddie's, Rawley ran into Doc. The crusty older gentleman asked, "How's our girl this morn?"

"Still sleeping."

"Any problems last night?"

Shaking his head, "Nope, slept solid, didn't even move."

Doc rubbed his face. "Humph, well then, she'll be alright," he said. Sticking the ever present matchstick back into his mouth, Doc tucked hands into his trousers' pockets and sauntered off.

Staring out the window sipping coffee, Lacy watched the two men converse silently, then go their separate ways. She turned toward the door as it opened.

Carrying the tray over to the table, Rawley sat it down. Casting a glance at the redhead standing by the window, he said, "Maddie sent some breakfast over, better eat while it's still hot." Studying Lacy, as she continued to stare back at him warily, Rawley thought, *she still has that hooded look about her. I'd swear something happened out there with her last night.* He wandered back to his desk and sat. His weight made the chair squeak. The noise broke into the thick silence. Picking up a pencil, he continued to watch his redhead, fingers twiddling it.

Silently drifting over to the table, Lacy lifted the napkin off the tray. She stared at the food. Finally she sat down and ate a few bites, and then just began shoving the food around on her plate. She wasn't hungry. A chair scraped against plank flooring, rising, she walked back to the potbellied stove and refilled her cup.

Focusing eyes out the window, Lacy's mind still tried to wrap itself around yesterday's revelation. Looking down she spied her filthy shirt. Spinning, the cup landed hard on the desk, splashing its contents.

Rawley stared at the dark liquid spreading its stain toward his paperwork. He moved it quickly.

Her hand reached for the bucket. Whirling, Lacy headed out back for water.

Rawley just sat watching her go. Lacy always clammed up when she was struggling with her emotions. He'd wished she'd talk to him, let him help overcome her fears, but as stubborn as Lacy was, as hardheaded as she was…well, he would have to dig down deep, bring up more patience. Something he was running out of mighty quick.

When Lacy emerged from her room, later, Rawley took note of her recently washed thick copper rope. A fresh blue and cream checkered shirt rolled to freckled elbows and tan canvas britches clothed Lacy's petite frame.

Rawley's gaze followed as the girl got another cup of coffee. She then continued staring out the window. Finally putting the cup down without taking a sip, Lacy walked over and pulled her rig off the peg, buckling it on as she went out the door without another word.

The chair squeaked as he stood and walked over to the window. Observing Lacy head toward the stable, Rawley stood thinking. *Damn girl is still the quietest female I have ever met. Conversation? Hell! With Lacy around, conversation was just a long word that contained a bunch of letters.* She did a one hundred eighty degree turn on him in less than twenty-four hours. That didn't set too well with him. Fingers scratching dark stubble, Rawley sighed heavily. She didn't just take a few steps back this time. No. Lacy had retreated far enough away it'd take a good day's hard ride to get there.

CHAPTER TWENTY SEVEN

A shock of grey cock's comb shadowed the open doorway; a body followed. Rooster slid in the office door. "Hey Rawley, Mike wants you at his place. Seems, there's some characters he's not too pleased about standing at his bar." Turning, he blinked, refocusing on the town's gadfly instead of Lacy. The marshal asked, "Oh…who?"

"Don't know," Rooster replied. "Mike…he jus' don't like the looks of 'em."

"Alright," Rawley said. Turning, he walked to the pegs holding his hardware. Reaching for his rig, he buckled it as he followed Rooster back to the saloon.

Coming out of the stable, chewing on a blade of sweet hay, Lacy watched Rawley and Rooster heading in the direction of the Mike's place. She wondered what was up. She tossed the blade as she picked up her pace, and followed them.

Palms resting on the bat-wing doors of Stewart's Saloon, Rawley stopped and surveyed the three men at the bar. Rooster peered around the marshal's broad back.

From the back, Rawley didn't recognize them. The trio took up one end of Mike's bar. The one closest to the barkeep, leaning on the bar, had thick arms and boulder like shoulders encased in a moth-eaten, molting piece of hide. The appendages appeared even bulkier with the old buffalo coat. Eyes drifted to the others, one tall and lanky dressed in buckskin, and the last of the three, also in buckskin, had dark stringy hair that dripped from under his hat ending below his shoulders. Rawley thought, *Hide hunters.* His gaze traveled to Mike's

FRECKLED VENOM
COPPERHEAD STRIKES

face.

Mike cut his eyes to the left at the three.

Rawley nodded, acknowledging the non-verbal heads up.

Moving toward the bar, Rawley said, "Coffee, Mike."

Sliding in the door behind the marshal, Rooster sat at a table with two others, slowly sinking into the chair. He kept his eyes focused on Rawley. Rooster wasn't about to miss this.

A cup tapped the well-worn shiny top. Steam rose as liquid splashed into the earthenware mug. Rawley's nose not only whiffed up the aroma of hot coffee, but, also, the thick, fragrant stench of hide hunters, smelling like a dozen week old elk carcasses in the heat of summer. Mike refilled his cup too.

Taking the cup Rawley raised it to his lips. As he sipped, he rested that elbow on the bar and turned to his right facing the trio. His right thumb tucked itself into a hip pocket closer to his pistol. The stench arrived first as the one in the ratty buffalo hide turned, throwing the unpleasant odor. He faced the marshal.

Rawley's eyes tightened as he recognized the grizzled mug of Big Joe Kannon. A hired gun, and bounty hunter, he worked for whoever paid the highest price.

"Well, if it ain't Rawley Lovett," a gravelly voice began. "Last I heerd you wuz deputy in Montana," Kannon said glancing at the badge. His tongue shifted the wad of chaw from one side of his mouth to the other before speaking again. "Took a step up, din cha? Course don't make as much as ya did bounty hunting, but, then, ya always did like the law a little too much."

"State your business, Kannon."

Sneaking in the side door, Lacy sidled in behind the big pot-bellied stove that remained cold. Her eyes roamed the room, taking in the tables with a few patrons. They had glanced up when she'd entered. Settling a hard look on the six men, Lacy jerked her thumb over her shoulder and silently mouthed, *out!* When they didn't leave, she zeroed a blistering look on Mike's patrons and jerked her thumb harder, mouthing, *move it!* This time the six seemed to get the message as chairs scraped against scarred planks and boots thumped out the door. Seeing Mike's surprised look, she warned him with a finger on her lips to be quiet. Lacy remained behind the stove.

Big Joe replied smugly, "Oh, jus' doing some scouting. Thought I might do a little fishing, too. Fresh trout'd be mighty tasty, right 'bout now, don 'cha think?" Rolling the wad around in his mouth, Big Joe leaned back and sent a long stream of tobacco juice through the air behind his boys, splattering a dark stain across the wood floor.

Mike rolled his eyes.

"Who you looking for, this time, Kannon?" Rawley asked tersely.

Pouring another drink, he sipped before answering, "I do believe that's my business, Lovett."

Jaw clinched, Rawley knew these men were trouble, always had been since he'd known them. Once they got liquored up, they could do more damage in one hour then five hundred head of cattle stampeding through town. "If you're planning to stay, you'll have to turn over your guns, you can pick them up when you leave town."

Kannon straightened, moving away from the bar, hand relaxed, fingers flexing above his gun butt. "You want 'em, you come get 'em, marshal," he challenged the big man.

Pulling her weapon, she stepped away from the stove. Lacy fired her pistol into the floorboards at Kannon's feet, surprising the five at the bar. Holding the weapon in a two handed grip, she stated quietly, "You heard the marshal, drop your gun belts."

Rawley's head spun. Hearing a pistol fire, he thought, *damn it, Lacy! She's gonna screw everything up.* He threw a *be-quiet* look across the room.

Lacy caught the look. *Like hell,* she thought, ignoring it.

Five sets of eyes rested on a freckled face with the skin

around one eye beginning to turn green with a scabbed scrape marking her cheek. The copperhead did not flinch from the ten eyes staring at her.

The girl's husky voice dropped into an even lower pitch, laced with venom. "You heard me, *boys*. Drop those rigs, now."

Mike had taken the time to lay his sawed off scatter gun on the bar.

Elbows resumed resting on the bar. Big Joe with his back to Lacy downed his drink, pouring another. "Don't think I care for your brand of hospitality, Lovett," he said.

"Well now…that's jus' too bad, ain't it," drawled Rawley.

Turning once again, Kannon faced the girl, the small of his back pressed against the bar, placing his elbows on the smooth surface behind him. "You must be goin' soft in tha haid, marshal," he said. Nodding at the badge pinned on the front of Lacy's shirt. "Hiring a li'l gal ta be yure backup."

Mike piped up. "That li'l gal happens to be tough and smart, which is mor'n I can say for you."

Deliberately turning slow, Kannan addressed Mike, "Barkeep…," Suddenly he grabbed the front of Mike's shirt, half pulling the barkeep's bulky frame across the bar. Big Joe's wonderful perfume of dead carcasses swirled through the air with his quick movement. "When I want yure opinion I'll ask fer it," he growled shoving him hard, back against the shelves behind him. Bottles clinked, when Mike's elbow landed in the midst. Two crashed to the floor, shattering. The sweet smell of sour mash rose mixing with tainted carcasses, saturating the saloon's air.

Lacy hadn't budged from her position. She continued to watch the tension, twenty feet away. Her weight centered on the balls of her feet. Waiting to see who might make the first move.

Rawley asked again, "Who you after this time, Kannon?"

"Ya always wuz a nosy sum bitch. Dillard brothers' trail ends here, they must be up in tha high country," Big Joe said. Upending his glass, he swallowed the liquid.

Clamping lips tight, Lacy tried to keep the smile from poking out.

Rawley grinned. "You're late. Those boys were caught months ago." Seeing surprise filter across Kannon's face, he added, "The last one alive, wuz hung jus' recently."

One eye tapered almost shut in Kannon's grizzled face. "Who caught 'em?"

"Me and my deputy," he said, his eyes gesturing back at Lacy.

Dirt crusted crow's feet grew darker as Big Joe's eyes traveled into slits. Directing his question at the lawman, he asked, "Who got the bounty?"

Lacy spoke before Rawley could. "I did. It went to the little boy whose family was slaughtered by the Dillards."

His pungent perfume swirled in the air as he turned facing the girl. "Well, now, ain't you jus' the Sister of Mercy," Big Joe said as tarnished teeth gave way to a counterfeit smile.

"You looking for bounty…," Rawley offered, hoping to get the trio out of town, before Big Joe and his boys reduced it to rubble. "Jack Drake jus' broke jail. Don't know what the bounty is yet, but, I'm sure it'll be a pretty penny, that is…if you're interested," Rawley stated.

Thinking about what the marshal just volunteered, Kannon said, "Jack Drake, huh? Seems like I 'member you and," snapping his fingers. "Luebker got 'em ah while ago." Pouring his glass full again, drinking it down, he asked, "Where wuz he?"

"Denver."

"Federal prison, huh? He comin' this way?"

"Don't know."

"You gonna be setting on a hot seat, Lovett. Drake's gonna be gunning fer ya."

"I know," Rawley stated quietly.

FRECKLED VENOM
COPPERHEAD STRIKES

Gesturing at Lacy with his glass, he told Lovett, "Drake's smart. That li'l gal ain't gonna be nuff back up to cover yure arse, this time, Lovett."

Sticking one thumb in his back pocket, the other hand resting lightly on his weapon, he spoke quietly, saying, "We'll manage."

"Uh-huh…how long ago he break jail?"

"Eight days."

Thinking, Kannon said, "Well, tell ya what Lovett, you let us keep our guns, let us get some supplies, we'll ride outta here, and try'n keep Drake outta yore purity li'l town. That suit ya?"

"That suits me just fine, Kannon," smiled Rawley.

Throwing a few bills on the counter, Kannon ordered, "Barkeep, give us a few bottles ta take with us."

Mike complied.

Bottles clinked as two men gathered them to their chests, and then walked out ahead of Big Joe Kannon. Big Joe doffed his hat to Rawley, saying, "Next time…Lovett." The trio headed out the door, noisily clumping down the steps, leaving the scented trail of rotting carcasses floating in the air.

Walking around his bar, Mike stepped over the tobacco stain gracing his floorboards, and flapped his apron at the tainted atmosphere, hopefully pushing that out the door, too. Turning, once again, he stepped over the stain and then resumed his post behind the bar, saying, "Whew…them boys wuz worse'n then a million skunks letting loose all at once!"

Picking up the coffee urn, Mike said, refilling the marshal's cup, "Mighty fine job, Rawley." Glancing over at Lacy as she stepped up to the bar, "You too, Missy. How 'bout a sasparilly?"

"That 'd be nice, Mike," Lacy replied.

The marshal turned toward his deputy. "Where'd you come from?"

Lacy turned the handle of the glass toward her. Lifting she took a sip, savoring the dark, sweet foamy brew. She swallowed. The back of her hand swiped across the foam she knew remained on her lip. "The side door," she answered. Then nonchalantly she took another sip.

"You and I need to have a talk."

Freckles closed in. Flashes of anger lit burnt coffee eyes. "Why? Jus' 'cause I was covering your ass? Doing my job? You hired me to be your backup. That's exactly what I was doing," she said angrily. Draining the last of her drink, she slammed the heavy mug on the bar. Whirling around, she walked out.

Mike looked at Rawley.

Rawley looked at Mike.

Mike waggled bushy eyebrows. Rawley sighed heavily and rolled his eyes. They landed on the hole still in the ceiling Lacy had put there last fall. *Scheesh, was it only last fall? Seems like a lifetime ago.* Sighing again, he said, "Winter's coming, Mike." Blue eyes refocused on the barkeep. "When you gonna fix that hole in the ceiling?"

The barkeep looked up. "Oh...don't rightly know...May never fix it. It kinda adds a little ambiance to the place," Mike said drily.

Rawley snorted. "Ambiance? Hell...Mike! You're as nutty as Maddie's fruitcake!" He turned and angrily stomped through the bat-wing doors.

Mike just grinned at the retreating back of the marshal.

* * *

Lacy had the log book pulled in front of her, open to record the incident with Kannon. Instead she held her forehead in her hand, staring at a blank page. Every time she tried to do her job, it seemed that Rawley had to give her a lecture.

Picking up the pencil, she had written down the day's date, when the door opened. A big shadow graced the desk. His warm masculine scent wrapped around her. A heart began banging around in a freckled chest. Lacy bit down on her tongue, to keep silent. But, the pencil kept agitatedly beating a fast tattoo against her fingers attesting to Lacy's frustration.

Easing down next to Lacy, he gazed at the top of that copper colored mop. Her forehead resting in a freckled hand, she continued ignoring him. *Damn kid is so hard-headed,* he thought. *But, I still love her.* Though, right about now, he began to question his judgment.

Rawley decided to try another form of tactics. "Sorry, I've been so hard on you lately, Sunshine." Seeing the hand holding the pencil go still, he continued, "I just have to keep reminding myself, that Sam taught you, and that you do know how to do your job." Waiting for a reaction, Rawley saw none was forthcoming. He rose, going out the door, closing it softly.

Looking up when she heard the latch click, Lacy leaned back in the chair. It squeaked, and the pencil picked up the frustrated tattoo, again. Shrugging her shoulders, she leaned back over the paperwork. The chair squeaked, breaking the silence. As lead touched the tablet, she began writing.

Thinking, as he crossed the street heading toward Maddie's, Rawley began to formulate a plan in his head, to leave the little spitfire alone, totally ignoring her. They had been doing everything together, the last several months, she even trying to keep up with his long legged strides. That thought brought a smile as he sat down. Reaching for the salt shaker, he tossed it back and forth in his hands. Rawley knew Lacy wouldn't like it, but it might make her come around, giving her a dose of her own medicine.

His coffee arrived. A smile curved rugged features upward as he took a sip of the brew.

CHAPTER TWENTY EIGHT

Phosphorus flared, lighting a face as the flame lit a cheroot. The flame traveled to the next face repeating the picture and then on to the third. The flame suddenly disappeared. Three crimson dots glowed in the moonless atmosphere. One crimson dot moved. "We'll wait here a bit longer...wait till the town quiets down some more," a voice instructed.

Another crimson dot moved. "Rawley Lovett finally gets to wear a real purity marble hat," a different voice added.

Three glowing dots danced in the darkness as soft laughter filled the air.

* * *

Lacy didn't really understand what had changed. Before, the marshal seemed to always be dogging her butt, joking around, now, *nuthing*. He wasn't even talking to her, except when he had to. They didn't eat together anymore, do rounds, nothing. Lacy missed that, a lot. She even missed hearing Rawley jabbering all the time.

If the tension was thick before, it was even thicker now. Rawley acted as if she had some kind of plague or something, avoiding her all the time, not even calling her Sunshine anymore. That had bothered her the most, she had kind of come to like that name. He even went so far as to go formal on her, calling her *Miss Carrigan,* most of the time, now, too. Lacy "Pifftt," blowing wet copper tendrils off her sweaty forehead.

Walking, her boot heels lightly clumped across the

wooden walkways of the town, which was settling down for sleep. She heard Baxter barking at some unseen critter behind Miss Liv's house. An owl warbled nearby, setting up more frenzied barking from the dog for a few seconds then he became quiet once again. Coyotes began their caterwauling in the distance. Baxter began yodeling in response. Lacy smiled faintly at the sound.

There was something in the thick, hot air tonight, and, it wasn't just the tension between her and Rawley. Sniffing the night air, Lacy figured out, *no, that wasn't it*. But, something felt out of kilter. The hairs on the back of her neck had been up most of the day, setting her on edge. Even the hairs on her arms had been tingling. Lacy had gotten that same premonition before when she came close to capturing her prey. If she listened to it tonight, it meant something was about to happen and happen very soon.

Pushing open the office door, she shut it with a soft click. Lacy spoke to the marshal for the first time in a week. "Umm...you need to be careful tonight making rounds," she said.

The newspaper Rawley had been reading crackled as he folded it up, laying it on his desk, he glanced up. "Why?"

Automatically pouring them both coffees, Lacy halted the coffee pot in mid-air realizing what she had done. Silently, she took in air avoiding his intense blue eyes.

A black brow quirked up at her hesitation. Maybe his little plan was working.

She quickly replaced the blackened pot on the stove with a slight click. Turning toward the window, she shrugged thin shoulders as she sipped at the coffee. Lacy continued to stare out the window into the moonless street. Dark eyes gazed at the gnats and a few bats converging around the coal oil lamps lit outside various businesses and across the street at Ezra's. Following the flitting, darting, dancing flights of the critters helped her to avoid Rawley's penetrating gaze that she felt boring into her back.

Still keeping her eyes forward out the window, she explained. "I don't know. Something has been...," she hesitated. "Well...something's up. The hairs have been standing all day on my neck. Oh...I don't know, but you be careful tonight," she said sipping again from her cup.

Dark brows rose in surprise at Lacy's warning, revealing just how much she did care about him. Despite the few stringy words that had passed for conversation between them the past week. *Bet, she doesn't realize what she just said,* he thought.

He knew what Lacy told him, to be true, as Rawley had felt that same way on many an occasion. He quipped instead, "You been reading that crystal ball of yours again, Miss Carrigan?" Knowing that'd get a rise out of her.

Lacy spun. "I'm tired of the little game you've been playing, Lovett," she snapped. Taking in air to keep her temper in check, she revealed, "Whenever I got close to my quarry, I'd get the same feeling, always paid attention. It kept me alive," she finished softly, eyes downcast into the black brew.

"I see," he answered.

"Well, jus' thought I'd warn you," Lacy said, sitting the cup down on the edge of the desk. She turned and trudged down the hall to her room.

The chair squeaked as he leaned back. Swiveling it, his gaze followed Lacy, noticing she'd lost weight. His little game, as she called it, was affecting her more than she let on. But then, Lacy remained a master at concealing her emotions.

Rawley didn't know where Jack Drake was, but, he'd had that same feeling all day too, like a feather had been tickling the back of his neck. And every now and then, that thought would send chills down his backbone, despite the overly hot air that seemed to have settled in the area. The chair gave its ever present squeak as Rawley stood. His hand plucked the weapon from its holster. After checking the cylinder, he slid it back into its rightful place. A wooden drawer scraped open. He picked up two extra cylinders, he kept pre-loaded, tossing them around in his hand before sliding them in his pocket. Grabbing his hat, he left the office.

*   *   *

Not only did Lacy feel something was going to happen, it had been uncommonly hot the last few days, setting everyone on edge. Conversation had monopolized on the likelihood of lightening striking the parched earth setting off rampaging wildfires, keeping all eyes toward the skies. Lacy knew now what that big brass plate in front of the office was used for, a fire alarm. Its heavy brass sound traveled for miles, alerting anyone within hearing distance.

Tonight, though, very little breeze blew through her window, making the air suffocating. Unbuttoning her shirt, she slid that off her shoulders, revealing a feminine piece of attire. A camisole edged in pink ribbon she'd bought from Lydia.

Pulling her boots off, they clunked to the floor next to her legs. Elbows rested on her knees, hands dangled between canvas britches. She heaved a tired sigh, while dark eyes focused on brown socks encasing small feet. Lacy watched as she flexed her toes against the floorboards working the kinks out of them. Her stomach hurt, that snarling barbed wire still seemed to slice her gut to shreds. Her mind still tried to wrap itself around the revelation that she just might be falling in love with the big handsome galoot. She had no business falling in love with anyone, or anyone with her. Lacy sighed. Pulling herself upright, her hands gripped her knees as she gazed at the beams above, focusing on dusty strings of cobwebs. A weird thought popped into to her brain. *I need to clean, but, I hate cleaning.* She tossed the odd thought out of her head.

Her past had tarnished any future she might have wanted. A man to love, family, babies and a home. *Those ideas are completely out of my reach,* her mind said. But a heart tugging inside a freckled chest said otherwise.

Sighing heavily again, she flopped back on the bright coverlet. An arm draped itself across her eyes. Lacy expelled more hot air into the already stifling room.

Run! Her mind said. But, she didn't want to run anymore. Never knowing where your next meal might come from. Eating rattlesnakes and rabbits got old quickly. Washing in cold streams, wearing the same clothes for weeks on end, they becoming so stiff from dust and sweat, you could barely move. Her senses, carrying that ever-present, heart-pounding fear of never knowing whether she'd survive the capture of her next bounty.

No. She'd lost the exhilarating excitement she once felt chasing fugitives. *Rawley Lovett is to blame for that,* her mind echoed. Bringing her legs up, she rolled over. Urging the cackling in her head to go away, Lacy drifted off.

* * *

Rawley's senses were on high alert. Making rounds, that niggling little feeling he'd had all day became stronger. Thinking back, he and Lacy had been on the same wavelength, tonight. Rawley had never been that close intuitively with anyone before or with the camaraderie he'd felt with Lacy. Despite her tongue always being glued to the roof of her mouth, leastways most of the time it was, except when she got mad.

That little freckled tomboy didn't have all those squirrely emotions like most women, thinking more with her brain than her heart. Not letting those crazy female emotions interfere, well, except for the few times, Lacy had let those emotions peek through. He took a moment to fondly remember the kiss they shared after the race and then, later in the office, before the dance. His stomach took a nose dive thinking how beautiful Lacy had been that night. She even allowed him to kiss her, again, after the reel at Cotton's instance before Doc had so rudely interrupted.

Rawley had to admit, he liked it when Lacy got emotional. Her vulnerability that popped up every now and again in her burnt coffee eyes made him want to protect her.

But then, she'd gain control again, shying away from him. Denying the love he knew she felt for him.

CRACK! A bullet ripped through flesh, tearing into his shoulder, rendering his gun arm useless. Rawley hit the scarred walk and rolled, his hat flying, gasping as the pain made his eyes water. Pushing himself closer to the barrels, outside of Ezra's store, he placed them between him and the flying lead. He peeked around a barrel. *Ping*...a piece of lead bounced off a bow-saw blade hanging behind him. *Ping*...a lantern shattered next to the front door of the bank. *Crack...crac...crack*, the store's big plate glass window exploded behind him. Rawley felt glass splinters nick the back of his neck and one ear leaving a stinging sensation, like he'd been hit by a swarm of bees.

Rawley gritted as his hand pulled the weapon from his holster. Switching to his left hand, he returned lead in the direction he'd spotted the flashes of fire. A hail of flying lead erupted, making him hunker down. When that had passed, he rose to his knees and peered from his cover. He couldn't see a damn thing from this position.

Whoever happened to be taking pot shots at him had made sure they hit the lanterns, too. It's a wonder a fire hadn't already started as dry as it had been.

No moon. Any shadows that should have stood out blended with the darkness. He held his fire for now.

Lacy rolled off the bunk. "Rawley," she whispered. Quickly shoving arms into her shirt, she tucked the front ends into her britches. Grabbing Vern's old buffalo gun, she lifted the lid on the humped back trunk. The tray held her extra ammo. A shaking hand helped to rid the box of its top. She stuffed a few linen encased cartridges and percussion caps into her shirt pocket. Emerging from the back of the marshal's office, stocking feet silently guided her toward the darker shadows of the building next door. The sharp acidic scent of spent gunpowder grew stronger, greeting her nose as she moved closer to the street.

Plastering herself against the wood siding, she peered around the corner. Smoky grey haze hung like puffy clouds in the still atmosphere at various points along the empty street. Gunfire erupted again; watching the flashes of flames in the dark, helped her to determine who was where. Her gut told her the flash of fire in front of Ezra's must be Rawley. That meant the others, were her quarry. She plastered her back against the wood again. Digging into her pocket, she brought out one cartridge. The slight click as she popped open the breech loader sounded loud in the sudden quiet. Another click sounded as she closed the chamber cutting the casing open, exposing the powder. Her thumb cocked back the hammer, two fingers dug out a percussion cap. She tapped that onto the nipple.

Lacy peeked around the corner again. She squinted into the murkiness, dissecting any darkness that did not exactly fit within the normal frame of the town's nighttime shadows. Spying the darker shadow of a lump besides the wheel of a wagon parked across the street at about fifty yards; she flipped up the ladder type site. Taking careful aim, focusing in, she held her breath, and smoothly squeezed the trigger. *Kaaboom!* The recoil flattened her back against the wall. She heard a scream, Lacy grimaced, knowing she'd made a solid hit.

Gritting his teeth, Rawley had tried to stop the flow of blood leaking from his shoulder. It was no use, the wound continued to pour, making him lightheaded in the process. Wiping the sticky, slippery stuff off his left hand, he picked up the pistol again. That's when he heard the *Kaaboom!* Along with a scream that pierced the dark. *Lacy!* He thought foggily. *She's got that damn buffalo gun!*

Digging into her pocket, she pulled out another cloth wrapped shell. A wild shot whizzed by the corner where she stood. Lacy looked up, hearing the sound of a *pl-ink* as the bullet dug itself into the log walls of the marshal's office. Popping the breech loader open, her nimble fingers slid another cartridge into the chamber, and then snapped it shut.

Quickly, those same two fingers once again tapped a percussion cap onto the nipple under the hammer.

One down, thought Lacy.

Maneuvering behind the barrels, Rawley willed his brain not to allow him to pass out. Breathing deeply, he began shooting at random, drawing fire, so Lacy would have a target. It worked, lead began flying. He slid lower behind the barrels.

In that prone position, Rawley dug out a spare cylinder from his pocket. Resting the pistol against his stomach, his fingers removed the pin. His left hand pulled the empty cylinder; a dull thud sounded when it dropped. Wiping blood slick fingers on his britches, again, he then clicked the full one in place, replacing the pin.

Blinking rapidly from the pain-filled watery eyes, Rawley gritted as he tried to maneuver into a better firing position. A blood draining weakness seemed to fill his soul. A hand stuck itself around the barrel and began firing at random.

Peeking around the clapboard, Lacy saw a dark shape, hunkered down behind the water trough, maybe fifteen yards to her left. Gun fire erupted from behind barrels in front of Ezra's store. The shape, to her left, too interested in what was going on across the street, kept shooting. Flames erupted every couple of seconds, lighting the hand holding the weapon. Lacy eased down on the steps. Doing a belly crawl up, she slithered across the boardwalk, hugging the edge in case she had to roll off. Lacy hoped she blended in with the shadows and weathered wood with the darkness.

Positioning the rifle against her shoulder, elbows resting on the wide planks, supporting the heavy weapon, she yelled, "Hey! You little pipsqueak! Why don't you try someone, yore own size?"

The shape turned giving her a full frontal view. Flames spit, the bullet whizzed into the boards, a foot to the left of Lacy. Holding her breath, she pulled the trigger. *Kaaboom!* The stock slammed into her shoulder. She watched as the powerful rifle lifted the body up, and sent it flying back, landing with a thud against the wall of the building. Lifeless, the body slid down the wood, leaving a dark, bloody trail, to crumple into a pile.

Hearing the fast tattoo of hooves pounding the dirt, she quickly reloaded. Racing to the middle of the street, Lacy plopped down in the dirt. She fired at the fast retreating figure; the sound ricocheted off the buildings. She then watched with satisfaction as the shadow spun out of the saddle.

She stood, calming a heart that acted like a thundering stampede. *Rawley,* her mind refocused. Spinning, she ran, meeting the staggering lawman half-way.

A heavy flow of blood had quickly saturated his shirt running down both belts blemishing dark britches even darker. She gasped realizing the extensive damage the bullet had caused. Dropping the rifle, Lacy's arms quickly circled Rawley's waist, catching the big lawman as he sunk to his knees, taking her down with him.

Gently removing the blood covered pistol from his left hand, she tucked it into her britches. Giving his wound a cursory glance, she saw that he'd been shot in the back. *Chicken-livered bastard!* She thought. The exit hole in his right front shoulder was a ragged looking, bloody mess. Rawley had lost a lot of blood, already. Her fingers probed his back pockets looking for his bandana. Not finding it, she reached for her own. Lacy pressed her palm over the hole in his back, and the bandana she pressed against the exit wound, trying to stem the flow of blood.

Rawley clamped his teeth down, sucking the wind in so hard, it whistled.

"I'm sorry," she said softly. "I don't mean to hurt you."

Then she smiled, trying to make light of the situation. "Who the hell did you make mad now, Rawley?" She teased. Her gut told her, Jack Drake had paid them his last visit. She continued to press both hands against his wounds.

"Shut up," he growled. His body began leaning a little too much in one direction.

FRECKLED VENOM
COPPERHEAD STRIKES

Her bloody hands dropped from the wounds as Lacy tried to hang on to him. "Oh, no you don't," she said, her fingers clawed into his blood soaked shirt. "Don't fade on me just, yet. You've got to help me get you to Doc's." Looking around she didn't see many people on the street, yet.

"Did you get 'em?" The words, spoken through clenched teeth, sounded like sandpaper going crossways against the grain.

"Yeah, I got 'em," Lacy smiled.

Nodding again, Rawley struggled to stand.

"Lean on me," she offered.

"No."

Red brows shot skyward. "Don't go getting hardheaded with me now, Rawley Lovett!" Lacy warned him. She felt him sag against her, almost buckling her knees.

Luke, Mike and Ezra came out of nowhere.

"We've got to get him to Doc's quick, he's bleeding heavy," Lacy intoned breathlessly to the three men.

Doc had the door open, waiting on them. "Get him up on the table, boys. Lacy get that shirt off, while I get dressed."

Turning to Mike, Luke and Ezra, Lacy said, "I'll be back down in a minute, thanks for your help."

Mike took Ezra's arm, saying, "Let's go find some wood to cover yore window, Ezra." Three sets of boots clattered down the steps, and then faded into the quiet darkness.

Lacy quickly grabbed Rawley's arm as he swayed almost toppling off the table. "Whoa now, you fall off, that's where you're gonna stay, on the floor," she said beginning to unbuckle his gun belt.

"No," Rawley whispered, his hand stopping hers.

"Don't go getting pigheaded on me," Lacy warned. Then she smiled into his face, "You've helped me, now it's my turn to help you. Besides being pigheaded is my department," she admitted. Her fingers quickly worked the belt loose, dropping the rig to the floor with a thunk.

Getting the big marshal's shirt off and trying to keep him on the table at the same time, taxed Lacy to no end. Finally climbing up and kneeling behind him to steady his body with her knees, worked. She eased him down, just as Rawley passed out.

Doc helped her to place Rawley's legs on the table; she took a huge breath. "Don't realize how big he is, till it's all dead weight," Lacy said smiling at Doc. "I'll be back soon, gotta check downstairs."

Doc called out, pointing. "You're covered in blood, young 'un, and where's your boots?"

Lacy glancing down, she saw that it was true. She was covered in Rawley's blood. Her eyes landed on dusty brown socks. Wiggling her toes, she smiled, exposing two rare dimples. "Guess I left them in the office. I'll be back soon as I can, Doc."

Turning back to his patient, Doc didn't like what he saw. Rawley was in bad shape, loosing that much blood. He would take a while to heal. Good thing this town had that little copper-headed spitfire to take over.

Lacy skipped down the steps. Hurrying over to the first little crowd, she asked, "Anyone know this man?" The story on their faces said no. "Okay, guess some of you men can haul him over to the parlor." Stopping in the middle of the street, she picked up her rifle. Going over to the first man Lacy had killed, she asked the same question and got the same answer.

Kneeling next to the body, Lacy had a gut feeling the face she looked into was Jack Drake, but Rawley's files did not have a picture. He was the only one who could identify him and he was out cold. She told some other men to take this one to the parlor too, pointing down the street, she added that one.

Entering the office, Lacy laid the Sharps on Rawley's desk. Plucking the bloody pistol out of her britches, she gazed at it before lying that, too, on the desk. Dusty stocking feet took her back to her room. She stopped at her looking glass and gazed at the figure staring back. She looked like the one

FRECKLED VENOM
COPPERHEAD STRIKES

wounded, not Rawley.

Stripping out of the bloody clothes, Lacy dropped them to the floor. Quickly washing and dressing, she pulled on her boots this time, and headed back to Doc's office.

Taking the stairs two at a time, Lacy reached the stoop. Her hand gingerly turned the crystal and brass knob. Stepping inside Lacy quietly closed the door, lock connecting with a soft click.

Doc looked up.

Coming to stand next to the crusty doctor, she asked, "How's he doing, Doc?"

Finishing up the thick bandage on Rawley's shoulder, Doc answered, "Would've been better, if I had to dig the bullet out, must've been a high caliber gun," he glanced at Lacy. "Like that damn thunder pipe you carry."

Red-gold brows rose at his comment.

"That little piece of lead did a lot of damage. It'll be awhile afore he's healed good."

Washing his hands again, Doc threw the words over his shoulder, asking, "Did you look for the bullet yet?"

Lacy shook her head no, saying, "It's still too dark out." Fingers slid into her hip pockets.

"Well, see if you can find it tomorrow, I want to take a look at it."

Doc walked over to his desk. Sinking into his chair, he pulled a drawer open. Retrieving a bottle and glass, he poured a generous amount of amber liquid into the tumbler. Doc swallowed half of it. Leaning back in his chair, he sighed deeply.

Doc's tired, she thought. "You go get some rest, I'll stay with him."

Doc acknowledged her comment with a nod. "Any change, you come get me, you hear?"

"Yes, sir," she said smiling, as she watched his tired shuffle take him to his room.

Covering the marshal, Lacy leaned over Rawley.

Fingers lightly brushed dark hair off his forehead, the shadow of his beard a stark contrast against the pale face. Long dark lashes feathered against high cheek bones, revealing his Indian heritage. Except for his bright blue eyes, he could've passed for a brave. Lacy wondered what his Indian name would have been.

Looking around, she spotted a spare chair. Picking it up, she brought it back sitting it down next to the table where Rawley lie so still and deathly pale.

She sat, placing her forearms on the edge of the table. Lacy rested her chin on her hands. Softly, hesitantly she began to empty her heart to the unconscious giant.

Lacy whispered, "I think I'm falling in love with you, Rawley Lovett...but, I can't." Tears began pricking her eyes, burning them, her nose began to run. "You like frilly females, who wear dresses and act like ladies. I don't know the first thing about being frilly and I hate dresses. And I sure don't know how to act like a lady," she sniffled.

A thumb brushed against her eyelids, it came away wet. "You're a good person, Rawley Lovett. I'm...I'm not. I've...I've killed, maimed...," thinking of Aubrey Dillard and Lowell Taylor, "Just for the money. You don't need someone like that raising your babies..." Lacy faltered. "I should leave, but, I don't want to run anymore. Chasing fugitives doesn't hold the excitement it once did, thanks to you, Lovett. But, I'm not the wholesome, pure, church-going individual you need, to raise your babies. So...I have to toss my feelings for you away and...and just be content to be your deputy. You'll find someone, someday," her already husky voice became more so with emotion. "And no matter what happens...I'll still be your deputy," she whispered. Knowing as she said that, if she had to stand and watch him marry someone else, it would rip her heart apart.

Tears began pouring in earnest. Lacy pressed her eyes against the soft cloth of her green checkered shirt. She stifled a sob.

FRECKLED VENOM
COPPERHEAD STRIKES

Later, when she had gained control over her emotions, Lacy raised her head. A small freckled hand tentatively slid into a big paw and rested there.

CHAPTER TWENTY NINE

A moan slipped into Lacy's sleeping mind. When she heard it again, she lifted her head, and then stood, watching Rawley regain consciousness.

A pair of eyes cracked open to see a freckled face grinning at him. A voice broke into his fuzzy brain. "Welcome back, Lovett. You know you're heavy when you're all dead weight," she said seriously.

Groaning, Rawley croaked, "Shad up, Sunshine."

Lacy flashed a bigger smile. Pouring a glass of water, she held the marshal's head as he drained the glass. "Feel better?" Lacy asked.

"No. I hurt like hell." Looking around, he saw bright sunshine filter through the window. Rawley asked, "What time is it? And where's Doc?"

"Sheesh…Lovett…" came the reply. "I don't know. I just woke up myself. And Doc's still sleeping," she added.

Rawley tried to sit up; his mouth dropped with the pain.

With a hand on his shoulder, Lacy stated quietly. "I wouldn't try moving just yet. Doc wouldn't be happy you bust open all his hard work."

"Shad up…Sunshine! I want to go back to my quarters, help me up."

Lacy retreated out of his reach. "No. You need to stay here for a few days, and then we'll move you back to the office."

"Sunshine, I'm giving you an order!"

"No. You rip those stitches out…."

Rawley butted in, growling, "You little snit! Fine I'll do it myself!" Easing his legs off the table, he stood, and remained standing, upright, but just barely.

Lacy's brows rose when he growled. It reminded her of when he tracked her back to the cabin when she'd run away last Christmas. "A little testy today, ain't cha?"

"Just you never mind," Rawley groused. He leaned back against the table, needing the support, left hand gripping the edge to steady him. His legs felt like strings of molasses drizzling over flapjacks. Looking around, he took in a big breath, expelling it. "Where's my shirt?" He asked.

"It'd seen better days."

Grabbing the blanket, he tried to throw it over his shoulders. The movement almost made him black-out. He locked his knees to keep from collapsing. Lacy standing by, watching Rawley struggle, did not offer to help.

Sagging back against the table, Rawley blinked rapidly, waiting for the pain to ease off, some. After a few minutes he threw a frosty look at the copperhead. Growling again, he said angrily, "Don't know why in the hell I hired you, you're no help." Rawley began a slow wobble toward the door.

"Maybe it's because I've got better sense right now. You leave…Doc's gonna have your hide," Lacy returned.
Rawley jerked the door open; sunlight poured in. Glancing over his shoulder, he snapped, "Shad up, Sunshine!" His left hand gripped the rail tightly as he took one knock-kneed step after another, descending to street level.

Rolling her eyes, Lacy followed Mr. Wise-Apple.

*   *   *

Eyes followed the tall lawman weaving his way back to his office, blanket thrown over his shoulders, followed by a redhead trailing him. Murmurs began to whisper in the air. Lacy threw a blistering look over her shoulder. The whispers ceased.

The short trek down the street toward his office and bed

had exhausted Rawley. Lacy saw that blood had seeped through the bandages when she helped him into bed. Standing back, after tucking the blanket in, she gazed at the marshal, now, sleeping in total exhaustion. *It's a wonder he's not dead with the amount of blood he's lost,* she thought. "Good thing, you're such a big galoot, Lovett, else you'd be dead," she whispered. Her heart gave a sharp jump when she said the word *dead.* She ignored the heart part, walking toward the door.

Tucking a tendril of red hair behind one ear, Lacy sighed closing his door softly. She refocused her mind. Doc wanted her to find the bullet that tore Rawley's shoulder to shreds.

Standing at the edge of the scarred planks, outside the office, Lacy tucked the tips of her fingers into back pockets. She pulled the scenes of last night's fire fight from her memory bank. Remembering the way she'd poked her nose around the corner of the building next door and what had greeted her eyes. Puffy grey haze hanging in the air, the acrid scent of spent gunpowder, flashes of sporadic gun fire.

She hopped off the walk, fingers still tucked into back pockets, Lacy strolled to the wagon still there, first. The sun glinted off brass casings littering the dirt next to the wheel. Squatting, her knees cracked, and she winced. Refocusing, Lacy stuck her hand out imitating a pistol, aimed it toward Ezra's. Standing, she began the trek toward Ezra's. Turning, she walked backward a few feet, her mind imagining the track of the bullet. Turning again, her eyes traveled the possible route that the slug would have taken. Stepping on the scarred planks, Lacy glanced down behind the barrels. Her eyes caught the shards of splintered glass shining like diamonds from the late afternoon sun, scattered from Ezra's now boarded up window.

The amount of dried blood she saw mingled with the shards of glass, and buzzing flies made her lips work themselves into a hard thin line. Tearing her eyes away from the blood of the man she finally figured out she loved, but couldn't have, Lacy refocused, thinking, *He was shot in the upper right shoulder, bullet passing clean through.* So that would have slowed the velocity down some, Lacy presumed. Configuring Rawley's height, she allowed her eyes to travel. There a few feet away, she saw it. In the porch post, a splintered bullet hole bright against the exterior weathered wood, the right height and angle. Digging out her pocket knife, Lacy dug into the wood. A piece of lead finally popped out, into her hand. Scrutinizing it, her eyes went wide then narrowed, drawing the freckles in closer. The tip had been cut, a cross or x marking, making the bullet splay out when it hit it's mark, causing a lot of damage.

Rawley was lucky he was a big man, strong and muscular, a picture of robust health. Anyone smaller, they would have been dead. Bouncing the lead in her hand, her thoughts were interrupted by Ezra. "How's Rawley doing this morning?" He asked. Dipping a broom into a bucket of water, he began cleaning the brown stain from the boards.

Studying the proprietor as he cleaned the walk, with her mind stuck on the piece of lead she bounced in her hand, she tried to gather her thoughts enough to reply. Lacy finally answered him, "He's still alive. Gonna be awhile afore he's healed good."

Ezra nodded, looking at his bordered up window. "Glad we didn't loose him last night," he said.

It was Lacy's turn to nod silently. "When do you expect the glass to come in for your window?" She asked, continuing to bounce the frayed piece of lead in her hand.

"Depends on how many times shipping breaks it," Ezra grinned.

One red-gold brow cocked upward. Lacy nodded, saying, "See ya later, Ezra."

"Yea-up," he replied.

Turning, Lacy hopped off the walk, boots landing softly in the dirt. She headed toward the office. When Rawley was better, she'd show him the piece of lead.

Toward evening, Doc banged open the office door.

Lacy jumped, her hand automatically wrapped around the butt of her Colt.

Doc spluttered. "Where's that young whippersnapper?"

She relaxed, releasing the taunt grip on her pistol. Silently, Lacy thumbed at the closed door behind her.

Doc went in, slamming the door in his passing.

She rolled her eyes, as she heard two voices, Doc's gravelly one, and Rawley's deep baritone arguing back.

The chair squeaked as Lacy rose. She poured more coffee while waiting for Doc to come out of Rawley's room. Hearing the door open again, she stood, the chair gave its ever present squeak. Lacy poured Doc a cup of coffee. Handing it to him, she asked, "Well, what's the verdict?"

Gratefully taking the cup, he sipped. "Humph, he's lucky I don't horse whip him, lucky he didn't rip those stitches out, or I'd 'ave ta charged him double!"

Freckles curved around deep dimples as she smiled.

Doc continued, "Changed the bandage, gave him something for the pain, he'll sleep most of the night."

Sitting back down in the chair, she swiveled it, making the chair give its customary squeak. Lacy reached across the desk and handed Doc a small envelope.

He opened it, and allowed the lead to slide into his hand. Doc gazed hard at it. "Humph, no wonder it did so much damage to his shoulder."

Lacy nodded. "That was done deliberate. Later, I'm going to wire Denver, see if they can give me a description of Jack Drake. Rawley's the only one who can identify him and he's out cold.

Doc glanced up sharply. "You think it was Jack Drake did this?"

"My gut tells me so, but I've never seen the man," Lacy finished.

Reaching into his bag, Doc pulled out some laudanum.

FRECKLED VENOM
COPPERHEAD STRIKES

"Put a spoonful in a glass of water for the pain when he needs it, tho' he's 'bout as hardheaded as you, young lady," Doc said. Then he rose and shuffled toward the door. Hand resting on the knob, he stopped and turned, giving Lacy a hard look. "I looked at those men you killed last night," he said.

A red-gold eyebrow shot up.

"Nice shooting through the dark," he said. "Well, come get me, if that young whippersnapper gives you any problems."

"Thanks, Doc I will.

* * *

Maddie pushed the door open with one hand, balancing a tray with the other. "Lass, how's me laddie?"

"Grouchy, grumpy, temperamental, the way all men get when their masculinity gets threatened," Lacy answered.

"I heard that, Sunshine," bellowed Rawley through the open doorway of his room.

Lacy thumbed over her shoulder. "See...what I mean?"

Maddie chuckled. "Ach, laddie's chust got his knickers all in a twist," holding up the tray. "Some 'o Maddie's good cookin' 'ill make him feel better!"

"Be my guest," Lacy gestured behind her.

Walking behind Lacy, the cherubic faced woman with the constant rosy cheeks entered Rawley's room. Maddie said, "Aye, laddie, ye aboot a done wit ye a fussing? Eat some of Maddie's good cookin', I brung ya?"

He struggled to sit straighter. Maddie sat the tray down on the bedside table and came to his aid, helping Rawley to sit further upright, while fluffing his pillows. She then placed the tray on his lap.

Gazing fondly at the Scotswoman, Rawley said, "Thanks Maddie." Picking up the fork in his left hand, he began to eat.

Gazing sternly at her friend, Maddie then walked back to the door and closed it softly.

The marshal glanced up in surprise. Walking back to his bedside, she placed fists on generous hips. "What ye being so hard on da wee lass fer, eh, lad?"

Talking around a mouthful of food, Rawley snapped, "She's smothering me to death!"

"Taint like you Rawley Lovett, speaking ill aboot the wee lass like that," she said. "Specially, when she saved yure arse."

Fork stopped in mid-air. "I know she saved my ass! But, I ain't interested in hearing you lecture me about it neither, Maddie!" Rawley growled.

"Aye, da wee lass, she chust care fer ye. I can see it in her eyes, is all. She loves you, Rawley."

"Like hell!" He groused poking more food in his mouth.

Puckering her mouth, Maddie looked at the dark seven days growth on Rawley's face, *the boy might feel better if he was cleaned up.* "May 'aps, ye let ol' Maddie give ye a shave and a wash up, ye'll be a feeling a bit more sociably, eh, laddie?"

Fork stopped midway to his mouth, again. "You just leave me be, Madeline Campbell! I'll clean myself up!"

"Ach, laddie, ye got a pickle fer that brain of yers!" Twirling, Maddie called out as she opened the door. "Lass, ye got, any hot water?"

The chair squeaked as Lacy hopped up. "I will in a minute," she replied. While the water heated, Lacy asked, "You sure you can handle him?"

"Lassie, me Angus wus't a big man like me laddie, and I could handle him," she said throwing eyes upward. "May God rest 'iss soul!" Going back into the room with the warm water, her high top shoes kicked the door shut in Lacy's face.

A deep baritone bellowed through the closed door. "Now Maddie, don't even think about, what I know you're thinking!"

FRECKLED VENOM
COPPERHEAD STRIKES

"Ye, hush up, laddie. Ye'll be feeling better, when ol' Maddie gets done with ye."

Smiling, Lacy knew the marshal was in good hands; she left to check the mail.

Reading over the telegram from Denver confirmed Lacy's suspicions. She wired back another inquiry. Wandering through town, giving Maddie time to work her magic with the grouchy lawman, Lacy stopped at Lydia's shop and stood staring at the dressmaker's latest creation, beckoning to her through the window. Sighing wistfully, she turned away and headed for Mike's to drink a sarsaparilly.

* * *

After wiping her hands on her apron, Maddie rolled her sleeves back down. She looked up as Lacy entered. Nodding over her shoulder, Maddie said softly, "Laddie 'ill be feeling much better, when he wakes up."

Lacy peeked in the door, seeing a clean shaven, hair combed Rawley. She asked, "How 'd you do it? I've tried for a week and he wouldn't let me get close to him!"

"Aye, he would have, if ye been married."

"Married? Hog wash! That ain't never gonna happen!" Lacy retorted, hiding her true feelings about the lawman from the Scotswoman. Knowing full well that kind of happiness would forever be out of her reach.

"Aye, we'll be seeing aboot that, lassie," said Maddie knowingly. Generous hips sashayed out the door, leaving Lacy with her mouth hanging.

* * *

A few days later as Lacy removed another tray from Rawley's lap. She noticed the ruddy color coming back into his high cheek-boned features. Walking out of his room, she sat the empty tray on the desk, and picked up the little envelope. Walking back to his bedside, she handed it to him.

Rawley looked up, mystified. "What's this?" He asked.

Jamming hands into her pockets, Lacy said, "Thought you might like to see what almost did you in."

Rawley opened it, letting the little piece of lead slide into his hand. Picking it up, he gazed at the splayed tip. "Where did you find this?"

"In a post in front of Ezra's," she said then added, "Doc wanted me to find it, he thought it might be from a high caliber gun, it's just a regular .38 but cutting the tip made it twice as deadly. Good thing you're such a big moose, Lovett. Anyone smaller would've been buried by now."

Suddenly shy, her face flushed covering tawny freckles. She darted eyes down as her boot scruffed at a crack in the floor. "It was Jack Drake and I guess what was left of his gang, got a reply from Denver, they gave me what I needed for identification."

"I could've identified him?"

"You were out cold most of the time. What with this heat, we needed to get them in the ground."

"Who were the other two?"

"Uh, Jess Hardin and," her eyes rose thinking. "And Pike…something or other."

"Pike Summers," Rawley offered.

"Yeah, that was it."

"There's reward out on those two, it'd be in the files. What about Drake, what was the reward on him?"

Lacy shook her head, shrugging her shoulders. "I do' no. A bank draft will be here in a few days, is all I know. Well, I've got to go make rounds," she said shyly. The words she wanted to say remained glued to the roof of her mouth; she bit down on her bottom lip.

As Lacy neared the door, Rawley's voice stopped her. "Sunshine, I owe you, you did a fine job backing me up."

Turning slowly, Lacy faced the marshal and tried to will her eyes to hide the emotion she knew existed there. She shook her head. Speaking softly, she said, "You don't owe me anything. But, my debt to you is paid up now, saving my neck like you've done in the past. We'll just call it even, okay?" Her secret would always be firmly locked into her heart.

Cutting her a funny glance, he read something in Lacy's eyes, but, couldn't quite put his finger on it at the moment. Rawley replied instead, "Okay, Sunshine."

Lacy was surprised to see Rawley sitting at his desk a week later. Shirt draped across broad shoulders, the bandage a little smaller now, his arm still remained in a sling.

"What are you doing out of bed?"

"Don't start with me, Sunshine," he said irritatingly. "I'm tired of lying in that bed. I need to move around some."

Lacy poured herself some coffee. "Okay, if you're feeling that good, you can just take me to breakfast," she said gazing at him over the rim of her cup. Raising her eyebrows, she waited on an answer.

CHAPTER THIRTY

Early Fall 1879

Things had been quiet for a change in White River lately. But ever since Lacy had come busting into town, activity had certainly picked up in this little river-side community. Rawley liked teasing her, saying, that since she'd been here, she'd made him earn every penny of his paycheck. Lacy's reply was to roll her eyes at Rawley's remarks.

He and Lacy had declared a truce, *sorta*, if one could call it that. Rawley still waited patiently for Lacy to figure out that she did love him. And if she didn't come around soon, he was just going to have to take her bullheadedness by the horns and force the issue.

* * *

Lowell Taylor had served his time after being slammed in the head by a rifle stock, crushing his skull. He should have died then, but didn't. Later, he was hit again, his cheekbone becoming mere pulp. The injuries were created by a copper-headed bounty hunter years ago, with the name of Lacy Watson. His left temple consisted of a big dent that flowed downward into a now non-existent cheek, flattening that side of his face. Gravity pulled the loose skin south ending in a slack jawed look. Folds over his eye socket drooped, along with that side of his mouth. All this left a grotesquely disfigured face. Taylor talked, it seemed, with an ever present sneer. Lowell Taylor should have died many times over. That's when the voices began talking to him; they'd kept him alive.

After his release, the voices quietly told him to find this bounty hunter. And when he did, the voices said they would instruct him how to create deadly chaos, turning the redhead's veins to ice with the sheer terror of what they would tell him to do. He grinned. He liked listening to the voices; they were his only friends.

Fire. The voices told him fire. He liked fire. Liked the way it licked, slowly becoming all consuming, destroying. She had destroyed his mind. He knew that, creating the voices who had become his friends. He did have her to thank for that. Now, fire would destroy where she lived, what she loved. He asked the voices when he could destroy her. The voices said, *wait.* He sighed.

* * *

Earlier in the day, Rooster delivered a telegram to the Marshal's office. Paper crackled when Rawley opened it. Reading the words, grimness navigated its way across his face. His chest and stomach clenched into a tight knot. Wordlessly, he handed the note to Lacy.

Rosy freckled cheeks altered instantly, changing to the color of rice powder when she read the telegram. Shakily, her hand crumpled the paper. Rising, Lacy opened the door on the wood stove and threw the wad of paper into the flames. She stood watching it burn. Finally closing the door, she latched it with a click. Turning, Lacy reached to pick a fresh cup from the shelf. Her hand wrapped around the handle of the hot pot, lifting. It quickly clattered back against the stove top. Air whistled through her teeth as she shook her hand. Reaching into her back pocket, she pulled out her bandana. Wrapping that around the pot's handle, she began pouring coffee into the cup. The spout rattled so hard against the earthenware, she quit pouring, resting the pot back on the stovetop. Lacy inhaled deeply trying to quell the sour bile sloshing in her stomach and to keep it from rising. She stared out the window at the sunny street. A few moments later, the coffee poured smoothly into the cup.

Quietly watching his redhead, Rawley knew Lacy's skeletons from her bounty hunting had come back to bite her with a vengeance. He wanted to say, *told ya so*. But he kept quiet.

Listening when she'd finally opened up, some months back, she had told him about some of her captures. Lowell Taylor had been one of her most frightening experiences. Even then he watched the skin whiten across freckled features and then tighten as fear skittered through her eyes.

She told him that she knew she'd cracked his skull. But in the same breath, Lacy defended herself, saying, it was the only means she had to protect herself, and had been told, that if he lived, he'd hang.

Apparently that did not happen, according to the telegram. All wardens were required to notify communities when someone had been released or escaped from prison. Lowell Taylor had been released instead of being hung. The warden saying the man had made a masterful transformation, prompting the parole board to give him a second chance. *Like hell*, Rawley thought. His eyes took in Lacy's rigid stance in front of the stove starring out the window. She turned. Deep downright cold fear radiated from her eyes. She spoke, "He lived…and they didn't hang him." The words came out more as a statement then a question.

* * *

A heavy frame lumbered as it hobbled like a horse in the velvety blackness of the night. The copperhead had shot his leg out from under him. It had never healed right causing the odd gait. When the voices told him, Lowell Taylor would do the same to her.

Moving around back of Ezra's, he listened. The voices

were quiet. They'd speak to him again, soon, he knew.

Stepping on the loading dock, he walked toward the double doors. Giving them a cursory glance, his eyes drifted toward the one window. Taking his fist, he punched out a pane. Glass tinkled against the wood dock. Cutting his hand, the blood dripped on the broken pane; he didn't notice. After pushing the lock out of the way, he slid up the window and crawled through.

Rummaging around the front of Ezra's store, he found the canisters of coal oil. Opening one, he sprinkled the bolts of colorful cloth with the oil. Picking up two more canisters, he took them back to the window and placed them outside. Turning, he walked back to the counter, eyes scanning through the darkness. He spotted the stacked boxes of matches on a shelf. Moving around the counter, his hand picked one.

Sliding the box open, his fingers dug out several matches. Striking them on the side of the box, the phosphorous flared. Staring at the flame, he heard the voices. *Good. Light the oil. Go to the stable next.* He smiled. Taylor liked listening to his friends. A hand threw the flame into the bolts of cloth. It ignited with a *Whoosh*.

Weaving his way past the loading dock, Rooster heard the *Whoosh* coming from inside Ezra's. He stopped turning toward the sound. That's when he saw a figure climbing out the window. Stepping forward, he yelled, "Hey…you thar…what the hell ya doing in Ezra's?"

The voice's said, *kill him, no witnesses.* Taylor jumped off the platform. Heavy arms wrapped around Rooster's torso. Two hands held his head in a vice-like grip. They twisted, and then quickly jerked, snapping Rooster's neck, silencing his yells.

Burn him, the voices told him. Removing the canisters from the loading dock, he opened one. Sprinkling the body with the oil, he lit the still figure. Standing back, he smiled. He liked fire, watching it turn skin into charred flesh.

The voices returned; he cocked his head and listened.

Good! Now the stables, they said. Lowell Taylor smiled.

Running, the canisters bumped against his legs. Sitting them down, he leaned against the logs of the stable while he caught his breath. Looking around, he could see the flames licking the inside of the store. No one had noticed yet. The voices returned. *You have time,* they said.

Peeking around the wall, the front doors remained open due to the warmth of the night. He smiled, *it's gonna get hotter then Hades,* he thought. Stepping forward carrying a canister, he walked into the stable. His presence caused the horses to begin shuffling and stamping in their stalls. Fancy's ears laid back, her nostrils picking up a scent she didn't like, smoke. Her head shook briskly.

Walking over to a loose pile of hay, Taylor opened the canister, and shook the contents over the dried grasses. Silently moving toward two buggies backed against the wall, he doused the leather seats with the oil, and for extra good measure, he splashed the rest on the logs. The can now empty, he threw it in back of one buggy. It clattered loudly in the silence. Backing up, he dug the match box out of his pocket. Scraping the matches across the sandpaper glued to the box, they flared. Taylor threw the flame into the buggy. The horses nickered. Backing up some more, he repeated the process, throwing the flames into the saturated pile of hay. Turning he ran. Picking up the canister, he scurried across the street between two buildings. He stopped to watch his handiwork beginning to lick the inside of the stable. Horses beginning to shrill as the flames grew. The voices returned. *Good. One more, then hide, we'll give more instructions later.* He smiled, he'd pleased the voices.

Running again, he randomly picked a building. Shattering the backdoor glass, his fingers twisted the cap off and threw the can inside. He listened to the *glug-glug* of the oil spilling from the can. The flame flew through the opening, igniting the oil with a *whoosh.* After watching for a few moments, Lowell Taylor disappeared.

* * *

FRECKLED VENOM
COPPERHEAD STRIKES

Sheer terror screamed, filling his barn. Luke sat up abruptly. Groggily he stuffed his feet into his boots. Standing, one hand slid a suspender over his shoulder. Running the short distance to his door, he flung it open. Flames rushed in grasping at more oxygen, licking at his hair, face and arms. The roar, heat and the shrill whinnying of the horses had Luke backing off. Taking a deep breath against the searing heat and flames, he ran through them. He yelled as he released the animals, they tore out of the stable. Running around to the side pen, he opened the gate, releasing those horses.

Luke ran to the middle of the street, looking toward Ezra's. It had become a towering inferno. His eyes saw yellow and orange and blue pouring out of Maddie's. The flames, like fingers stretching, reached and inched toward the eaves. The roar became deafening, as smoke filled the street.

Where the hell is everybody? He thought. *The town's going up in flames!* Luke ran to the huge fire gong by the marshal's office. Wang gave it to the town when he'd opened up the laundry. Said it might come in handy one day.

His hand picked up the large padded stick and hit the round brass plate with everything he had. The air vibrated with the deep sound, making Luke's ears ring. He hit it again and again even after he began to see folks emerging.

Rawley sat up, grabbed his pants and stepped into them. He shoved feet into boots. Running out his bedroom door, he buttoned his pants. Lacy had already flung open the office door. They both scrambled outside, stopping at the edge of the porch.

Both saw the flames eating the stable. Looking up the street saw the inferno that had once been Ezra's and Maddie's businesses. Their feet, rooted down in the scarred planked walkway, wouldn't move. They stared at Luke, banging away on the gong.

Luke stopped and shouted, stupidly, "Fire!" He aimed his comments at the marshal and his deputy. "It's too late to save Ezra's and mine, but maybe we can save the rest of the town!" He yelled.

Lacy hopped down, "The horses..." she began.

"They're safe," Luke replied. Rawley's deep baritone bellowed through the commotion that had begun filling the street. "Bucket brigade! Bucket brigade!" Dressed in their night clothes, citizens began converging with buckets around the water troughs. The men took the buckets from the women, throwing the water as high as they could and as often as they could.

Yells accompanied the sharp cracking and popping as the flames ate the wooden buildings. Intense heat surrounded everyone. Bodies dashed here and there in a semi-organized frenzy with buckets sloshing precious water. The street became even thicker with smoke as water hit the flames, making them sizzle, if only for a moment before they took off again.

Billy showed up out of nowhere. Filling his bucket he yelled above the din at Lacy. "I'm here!"

Looking up, she gave a tired smile, "Thanks, Billy," she said. Nodding over her shoulder, she told him, "Go help Rawley and Luke soak the roofs," handing him another full bucket.

"Right," he said, taking off. Precious water sloshed against his britches, soaking them as he ran. Reaching the ladder, he climbed each rung precariously, juggling two full buckets. Rawley threw his empty ones down, and came over to Billy. Kneeling, his arm reached out, taking the filled buckets. "What are you doing here...you should be with Liv and Cotton," he said.

Billy gave him a squirrely look. "You need as many hands as you can get. Besides...they're safe at Mike's place," he said.

The kid's half-growed, somewhere between grass and hay. Rawley smiled, "Thanks, son." Turning he threw the water on the roof. Pitching the buckets down, he began to descend the ladder. Billy waited on the ground for him.

FRECKLED VENOM
COPPERHEAD STRIKES

Shouldering the ladder, Rawley said, "I'll meet you over at the hotel, we'll soak that roof, next."

Gathering the buckets, Billy nodded, running for the nearest water trough.

CHAPTER THIRTY ONE

Gazing over his still smoldering town, sunlight poking itself through the thick haze, Rawley sighed. A soot covered hand rubbed against his chest, realizing then he'd never put on a shirt. The stench of charred remains permeated the air. Right now, he didn't think he'd ever get the stink out of his nostrils. Trudging tiredly, he headed toward Mike's where everyone had gathered. Boots tread heavily up the three steps. He paused as tired soot-bruised eyes looked over the bat-wing doors. The only noise a soft murmur, everyone was too tired to speak normally. Doc had set up shop in a corner tending to burns and what-not, with Liv helping. Rawley searched for Lacy, and found her comforting Maddie. Her girls were there, too. Billy and Cotton were quietly sitting with them. Cotton's short legs swung back and forth under the table, his hands resting in his lap.

Rawley smiled at the picture. Walking through the doors, he stopped by Doc, asking, "How many are hurt?"

Not bothering to look up, Doc replied, "We're good. Not as bad as what's out there, though," he nodded toward the doors.

The marshal agreed. Turned his attention to the rest of the folks, he saw Lydia Marshall come out of Mike's kitchen toting a heavy pot of coffee. The sound of it, clattering against the bar top as she hoisted it, made everyone jump. Rawley pursed his lips together and blew hot air.

FRECKLED VENOM
COPPERHEAD STRIKES

The top of the bar had been littered with all the glasses Mike owned, filled to the brim with whiskey, known in some circles as Kansas sheep dip. Rawley took one and downed it, burning the soot and smoke out of his mouth and throat. Setting the empty glass down, his hand reached for another. Turning, he leaned tiredly against the bar. Rawley found Lacy sitting quietly, now. Slouched in her chair, shirt tail hanging, face, hair, hands and clothes covered in soot, same as everyone else in the room, bringing the stench from the outside – in. Her hands clenched tightly, grimy white knuckles held her chin. Her eyes were a million miles away, Rawley noticed. Tearing his gaze away from his redhead, his eyes continued to roam the room. Lydia Marshall had walked over to sit with Ezra and Cody Brown. She'd placed a hand on Cody's arm. He glanced up, giving her a tired smile. *Never figured on those two hooking up,* Rawley thought. Cody and Lydia had been an item since the dance this past summer. Thinking again, *maybe it's true that opposites do attract.* He flicked his eyes toward his redhead once again.

Sighing, Rawley searched for Luke, finding him in the corner. His hand reached back. Picking another full glass, Rawley walked over to Luke. He sat the glass in front of the man. Pulling out a chair for himself, he collapsed into it.

"Talk to me, Luke," he said, nudging the glass closer to Luke's hand.

Coming out of his stupor, Luke gave a mighty shrug as he picked up the glass. Opening his mouth, he poured the tawny liquid in. Swallowing, he began to cough. A bandaged hand swiped across his mouth, and he heaved in air, saying, "Don't know, Rawley. Hain't gotta clue."

He gazed at the burnt face, eyebrows singed off, hair, too. Doc had put some burn ointment on the raw skin, which made it glisten. "Did you hear anything? See anyone?"

Bleary red eyes stared back at Rawley, as Luke shook his head. His voice sounded like a burro with a bad cold when he answered. "The only thing I 'member...I knowed, them fires wuz set...too many buildings caught fire at once for hit to be accidental. Too, I 'member smelling coal oil," he said, settling tiredly back in the chair.

Rawley settled back, too, his hand swirling the brown liquid around in the glass. Finally he nodded in response. Hearing a chair scrape back, his head rose. He watched Lacy leave the saloon. He upended the rest of the liquid into his mouth. The glass tapped the table as his chair scraped back. Rising, he told Luke, "Thanks, Luke. Take care of those burns."

* * *

Lacy's insides were knotted so tight she found it hard to breathe. Picking up a piece of still smoldering wood, she tossed it aside. She could smell the coal oil. Maddie's place reeked of it. Tears begin running in rivets through sooty cheeks. *All this is my fault,* she thought. She struggled, climbing out of the debris, walking some ten feet away. Lacy plopped to the ground Indian-style. Her face resting in her hands, she began crying in earnest.

Looking beyond the ruins of Maddie's restaurant, Rawley spotted Lacy sitting in the dirt, face in her hands. He moved toward her.

Hearing the strains of sniffles, he knelt next to his redhead. His hand touched her shoulder.

Lacy jumped.

Rawley saw the sheer terror flit across her face, then disappear when she recognized him. *She's as nervous as a long-tailed cat in a room full of rocking chairs,* he thought. "It's just me, Sunshine, he said softly. "You okay?"

She sniffled. "No!" Taking the tail of her grimy shirt, she wiped her tears. "No, I'm not," she replied tersely. Standing, hands angrily swiped at her cheeks, smearing soot across tawny freckles. "No, I'm not okay..." she repeated. Waving an arm around at the smoldering ruins of the town, Lacy shouted, "All this is my fault!" She whirled on him, "If I'd left when my gut told me to, none of this would have happened! My grandfather would still be alive and the town would still be here! This is my fault!" She cried.

Rawley blinked when she mentioned her grandfather.

Taking a few steps closer, Lacy said, "You know who is behind this, as well as I do…Lowell Taylor. He's come to torture me first, by doing things like this. Punishing them," her hand waved toward Mike's place, "to get at me. Then he'll come after me, to kill me."

"I won't let that happen, Sunshine."

"How you gonna stop it? He floats around in the dark like a ghost!" She shrieked. Her arm flew again, "Look at what he did last night, while we were all sleeping, snug in our beds!" Taking in a huge breath, she plunged on, "He's a master at terrorizing and he'll do that to this town, too! How do you plan to keep that from happening, Rawley Lovett? Just how do you plan to keep everyone from coming unglued? Keeping the fear from overrunning this town, slowly killing it!" She jabbed a finger into his shirtless chest, "And how do you plan to keep *your* sanity, during all of this, Rawley Lovett?" She glared at him for a moment longer, and then took off running toward Ezra's burned out structure.

Tired eyes just watched her go. This incident really had Lacy spooked, her fear more along the line of sheer terror. He didn't doubt for a moment why she'd smacked Lowell Taylor in the head with the butt of that thunder pipe.

* * *

Turning the handle, Rawley entered the office. He sniffed. The stench had permeated the air in here, too. He sighed, it would be a long time before that smell left town. That's when he heard the scream. Dashing outside, Rawley listened; someone screamed again. It came from Ezra's.

Folks ran out of Mike's. Standing in the middle of the street, they listened. Long legs pumping, Rawley flew past them.

He found Lacy screaming and sobbing hysterically

while her feet danced a jig. Grabbing her arms, Rawley shook her roughly, abruptly cutting off her screams. "Lacy...Lacy! Take it easy!" He shouted. *This is not like her,* he thought. *Taylor's got her spooked good.*

Her eyes looked beyond him. Rawley's head swiveled. That's when he saw the charred figure of a body. Dropping her arms, he walked over and stood staring at what remained of someone. Swallowing the bile that popped into his throat, he forced himself to examine the remains.

Doc and Mike began walking toward Rawley and Lacy behind Ezra's burnt store. A body, burned beyond recognition, lay in the blacken earth. Bones that should have been white were charred. Blackened teeth stared back at him, tongue burnt away, jaw grotesquely welded open. Eye sockets stared emptily at a blue sky.

Taylor did this, Rawley thought.

Coming to stand next to the lawman, Doc harrumphed. Over the years, he'd seen just about everything. Nothing fazed Doc anymore. "Rather crispy, ain't he?" He said casually, and then added, "Neck's been busted," looking at the unnatural angle of the body's head.

Mike came closer, felt his stomach heave. Turning, he walked a few feet and puked.

The sound made Rawley realize that someone stood next to him. He looked up. "Mike? Doc...who we got missing?" He asked.

The two looked at the barkeep, Mike swiped at his mouth. "Uh..." he cleared his throat and spit. He did a mental tally of the folks in his saloon, saying, "Uh...don't know, right off hand."

Giving Mike a disgusted look, Doc said, "With all the free booze, you've been handing out...who's missing?"

Brows closed the gap between his eyes. Thinking, Mike said, "Rooster?"

Two sets of eyes swiveled back toward the marshal.

"Rooster," Rawley sighed softly. "Awright, find something to put the remains in...I need to talk to Lacy," he said.

"I'll see if I can find a shovel," Doc said.

Mike gagged.

Rawley threw Doc a dirty look.

Catching it, Doc returned one of his own. "Well...," sounding more like *way-ell*. The condition he's in...can't pick 'im up," he retorted.

Sighing again, Rawley just nodded.

"I need another drink," Mike said.

Doc harrumphed.

* * *

Standing in front of his redhead, thumbs tucked into back pockets, Rawley gazed at Lacy. Burnt coffee eyes huge in an ashen face, a million tawny dots the only color, she searched his for answers.

"Rooster?" She asked.

He nodded.

Lacy stared at the dirt. She spun and walked off a few feet. "All this is my fault," she whispered.

Following her, he said sternly, "Talk to me, Sunshine."

She whirled. An arm flung out, gesturing toward the burned remains, "About what...this?" Eyes narrowed into slits, "This is just the beginning...Lovett. You don't know Taylor...I do," she said.

"Damn right...you do!" He barked. "And you'd better start talking!"

"I...I can't think right now," she said lamely, beginning to turn away from him.

He exploded, "Tough Shit!"

She spun. Dark eyes grew wide unaccustomed to Rawley's choice of words.

"You'd better start thinking and talking!" He growled. "This is my town...your town," his arm waved toward Mike's, "And their town! We are going to do whatever it takes to keep them safe! Do you hear me, Sunshine?" He'd spat out each word as if he were ejecting empty brass casings from his Henry rifle.

Lacy blinked, her eyes huge as she sensed Rawley's barely controlled anger.

She finally nodded.

"Then…damn it! Start talking to me!"

CHAPTER THIRTY TWO

"Here comes, Mike," Lacy announced, looking through the window, watching him slosh through puddles toward their office. She turned toward him when he opened the door.

Droplets splattered the floor as he shook himself. "I hate a cold rain," were the first words out of Mike's mouth. Water continued dripping off of his hat and poncho, building a puddle around his boots. He kept looking back and forth between Lacy and Rawley.

"Umm...I know you said anytime...we went anywhere...we weren't to go alone. We need Joe Jenkins's wagons to help remove the debris," he said. "So I thought...maybe, you, me, Luke and Cody Brown...I wou'da asked Ezra, too, but he's kinda busy trying to get his insurance settled. But the rest of us could go out there and get them, bring Joe back to town with us. Those big draft horses of his would be a help, too..." he left the rest hanging in the air.

The chair squeaked when Rawley leaned back. An odd thought entered his brain, *too late now to get oil from Ezra's for this chair.*

Rawley looked over at his redhead. He'd kept a tight rein on Lacy since the fire, not letting her out of his sight. As she had said, 'Taylor floats around like a ghost.' He had even followed her to the outhouse in back; she'd really bucked at that. Then she settled down and for once *actually* listened to him. He sighed. He'd have to leave her to go with Mike and the others.

The chair squeaked again as he sat up. "Sunshine? You gonna be okay...if I go with them?" he asked.

Eyes rolled in her freckled face. "I can take care of myself, Lovett!" She spat.

CHAPTER THIRTY THREE

Under a weepy drizzle from the low ceiling of slate-gray skies, hooves sloshed through puddles and mud. A slow, steady, cold rain had been falling the last three days, saturating everything. The parched earth swallowed up every drop. Having had its fill, it offered up sloppy conditions throughout the area.

Four men rode through the gates fronting Joe Jenkins property. A nondescript log home seemed to squat in front of the riders. A porch ran the length of the front. The door centered the wall with two windows placed on either side of that under the porch roof. A stone chimney faced the barn and pens. A lean-to held the wagons they were hoping to borrow, with more pens to the right of that.

Something nudged Rawley between his shoulder blades. Nothing seemed to be out of the ordinary as he looked around, so he shook it off. Then, he noticed no smoke coming from of the chimney of Joe's house. That feeling came back, nudging him harder. His eyes roamed, dissecting the muddy yard, *nuthin'*, he thought.

Rawley called out, "Joe? Joe?" Silence answered him. No wind, no animal sounds, nothing, except the rhythm of the rain softly dripping off their hats, the eaves, and their mounts shuffling through the mud.

Leather creaked as four men dismounted, uttering not a word as ears listened to the extreme silence. The four glanced at each other. On cue, three of them pulled their pistols from under the ponchos as if reading each other's minds. Mike slid his sawed-off scatter gun from the scabbard.

Rawley's voice sounded eerie in the stillness. "Luke and I will take the house and grounds," he said. "Mike...you and Cody check out the barn and pens."

Stepping on the porch, Rawley and Luke paused, listening again. Luke sidled against the log wall, elbow crooked, pistol held in the air, ready. He peeked into a window. All that greeted him was the dark inside. Looking at Rawley, Luke silently shook his head. The marshal nodded acknowledgment.

Placing his hand on the door knob, Rawley put more of the log wall between him and what might lie inside. Twisting the handle, he suddenly shoved the door open, hard. He drew back. It bounced against the wall with a dull thud and swung back squeaking. He and Luke waited. Silence greeted four ears.

A long leg with a boot attached pushed the door open further. Both waited again, nothing flew out to surprise the two men. The filtered light followed them inside. Through the gloom, they saw the room had been tossed. Table and chairs upended, cupboard on its front, glass and dishes shattered.

Luke knelt by the hearth, and his hand dug in the ashes. He looked up. "Cold," he told Rawley.

Mike and Cody waited until they saw the marshal and Luke enter the house without gunfire erupting. Squishing through the rain soaked yard toward the barn, they slowed as their noses picked up an unpleasant odor. Heads swiveled, cutting each other a quick glance before stepping up to the doors. Both rested an ear against the wood and listened. Thick buzzing greeted their ears.

* * *

Pulling the office door shut behind her, Lacy moved to the edge of the walk, listening. Just the slow rain dripping off the roof reached her ears, splashing into puddle water at the edge of the walk. She stared down at the row of droplets cascading from the eaves into the puddle. Looking up, she allowed her eyes to roam the dark town, flitting here and there, resting on the scattered skeletons of the burned businesses, before moving on. With the heavy slate-grey skies, darkness arrived early. She wondered what was taking Rawley and the others so long out at Joe Jenkins' place. Her boot heels thumped along the planks, ceasing every once and a while to stop and listen.

* * *

Opening the huge barn door, Mike and Cody recoiled at the stench that seemed to burst through the opening. The humming became more pronounced. Mike took in a lungful of fresh air, and holding his breath walked into the dusky interior. Cody followed, his hand covering his nose and mouth, trying to block the putrid odor. It did no good, the smell permeated, stinging and burning his nose hairs down to bristle.

They advanced on the buzzing, reaching the stalls where Joe kept his big draft horses. Tentatively the two men peeked over the partition.

The huge animals had collapsed on themselves, single bullet hole between the eyes. The bodies were bloated and beginning to ooze fluid. They had begun collecting numerous flies and maggots, crawling in and out of eyes, the nostrils and mouths, beginning the slow but meticulous work of demolishing the flesh, until the bones had been picked clean.

Cody's stomach heaved, and he barely had time to turn before he puked. Mike gagged hearing Cody upchucking, but managed to keep his own contents from coming up.

Stepping toward Cody, Mike rested a hand on his shoulder. "Let's go tell Rawley what we found," he said. Cody nodded, anxious to return to fresh air.

Moving quickly for the door, Mike abruptly slowed, catching something out of the corner of his eye. He grabbed Cody's arm stopping him. Slowly he turned and stared into the back of a stall. Taking steps closer, Mike drug Cody along with him, not willing to make the discovery on his own.

A man sat in a chair pushed up against the wall. Releasing Cody's arm, Mike took a few more steps. The face and upper torso was covered in black flies. He waved them away. They flew at the disturbance of their meal, buzzing around Mike's head. The barkeep sucked in foul air, as words ripped from his throat, "Oh...Gawd!" Mike fled the stall with Cody on his heels. They both stumbled out of the barn, puking their guts out on the muddy ground, the contents washing away with the rain. When finished, they rested against the door, their faces lifted to the cleansing drops, too weak and shaken to move.

Holstering their weapons and stepping off the porch, Luke and Rawley strode toward the two leaning against the barn. The air became more pungent along, with the increased humming noise, as they approached Mike and Cody.

Luke said, "You two look like ya seen a ghost." Sniffing the air, he didn't like what it meant.

The hair on the back of Rawley's neck began to tingle, as he breathed the foul odor.

Cody gulped air. "It's a lot worsen then seeing a ghost, Luke," he squeaked. "I wished I'd ah seen ah ghost. That'd jus' scare the bejeebus outta me, instead of making me puke ma guts out," he finished, swiping his hand across his mouth.

"Rawley...you done ate today?" Mike asked stupidly.

Glancing at the opened doorway where the smell and humming came from, he asked, "Why?"

"Cause effen ya hain't...it won't hurt so bad, losin' yure cookies with an empty stomach," he replied.

"Joe?" He asked simply.

Mike gave a weak shrug. "I 'spect that might be who that man in there is, but, he's kinda hard ta recognize...with what's been done ta him," he said.

His gaze drifted downward, staring at the saturated ground. The water cascaded off the brim of his hat, splashing his already mud splattered boots and britches. Rawley sighed. Looking up he said, "Thanks for the warning, Mike." Steeling himself, he strode into the barn, with Luke on his heels.

Black flies hummed, increasing in intensity as Luke and Rawley walked deeper into the barn. Both he and Luke had pulled bandanas out of back pockets to curtail the stench of rotting carcasses, to no avail.

Winding their way through the fumes and flies, they didn't see the body at first, finding the draft horses instead.

"Lordy...Rawley...Who the hell would do sometin' like that to those good harses?" Luke asked.

"A real mean...sum bitch, that's who," he replied bitterly, thinking, *Lacy is right again...Taylor terrorizing as she said he would do.*

"Hell...Rawley! Ah damn rattler wouldn't set down tae dinner wit someone lak that," Luke added.

Looking around, Rawley nodded absentmindedly. His height enabled him to spot the body before Luke. Moving, he stood at the entrance to the stall, staring at the figure in the chair. The head rested on the man's chest. Barbed wire had been strung around his shirtless torso, holding him upright. Barbed wire also strapped down the wrists and bootless ankles to the arms and legs of the chair. The body had bloated to the point where the wire almost disappeared. Dried blood caked the man's belt and britches. Black flies feasted on that, too.

Luke had stepped around Rawley, stopping by his side. His eyes popped when he saw the black draped flesh. "Good...Gawd Almighty!" Luke exclaimed. "He's been skinned...from the waist up! Even his face and scalp! Like a damn hide skinner would skin tha hide offen ah critter!"

Rawley heaved in the foul air. It seemed to settle in his mouth and on his tongue like oil, killing his sense of taste. He continued to breathe out of his mouth. His feet finally moved toward the figure in the chair. Kneeling, Rawley took his hat off and fanned the flies. They hummed and buzzed in irritation, being shooed from their meal.

Following, Luke bent over, bandaged hands gripped his knees. Brow less eyes squinted at the body, then he announced softly, "He was skinned while he was still alive...Rawley."

With his elbow resting on his knee, Rawley pressed the back of his hand against his mouth. Bile seemed to inch upward from his stomach. He swallowed it back down. He, too, had noticed the uneven skin tags left under the barbed wire.

Straightening, Luke whispered, "Gawd Almighty! I hope he died quick...That's a hell 'ave way to die. Joe was a good man, too."

"Let's get outta here," Rawley said, standing. Both exited the stall and then stopped, staring at the inside of the barn door. Hordes of black flies had covered the skin and scalp nailed into the door, giving the appearance of a dancing silhouette.

"Lord...Gawd Almighty...," Luke began, swallowing. "We're dealing wit one sick sum bitch...Rawley."

"Yeah," Rawley replied. *And Lacy's next,* he thought.

Thinking as one, the two hurried outside into the rain that continued to fall.

Tilting his head to the dark skies, Rawley let the rain begin to wash his senses clean, as Mike and Cody had done.

After a few moments he jammed his hat back on, and turned toward the three men who had quietly watched him. "Nuthin' more we can do here. After it stops raining, we'll come back out and burn the barn." Three sets of eyes just stared at him when they heard that remark. Rawley shrugged. "I know it's not really a fitting burial for Joe, but we can't move those big draft harses, and Joe...well...," he trailed off. He didn't want anyone to have the responsibility of burying Joe. They'd have nightmares the rest of their lives. "It's just better we burn everything." He waited; finally three heads nodded.

Rawley looked over at the two wagons. "Might as well unsaddle our harses, hitch them up to the wagons, and head back to town," he said, *and Lacy. Taylor is still out there...like she said he floats around like a ghost,* he thought.

Looking up, he suddenly realized how dark it had become. Rawley's stomach and chest clenched into a hard little ball, cutting into his air supply. Darkness came early today with the heavy skies. The hairs on his neck rose, sending a chill skittering down his spine.

CHAPTER THIRTY FOUR

Something slammed into Lacy's back, sending her sprawling into the mud. The rifle splashed into a puddle, out of reach. Her hat landed on its crown. Rain began filling the makeshift bowl. Thick hands clawed into her shoulders, yanking her up. Furry arms wrapped around her neck beginning to slowly cut into her air supply.

Taylor..., her mind screamed. She panicked, her mind tumbling. She struggled against the arms that enslaved her throat. Lacy caught the thick musty scent of wet wool, realizing then, it wasn't furry arms but a coat.

Easy now, the voices told him. *Play with her.*

Feeling the wet wool relax around her throat, Lacy went into survival mode. She slumped, acting as if she'd passed out. The arms let her go, and she collapsed into the mud. Rain peppered her face. Keeping her eyes closed, she forced her senses to magnify, picking up any slight delicate difference. She felt the figure move closer, terror rose in her throat. She swallowed it back down, forcing herself to think calmly. Lacy continued to lie in the mud like a possum, ever so still. The cold wetness seeped into her britches. The poncho kept the upper half of her torso somewhat dry, but prevented her from reaching for her pistol. *Damn it!* Her mind exclaimed. *I've got to reach that rifle!*

The figure moved closer. She felt him kneel, and then hands roughly shoved her over. Water seeped in, soaking first her coat then her shirt. Lacy tried mightily to keep the shiver that wanted to claim her body under control. Hands pulled up her poncho. Her heart jumped into her throat; she swallowed it back down. Lacy kept her breathing as normal as she could. The hands found her pistol and whisked it out of its holster. She felt the figure stand, felt his eyes piercing her prone body.

Roll! Her mind said. She did, rolling towards the rifle. Lacy's hand reached out, laying fingers on the stock. A boot smashed into her hand. She yelped. Lacy rolled onto her back. Her leg struck out, boot smashing into his knee, jammed it backwards. He yowled.

Rolling again, Lacy placed her knees under her. She struggled to rise in the soupy mess, mustard colored poncho hampering her progress. The mud, sucking at her like molasses, slowed her movements. Her boots slip-slided every which way in the muck.

"You bitch!" Taylor yelled.

She heard the threat in his gravelly, sandpaper-scraping tone. Lacy tried to move faster toward the rifle. She didn't make it.

Thick hands grabbed her shoulders, whirling her around. Her braid flew with the force. Taylor sent a fist into her jaw. Her head jerked back. Lacy saw stars and then blacked out, slipping back into the cold mud.

Picking her up, Taylor threw her over his shoulder like a sack of feed. Boots squished through the mud toward his horse in back of the bank. Reaching his mount, he slung her over the neck of the horse, the animal jumped at the unusual placement of the weight.

The voices returned. He cocked his head listening. *Good, take her to where we told you.* He smiled. Climbing into the saddle, Taylor guided the animal toward Lacy's final resting place.

* * *

Wandering through town, Rawley frantically searched

for Lacy. Peeking in the saloon, he saw Mike and Maddie talking behind the bar. The barkeep had offered her the use of his kitchen, until she could build a new place. Now folks could get a beer or a whiskey with Maddie's good meals.

Backing away from the bat-wing doors, Rawley walked to the end of the porch and leaned against a post. It had been uncommonly warm and muggy for this time of year. His chest and gut clenched and unclenched. It felt like Luke's anvil had taken up permanent residence in his stomach. He tried to breathe and think.

His eyes picked up movement heading toward the office. Rawley stepped off the walk, *Lacy,* he thought, heaving a huge sigh. *Finally.*

* * *

Bouncing across the neck of the horse, Lacy lost her breath with each step the animal took. She pretended to still be unconscious, but her mind had kicked into a fast trot.

She had no clue as to where Lowell Taylor planned on taking her. The rain had slacked off to a miserable drizzle for the moment and it was dark as tar pitch. Lacy could only stare at the ground as the horse moved. Her ears picked up the soft thuds...*we're on the prairie*...she thought.

The grasses would be flattened with the rain, but she could still hide in them, if she got rid of the dingy mustard colored poncho. Lacy moved her hips, so that her legs dangled further down the other side. She tightened her muscles, and flung herself off the horse. Landing hard on her backside, Lacy scrambled up and took off running behind Taylor giving herself the few precious seconds it would take him to whirl the horse around and chase her.

He yelled, "You damn bitch!"

Her heart in her throat, Lacy forced the air into her lungs as her legs pumped through the grasses.

Thwack!

A bullet whizzed by her head. She ducked and nosedived into the wet grasses. *That's one...* she thought, her mind beginning to count the bullets. Hurriedly, Lacy removed the poncho and threw it across the grass. She looked up. Taylor was only about fifteen yards away, now. The sky so dark and black, she could barely make out his silhouette. Lacy skedaddled backwards on her belly away from the tell-tale poncho.

Lacy had jumped her prey from the ground before, but, this time it became a matter of life or death. This time she couldn't lose. Judging the distance, she rose into a squatting position. Adrenaline pumping, she waited.

* * *

Pushing open the office door, Rawley spoke, "Lac...," then stopped when he saw Billy standing by the desk. "Damn it, Billy!" He growled angrily. "What are you doing here? You should be home where it's safe!"

Ignoring the marshal, Billy nodded toward the desk. "Found these between Miss Lydia's and the bank. They're Miss Lacy's, ain't they?"

Rawley flung a look at the muddy rifle and water logged felt hat, beginning to leave a puddle on his desk. His heart clenched recognizing the items. *Taylor's got her,* his mind buzzed. He raked knuckles across four days growth of beard, "Yeah," he replied. *Think! You damn fool! Think!* He told himself.

Moving toward the desk, a sudden thought burst into his brain. *Baxter...* Rawley knew Billy used the dog to hunt prairie chickens. Maybe, just maybe...he might be able to sniff out Lacy. "Billy, think Baxter might be able to find Lacy in this rain?" He asked, opening a drawer and taking out a box of cartridges.

The boy shrugged. "I do' no...he's pretty good about finding Cotton when he's hiding," he said.

Rawley leveled a strong gaze on the boy, *he's growing up.* "Awright...go get him. And find Luke, tell him to saddle three harses...meet me back here as soon as you can," he said.

Straightening like a cadet at West Point, Billy clacked his heels together and saluted the marshal. "Yes...sir!" Rawley gave a tired smile at the gesture. Turning, he mustered an orderly, but restrained control, belying the frenzy he felt inside. Removing his three best rifles from the gun rack, he opened the box of cartridges and began sliding the brass casings into the breech of each rifle.

* * *

Lacy knew she was no match for Lowell Taylor's physical strength, but she had to try. Thunder rolled in the distance and then lightening flashed, silhouetting the figure on horseback. In that split second flash, she saw Taylor take aim and fire at the poncho in the grass. Nothing happened. *The powder's damp,* she thought, *good.* The one time she was thankful for that old cap and ball Navy Colt to miss-fire.

Thunder rolled again, followed by another burst of light. A raw wind surrounded her, bringing with it a blast of cold air, Lacy shivered. Her gut told her, *Now!* Bouncing up, Lacy ran the few short yards toward Taylor. Jumping, her fingers clawed into the arms of his wet coat. She let her weight drag him off the saddle in surprise.

Twisting, Taylor pushed the muzzle into her coat and pulled the trigger, this time it went off. Lacy screamed as hot lead sheared her ribs. Her coat and shirt caught fire momentarily then quickly extinguished by the wet material. Doubling over in pain she crumpled into the grass.

Scrambling up, he stood over the figure; Taylor pointed the muzzle at her head. His thumb cocked back the hammer, creating a dull metallic click as the cylinder rolled, stopping under the nipple. His finger slowly pulled back on the trigger.

* * *

After giving the scruffy canine a good sniff of Lacy's shirt, Baxter led the two men and a half-growed boy, somewhere between grass and hay, back to the alleyway between

FRECKLED VENOM
COPPERHEAD STRIKES

the bank and the dress shop. Rawley gave him another whiff. Lifting his nose in the air, Baxter set off towards the Northeast. Three figures slipped quickly into their saddles and on horseback followed him.

Lightening flashed illuminating Baxter's tail up ahead waving in the grasses, and then the area plunged into darkness once again. Thunder followed a few moments later.

"Hell...Rawley," Luke began, "Ya don't really expect that dog to find Lacy in this weather, do ya? It's black as tar pitch out here! The rain'll wash out her scent again, fore too long."

"It's the only thing we can do, Luke," he answered. "We have to find her before Taylor kills her." Looking over at Billy, Rawley shouted, ordering, "Don't lose sight of Baxter, Billy!"

The boy nodded, nudging his horse into a faster pace.

* * *

The hand holding the pistol moved slightly, the finger continued to pull back on the trigger. Flames spit, a loud *thwack* entered the storm plagued air. Lacy screamed again as a pea-sized piece of lead tore through her calf.

Baxter stopped, head turned toward the sound. Three riders pulled up short behind the dog. They too, had heard the scream.

"Billy, get a rope on him," Rawley ordered crisply.

Scrambling off the horse, Billy slipped the noose over Baxter's head, and then climbed back into the saddle.

Two men slid their rifles out of the scabbards. Cocking the levers back, they injected a cartridge into the chamber.

Another *thwack* reverberated through the air. This time no scream accompanied the shot. Rawley's gut clenched even tighter when he didn't hear another scream.

* * *

The third piece of lead entered high, throwing Lacy

back into the grass. The ball nicked her collarbone as it dove under, lodging next to her spine.

Flashes of her life passed through her mind; a Christmas, long ago with a little girl in an emerald dress. Cradling, her mother's head on her lap, a bloody hand banging on Vern's door. Running, always she seemed to be running. Images of Sam and Sally…the boys…Mike, Maddie, Olivia, and Doc flew by. She and Fancy winning the race. Rawley…her new dress, the dance…his kisses, the way she felt that night.

A light seemed to fill the inner reaches of her mind, and suddenly Lacy felt like a feather floating in the spring breezes. Her sights fell on the tunnel of light; she floated toward it. The door slammed shut, suddenly blocking the light. She fell back to earth, landing hard. Lacy moaned, and then fell silent.

* * *

"Let's go!" Rawley yelled. A hundred yards later, he held up his hand, slowing the three riders to a standstill. Six ears listened, trying to pull a smidgen of human sound from the storm-tossed prairie. They heard nothing, except the wind beginning to build high in the air from the northwest. A chill seemed to surround the three.

With the storm closer, thunder rolled and lightening flashed once again. Rawley and Luke both saw in that instant, a lone figure standing thirty yards away. The two men dismounted as one and silently handed their reins to Billy.

"Stay here son, and don't let that dog loose for nuthin'," Rawley told the boy.

Rain abruptly came down in sheets. Water funneled off the brims of their hats like gutters. Crouching low, Luke and Rawley ran through the downpour toward the figure. Slowing when they heard more thunder, they waited on the flash of light they knew would follow, pinpointing their prey. It did, accompanied by a blood-curdling yell that seemed to shake the inner core of the storm that surrounded them.

"Damn…" said Luke, "Minds me of them victory war-hoops from the Sioux during the Indian Wars."

Rawley didn't bother to answer. His mind concentrated on the other figure the lightening pointed out, lying on the ground not far from where Taylor stood.

He whispered. "Cover me, Luke," and took off winding his way through the flattened grasses.

Luke wasn't waiting, his gimpy hobble followed Rawley five yards behind the lawman.

Thunder rumbled far off in the distance. The wind had died suddenly, leaving the air too quiet, permeated with bitter cold. Another blood curdling yell pierced the black air surrounding Rawley, sending shivers down his backbone. Lightening flashed. Ten yards away stood Taylor. Rawley straightened and barked, "Taylor!"

Whirling, Lowell Taylor shot blindly. The fire spit from Lacy's pistol he held in his hand. Before the marshal's reflexes could react, a rifle blasted from behind him and quickly fired again. Rawley watched Taylor drop like a sack of rocks. Turning he saw Luke lower the rifle from his shoulder. "Couldn't let you do it…Rawley. It was best I kilt the sum-bitch," Luke said lamely.

CHAPTER THIRTY FIVE

Soft big flakes began filtering through the still atmosphere. Thunder echoed in the distance, followed by lightening flashing sporadically heading southeast.

Sprinting toward the small figure, Rawley reached Lacy's side. Dropping his rifle, he knelt. His shaking hands slowly turned her over. Fingers gently pulled her wet coat collar from her neck. His hand touched the freckled face he'd come to love so dearly. The skin was as icy as a mountain stream. Fingers slid toward her neck. Finding the vein still pulsing, Rawley gave a relieved sigh.

Luke walked over to the bulky form he'd killed. Taking the toe of his boot, he shoved the body over. He stared into a grotesquely deformed face. "Gawd…damn! He's one ugly sum-bitch," he said to no one in particular.

His hands full of reins and the rope keeping Baxter in check, Billy rode upon the scene. He sat staring at the two men and the bodies of the others. Flicking eyes toward the marshal, Billy nudged his horse closer. Tying Baxter's rope around the saddle horn, he slid off the leather seat. He swished through the flattened prairie grasses, coming to stand next to the marshal. "Mister Rawley…" Billy began then trailed off leaving the unspoken question hanging in the stillness.

Luke tramped through the wet grass, kneeling across from Rawley. He flicked eyes at Lacy then back to the marshal. "How bad…" he began.

FRECKLED VENOM
COPPERHEAD STRIKES

Suddenly Rawley realized someone had spoken. He glanced up seeing Luke and then Billy standing close by. "She's still breathing," he replied.

Laying the rifle down, Luke's fingers began roaming across the soggy coat. "Hell...she wuz shot at close range. Her coat caught on fire," he said. No one bothered to reply to his statement. Glancing up at the lawman, Luke noticed Rawley seemed to be in a stupor. Unbuttoning Lacy's coat and brushing it aside, he saw blood had saturated her shirt by the collarbone and ribs. Checking further, he found her bloody calf. "Dammit to hell...she took three bullets, Rawley!" he said.

The words seemed to jerk Rawley out of his stupor. "We've got to get her back to Doc...quick!" Scooping the girl into his arms, he rose. The three hurried back to their horses. Rawley handed Lacy to Luke. He swung himself into the leather. Reaching down, he gathered his redhead into his arms. Cradling her across his lap, his free hand took the reins Billy handed him. Wordlessly reining the bay around, Rawley nudged the animal into a trot back toward town. "Stay with me, honey. Stay with me, Lacy," he whispered to the still form in his arms.

CHAPTER THIRTY SIX

An early fall snowstorm had laid about three inches, and was still coming down making the thick silence feel even deeper, turning a black as tar-pitch darkness to silver grey when three riders pulled up in front of the stairs leading to Doc's office.

Wordlessly, Billy slid out of his saddle and took the stairs two at a time, leaving defined boot prints on the snowy steps. His fist reached out and began banging on the door.

Reaching up, Luke took Lacy from Rawley. Slipping from the saddle, Rawley relieved Luke of his redhead. Turning, he saw the soft light filter through Doc's window and open doorway, creating a block of yellow marking the fresh snow.

Gently taking the steps, he carried his ever-so-still copperhead. Stopping on the stoop, the marshal just stood staring through the doorway at the boy and Doc returning his gaze.

Placing a hand on Billy's shoulder, Doc said, "Son...go get Miss Liv, and get out of those wet clothes while yer at it. Don't need you catching pneumonia."

The boy clattered down the steps heading towards Liv's. Luke watched the boy run up the street. The chilled air clung to the fog rising from the stable owner and the horses as he gathered the reins. Then he remembered Baxter, and relieved the rope from his neck. Straightening, he watched the dog scamper after Billy. His eyes flicked toward Doc's, the yellow block of light from the open doorway disappeared as the door closed.

Turning, Luke sighed heavily, releasing a thick fog into the cold atmosphere. Pulling on the reins, he muttered, "C' mon…ya mangy hay-burners."

He led the mounts toward his temporary corral until he could get his livery rebuilt. After giving the horses a ration of oats, his gloved hand brushed at the three inch layer of snow that had balanced itself on the top rail. He leaned his arms on the bare wood, as his gaze shifted towards Mike's. Beams of weak light, from a few coal oil lamps, poked itself through falling snow further up the street. The darkness hid the still burned skeletons of buildings. His tongue snaked out wetting his cold lips, thinking how that amber liquid would feel on the way down warming his chilled insides. An uncontrollable shiver began rattling from his shoulders clear down to his toes. Luke hadn't felt this chilled since the Indian Wars. The events of the last week had brought all those horrors back. Lowell Taylor had dispersed the sunny, calm disposition of this town, as if he'd blown dandelion seeds into the air, leaving only the stem bending to the will of the wind. Taylor had created a heart-pounding, heart-stopping fear within the close-knit community. Luke's senses always came alive when faced with that kind of terror, not knowing if he would live or die in the next few seconds. He'd gotten that same fear during the Indian Wars. Shaking the chill off, the accumulating wet snow on his shoulders tumbled off in clumps.

Then he did something unaccustomed for Luke Castleberry, he prayed. "Lord…I knowed you ain't heerd from me in a long while…but I's got a special request. Got a li'l gal up thar in Doc's office that's gonna need some powerful healing…and I knowed you're the only one who ken do that. So…please Lord…" Luke trailed off. He sighed heavily, fog erupting like he'd been sucking on a cheroot, sending thick smoke into the air. He opened the gate and walked through, latching it behind him. His gimpy hobble headed him toward Mike's.

CHAPTER THIRTY SEVEN

After laying Lacy on the table in Doc's office, Rawley shucked out of his rain gear. He hung it on the coat tree, followed by his sopping coat and hat. A puddle of water soon graced the floorboards underneath. Turning, he walked back over to Doc, leaving muddy boot prints on the floor. Rolling wet sleeve cuffs back, he asked softly, "What do you want me to do, Doc?"

Hooking his glasses on his ears, Doc peered over the rims at the marshal, his face as white as the girl's on the table. "Let's get her out of these wet clothes first…don't need her catching pneumonia," he said.

Eager hands quickly assisted Doc in removing her dripping coat, then her shirt, leaving an attractive undergarment with pink ribbons exposed. An empty gun belt thudded to the floor, followed by boots and canvas britches revealing pretty pantaloons edged in lace. Rawley blinked at the feminine underclothes. A strange thought entered his head. *When did she buy these?* He asked himself.

Noticing Lacy's skin tone and her struggle for air, Doc quickly reached for his stethoscope. Listening, he knew one lung had collapsed. Ripping the earpieces from his ears, he told Rawley, "Damn bullet nicked her lung, making it collapse." Then Doc ordered, "Go over to that top drawer and get me that new-looking leather case," Doc ordered.

Rawley hesitated.

Seeing the lawman stall, Doc gruffly commanded, jerking Rawley out of his stupor. "Get a move on, boy. We hain't got all night, if you want me to save this girl's life!"

Long legs made it to the three drawer bureau quickly, wood scraped as he pulled the drawer open. His eyes searched for the case Doc wanted. Finding it, he turned, holding the leather in the air. The crusty doctor nodded; Rawley handed it to him.

Moving the rolling table closer, Doc opened the case, pulling out one of his new glass tube syringes. Attaching the metal needle, he depressed the plunger expelling the excess air within the tube. He then poured alcohol on the needle.

One hand untied the pink ribbons and opened the garment further exposing more freckles. Doc heaved in air before he gently inserted the needle deeply into the flesh. He slowly pulled back on the plunger pulling the excess air into the glass tube. His eyes remained on the redhead. He watched the rhythm of her chest rising and falling; Lacy began to breathe easier. Doc pulled the syringe out. Laying it aside, he stuck one earpiece from the stethoscope in his ear, and listened. The stethoscope moved, stopped and moved again. Finally satisfied, Doc nodded.

Doc looked at Rawley, the dark stubble gracing the boy's face made a sharp contrast against the white background. "The lung inflated again, son," he said.

Rawley let out the breath he had been holding, for how long he didn't know.

A sharp pitter-pat climbed the stairs. The door opened and Liv breezed into the heavy air. "Gaylon...Rawley...Billy said..."

"Liv, stoke up that fire and start heating some water," Doc interrupted her. Then his eyes softened, "Thanks for coming, Liv," he said.

Sliding the heavy wool cape off of her shoulders, Liv threw it across a chair and began doing as Doc had instructed.

Gentle fingers touched icy skin as Doc began to examine the hole near Lacy's clavicle. The flow of crimson had slowed considerably. His hands then moved to Lacy's ribs, "Bastard shot her at close range," Doc grumbled, noting the powder burned material. He reached behind him for the scissors, snipping the cloth away from her side. A neat round little hole stared back at him. Fingers pressed the skin around it. "Her ribs stopped this one," he said reaching back for the instrument. A few seconds later he pulled the pea sized piece of lead from Lacy's side. The sharp *pl-ink* sounded loud in the quiet room as it hit the metal pan. Doc spoke. "Liv dress this wound please," he said, moving to the wound in Lacy's calf. The scissors once again cut bloody material from a wound. The lead had gone all the way through catching mostly tendons and muscle. Looking up, he focused on Liv's always neat bun at the base of her slender neck. "This one too," he added.

Liv nodded.

Moving back toward Lacy's shoulders, Doc rested a hand on her wrist, taking her pulse. It remained light and fluttery. Breaking the quiet, he said, "She's as cold as an iced down cucumber."

Her hands stopped the task of bandaging Lacy's wounds. Liv glanced up, her mouth dropping.

Tired blue eyes suddenly threatened the crusty doctor.

Hand rising Doc fended off the threat, explaining, "That's a good thing, son. The hypothermia slowed her circulation down so she didn't lose as much blood as she could have."

Retrieving another pan, Doc filled it with steaming water. Carrying it back to his rolling table, he sat it down. Shuffling over to his bag, Doc dug out the probe and another leather case holding his various scalpels. He pulled two out. A box held his thread and needles. Selecting black thread and a needle, along with his extraction instrument, he dropped those into the boiling water, too.

Examining the wound, sweat began popping out across the crusty old bachelor's brow. Gently sliding the probe in following the track the bullet made, his eyes squinted as he tried to find the piece of lead.

Doc's voice remained calm. "Son, this ain't good," he said, pulling the probe out.

"What 'da mean this ain't good?" Rawley demanded, his voice turbulent with worry. "You've got to do something. I don't want to lose her Doc. Hell...I just found her. Do you understand me? I can't lose her!" Rawley cried.

The turmoil in Rawley's voice had Liv reaching across Lacy. She silently touched his arm as she tried to reassure him with her eyes.

Blue eyes flicked briefly at Liv and then back to Doc.

Narrowing tired eyes, Doc said, "Son, I'm doing the best I can, the bullet's lodged next to her spine, near as I can figure." Raking a hand through his salt and pepper hair, making it stand on end, he glanced over at Rawley. "I can take the lead out, but one misstep from me and she could be paralyzed for the rest of her life. Or we can leave it in there, where eventually the bullet could move and cause more damage," he explained quietly.

Drawing more air into his lungs, Rawley spoke softly. "Do whatever you think is best, Doc," he said.

"Alright, we need to turn her over. Gentle now, we don't want to cause more damage," Doc said, seeing Rawley a little too eager to comply.

Taking the scalpel, Doc slit the undergarment, pushing it out of the way, exposing Lacy's freckled skin. "Sheesh, the girl's even got freckles on her back," he said.

Giving Doc an unaccustomed dirty look, Liv shook her head at his attempt to break the tension in the room.

Glaring at Doc, Rawley growled, "Shad-up Doc, this ain't funny."

Doc squinted back at the boy. Eyes softening at the upheaval he saw reflecting from Rawley's face, he spoke quietly. "I know, son," he said.

Laying the probe at an angle across Lacy's back, he determined approximately where the bullet might lay. Fingers gently tapped across the skin, picking out a three inch area next to her spine to begin the surgery.

Doc walked over to his cabinet and pulled out a bottle of ether. Reaching into a drawer, he pulled out a clean cloth, and handed the items to Rawley. "She shows any sign of coming to, you pour some of this on the rag and hold it to her nose. I don't need her moving. You got that, son?" He ordered.

Flicking eyes at the items, Rawley nodded. Then throwing his eyes heavenward, he whispered, "Lord, you know I'm not much on prayer, but somehow I feel you sent Lacy to me and I to her, for whatever reasons you had. Guide Doc's hands, Lord. You know I love her, please let her live, please…" Rawley trailed off.

Sending her own silent prayers to the heavens, Liv whispered, "Amen."

Doc cocked a salt and pepper eyebrow hearing the young man's words and Liv's 'Amen.' Silently, he began the surgery.

Lacy's vitals' remained light and fluttery, her breathing still shallow. But, Doc hoped because she was young and in excellent health, Lacy would make it, only time would tell.

Rawley held his breath, sweat running down the sides of his face watching Doc proceed with the delicate surgery. Standing by Lacy, he held her hand, squeezing it every few minutes. He also whispered in her ear to hang in there, stay with him. He felt as if he had been shot himself, the air in his lungs slowly being siphoned out of him.

Wringing the extra bandage into a tight rope, Liv realized what she'd done and dropped the article. She continued to stand next to Doc. Picking up a fresh cloth she dabbed at Doc's brow soaking up the sweat that cascaded down his face.

Finally Doc said, "There's the little bugger." Pulling out the piece of lead, he held it in the air before dropping it into a basin. The sound of it hitting the metal released a sigh of relief from the three.

*   *   *

Watching Liv's fingers make neat little stitches binding

Lacy's wound, had Doc placing a gentle hand on her shoulder. She looked up. He gave her a tired smile. Love showed from grey eyes as Liv gave him a quick smile, she then returned to her task.

Doc turned. Shuffling toward his chair, he slipped tiredly into it. Glancing over at the haggard face of the marshal sitting a few feet away, he thought, *the boy is still in shock.*

Pulling open a drawer in his desk, Doc retrieved a bottle and two glasses. They tapped the top of the desk, and the cork squeaked as Doc twisted it out of the bottle. Generous amounts of amber liquid splashed into the two glasses. Doc picked one up and gestured for Rawley to take it. The marshal continued to stare off into space, a million miles away. Doc lightly touched his arm. Eyes slowly came back into focus, and Rawley glanced at Doc. The doctor gestured with the glass once again. Staring at the tumbler in Doc's hand, a big paw finally took it. Opening his mouth, Rawley poured the amber liquid into his throat, prompting a coughing spell from the whiskey. It landed in the bottom of his empty stomach with a thud.

Something made him glance at the clock. Rawley was surprised to find only an hour and a half had passed. He felt as if it had been a lifetime, he heaved in more air for his oxygen starved lungs.

CHAPTER THIRTY EIGHT

A heavy dark cloud seemed to hang in the room, as Rawley kept a vigil at Lacy's side, waiting for the Sunshine in his life to once again shine. Sleeping off and on in a chair by her bed, he kept a running stream of one-sided conversation going until his voice gave out. When that happened, he would continue to whisper in her ear, as he tried to bring his Sunshine back to consciousness.

Doc came in, placing a hand on the marshal's shoulder. "Son, go get some rest, I don't need two patients to take care of."

Rawley hesitated.

"Go on son, I'll be here, and Liv will be here soon. Go on, son. Get some rest," Doc said.

"You'll let me know if she wakes up…any change?"

Doc nodded.

Smoothing the curls off Lacy's forehead, as he'd done countless times before, Rawley leaned over and kissed his redhead. Rising stiffly, he took a few steps toward the door, and then hesitated again.

"Go on, son. I'll be here," Doc reassured the tall lawman.

Nodding, Rawley let himself out of Lacy's room.

Sitting in the chair Rawley had vacated, Doc rested his head in his hands. Memories of this little spitfire kept flitting through his mind. Remembering how even though she had been wounded and loaded with fever and blood poisoning, Lacy still managed to land Rawley on his arse in Mike's place.

His head rose; Doc gazed at the redhead, and smiled. Taking her hand, Doc squeezed it. More memories invaded his thoughts. Rescuing Cotton and bringing the bastards to justice who had killed the little towhead's family. The hard time she always gave the marshal, exasperating the hell out of Rawley. Standing up to her grandfather for the atrocities, wickedness he'd committed. Doc sighed heavily remembering how she rode that mare and won that damn horse race. How he had enjoyed dancing with her wearing her new dress, and hearing Lacy laugh for the first time. Watching as the big marshal gradually fell in love with the freckled, venom-packed copperhead. And he knew Lacy had been falling in love with the big galoot, too. He'd seen it in her eyes when Rawley had been shot.

Doc's voice became hoarse with emotion as his eyes blinked rapidly. "C' mon, you little catamount, after what all I've been through with you, you'd better live.

Noticing the bright light, Lacy began floating toward it. Looking back she saw herself still lying on the bed, Doc sitting bedside holding her hand. She turned once again toward the light.

A figure was there waiting for her. *Mama*, Lacy whispered. *Mama, is it really you?*

The figure held up her hand, stopping Lacy's travel. *Yes, my child, it is me*, the voice replied softly.

Mama, I've missed you so.

I know, but, you must go back, it is not your time yet.

But Mama, I've missed you. I want to be with you.

I know child, but, you must return, you have a family to take care of, a life full of joy and love, yet to live.

A family? I don't understand?

You will soon, I promise you. You must go back. I love you little one.

Lacy watched as the figure in the light faded. The redhead sucked in air. It felt as if she had been holding her breath for days.

Doc jumped, hearing the sudden intake of air. Taking her hand he gently squeezed.

Lacy opened her eyes.

"Well, young lady, it sure is good to finally have you back," he said smiling, taking her pulse.

The first words out of her mouth surprised Doc. Her voice, thick and raspy as new rope scraping across a wood beam, she whispered, "Where's Rawley? I need to see him, Doc. I need to see Rawley!"

"Here now, simmer down," Doc's gravelly voice soothed her. "I sent him to get some rest. He's been sitting here, the last ten days. I didn't need two patients to take care of. Let's give him a few more hours of sleep, okay? Then I'll go get him," he reassured her.

Shifting against the bed clothes, Lacy gave a short nod, closing her eyes.

Now, you go back to sleep, I'll get him in a little while," Doc finished. Standing, he adjusted the covers. Stepping away from the bed, his hand reached for the knob. Giving the girl one last glance, Doc heaved a sigh of relief, opening the door he walked out. The latch clicked softly closed.

Walking over to his desk, he sunk into his desk chair. A bone weary numbness seemed to affect every part of his body. Leaning forward, the drawer scraped open. He retrieved the ever present bottle and a thumb printed glass. The cork tweaked as he removed it from the bottle. Amber liquid splashed into the tumbler. The bottle tapped the desk. Picking up the tumbler, Doc settled back into his chair. Lifting the glass, he said, "Thank you, Lord." Then he drained the amber liquid.

* * *

Doc lightly touched Rawley on the shoulder. The marshal flew up, fear registering on his face.

FRECKLED VENOM
COPPERHEAD STRIKES

"No, son, nothing like that. Lacy woke up. She wants to see you."

"When?"

"About five hours ago."

"Why'n the hell didn't you come get me then?" Rawley growled, boots hitting the planked floor. He pushed past the doctor, sprinting toward his hat. Lifting it off the peg, he slammed it on his head. Long strides quickly had his hand reaching for the knob. Jerking it open, he disappeared.

"You were 'bout done in, son, both of you needed the rest," Doc tossed the words at the marshal's back.

Coming out of Rawley's room, Doc stopped by the desk chair, looking around. He realized his words had been said to an empty office. Hazel eyes cut a glance toward the open doorway. Doc tugged on his ear and smiled. Boot heels thumped across the office floor, stepping through the door onto the planked walk. His ears picked up the sounds of hammers pinging nails into new wood. Voices shouted commands as the community came together to rebuild the town after Lowell Taylor had destroyed half of it.

Reaching into his vest pocket, Doc pulled out a matchstick and stuck it in his mouth. Shifting it around, he leaned tiredly against a post. Gazing up and down the street, the new buildings bright against the older ones, the smell of fresh cut wood reached his nose. He breathed deeply, thinking, *Things just might be pert near to getting back to normal, now. Lacy not out of the woods, yet, but showing good progress.* Doc pushed himself away from the porch post. Using a hand to steady himself with the weathered post, he gingerly took the steps. He ambled slowly toward Mike's place. He needed to tell everyone the good news. *That little freckled, venom-packed copperhead was gonna live.*

CHAPTER THIRTY NINE

Standing before Lacy's closed door, Rawley heaved in air for his starved lungs. It had been the longest dark days he'd ever spent, waiting for his Sunshine to regain consciousness. His hand reached for the knob, and then he remembered his hat. Whisking it off his head, he opened her door.

Stepping inside a few feet, he nervously twirled the hat on his fingers as he gazed at the woman he loved and almost lost. Flicking eyes at his fingers twirling his hat, he stopped it, tossing the hat toward the end of the bed.

Stepping closer, he eased down in the chair. Taking Lacy's hand, he whispered, "Sunshine?"

Lacy stirred hearing the deep familiar caramel baritone.

"Sunshine, I'm here," he said squeezing the freckled hand he held. The other smoothed those sun-kissed copper tendrils he'd come to love, that always curled across her forehead.

Feeling fingers lightly caress her forehead, she opened her eyes. Lacy's brow furrowed, pulling freckles in closer as she looked at Rawley. Thick dark stubble graced his handsome face. Now haggard and thin looking, it made his cheekbones more prominent. Dark circles reminded her of bruises under bloodshot, tired, blue eyes that barely mirrored a Wyoming summer sky. His hair looked like it hadn't been combed in a month or his clothes changed, either. His dishevel prompted Lacy to ask in a dry hoarse whisper, "What the hell happened to you? You look awful."

Laughter bubbled up from deep within a broad chest, releasing the vice that had been clamped around his heart for ten days. "Only you...Sunshine, would come up with a comment like that, at a time like this," he said, gently kissing her forehead. Her eyes closed at Rawley's tender gesture. His hand continued to smooth the copper tresses over her ears.

Eyes popped open, revealing their dark color, a stark contrast to the paleness of her skin. "Rawley, I...I need to tell you something."

He leaned in closer, hoping to finally hear the words he'd waited for, for so long. Instead, Rawley was taken aback by Lacy's next statement.

"Rawley, I saw Mama."

Suddenly sitting straighter in the chair, he waited.

Lacy plunged on. She couldn't seem to get the words out fast enough. "I saw Mama; there was this bright light behind her. Ooh, she looked so beautiful, wearing her favorite blue dress, the light behind her making her hair seem like flames."

Tears began sliding out of those burnt coffee eyes, running down her cheek, across that little freckled nose.

"She was so beautiful. Just the way I remember her." Lacy hesitated, catching her breath, and then plunged on, " Rawley?" A freckled hand squeezed his, tightly hanging on. His eyes flicked at the strong grip Lacy maintained on his hand. His head rose at her next words.

"She wouldn't let me go with her. I told her, I missed her so, I wanted to go with her, but she still wouldn't let me. Mama said I had a family to take care of, I had to come back. I don't understand, I don't have a family."

Watching Lacy's tears continue to trickle through a face the color of rice powder, her freckles still the only color, made his heart melt. He didn't know why, but he always became a sap whenever he'd see tears welling up in those big burnt coffee eyes. Wiping the moisture from her face, he smiled, replying softly, "Yes, you do, Sunshine. You have

Billy, Cotton, Doc, Liv, Maddie, Mike, me. In fact, you have this whole town wrapped around your little finger." Rawley paused, and then added, "Especially me. We have all become your family. Oh...and we mustn't forget Fancy and Baxter, either," he said as an afterthought, grinning at the petite face.

Sniffling, Lacy's tears began to flow more fluently. Her soft throaty voice croaked out the words, "You sure?"

"Yes, Sunshine, I'm sure."

Lacy gave her customary little nod, tears still streaming. "Mama...mama told me she loved me, Rawley. Then she just...just faded away. I guess I woke up then, and Doc was sitting here."

He realized God had sent his little copperhead back, allowing Lacy's mother to give her daughter the message. So that Lacy could see her mother one more time – whole – and not a bloody mess, the way Lacy had found her many years earlier.

Blinking fast and furious, he tried to keep the moisture in his own eyes from leaking. Rising abruptly, Rawley went and stood by the window, staring at the cloudless azure sky. "Thank you, Lord," he whispered as he tried to compose himself before walking back to the woman he loved.

Lacy had drifted back to sleep when Rawley finally turned and walked back to her bedside. Drying her tears, he kissed those soft pale lips. Now, he felt he could get some much needed rest, too.

Liv bumped into Rawley as he opened Doc's outer door. "Oh, Rawley..." wrapping her arms around his thick torso. "I'm so thankful...Gaylon gave me the good news!"

Treasuring the hug from his friend, Rawley hung on to Liv. After a few moments, she pulled out of his arms and stepped back. Liv gazed into a drained and haggard face, his bloodshot eyes creating a border around the blue. She tenderly touched the thick beard-like stubble, saying, "Go home and get some rest. I'm here now."

He hesitated and then finally nodded.

FRECKLED VENOM
COPPERHEAD STRIKES

    Liv watched Rawley's tired step slowly take him down the stairs and to the street. Grey eyes followed as he made his way toward the office. Closing the door with a soft click, Olivia Johnston turned her attention toward a spirited, copper-headed young woman, who by the grace of God had defeated the devil's demons, once *again*.

CHAPTER FORTY

Sitting out in front of the marshal's office, a cane hooked over the arm of the chair, Lacy breathed in the smells that surrounded her. It had been over a month since she had been shot three times. Her mind flicked tentatively at the memory, sending a chill down her back bone. Lacy shook it out, concentrating on more pleasant things, like enjoying being outside, *finally*, observing the town's bustle.

The mid-fall weather remained perfect, at least for today. Rawley had filled her in on the freak early snowstorm. He'd told her that the bitter cold had probably saved her life.

Gazing across the street, Lacy marveled at Ezra's brand-spanking new Shemwell's Mercantile Store, as he called it now. Even from her seat, her nose could still whiff up the smell of fresh cut wood and the lime whitewash, Ezra had painted the exterior with. This made the building almost too bright to look at, with the sun's rays bouncing off the siding.

Sounds of men shouting reached her ears. They were putting up the log walls of Luke's new stable, trying to finish it before the first big snow flew. Lacy had stayed with Olivia and the boys while Rawley and other men from the town and the outlying areas had gone into the mountains to cut the logs for Luke's livery and blacksmith shop. Rawley had deputized Mike before he left for the mountains. The barkeep had strutted like a peacock wearing that piece of tin and carrying his sawed off scatter gun everywhere. Dimples graced freckled cheeks as she smiled at the memory.

Heaving a huge sigh, Lacy settled more comfortably into the chair, when she spotted Miz Birdy Dawson striding purposely toward her. That bone-handled parasol tapped in rhythm with her heels. This time, however, her severe black had been replaced with a new navy blue dress, and resting on her pewter-colored hair a softer, more appealing hat. Lacy slunk down further in the chair, dreading the upcoming meeting with the wicked witch of the west…ah…White River.

Widow Dawson stopped in front of the redhead and then looked disdainfully down that long nose.

Lacy blinked.

"Young lady, may I have a word with you?"

Sitting up straighter, Lacy replied, "Yes, m'am."

"As you know, I don't hold with women doing men's work. However, I did some checking on you."

Cocking a brow, Lacy waited.

Miz Dawson continued, "Apparently, you have quite a reputation, for being a *lawwoman*."

Resuming her dour expression by sticking her nose back into the air, like a bird's beak, the widow sniffed, "I'm glad you survived those bullet wounds and are doing much better." Tilting her head, beady eyes at first gazed hard at Lacy, and then softened. "Maybe it wasn't such a bad idea after all…hiring a female gunslinger." And with that the old dowager spun on her toes, and flounced off, back the way she had come.

Well, thought Lacy. *That was a surprise!*

Rawley continued across the street with the mail. He had seen Miz Birdy Dawson talking with Lacy. Climbing the steps, Rawley squatted next to his deputy. His hand, reached out, and fingered that silky copper rope draped over Lacy's shoulder. He grinned, asking, "Well, what did the ol' battleaxe have to say this time?"

Lacy smiled back, exposing two dimples in full bloom. She gazed into the face she finally figured out that she loved.

"Not much, I think you could say she paid me a compliment."

"Miz Birdy?"

"Yep!"

Gazing after the woman striding down the street, Rawley exclaimed, "Well, I'll be!"

Turning back to Lacy, Rawley asked, "Sunshine, you want me to get Doc's new rig, and we take a ride? Pretty soon the weather's gonna turn, won't be many more fine days like this one."

Lacy softly touched his cheek, and whispered, "I haven't seen Fancy for a while. Could you hook her up to the buggy?"

"You sure?"

She nodded.

"Okay, be back in a jiffy."

Lacy would tell him on the ride, that she loved him. She hoped that it wasn't just her imagination, but she felt he might love her, too. Lacy prayed that she wouldn't make a fool of herself. That barbed wire returned and snarled her stomach. Lacy heaved in air.

CHAPTER FORTY ONE

Bouncing across the prairie in the buggy, Lacy quickly began to tire. She asked if they could stop and rest.

"Maybe this wasn't such a bright idea," Rawley said, helping her down, and handing Lacy her cane.

Her hand rested lightly on his arm as Lacy reassured him. "It'll be alright...really. I just haven't had time to build my strength back up, yet."

"Well, you've a few months to go, before next year's Fourth of July race," he said, tucking his thumbs into his back pockets. Suddenly shy, Lacy dropped her eyes. She nibbled on her bottom lip. Giving him that silent nod of hers, it made his brows draw closer above blue eyes.

Using the cane, Lacy slowly hobbled toward Fancy's head. That barbed wire had turned into a snarling ball in the pit of her stomach. Right now she didn't have enough courage to fill a thimble. Much less, the courage to tell Rawley that she loved him.

Pushing his hat back on his head, Rawley watched Lacy struggle to walk through the thick grass with the cane. It would take some time for the leg to mend. The other two wounds had healed nicely. He still thanked God every day for giving him his feisty redhead back.

As he continued to observe her, Rawley knew something else was going on with Lacy today. Since she'd regained consciousness, his copperhead had become warmer, more open with him, her quick laughter music to his ears. But still, just like a few moments ago, Lacy would suddenly go shy on him, locking those lips tighter than the Denver Mint and go somewhere inside her head. Even though he had become pretty good at reading Lacy's mind, sometimes he couldn't go there unless she allowed him. And this was one of those times, when the door remained shut. Rawley sighed inwardly. *Maybe one of these days...*, he thought.

Patting Fancy, the big grey nuzzled and nibbled at her shirt. Lacy looked around at the bright fall colors gracing the landscape. Gold coins seemed to dance from the aspens, and silver-green of spruce mingled with the darker greens of lodge pole and ponderosa pines. Golden and purple-red heads of grasses waved in the slight breeze.

Breathing deep, her senses relished the sights and sounds of fall after she almost lost her life. The quail calling, *bob-white, bob-white,* a lone cry of a hawk circling the skies, and numerous black birds and crows sitting in the trees, chattering amongst themselves.

Dropping her hand from Fancy's jaw, Lacy hobbled over to one of the downed trees. Setting aside the cane, she leaned across the big tree, her fingers picking at the bark, dotted with silver lichen, and moss.

Following her, Rawley took up a position a few feet from his redhead. Resting his backside against the large tree, he crossed his feet and folded his arms. Rolled up sleeves exposed his muscular forearms. Thinking as he waited. *She's more at home on the back of a horse, toting a sidearm, riding the prairies, then in dealing with her emotions.* His eyes softened.

Facing Rawley, she squinted while her hands played with a piece of bark, "Um, we need to talk."

"We do?"

"Yeah, well...maybe I talk, and you listen."

"You talk?" He teased her. "Well, now, I'm all ears, Sunshine."

"Don't tease, this is serious, I mean it is for me."
Rawley waited.

Backing a few paces away from the man she loved - he was cutting into her air supply again - Lacy stopped. Shyly glancing in his direction, she began, "You know I'm not good with words." Bending, a hand reached, pulling a blade of grass. Lacy feathered the seed pods back and forth across her hand. Her gaze drifted everywhere except at Rawley.

He continued to wait.

Inhaling deeply, she brought dark eyes back, scrutinizing his rugged features. The ones she had fallen in love with. "When I left over nine years ago, I thought I would never return," Lacy said. The seeds trickled through her fingers. Reaching down, she pulled up more grass, and repeated the process.

Lacy is as nervous as a long-tailed cat in a room full of rocking chairs, he thought as he continued to wait, wondering what this was all about.

"This is harder then I thought it would be," she announced, sucking in more air.

"I'm listening," Rawley prompted her.

His words gave her the courage she needed to continue. "Well...I never thought I would meet a big moose, who drove me nuts. Making me mad, interfering in my personal business, pushing me, crowding me to confront my fears and my past."

Heaving in another big breath, that ball of barbed wire in the pit of her stomach snarled a little tighter. "Who knew me better then I did myself. Who could take what little information he had and patch it all together like a quilt, and...and figure me out."

Limping closer, her eyes searched Rawley's face for some sort of expression. There was none, at least, not yet. "I thought I'd never be saying these words...ever, to anyone." Lacy hauled in more air for her starved lungs and willed that snarling ball in the pit of her stomach, to quit cutting her belly into shreds. "But, I love you, Rawley Lovett," she finally announced, exhaling a plume of air in the process.

Biting his tongue, he guarded his expression. His arms still folded across his chest, tightened, as he tried to keep them in place instead of reaching out for his redhead. *Finally,* he thought.

Burnt coffee eyes darted down. She stared at the ground for a moment, then brought her eyes back. They canvassed Rawley's face, the face she'd come to love. "I want to marry you, raise those two boys as our own," Lacy admitted taking a hobble closer. "I want to have your babies. I want to be able to laugh, to smile, to dance always in your arms. I want you to show me how to live, how to love," she hesitated, "again."

Glancing at the marshal's face, his expression remained vacant; Lacy groaned inwardly, *I'm making a fool of myself.*

"Did you hear me, Rawley Lovett? I said I love you!" Still, no reaction from the big moose, the barbed wire in her gut twisted, making her stomach hurt even more. Lacy retreated a few hobbles. Her husky voice filled with additional emotion as she whispered, "I knew it was hopeless telling you how I feel." She gave him one last pleading glance, but his silence remained along with his face imitating a marble bust. Lacy knew then, that was his answer, he didn't love her. Shaking fingers finally wrestled the badge away from her shirt, tearing the material. Limping toward him, she pried his hand loose from his arms.

Lacy's bottom lip quivered, Rawley noticed. She grabbed that lip with her teeth hoping that would stop the quiver. It didn't. He tilted his head gazing across her sun-ripened curls gracing a forehead with a thousand freckles. Blue eyes found dark ones beginning to fill to the brim with moisture. His heart melted.

Laying the piece of metal in his palm, she closed his long fingers over it. Her hand lingered on his, tears began to dribble down freckled cheeks. "My past will always come between us," she whispered. "I'm sorry." She dropped her hand. Withdrawing further, Lacy added, "Would you please take me back to town? The sooner I can pack, the sooner I can be out of your life." She turned her back on the man she finally figured out she loved, but still couldn't have. Lacy limped over to her cane, with a heavy heart. Her feet felt like she was wading through molasses, as she began hobbling toward Fancy and the buggy.

A big grin plastered itself across his face as he watched the back of his redhead slowly trudge away. Rawley straightened, wiping off the grin. He said, "Sunshine? I do declare, that's the second longest string of words, you've put together, since the Dillard brothers."

Hearing that, Lacy stopped. Her hand gripped the decorative iron on the seat of Doc's new buggy so hard her knuckles turned white. She didn't dare turn around with her heart banging against her ribs. That pounding made it tough to breathe. She swiped the sleeve of her shirt across her face, trying to dry the tears.

Coming to stand behind her, Rawley spoke in his soft, caramel baritone, "I love you too, honey, have for a long time."

Lacy spun. Color rising from the V of her shirt quickly covered pale, freckled cheeks. Her temper flaring, she asked, "You mean to tell me, you've loved me all this time and never said a word?"

Grinning at her spit and vinegar returning, he replied, "Well, you see...sometimes, one has to travel a long distance to find the shorter road...I had to let you do that, Sunshine. If I'd said anything earlier, you would have just run. Like, I just said, sometimes you have to take the longer road to find the short cut. I had to let you figure it out for yourself, that you loved me. I couldn't push you into loving me."

Ignoring what Rawley had just said, Lacy grumbled, "You mean you just stood there, letting me spill my guts, embarrassing myself?"

"Uh-huh," he answered, rocking back and forth on his heels. Rawley took another step closer. Warm callused palms gathered her face between them. "That is the nicest string of words I've ever heard, music to my ears, Sunshine." Softly he kissed her, she didn't pull away. He deepened the kiss, sliding his tongue into the soft sweetness.

Pulling back abruptly, Lacy questioned, "Wait...my past doesn't bother you?"

Rawley shook his head. "Nope. It's not about what happened in the past, it's the future that counts." Continuing to hold that freckled face in his hands, he gazed intently into burnt coffee eyes.

"Your mama sent you back down here for a reason. Just thinking about losing you, I was beside myself. If you had of died, I wasn't sure if I could go on living."

He paused, and then continued, "I want to see a woman finally able to realize a little girl's dreams. I want to see her wear a beautiful white dress, with imported lace, walk toward me down the aisle. I want to hear her say *I do,* promise to love me the rest of her life. I want her to have my babies, raise those two boys together, be the family that little girl always dreamed of, but thought she could never have. I want to hear the music of her laughter, see her smile. And you're the only one I want dancing in my arms. The only one I want covering my butt and me hers in a tough situation."

Taking the badge, he pinned it back on Lacy's torn shirt. "I want you to be my deputy, for the rest of our lives. I love you, Lacy Carrigan, will you marry me?"

Tears continued to spill out of dark depths, cascading down freckled cheeks. Rawley brushed them away with his thumbs, just to have them flow again, dripping off her chin.

Sniffling, she croaked, "You mean that, all of it? You're not just saying that? You're not teasing me, are you?"

Rawley grinned, listening to her rapid fire questions. "It's the truth, Sunshine, I meant every word." Throwing his little finger in the air, he mimicked Cotton, "I inky thware!"

"You what?"

"That's Cotton's way of make a promise and keeping

it." Rawley gestured again, "C' mon, wrap your little finger around mine and say, 'I inky thware',"

"You're as nutty as Maddie's fruitcake!"

"That's right, nuts 'bout you. C'mon now, say 'inky thware'."

Finally complying, dark eyes smiled. That smile spread, enveloping a petite freckled face, and two dimples erupted. Lacy began giggling, laughter bubbling to the surface. That snarling barbed wire in the pit of her stomach disappeared. She collapsed on the ground. Finally, she was able to catch her breath. With her eyes closed, she remained quiet and peaceful, basking in the glow of knowing that Rawley loved her, too.

Dropping to the ground, Rawley stretched out next to her. He took Lacy into his arms, holding this crazy woman he'd come to love so deeply. She snuggled into his embrace, giving a huge sigh. He smiled, resting his chin on fiery copper curls.

Eyes popping open, she sat abruptly, and asked, "You think we can make this work?"

Tucking hands under his head, he laced them together. Rawley lazily asked, "Make what work?"

Lacy punched him in the stomach.

"Oww, cut it out, Sunshine."

"Be serious, a marriage, between us?"

Rawley closed his eyes. "Sure, as long as you don't boss me around too much." He teased, cracking an eye open, as he waited on the copperhead's reaction.

"Me? Boss you around? Just so long as you don't boss me around!" She fired back.

In response, Rawley reached up pulling Lacy down on top of him.

Beginning with her mouth, he kissed her softly. Rolling her over, Rawley pressed Lacy into the sweet smelling grasses. The kisses began in earnest, sliding across and down her neck, to the V of her shirt. A hand slid south, feeling the soft tenderness of a breast through the material. He'd waited a long time for this moment. Rawley was going to make it last as long as Lacy would permit.

She gasped at what his touch made her feel. Lacy had never allowed such emotions to take over before, but this time the walls tumbled down. She reached up and pulled his face to her lips.

Unaccustomed to Lacy's passion, he relished the significance of that intense emotion as her lips smothered his face. His hands found her shirt buttons, and gently opened the green and cream fabric, exposing pink ribbon underclothes. Untying the ribbon he pulled the lacing loose. His hands slid south, pulling her undergarment and shirt from tan canvas britches. Then, Rawley slid both garments off her shoulders, exposing more of those tawny freckles, he'd grown to love. A red, raw scar stared back at him from her collarbone, a smaller one near her ribs. His lips touched the scar on her collarbone, sending tingles all the way down her back, and then they trailed down kissing the one near Lacy's ribs. Her stomach plummeted to her knees.

Fingers still tangled in his black hair, she marveled at how her body responded to his lovemaking. The sensations this man stirred deep within her inner core had goose bumps popping out, sending Lacy's head spinning and her heart to just a thumping against her ribs.

Hearing his redhead gasp, Rawley looked up. Lacy's eyes were closed, soft lips slightly parted, her breath ragged with emotion. He resumed. His tongue left a hot trail, stopping at a freckled covered breast. His fingers took over, beginning lightly at first, drawing circles, ever closer, finally reaching their destination.

Lacy gasped again as a finger lightly circled her breast, touching the perky tawny nipple. Watching Lacy's emotions glide across a million freckles, Rawley pushed the clothing further off her shoulders and lowered his head, his tongue continuing to trace where his finger had left off. Releasing her nipple from his mouth, he feathered his tongue up along her collarbone, following it to her shoulder and back to her neck.

Lacy arched her neck, allowing Rawley to continue tasting her. Trailing his tongue down to her belt buckle, he felt her arch against his mouth. Her hands, still tangled in his hair, pulled him tighter against her. His tongue found its way back to her mouth.

Lacy's hands found his shirt and began with the buttons. He helped her slip the fabric off his shoulders. Pulling her into a sitting position, he slid the two garments off her arms as he kissed her collarbone again. His tongue followed it to the nape of her neck, leaving a hot trail that sent her gasping for air. Laying Lacy back in the sweet smelling grasses, Rawley gazed at this crazy freckled woman he'd come to love so much.

His finger traced her jaw line. "You're beautiful, you know that."

Pinching her lip with her teeth, Lacy hesitated. This man loved her unconditionally, something she thought she would never know much less experience. Realizing that seemed to set her free. She whispered, "Would you...would you, make love to me, please? Like a man would to the woman he loves," she asked softly.

Rawley's answer was given by covering her mouth with his, plunging his tongue deep. Lacy tentatively allowed herself to respond to his kiss. His hand roamed, lightly tracing the scar on her ribs, then dancing to her breast above.

Once again making her gasp as his finger touched the nipple, he moved his head down, licked the little beacon. His mouth then kissed the concave of her shoulder, running his tongue across the ridge of bone.

Rekindling the kisses on her stomach, he continued to trail them with his tongue. Rawley took his time, showing Lacy how much he loved her by being gentle, allowing new memories to take root, erasing the old ones.

CHAPTER FORTY TWO

Holding Lacy afterward, Rawley felt something warm and wet running across his chest. He turned his head. Tears trickled from under those red gold lashes, and his insides melted, once again. Kissing them, he softly asked, "What is it, Sunshine?" Smoothing loose tendrils of hair from her face and not receiving an answer, prompted him to say, "Sunshine?"

Her head moved slightly against his warm chest. Opening damp eyes, Lacy hesitantly began speaking. Her soft throaty voice whispered, "I...it...it was beautiful. I never thought, it could be so beautiful."

"There's a big difference when you love someone and that love is returned," he said pulling her closer. Rawley kissed red-gold lashes again, tasting her salty tears.

Lacy's answer was to snuggle deeper into his strong, warm and gentle embrace, feeling safe.

* * *

It was dark when Rawley woke with a jerk. He then realized Lacy still remained enclosed within his arms, sleeping.

The stars shown from above as he sighed deeply. He too, once thought as Lacy did. That he would never find love. Oh, he'd come close a few times, but then found out the true color of those women he was involved with. He had sworn off ever becoming involved with another female. He'd kept that

FRECKLED VENOM
COPPERHEAD STRIKES

promise to himself, too, until he found that copper-headed, freckled, venom-packed firebrand on the riverbank, her temper striking more often than not, along with her fists. His world had turned upside down that day and had stayed that way, until this afternoon, when Lacy had finally told him that she loved him.

But, one thing remained different with Lacy than those other women he had known. What you saw with her, is what you got. Whether it be a fist or her pistol coming out of nowhere, surprising the hell out of you. Or dimples that suddenly blossomed amongst a million freckles, lighting her face like warm sunshine. Or how beautiful she looked when he first saw her in a dress. No. Lacy was real, from the top of her burnish copper curls to the tips of her scuffed and well-worn boots. Lacy was real.

Smiling, Rawley mused, *Maddie won't let me hear the end of it now, once word gets out there's going to be a wedding in town.* Liv had been right, too. Lacy had come around in her own timeframe.

Rubbing her back, his hand softly caressed the scar near her spine. Rawley spoke softly, "Up and Adam, Sunshine, time we got back to town." His hand slid down a freckled back and lightly slapped her fanny.

Lacy rolled away from him. "Watch it, Lovett!"

Hauling her to her feet, Rawley helped Lacy get dressed, and then began dressing himself.

"I'm hungry? You hungry, Sunshine?"

"I guess," she stated quietly.

Taking Lacy by the arm, he pulled her to him. "Hey, now...don't go getting bashful on me." Lifting her chin up, he made her look him in the eye. Rawley pulled a few stray pieces of grass from those copper curls. "I know every square inch of you now, Sunshine, and I'm not gonna let you go. I love you too much to do that. You understand me, Lacy?"

She gave that short nod, which had become so characteristic of her.

Smiling at Lacy's response, Rawley said, "Good, let's get something to eat."

CHAPTER FORTY THREE

Maddie knew something was different with the pair that walked into her café.

Both had an uncommon glow. Lacy's face, more rosy than usual, highlighted all those freckles and Rawley's eyes shined brighter. The matronly woman surmised that the lass had finally figured out she was in love with her laddie.

Maddie sashayed over with milk for Lacy and coffee for Rawley, a devilish gleam in her eye.

Two sets of eyes stared back.

"Well…it looks as if ye two aboot a done wit ye a fussing," Maddie said, cocking a brow at the pair.

"Ya think, Maddie? What's your special tonight, we're hungry."

"Aye, spect ye be," giving the pair a knowing look.

* * *

"She knows," Lacy stated flatly.

He'd slowed his long-legged strides, so that Lacy could keep pace with him as she limped alongside, her cane thumping out a rhythmic cadence. Rawley looked across at his redhead, "Who?" He asked. They were heading back toward the office after making final rounds in the dark town.

"You know who? Maddie."

"Well…so what! Soon as you pick a date, everyone in this town will know."

CHAPTER FORTY FOUR

Swiping the razor over the last of his stubble, Rawley stopped when his door opened. Lacy limped in, the door clicked softly closed. She just stood there, leaning against the wood, not saying a word.

His breath caught at the site of Lacy reflected in the looking glass, red waves flowing over her shoulders and cascading down her back. That pretty pink and white nightgown, showing her delicate side. He swallowed and slowly turned toward his deputy.

Hobbling over to him, Lacy removed the razor from his hand, laying it aside, saying, "Umm...I have a favor to ask of you."

A rosy flush began from pink ribbons at her throat and advanced upward to the roots of copper hair, covering a million tawny freckles on the way. Rawley waited, not sure what Lacy was up to.

Stepping closer, her nose whiffed up his masculine scent, a touch of pine mingled with a trace of store bought soap, making her knees suddenly weak. Stepping closer still, her finger lightly raked along his ribcage, making goose bumps pop out across his skin.

Big round dark eyes gazed intently into blue ones. "Would you show me how to make love to you?" She asked huskily. Again her nail dragged across his stomach, trailing up the other side. "Would you, please?"

His eyes flicked briefly at her nail dragging across his ribs, then back to his redhead. Rawley breathed deeply trying to put his heart back in its rightful place and more air into his deflated lungs. "Uh...Sunshine, I think you're doing a pretty good job of that right, now. You don't need me to teach you."

Lacy's hand slid the towel from his shoulder, and gently wiped the remaining soap from his face. She dropped that to the floor. The other hand resting lightly on his ribs; began its own travels. A finger drew circles in the thatch of dark hair on his chest, dancing through the scar on his shoulder. Winding its way, it circled each nipple, lightly dragging her nail over one.

Lacy's eyes never left his face, watching the need he had for her build in those summer sky eyes. Stopping abruptly, she dropped her hands and backed away a few feet. Lacy slowly pulled the pink ribbons loose so she could lift the gown over her head. She continued to stand in front of him. Lacy allowed the gown to trickle through her fingers to the floor.

This little copperhead's seductions only made Rawley want her now, more than ever. Stretching out his arms, his voice husky with emotion, he said, "Come here, Sunshine."

Lacy went willingly into his warm embrace.

Two hearts, two souls, became buried deep within a love finally recognized.

CHAPTER FORTY FIVE

After reading Cotton a story, Lacy tucked him in snugly within the folds of his quilt. Giving him a swift kiss on the forehead, she blew out the lamp and left the boy to his night-time sweet dreams. Closing the door softly, she headed back into the kitchen and another visit with Liv.

Settling down at the table once more, elbow on the top, her chin resting in her hand, Lacy asked, "Where's Billy?"

Turning, Liv wiped her hands on her apron, gazing fondly at her newest boarder. At least until she and Rawley were married. It took a while for she and Rawley to convince Lacy to move out of the office, six weeks ago. The copperhead had fussed and fumed, but finally gathered a few belongings and now resided in Liv's other spare bedroom. "Somewhere, with Rawley, I think," she replied.

Chin still resting in her hand, Lacy's brow puckered in thought. Fingers began drumming on the top. "Oh..." she said. Abruptly she pushed herself back from the table, saying, "Well...I need to go make rounds. Thanks for supper, Liv."

Hearing the front door give its soft click, Liv exhaled loudly. "Lordy...I hope she doesn't figure out the new house going up here in town will soon be hers and Rawley's."

Everyone had been working in secret, around the clock, the last five, six weeks, trying to finish the house in time for their wedding day. Rawley wanted to hand Lacy the key for her wedding present from him and the whole town at the reception in Mike's place. Liv "pifftt" blondish-grey tendrils off her forehead. "Lordy...I sure hope she doesn't figure it out," she repeated to the dishwater as she resumed cleaning up after supper.

Sitting on Liv's steps, elbow on her knee, chin resting in her hand again, but with fingers drumming a light cadence against her cheek this time, Lacy thought *Something's going on.* Her eyes narrowed, drawing the freckles in closer. Her mouth puckered into a frown. *Something's going on,* her mind repeated. *But, what?*

Burnt coffee eyes gazed down the street, everything seemed normal. The town was shutting down for the night. Her eyes shifted to the new house going up about fifty yards away in a stand of oaks on the outskirts of town. She'd been watching the building going up over the last month or so. Lacy hadn't heard anything about who the new owners might be, or when they might be arriving in town. *Must be someone with money, to build a house before they get here,* she thought.

Her interest growing, she pushed herself up off the steps and strode toward the lighted house. As Lacy neared the new home, her nose picked up the sharp scent of fresh cut wood and her ears, the murmur of male voices coming through the spaces left for new windows. She tip-toed up the steps and quietly opened the door. Stepping inside, Lacy gazed around in wonder. "Oh...wow," she whispered.

In the dusky twilight, the floor littered with sawdust and shavings didn't detract from the warm inviting interior. Even though void of furniture, it made Lacy want to drag her rocker from her room in the office and place it by the huge granite fireplace and plop herself down.

Her eyes drifted to the staircase going to the second floor. She wondered what might be up there, but that was another day for her to explore before the new owners moved in. Seeing a door-less room to the right of the fireplace, Lacy headed in that direction. Stopping just inside the door, she gazed around the large room. Boots thumped their way to where double windows would look out the front of the house. She could see Liv's house from where she stood. Soft light spilled out of curtained windows in the twilight. Spinning, she walked to the opposite wall where another set of double windows would take in the prairie with the mountains for their backdrop as the view. Lacy sighed wistfully; she'd fallen in love with this house already. But she also knew it belonged to someone else. She gazed longingly at the purples, reds and golds of the setting sun behind the mountains one last time, then spinning on her toes, she headed toward the voices.

Arriving at what would eventually be the kitchen, Lacy stood quietly in the doorway. Mike, Ezra, Doc, Luke and Billy were there. Along with Rawley, who laid submerged under the sink attaching the plumbing.

Doc grumbled as he slid a wood shaver across a cabinet door, smoothing it. "I sure am glad I became a doctor instead of a craftsman. I'm gonna ache for months after..." he looked up and saw Lacy standing in the doorway.

Billy and Luke turned from hanging a cabinet over the counter at the abrupt silence. Luke's mouth dropped and Billy's eyes widened.

Noticing the quiet, Mike and Ezra both looked up. Lacy stood at the door. Mike edged closer to a long leg sticking out from under the sink. He kicked a boot, "Rawley..." he kicked the boot harder. "Rawley...git yore arse outta there."

"Mike...damn it...I'm busy!"

Doc spoke. "Son, ya need to do as Mike said."

"What the hell...for?" Half rising, he banged his head on the bottom of the cast iron sink. "Owww...damn it, you two..." Rawley growled. That's when he saw Lacy standing quietly in the doorway, her hands tucked in her britches' back pockets, carrying questions in those burnt coffee eyes. Two hands grabbed the outside of the cabinet above him, and he pulled himself out the rest of the way.

Slowly Rawley stood, stalling for time. Brushing his pants and shirt off, all the while racking his brain on how he was gonna cover his butt this time.

One could hear a pin drop, the silence was so thick.

Lacy just stood there, her eyes bouncing from one man to the other, picking up on the nervous tension in the room.

Five sets of eyes kept their focus on the tall lawman, avoiding Lacy's scrutiny, waiting on Rawley to say something.

Clearing his throat, Rawley asked, "Sunshine...what are you doing here?"

"What are you doing here?" She returned.

Stalling for more time, willing his brain to come up with a good excuse, he said, "Last I heerd, you wasn't 'sposed to answer a question with a question."

Pulling her hands out of back pockets, she folded her arms across the front of her shirt as she rolled her eyes. Lacy settled a black look on the six, the one that would make a skunk roll over and play dead. Everyone flinched except Rawley; he was used to receiving those black looks.

Flicking a glance at the five staring at him, Rawley sent them a mental message, *help me out here, boys.* They continued to just stare at him. He groaned inwardly. A voice interrupted his thoughts.

"Well..." prompted Lacy.

"Uh..." Rawley began. "The new owners wanted the house finished pronto...so...uh...we decided to help out," he finished lamely.

Lacy flicked dark eyes over the six, *They're lying,* she thought. "Really...now..." She watched six heads nod. Her brow puckered, drawing her mouth into a frown. Rolling her eyes, Lacy spun on her toes. She left the six with their silence, heading for the front door.

Hearing the door open and then close, the six let the breaths they'd been holding escape. Mike said, "Whew...that was close."

Rawley heaved in air, "Too...close," he agreed.

Doc harrumphed. "Son, she ain't no dummy. She's bound to figure it out pretty quick," he said.

Squatting, Rawley threw a look over his shoulder at the five faces who continued to stare at him. "Well...then...we'll just have to tell a few more little white lies," he said, crawling back under the sink.

Doc snorted. Wiping his salt and pepper mustache, he picked up some sandpaper and began sanding the cabinet door. The others went back to their previous tasks hopefully finishing the house in time for Lacy's wedding present.

CHAPTER FORTY SIX

Lacy seemed surrounded by women, all voicing their opinion. Telling her what was right and what was wrong. The proper way to 'stage' her up-coming wedding. She felt like a ricocheting bullet, spinning, hitting, pinging, bouncing back and forth within a circle of giggling, squawking women. All of them clucked at her, like a yard full of hens at feeding time. Lacy was going insane.

Slamming the door shut in her wake, Lacy angrily marched further into the office, stopping in front of the desk. Her dark expression scorched the air across the space zeroing in on her husband-to-be.

Blinking in surprise, Rawley watched as Lacy would alternately suck in wind, and then expel it just as hard while she aimed that deadly blistering look in his direction, and still, did not say a word. "I take it your last meeting didn't go so well," he said.

"Who do those women think they are?" Burnt coffee eyes sizzled as she waved her arms in all directions. "This is supposed to be my wedding! Not theirs. They're acting as if it was their own personal wedding they're planning. Not mine. Clucking around like hens, watching the new rooster strut into the yard, except in this case," she said, thumbing at herself. "I'm the new rooster!" Lacy finished, crossing arms with a jerk, her face registering her bad mood.

"Sunshine, you were the one who asked for help…"

"But I didn't expect the whole town to get involved," Lacy interrupted.

"The more...the merrier," he tossed out. Rawley received one, nasty glare for his comment. She said decisively. "No! It's off." She threw a snarl as she drew her finger across her throat in a cutting motion. "The whole thing is off."

Rawley's eyes grew round at her last gesture. "What...and ruin everyone's fun?" He teased.

"It ain't funny, Lovett!" Placing her hands on the edge of the desk, Lacy leaned into Rawley's face. Her dark eyes pleaded with his twinkling blue ones. "Let's just run away tonight and get married someplace else, forget all this nonsense. Please?"

Leaning back in the chair, prompting it to give its always present squeak, Rawley bit back the grin. "Seems to me you've got pre-wedding jitters," he said.

Straightening, she argued, "I do not!" Throwing her hands into the air, Lacy wailed, "Maybe I do. Ooh...I don't know!" Whirling, boots thumped across the floor toward the window. Lacy tucked her fingers into her back pockets as she stared at the street, taking calming breaths. After a few moments, she spun around, demanding answers. "How can you be so calm? Those nosy ole biddies are driving me nuts! I haven't been able to say one word about what I really want!"

Eyes still filled with mirth, Rawley asked, "Do you know what you really want?"

Lacy's mouth worked silently. Finally, shaking her head, she said, "No." She continued to stare at the floor. "But I do know I don't want the circus those ole biddies are planning!" Lacy replied adamantly.

"Tell ya what. Why don't you take Fancy for a ride, figure out what you really want, then...when's your next meeting?"

"Tomorrow night."

"Then, go to them, tell them how you feel." Rawley

thought, *Lacy expressing her feelings to a bunch of cackling women, now, that would be a miracle.* He added instead, "And then wait and see what they have to say, okay?"

Pinching a corner of her bottom lip between teeth, Lacy nodded.

"Sunshine, it'll be all right. Things have a way sometimes of working the kinks out all by themselves."

Heaving in air, she leaned toward him. Lacy planted a wet kiss on her husband-to-be, then grumbled, "You'd better be right, Lovett. You'd just better be right."

A big grin plastered Rawley's face, as he watched his bride-to-be slam out the door. Lacy could handle fugitives without the blink of an eye, but, planning her own wedding, was tying his redhead up in knots. Shaking his head, he smiled, *Nope. Life sure wasn't dull with Lacy around!*

CHAPTER FORTY SEVEN

With pins stuck in her mouth, Lydia Marshall slowly moved around the bride-to-be. Lacy had arrived for her final fitting of the dress before her wedding. Lydia noticed the redhead focused on the ceiling, alternately heaving in air then expelling it. "You okay?" She asked, while fingers tugged, placing a pin here and there around Lacy's slim torso for a tighter fit.

A stiff nod from Lacy was her reply. Burnt coffee eyes didn't recognize the person she viewed in the reflection of the full-length looking-glass staring back at her. Lydia had certainly outdone herself creating her wedding gown. A square necked bodice surrounded a slender neck with a million freckles. The bodice and three-quarter length sleeves were lavishly accented with lace ruffles and beaded fringes. Layers of lace and ruffles cascaded down the full silk skirt of the dress to the floor. Satiny ribbons crisscrossed the bodice in front, so that Lacy could tighten the material as she lost weight. This wedding had her insides snarled so tight, she couldn't eat. That barbed wire cut into the walls of her gut constantly, making her stomach hurt all the time. She exhaled another noisy sigh.

Lydia looked up again, hearing that. "You sure, you're okay? She asked once more. The redhead just nodded silently. Standing, Lydia moved behind her customer. Dove grey eyes narrowed as she looked at the over-all picture reflected in the looking glass. Those same eyes came to rest on the still raw red scar on Lacy's collarbone.

"Ummm..." she began. "If you want, I can add some lace-trimmed silk to the bodice, bring it closer to your neck, to hide...to ah...well, to cover that scar," Lydia offered.

Dark eyes found grey ones reflected back at her in the looking glass, holding the question. Lacy's fingers slowly rose and gently touched the rough skin that had healed over her wound. Memories suddenly invaded her mind. The night Lowell Taylor had tried to kill her, shooting her three times. Rawley's unconditional love for her, his gentle lovemaking leaving her begging for more. Her gaze refocused on the figure dressed in the beautiful white gown reflected in the looking-glass, witnessing something she never thought she would experience, love, marriage and a home.

Turning toward Lydia, Lacy dropped her hand. She finally answered, "No. It's a part of me, it's who I am." Seeing Lydia's skeptical look, she reassured the dress-maker. "It's okay...really. The dress is beautiful, and...and you are making..." a rosy hue began climbing from a white bodice sprinkled with lace and bead work, through tawny freckles to the roots of copper hair. Her hands began twisting in front of her waist. "You are making a dream I never thought I could have, become real," Lacy whispered shyly, explaining. "And...and I thank you for that." Abruptly realizing she'd twisted her hands into knots, she quickly hid them behind her back, as her eyes dove downward settling on dusty boots peeking from under a pristine white skirt.

Grey eyes softened as a slight smile peeked through. She and Lacy weren't the best of friends. But Lydia had come to respect the hard-nosed, and now nervous as a long-tailed cat in a room full of rocking chairs, deputy. Her smile deepened. "It doesn't matter anyway. You'll be the envy of all the women in this town, when you walk down the aisle," Lydia said.

Lacy heaved in more air for her starved lungs and gave that half-nod that was so characteristic of her.

CHAPTER FORTY EIGHT

Late to yet another one of those crazy meetings, this time though, Lacy was late on purpose. She knew now what she wanted for that special day between her and Rawley. Come hell or high water, Lacy was going to take back her wedding.

Taking a deep breath, she quickly exhaled as she pulled open the church doors. Closing them softly, Lacy leaned quietly against the wood, as she listened to all the cackling and laughter that had been driving her nuts.

Rolling burnt coffee eyes, her boot heels began their solid cadence against the planked floorboards. She walked down between the rows of pews. A week from now, the aisle she would soon be walking to become Rawley's wife. Stopping just below the pulpit, Lacy turned, her eyes drifting over all the expectant faces.

Shushing sounds began floating through the air, waiting on the bride-to-be, to speak.

Lacy's heart hammered in her chest, cutting into her meager air supply at the moment. Shaking herself mentally, she told herself to think of them as...*well, fugitives from the law..., no, I can't do* that...Taking another deep breath, Lacy jammed fingers into her back pockets, hiding her nervousness. *Hurry up...get this over with,* her mind said. She began, "Ladies, I want to thank you for all that you've done in planning this wedding. But, I won't need your help anymore. I'll be planning this wedding myself."

Loud gasps echoed around the room.

"By yourself? You don't know what you're doing!" Piped up one woman in the back.

Anger began sizzling within burnt coffee eyes. Her color rising, Lacy threw an ominous look toward the woman who'd just spoken. That woman began squirming on the hard bench, averting her eyes and then dropping her head. A blistering gaze settled across the rest of the women sitting in the church pews. Daring anyone else to speak up, she replied sharply, "Maybe not, but it's my wedding. And all of you cackling hens have just been turning it into a circus!"

Sitting quietly to the side, Olivia glanced at her hands folded in her lap. A smile peeked out.

Heaving in more air, she tried to tamp down the anger she knew could explode any minute. It didn't work. "I haven't had one piece of say in what is supposed to be the happiest day of my life!" She shouted. "I'm bounced around like a ball! No one has even bothered to ask me what I want!" Heaving in another batch of air, she continued in that husky voice lowered just a notch. "No, it ends now, you all are fired. Do you hear me? I said you're all fired!" One last venomous gaze danced over the women, and with that, Lacy marched out of the church.

Bedlam ensued. "She can't do that!" One said.

"We were just helping!" Another stated.

"Why that ungrateful little…"

Olivia stood, holding up her hands, palms down, patting the air, quieting the verbal onslaught.

"Ladies, ladies please. I know we were all so excited that Rawley is finally getting married. I was especially pleased and excited, that two of my favorite people had finally found love. I guess, I, along with the rest of you, just got a little too carried away."

"Lacy is right, we are turning this into a circus and we have not exactly included her in our plans. It is after all her wedding."

"But, we were just trying to help!"

"Maybe a little too much," Olivia offered, then continued. "Lacy is a very private and strong willed young woman. She has seen and experienced things that we, if had to live what she has gone through, wouldn't last two days. The fact that she asked for our help was a big step for her. Unfortunately, we got a little too excited and carried away. Taking the pleasure of planning something she always dreamed of, but never thought she could have, away from her. I think it would be best if we allow her the freedom to do her own planning, agreed?"

"But, Olivia, that girl has no graces, no culture, why she's libel show up at her own wedding in men's britches and toting that gun she always wears!"

Rapping the plank flooring sharply with the tip of her new blue parasol, Miz Birdy rose and spoke. "Olivia is right, ladies. Lacy may not be the picture of what we like to think of as culture. But, she is an intelligent young woman, doing what she had to do to survive and...and we are lucky that she is still alive and to have her as deputy in this town.

Smiling at Emma and Miz Birdy, Olivia answered. "I do believe you will be pleasantly surprised, ladies. Now, shall we retire to my house and have a cup of tea?"

"Do you have any of those wonderful cookies to go with that cup of tea? Emma asked.

Olivia smiled. "I think I can manage," she said.

*   *   *

Wandering around town for the past hour, Lacy tried to calm down. She figured from now on those women would ignore her for what she had just done. But, fiddlesticks, she wasn't close friends with them and didn't care to be, either.

Sitting on the edge of the water trough, she let her hand swirl in the cool water. She ought to run away, go back to her old way of life. But she didn't want to run any more, she wanted to stay. Basking in the warmth and security that Rawley's arms gave her, his strength, gave her strength. Even if his jabbering did grate on her nerves some days, she wanted to stay.

Lacy knew she wasn't good at dealing with town life; she'd been traveling the territories for too long, isolating herself from the world. In a small community, everyone knew your personal business. Gossip flowed like a river. It was more up to date than the weekly paper and traveled faster than the singing wires of the telegraph. What she didn't like were those smirky little grins, folks gave behind your back. But, this was her home now, standing beside Rawley.

Lacy had been keeping up appearances for Liv's sake, but only during the daylight hours. In the wee hours of the morning, she'd been sneaking out of her bedroom window at Liv's house. Sticking close to the town's dark shadows, she followed them to the office's back door. So she could still sleep in the big bed next to Rawley, even if only for a few hours. Whiffing up his masculine scent of fresh air, pine and store bought soap, sharing the love they felt for each other. Lacy sighed heavily once again. She was going to have to go through with this wedding even if it killed her, because she loved the big galoot. Swirling her hand in the cool water once more, Lacy finally stood, and wiped the wet hand down her britches. She had to 'face the music' as the old saying went. Inhaling deeply again, she trudged toward the office, to tell Rawley what she'd said to the cackling hens.

Rawley had been waiting on Lacy to say something ever since she had walked through the door. She kept averting her gaze from his piercing blue eyes. Cocking an eyebrow, he leaned back in his chair. It squeaked as he laced fingers together across his flat stomach. "Well?" He asked finally.

A copper head swiveled. She angrily returned, "Well… what?" Just thinking about those old hens pissed her off.

"Did you tell them?"

"Yes, I told them."

"And?"
"And...I fired them!"
"You...Did...What?"
"I fired them!"
"You can't fire them! They volunteered!"
Lacy shot a blistering look toward Rawley, her face flushing with anger. "Yeah...well, I fired them anyway!" Giving him another dirty look, she spun on her toes, hurrying down the hallway, opening and then slamming the door to her quarters.

Rawley's brows shot to the ceiling, then a grin busted out.

A few moments later, the door reopened. Realizing she didn't live there, anymore, Lacy marched across the office floor. Opening the front door, she stormed out, slamming it and making the window rattle.

He sighed noisily at the window rattling as he rose, the chair squeaking again. Boot heels thumped across the planked flooring. Pulling his hat off the peg, he jammed it on his head. Rawley walked out the door, in search of Doc; he needed a drink. Long strides headed him toward Mike's place. Rolling his eyes toward the stars above, he thought, *Well...maybe more than one drink.*

* * *

The window slid up quietly and easily, from the wheel grease she'd put in the tracks. Even though she knew they had her best interest at heart, Lacy still mumbled and grumbled at what Liv had said. 'It's not proper for you to be living in the marshal's office now, with your upcoming wedding.' She made a face remembering Liv's words, mumbling in a sing-songy cadence, under her breath. "Nah...nah...nah-nah...nah."

But, she still escaped from her bedroom in Liv's house several times a week to visit Rawley in the dark of the night. One leg stuck itself over the window sill, followed by the other. She hopped down. *Hang...what all those old biddies would have to say...* Lacy thought as she maneuvered through the darkness, toward the back door of the marshal's office.

The latch clicked softly, waking Rawley. He focused through the darkness as the slight shadow moved quietly toward him. He waited.

Bed springs creaked as she crawled onto the bed, giving him a quick peck on the lips. His nose whiffed up Lacy's light lavender scent when she moved to sit on the edge of the bed. He heard one boot thump to the floor and then the other. Bed springs creaked again as she stood. Slight rustling sounds came as she removed her clothes. Throwing the covers back Lacy slid her naked body in, close to his.

"Sunshine...you're impossible," he whispered.

Taking a finger, she traced his strong jaw line. "I know...that's why you're marrying me," she teased, as a hand slid south under the covers.

White teeth flashed in the darkness. He pushed Lacy into the bedclothes. His mouth and hands became busy as Lacy sighed happily.

CHAPTER FORTY NINE

Finally her wedding day had arrived. She was supposed to be happy, right? *Wrong.* That snarling bit of barbed wire had returned. Lacy tried to swallow what seemed to be a permanent piece of cotton, which seemed to have swollen and closed her throat.

Her tongue worked inside her mouth, trying to dredge up some moisture as she traveled the distance from Liv's house to the marshal's office. It didn't work. She pushed open the door and walked into the office. Facing the man who would be her husband in a few hours, Lacy's words came out as sandpaper gargle. "I can't do this Lovett. It's too, too..." her voice trailed off into the air.

Surprised at Lacy's comment, Rawley gazed at his bride-to-be; she looked like death warmed over. "It's too what?"

"It's too permanent," Lacy whispered. "It makes me want to..."

"Want to what?"

"To run that's what!"

The chair squeaked as Rawley came to his feet. He studied his redhead. *She sneaks around in the middle of the night like a fugitive, coming into my bed so we can make love...then tells me she can't marry me because it's too, permanent?* He blinked as his mind tried to wrap itself around that revelation. Scratching his head, Rawley said, "Sunshine, I thought this is what you wanted?"

"I do, did, but now, I don't know."

The girl was having the worst case of wedding jitters he'd ever seen. "Lacy, I love you. I thought you loved me too?"

"I did, do, oh, I don't know."

Smiling, Rawley took the little redhead in his arms. Holding her, while he kissed that flaming mop, he said, "Honey, it'll be all right. You've faced worst and survived, you'll survive this too. It'll all be over in a few hours."

Lacy just looked at him like he had the plague or something.

"Go on back to Liv's, have her give you some of that soothing tea she has. I'll see you in a couple of hours," he said, pushing her out the door.

Lacy didn't like being the center of attention, Rawley knew. She still wasn't comfortable in social situations, even after being in this town for a year, now. Here the last couple of weeks, she had been the main attraction. Most women would have fawned over all that attention. His redhead cringed instead, making her feel like running again.

Lacy was comfortable chasing fugitives, being a peace officer. Wearing britches with that Colt tucked securely under her left arm. Outside of that comfort zone, she felt her life out of control and in chaos. Rawley did what he could to calm those fears; sometimes it worked, most often it did not.

If truth be told, he was kind of surprised that she hadn't taken off already, *still a couple of hours to go,* he thought, glancing at the clock. Lacy might still take it into her head to run, anyhow. He crossed his fingers, his toes and his eyes, *Here's hoping she stays put long enough for me to slid a ring on her finger,* he thought, then added, *Maybe I ought to put it through her nose, instead.* Rawley chuckled. Lacy would really swat him clear across Wyoming then, if he did that. He dropped that thought rather quickly, but the grin remained.

* * *

Forcing a glass of brandy down Lacy's throat, Liv stepped back and observed the redhead. The girl was wound so tight, she was afraid she'd snap. Most brides, Olivia had known, were happy, giddy on their special day. Lacy acted like she was going to the gallows, to be hung.

Liv worked the copper tresses into the latest fashion from back east that Lydia had shown her to use for the bride. "Honey, you couldn't be marrying a better man, he truly loves you."

"I know that," Lacy mumbled into her arms. "But I'm losing my freedom, I can't just take off now, do what I want. I feel like I have to ask his permission, I didn't have to before."

"Is that what this is all about?"

Raising a face wet with tears, Lacy nodded.

Quickly, Liv pulled a chair closer to Lacy, sitting down. Tenderly, her hands encased a freckled face. Thumbs caressed the tears spilling from burnt coffee eyes. "Oh, honey. That's what Rawley loves about you. Your independence, your free spirit. He may not agree with you, but, he'd never keep you from doing what you might want to do."

She sniffled. "You mean that?" Lacy's palms swiped at the wetness on her face.

Smiling, Liv's finger wiped a tear dripping from Lacy's chin. "Yes. Yes I do. Now let's finish getting you ready for your wedding," she said, standing and pushing the chair back out of the way.

Swallowing down that wad of cotton in her throat, Lacy abruptly pushed herself away from the dressing table.

"Miss Liv, I've forgotten something back at the office I want to have," Lacy lied, picking up the full skirts of her wedding gown and moving quickly toward the front door.

"Lacy? I can send Billy for it. What is it?"

"No. I...I've got it hidden, I'll be back in a jiffy," Lacy lied again scurrying out the door, lifting skirts higher, and picking up her pace, running.

Standing at the edge of her porch, Liv watched the girl

run back toward the marshal's office. Her brow puckered and her eyes narrowed, marking her pretty features. Liv knew something remained afoot, but she was not sure at that moment what it could be.

Lacy slid in the office door, closing it softly behind her, and leaned against it to catch her breath. Her heart crashed against her insides, feeling like a buffalo stampede thundering across her ribs.

Burrowing her face in her hands, Lacy's mind tumbled over itself. *I should be happy! I have someone who loves me more than I deserve. Yet, I don't have the courage to marry him.* A loud groan escaped her lips. *I'm not normal!*

Letting her hands fall, Lacy stared up at the ceiling. *I can't get married in a church, I don't believe in God.* She made this excuse to herself.

Suddenly, Lacy seemed to understand her turbulent emotions. *I'm afraid...afraid of letting my heart open, allowing love in, to stay and take root and grow.*

Everything became so gosh darn permanent when one got married. So, damn permanent. Her confused brain rattled on. *I've never had anything permanent in my life, and now I'm being given that chance, to have something permanent. And, oh...hell! I'm still losing my freedom, no matter what Liv said.* Her mind argued with her heart, creating further turmoil.

Her emotional train of thought continued. *What if I find out I married the wrong man? What if? Oh...there's way too many ifs! I'm too scared to trust a man I've fallen in love with, who loves me, freckles, temper and well...everything!*

Lacy groaned out loud, again. She had gotten herself into a real pickle this time, admitting to Rawley that she loved him. *Well...I do, I'm just, too, chicken to marry him...is all.* Her heart continued to do battle with her brain. Her brain won.

Pushing away from the door, Lacy hurried to her quarters. Changing clothes quickly, she stuffed her saddlebags. Wrapping the Colt around her waist, she gathered up her gear. Coming out of the room, her boot heels thumped toward the front of the office. Peeking out the window, she noted, that the street remained empty. Everyone was at the church waiting on the bride to make her entrance. *They'll have a long wait,* Lacy told herself. *Hopefully I'll be a long way from here, before they figure it out.*

Sneaking out the door, Lacy ran to the stable, gear and saddlebags banging against her legs, slowing her pace.

Quickly saddling Fancy, Lacy vaulted easily into the seat and headed off in a different direction this time. Knowing that it would throw Rawley off some, though not for long with his Indian blood and tracking skills. He would eventually find her. Maybe by then, she would have calmed down, got some sense into her stupid, confused brain. But Rawley wouldn't have, he'd be madder than a wet hen. Lacy was already dreading that confrontation when he finally caught up with her.

Urging Fancy faster, Lacy wanted to put as much distance as she could between herself and the man she loved, but still thought she didn't deserve.

* * *

Striding briskly toward the marshal's office, Liv thought, *Lacy's been gone just a tad too long for me to be comfortable.* That niggling feeling Liv had in the back of her mind continued growing.

Opening the door, she called out, "Lacy?"

Hurrying down to Lacy's old room, Liv knew when she saw the wedding gown lying on the bed. She groaned and whispered to the ceiling, "Lacy, Lacy...what in the world are we going to do with you?"

Spinning, Liv scurried out the door. As she reached the street, she picked up her skirts, running as fast as she could toward the church.

Mike seeing Liv's face as she quickly took the steps, asked, "Liv? What's going on? Where's the bride?"

Liv flew past him, through the open doorway, and continued running down the aisle toward Rawley.

Stopping as she grabbed two muscular arms, Liv heaved in a breath. "She's gone Rawley! Lacy is gone!"

When he saw Liv running toward him, his heart dropped into his boots. The way Lacy acted this morning he'd had a gut feeling that if she showed up at her own wedding it would be a miracle.

Taking Liv in a calming hug, Rawley assured her, "It's okay Liv, I'll find her." Pushing Liv away from him, his eyes studied her turbulent grey ones. He asked, "Do you know which way she went?"

Liv shook her head no, saying, "She just said she had to get something from the office. Oh...I should have known not to let her go!"

"It's okay, Liv," he reassured her. And then he voiced his own thoughts, "I figured from the way she was acting this morning, it would be a miracle if she showed up at her own wedding," Rawley said.

Voices murmured from the folks in the pews hearing the news.

Her hands wringing in front of her, Liv watched Rawley head back down the aisle in his nice new grey suit.

Pushing himself through the throng of surprised attendees, now crowding into the center of the church's aisle, Rawley stopped by Mike.

"Guess, I'll be gone for a while, Mike. Take these folks over to your place, don't let all that good food go to waste," he said, hurriedly skipping down the steps.

"Hey, Rawley?"

The marshal stopped and turned.

"Think you can get her to change her mind?"

Raising arms, palms up, Rawley replied, "Don't know, Mike."

CHAPTER FIFTY

Quickly picking up Lacy's trail out back of the stable, Rawley knew she was trying to be slick, thinking she'd thrown him off her course. The little redhead couldn't be that far ahead of him.

Rawley was mad, just plain spitting mad. He had finally lost patience with the girl. He was insane to have fallen in love with the fire-breathing, gun-toting freckled venom-striking copperhead in the first place, but it had happened. He'd chased after her once before; last Christmas, bringing her back down the mountain. He should have learned his lesson then, but here he was chasing her down again. Rawley groaned inwardly. He loved her and he was gonna marry her come hell or high water, whichever came first. *Probably hell,* he thought dryly.

They would have been married by now. Enjoying Maddie's meal, dancing, laughing, kissing. Giving her the key to the home she never thought she would have. Carrying Lacy over the threshold of her new house and later making love for the first time as man and wife.

What was he doing instead? Chasing her down. He was insane; that's all there was to it. He was insane. Right now he felt as nutty as Maddie's fruit cake!

* * *

Stopping an hour later to let his mount breathe, Rawley

still had Fancy's trail in site. The damn girl was heading northeast, probably into Montana. Wiping his brow with the sleeve of his shirt, he resettled his hat more firmly on his head.

"Hup, son," he said, guiding the bay forward once again after the woman who was supposed to be his wife, by now.

Easing his horse down a scree embankment, Rawley continued to follow the deep marks Fancy had left. Pulling up on the reins when they reached flat ground, he glanced down, noticing the trail going in a more northerly direction now. Looking up, Rawley nudged the bay into a lazy canter.

* * *

Lacy knew Rawley was not far behind her, she felt it in her bones. That's why she took refuge behind some boulders, Fancy remaining behind her. Hopefully, the big grey would keep her mouth shut for once, so Rawley couldn't pin-point her location. But she also realized it was hopeless, trying to hide from Rawley. That man had tracking skills that would put most Indians to shame. And he was half-Indian, doubling the threat. Lacy exhaled noisily. Fancy blew, shaking her head, making the bit jangle. Her head swiveled; Lacy shushed the horse.

Peeking over the rim of the rock, Lacy saw the lone rider coming her way. Sliding back down, she groaned, he'd found her quicker then she thought he would. Flipping up the site, she rose again. If nothing else, maybe firing a few rounds would give him the message. Lacy aimed for his hat. Holding her breath, she squeezed the trigger. *Kaaboomm!* She disappeared behind the boulder. Quickly reloading, she rose, laying the rifle on the rock, and fired at the bay's feet. *Kaaboomm!* A puff of dust rose in front of the bay, making him rear.

The first shot took Rawley's hat off, catching him by surprise. Keeping his seat, when his horse reared, he squinted into the setting sun as they followed the sound and found the rifle barrel blinking in the early evening sun's rays.

He roared, "Damn it, Lacy! Put that thing away!"

"Don't come any closer, Lovett. I don't want to hurt you." A voice announced from the rocks.

"Damn it, Lacy! What the hell's gotten into you, running like that!"

The rifle barrel slid out of sight, making Rawley hop off quickly, taking cover. No telling what the girl would do with that damn thunder pipe.

Resting her head and back against the boulder, her eyes closed. She tried to stay calm. It didn't work. Her heart just kept a stampeding against her ribs. Heaving in more air, she rose slowly, edging back over the stone rim. Lacy didn't see Rawley. *Damn it,* she thought, *he's probably coming 'round back of me.*

She yelled down, "I can't do this, Rawley!"

A deep baritone answered. "Can't do what, Sunshine?"

Okay, he ain't coming up behind me.

"I can't marry you," she said, sending the words over the space.

"Why?"

"I...I just can't."

Squatting against rock cover, Rawley rubbed his forehead and sighed. It wouldn't do any good to argue with her, that head of hers was as hard as those boulders she hid behind.

Rising, he walked over, picking up his hat. He glanced briefly at the hole gracing the crown, then jammed it on his head. Taking the reins of the bay, his foot stepped into the stirrup. Leather creaked as Rawley slipped easily back into the saddle.

He yelled up at the rifle still glinting in the sun. "Alright, Sunshine, have it your way. Maybe one of these days we'll meet again," Rawley said, and then added. "I hope you have a good life." He turned the bay toward home.

Peeking over the rock, her mouth dropped at what Rawley just said, and then seeing him begin to ride away, made her drop that thunder pipe. The rifle clattered against the rock. "Lovett? Wait!"

FRECKLED VENOM
COPPERHEAD STRIKES

Sliding down the loose scree, plumes of dust following her, she landed on her butt. Lacy scrambled up, running after him. Catching up to him, her hand grabbed his pants leg, stopping him.

Blue eyes held a hint of merriment in them as he gazed at Lacy. Tears had left wet streaks on freckled cheeks. Flowers a little a-skewed, were still in her hair for their special day.

"Lovett, I'm sorry. I didn't mean what I said."

"You didn't? Sure could have fooled me, taking those pot shots at me like you did."

"I just...I didn't want to hurt you, just make you listen."

His temper rose, he angrily demanded, "Listen...to what?"

Burnt coffee eyes dropped. Focusing on his dusty stirrup and boot, she remained silent.

Angry eyes tapered at her wordless reply. "Well, Sunshine, it's too late now, I've had enough. You go your way and I'll go mine," he said, touching the brim of his hat with two fingers. "I hope you find what you're looking for, one of these days, Sunshine." Tapping the bay's ribs, he set off at a trot.

Lacy's mouth fell a mile.

"But, Lovett!" She cried, running a short distance. "I did find what I was looking for! Lovett? You hear me? I love you!"

His anger dissipating as quickly as it had rose, Rawley tried to keep the grin off his face, and to keep from turning the bay around, jumping off and taking Lacy in his arms. He kept riding. He'd give her a few more minutes.

Lacy couldn't believe it. The man she loved was riding out of her life, for good. Turning her back on the solitary rider, her hand touched trembling lips. Rawley always kissed her so tenderly, leaving her begging for more. And the way he made love to her, erasing old memories, beginning new ones.

Turning, her eyes filled with tears once again as she watched the distance between them grow. Lacy collapsed in the dirt. Holding her stomach, she bent over, crying silent sobs. The last year, flashing though her brain, made her realize what a fool she had been, and that just made her cry harder.

About fifty feet out, Rawley reined up the bay. Leather creaked as he turned in the saddle. One hand resting on the cantle, he looked over his shoulder. The lone figure sitting huddled in the dirt tore at his heart.

Reining the bay around, he slowly walked the horse back. Pulling up fifteen feet from his feisty copperhead, he sat observing her from the back of the bay. The silent sobs, racking her small shoulders, made his gut twist.

Leather creaked as Rawley slid out of the saddle. Ambling over to Lacy, he squatted in front of her. Placing his palms on her arms, he squeezed gently, making her look up at him. Pulling the bandana out of his back pocket, he gently wiped the tears running in rivets down those cute freckled cheeks.

"Here now, blow your nose," he said softly.

Lacy did; then handed the snotty bandana back to him, hiccupping and still sniffling.

Rawley grinned. "Now, you wanna tell me what this was all about?"

Taking a finger, Lacy began drawing in the dirt. She finally nodded.

Watching that finger trace designs in the dirt reminded Rawley of the first night they spent together on the mountain beginning the chase for the Dillard Brothers after finding the bodies of Cotton's family. Lacy always did that, when she was trying to unglue her tongue from the roof of her mouth. He waited.

"I can't get married in a church. I don't believe in God," Lacy finally offered up.

Taking a finger, placing it under her chin, Rawley made her look at him. He asked, "Is that the only reason?"

Eyes searching his, Lacy swallowed that wad of cotton in her throat and eventually she answered him. "No." Dark eyes darted away from his penetrating gaze. They squinted at the dusty rock strewn landscape. "It's because...because I'm...I'm afraid, and...and I don't deserve someone as good as you."

"I know you're afraid, Sunshine," he said softly. "I figured that out a long time ago."

"You did?"

"Uh-huh," he said. Rawley tilted his head, and watched the waves of insecurity still flit across her eyes.

Heaving in a huge breath, she began, "I'm afraid...afraid that I can't love you as deeply as you love me. And, and that I won't be able to open my heart big enough to allow love to take root and grow and, and...," averting her eyes. Lacy added softly, "I don't know if I can do that."

"Sunshine, you've already done that, and I know that you love me as deeply as I love you."

Thoughts flickered through her eyes. "You do? How?"

"I just do."

"But, why...why did you just leave me like you did?"

"You needed to be taught a lesson."

A bright flush began climbing, covering a million freckles. Her mouth opened ready to fling a retort.

Seeing that, Rawley wagged a finger in her face. "At, ah, Sunshine...don't you dare." Lacy's mouth snapped shut. "I figured I'd give you a dose of your own medicine. Make you realize how much you really did love me, finally...placing all your trust in me. You don't have to be afraid anymore; I still love you and still want to marry you. Though, only heaven knows why, after this last little escapade of yours."

The blush grew deeper as silence followed.

"What? No sharp comment? No argument?" He teased.

Finger tracing in the dirt again, a head said no.

Sighing, he asked, "Okay, so you don't want to be married in the church. Where do you want to be married?"

A shrug was her answer.

Rolling his eyes, then closing them, Rawley rubbed his

forehead with the heel of his hand. He proceeded again. "Alright, you wanna get married at Miss Liv's?"

No said the head.

Rawley thought they had made it past the one-sided conversation phase, *guess not.*

"Mike's place? The office? How 'bout the middle of the street?"

Lacy's head popped up.

Well, that got a response.

"Sunshine, you gotta help me out here. I'm pretty good at reading your mind, but, I've 'bout run out of ideas." Rawley was running out of patience here and mighty quickly, too. He wanted to get back to town, and get that ring on her finger before she decided to pull any more cockamamie stunts.

"How 'bout the river?"

Nothing but more silence greeted him.

Rawley sighed noisily.

"The downed trees," a small voice said.

"What?"

"The downed trees," the voice said, a little stronger now.

"Where I first made love to you?" Rawley asked. His mind tried to wrap itself around that thought.

Another silent nod.

"It'd mean that much to you?"

Lacy nodded.

"Well, it's gonna be dark soon, we'll have to do it tomorrow."

"No," a small freckled hand reached out and lightly touched his arm. "It would be real pretty with torches lit."

Rawley suddenly understood why Lacy had said the downed trees. It was where she had begun to live and love again, allowing him to make love to her there. Now she wanted to be married in that very special place to her, to both of them.

"Well, if you want to get married tonight, we had better get going," he said as he reached down pulling her up.

FRECKLED VENOM
COPPERHEAD STRIKES

Lacy went into his arms willingly, allowing his kisses to wash over her. Her knees buckled; she locked them into place. Finally, stepping back, she spoke softly, tears beginning to glimmer again. "I'm going home, Rawley. I'm finally going home."

He smiled.

CHAPTER FIFTY ONE

Billy remained on lookout. Finally, spying the pair riding back into town, holding hands, he thought, 'Bout *time*.

"Hey everybody! They're back!" He yelled over the swinging doors, quickly stepping out of the way, lest he be trampled from the onslaught.

Lacy stiffened, seeing what seemed to be the whole town streaming out of Stewart's Saloon. Rawley continued to hold her hand tight, squeezing gently, reassuring her. He looked over and smiled at his redhead. Lacy shyly allowed those dimples to peek through.

Both riders reined in, as the crowd surrounded their horses. Still holding tight to Lacy's hand, so she couldn't escape, Rawley made an announcement. "Folks, seems there is a little change in plans."

The crowd groaned.

"No, nuthin' like that, the wedding will be held at the downed trees."

Glancing at Lacy, he held her gaze. "It's where I proposed to Lacy and she accepted, so that's where the wedding will be. In one hour. Luke, get as many torches together as you can. Mike, is there any food left?"

"Plenty!"

"Aw right. Doc, think you can get the Reverend out there?"

Doc harrumphed.

Rawley grinned at Doc's grumpy reply. "Thanks. Everything else will be as planned, that suit everybody?"

Mummers of agreement went through the crowd.

"Thanks everyone, see you all in an hour."

Liv stood next to Lacy's leg. She touched it lightly, saying, "Honey, you okay?"

Looking down at her old schoolteacher, now her best friend, Lacy replied, "Yes, m'am."

"Well, get down then. Let's get you ready for this wedding!"

* * *

Liv fussed with Lacy's gown one last time.

Holding onto Billy's arm, Lacy's fingers bit into his skin through the new coat and shirt he wore. She relaxed her fingers; Billy grinned at her. She shyly smiled back, allowing two dimples to blossom in her face. Lacy had no reason to be afraid any longer.

Billy agreed to give her away, if he could begin calling her mom.

Mike gave Lacy a quick peck on the cheek. "You're beautiful, Missy."

Billy and Lacy slowly advanced into the circle of light the torches were casting. Folks littered the ground, while some stood or sat on the downed trees, waiting for that special moment to arrive.

Her gaze traveled over the towns' folk. She saw Madeline Campbell, with a pretty new hat sitting on her frizzy brown curls. Her smile was as wide as her cherubic face; Lydia Marshall, approval showing in her dove grey eyes and Cody Brown, dressed to the nines due to Lydia; Luke Castleberry, as rumpled as ever in his brown suit, but, with pride written all over his face; Miz Birdy Dawson, wearing an attractive sage-colored dress ensemble; Luis and Maria Garcia; Ezra Shemwell, his nicely cut coat hiding his colorful sleeve garters for today; And Doc. Yes, crusty old Doc. He didn't look so frumpy, tonight. *Liv must've had something to do with that,* Lacy thought. Even from that distance she could see the moisture rise in the hazel eyes of the grumpy old coot. Then, her eyes came to rest on Rawley. Her steps hesitated. Tears spiked the back of her lids. The handsome man, who loved her so much in spite of everything, and little Cotton, standing so proudly next to the big tall lawman, in his brand new suit, made Lacy want to bawl all over again.

Tears coursing down her cheeks had Lacy stopping as palms quickly swiped at them. Liv handed her a handkerchief, to finish drying the tears, happy tears, finally.

When Lacy stepped into the firelight, Rawley's heart stopped. His eyes went soft, at her tears glistening in the glow of the torches. The little copperhead, he had found on the river bank, had turned into a beautiful woman. In spite of what had happened earlier today, he thought, *She's come full circle. Lacy had finally come home.*

It all proceeded very quickly then. Proudly, Billy stating, "I, give this woman."; Rawley squatting as Cotton's pudgy little fingers placed the ring in a big palm; Rawley sliding the band of gold on Lacy's finger.

He watched as more tears slid out of Lacy's eyes. His thumbs, brushed them away as he gave her their first kiss as man and wife.

Rawley picked up Cotton, while Billy came to stand next to Lacy as the Reverend announced, "Mr. and Mrs. Rawley Lovett and family."

*   *   *

The noise in Stewart's Saloon seemed to be maintained at a low roar. Mike had gotten the White River String Dusters to provide the music. The sounds co-mingled with the burble of voices and laughter that would occasionally bust out above the din. Ezra had passed out cigars. Their pleasant perfume mixed with the scent of roasted meat and onions, along with the faint sweet smell of good rye and iced down champagne. Cigar smoke swirled in pockets of fog above heads, then floated up, where it rested, hanging half-way to the ceiling. The hole Lacy put there about a year ago, still very much in evidence, adding ambiance to Mike's business as he liked to say.

The tables had all been pushed back against the walls, creating a dance floor in the middle of the saloon. Abruptly the floor cleared. Hands began banging on tables and boots thumping the floorboards, along with silverware tapping glasses resulting in a high-pitched pinging sound. Voices urged Rawley to take his bride in his arms and make that first spin around the floor as husband and wife. The White River String Dusters softly began to play the waltz Lacy and Rawley had danced to during the Fourth of July dance.

Turning toward his wife, Rawley asked softly, "Mrs. Lovett, may I have this dance?"

Closing her eyes, Lacy allowed that warm, smooth caramel baritone to wash over her. Tears began burning her lids, again. Dark eyes opened as she gave that wordless half-nod that was so characteristic of her.

He smiled catching a glimpse of tears from those burnt coffee eyes he'd grown to love. Taking her hand he brushed a kiss across it. Lacy's stomach plummeted to the soles of her new shoes. Rawley pulled her up and led her to the center of the saloon floor. Cheers erupted, but having eyes and ears for only each other, the two in the middle of the floor didn't hear a thing.

Cotton slid off the chair, where he'd been sitting with Liv and Doc. Reaching the couple, his hand stretched out and tugged on Rawley's coat. The pair stopped and looked down at the little towhead. His arms reached up. The couple smiled. Rawley swung the towhead into his arms, creating a threesome. That seemed to signal to others as the middle of the saloon soon filled with couples dancing.

Sitting later, at their table, Rawley nuzzled Lacy's ear. Her stomach flipped at his touch. "You happy, Mrs. Lovett?" Gazing back into smiling summer sky eyes, she whispered, "Yes, Mr. Lovett, very happy." And her lips brushed his. Abruptly, Lacy leaned back as her hand squeezed his arm, her fingers pinching through the cloth.

"What is it, Sunshine?"

"I...I need to tell you something," she whispered.

Rawley waited. Lacy still had trouble expressing her emotions.

Her eyes spoke volumes, though, exposing her feelings. She began, "Thank you...for...for giving me a second chance to learn how to...to live, and...and love again," she whispered. Tears glistened once more, melting those chocolate eyes.

Rawley's own eyes softened at her tears. "Sunshine I'm glad, too," he said, kissing her thoroughly. His wife didn't pull away from him. In fact, Lacy allowed her lips to linger on his. *We're making progress...*came the sing-songy cadence in his head.

Later sitting next to Liv, Rawley gazed in wonder as Lacy took the floor, dancing with each of the men in her life. Luis, Mike, Ezra, Luke, Billy, Doc and Cotton. He watched as she'd throw her head back in laughter at what one, or the other, said to her.

Liv gazed fondly at the man seated next to her, who seemed mesmerized by the redhead in the middle of the room. Speaking softly, Liv said, "She's beautiful, isn't she?"

The voice jerked Rawley out of his stupor. Tilting his head, he looked at Liv and smiled. "Yes."

"Do you remember what I told you when the two of you came back to town after capturing the Dillard brothers...Let's see...about a year ago?" Liv asked, grey eyes searching Rawley's face.

Black brows furrowed, pulling a frown. "No," he replied.

FRECKLED VENOM
COPPERHEAD STRIKES

"I said, that if there was anyone who could give us back the real Lacy, it would be you. Remember, now?"

"Yeah," he said, smiling.

Laying a gentle touch on his arm, Liv said, "You did."

Rawley laid a big palm over Liv's small one and gave it a squeeze.

* * *

Sighing happily, Luke straightened. He'd finished attaching the board which said *Just Married* to the back of Doc's buggy. Fancy waited impatiently, ready to pull the rig to Rawley and Lacy's new home. Billy and Angela had attached the wires holding strings of horseshoes to the back of the buggy.

Gazing around, Luke's brown eyes took in the new morning sun rising, blessing the landscape with its glow. A light grey fog shrouded the prairie; golden rays poked themselves through the mist giving it a shimmering quality.

Luke's mind retrieved the memories of when that copperhead had landed in this towns' lap, turning it on its ear. He grinned remembering Rawley's constant exasperation with the little fireball. The kid had a mind of her own, and a temper to match. Turning, Luke headed back into the saloon. His grin grew wider as he peeked over the bat-winged doors when his gaze rested on the couple. Rawley had finally managed to lasso his copperhead. White River would remain well protected with that freckled venom-packed redhead and the commanding presence of Rawley Lovett. *Anyone thinking they could come into town and create a roocus, had better think again,* Luke thought, dryly. He pushed open the doors, and walked over to the bar. He whispered something into the barkeep's ear. Mike nodded, and then he banged on the bar for quiet.

"Folks? Folks, let me have your attention, now," Mike bellowed. The White River String Dusters instruments gave one last twang and fell silent as did the crowd of attendees. One could hear a pin drop; the silence was overwhelming after the dull roar that had previously filled the room. Lacy's ears pricked up at the abrupt silence; she glanced around, wondering what was going on.

Reaching under his bar, Mike picked up the small box, tied with a colorful ribbon. Stepping around the counter, he came to stand in front of the dark scarred bar. Clearing his throat, he said, "Uh...Rawley and Lacy would you please come up here?"

Furrowing those red-gold eyebrows at her husband, Lacy threw a questioning look in his direction. Rawley just grinned. Taking her hand, he pulled her up and along behind him toward Mike. The barkeep handed the small box to Rawley.

Giving the box to his wife to open, he stepped back a pace to watch her expression. Confusion puckered up a freckled face. Lacy gestured with the box asking, "What's this?"

Shoving his hands deep into his trouser pockets, the anticipation was killing him. Rawley rocked back and forth on the balls of his feet. "Open it," he said.

Giving him a squirrely look, Lacy slipped the ribbon off the box, and removed the top. Inside, a key lay nestled in blue velvet. "A key? A key to what?" She asked, mystified.

His toothy grin spreading from ear to ear, Mike said, "Well now, you don't think we'd let the marshal and his deputy set up housekeeping in that ole jail, do ya?"

One could still have heard a pin drop; everyone seemed to be holding their breath, waiting on the secret to be revealed.

Burnt coffee eyes bounced from Mike to Rawley. Her heart began pounding a rapid tattoo against her ribs. "What did you do?" She softly asked the man standing in front of her. His smile as wide as his shoulders, he seemed to be wiggling like a new puppy in anticipation of a juicy bone.

She asked again, "What did you do?"

"Well..." Rawley began. One hand pulled itself out of his trouser's pocket while he said, "It wasn't only me,

Sunshine." One long arm gestured, sweeping in a wide arc, encompassing all the folks in the room. "It was all of us, the whole town. We...uh...all came together to build you the home you thought you could never have." That one hand jammed itself back into his trouser pocket, to keep from taking Lacy in his arms. He began rocking back and forth again on the balls of his feet. Rawley waited.

If silence could echo, it would have echoed loudly off the interior walls of Stewart's Saloon. Her mouth dropped in a very un-lady-like bride expression. Lacy's gaze drifted around the room, resting on the familiar faces, she'd grown to know and love. Abruptly, her mouth snapped shut, realizing that like Rawley, who loved her unconditionally, these folks did, too. Her past didn't matter to them. *They have accepted me, warts and all,* Lacy thought. Tears rose in dark eyes; she dropped her gaze. Wet splotches landed on the blue velvet, marking it. Her nose began to run; a freckled hand brushed her nose and then wiped at the tears cascading down her cheeks. Lacy's head rose. She spoke so softly, they could barely hear her words. "Thank you...I can never thank you...all of you, enough."

Luke piped up from the back.

Looking around, Lacy finally found him, leaning against a wall.

"No need to thank us...hit was our pleasure. But, jus' in case I decide to tie on a twister...you haul me to my bed...and not to jail, ya understand?" Luke said.

Laughter lightly twittered through the crowd.

Two dimples blossomed amongst a million freckles and tears; Lacy nodded.

That seemed to break the quiet mood that had penetrated the saloon. Whistles competed with boot heels hammering against the planked floor. Hands clapped, and silverware tapped glasses. Voices rose in chatter again. The White River String Dusters began playing *Turkey in the Straw*. Folks began crowding the floor once again, sending vibrations through the floorboards from shoes and boots pounding out a rhythmic cadence.

Taking a few steps closer to his bride, hands still tucked into his trousers, Rawley's warm caramel voice brought Lacy back to earth. "Well..." he asked.

Turning, she faced the man she loved. "The house..." her voice choked with emotion. Lacy cleared her throat, "Um...the one you were working in...that night I paid...a visit to?" Her eyes scanned Rawley's smiling face.

Moving closer still, hands came out of the pockets and circled Lacy's waist. "Yep," he grinned.

Throwing her shyness, and her cares of what folks would think, into the wind, Lacy flew into his arms.

Picking her up, Rawley swung her around. His warm laughter music to her ears, two small freckled palms held his chiseled face in her hands. Rawley gazed into those burnt coffee eyes he loved. Her eyes spoke volumes to him, telling him how much she loved him. Lacy's mouth lowered, tasting her husband.

After returning her kiss, Rawley leaned back a tad, and whispered in her ear. "Think, it's about time we got out of here, Sunshine?"

Eagerly, Lacy nodded.

Swinging his redhead into his arms, Rawley made a beeline for the bat-wing doors.

A voice bellowed, slowing Rawley's steps. "And, chust where ye plan on taking tha wee lass, now, eh...laddie?" The twinkling green eyes of Maddie watched as Rawley turned, his arms full with his bride.

A big grin plastered the lawman's face as he replied, "I'm taking my wife home and then I'm going to make mad, passionate love to her." Lacy's face turned cinnamon red. She clapped a hand over his mouth. Blue eyes smiled over the hand.

Wolf whistles and cat calls greeted his statement, boots thumping the floorboards once again.

"Aww...git along wit ye then," Maddie teased, her arm

giving them a dismissive wave.

Abruptly, the marshal's gaze turned threatening as it traveled across the crowd in the saloon. His voice carried a warning, "I don't want any of you getting any bright ideas of giving us a shivaree, either." Then he added, as blue eyes took on the look of a polished rifle barrel, "I mean it, too." Rawley noticed the looks that passed from one to the other in the room. Addressing the barkeep, he threatened, "I mean it, Mike."

Eyes growing round in a square face, Mike thumbed at his chest, saying, "Who...me?"

"I warned you, Mike." With those words, Rawley turned, and still carrying his bride, pushed through the batwing doors.

After watching the bride and groom leave, all eyes swiveled toward the barkeep. They waited.

Resting his burly arms on his bar, Mike threw a look at the crowd. He announced, "Well...since our marshal kinda stomped on that idea and squished that sucker flat. Guess...we could still follow them to their new home and wish them well." His eyes traveled across the room. "Don't cha think?"

His answer was the sound of chairs scraping back and the crowd beginning to move toward the swinging doors. Folks funneled out and down the steps. Whistles and cheers followed the couple as Rawley drove Fancy toward the home he and Lacy would share together. He grinned broadly at his bride, *finally*, he thought. Lacy's cute dimples exploded in a wide smile as she gazed over her shoulder at the town following them.

Reining Fancy to a stop, Rawley hopped out of the buggy. He sprinted to Lacy's side. Plucking her out of the rig, he swung her around, and firmly planted a kiss on her lips. Her bubbling laughter remained music to his ears after not hearing it for so long. Sitting her down, and holding her hand, they both looked at their new home. Rawley heard Lacy give a happy sigh. He smiled.

The sign by the front gate said: *Marshal Rawley Lovett*

and Deputy Lacy Lovett. Rawley pushed open the gate on the picket fence. They entered the little yard together and walked up the steps. Love shown from burnt coffee eyes as Lacy said quietly. "I'm home, Rawley. I'm finally home."

A finger reached out, caressing a million freckles, and then traced her jawline. "I know, Sunshine...I know," Rawley said. His head bent, as lips tenderly brushed hers.

Swinging his bride into his arms, he turned and faced the crowd. Lacy threw a wave.

"I'm warning you, Mike. You just leave us be." Rawley threatened the barkeep one last time.

Mike replied. "Who...us? Naw...we wouldn't think of it," he said, his toothy grin spreading across a square face.

"See that you don't," Rawley threw out, and with that, he carried Lacy over the threshold, closing the door with his foot.

Cheers, whistles and clapping echoed loudly outside. Inside, a groom and his bride became busy...very busy...very busy, indeed.

CHAPTER FIFTY TWO

Spring 1880

Resting on the three-pronged fork she was using to mix the soil with manure and old hay in front of the house. Lacy was determined to have as beautiful of flower gardens as Liv did. She had instructed Lacy on how to turn the earth and haul old hay mixed with manure from the pile out back of Luke's stable, turning so-so dirt into rich soil. Enlisting Billy and Cotton's help, Lacy was now ready to begin planting the bulbs from Liv and seeds she'd bought at Ezra's store.

Letting go of the three-pronged fork, it thumped the ground, and she dropped to her knees. Lacy's hand reached out pulling the small wooden box, filled with bulbs and seed packets, toward her. Plucking that first bulb out, Lacy held it tenderly in her hand. Re-arranging her legs, she sat cross-legged staring at the little bulb she held. Her head rose, and burnt coffee eyes took in the vista that seemed to hang in the warm spring air. The mountains in the distance still had their white caps on. *Angel Dust* her mama had called the snows. Lacy smiled at the memory. Trees had begun pushing new growth leaves out in the lower elevations, creating a lime green cast to the picture, mixing with the darker greens of spruce and pine.

Pulling her knees up, she rested her chin on them as she reflected on the past year and a half. She continued to marvel at the fact that she was married and madly in love with her husband. Somehow, that crazy love had wrapped itself around her heart, taking root, continuing to grow daily. Lacy savored the glow of a love she never thought she would get to experience.

Or that she and Rawley would get the chance to raise those two boys as their own. Or that she would be planting flowers in front of their home during springtime instead of chasing fugitives across the territories for bounty. Again, something she thought would never happen.

Sighing happily, Lacy hoped her flower garden would do the same as her heart, take root and grow. She began planting the bulbs and seed to make her own spectacular flower garden.

*   *   *

Lacy's rolling stomach woke her. She barely made it out the kitchen door before everything came up. Fixing breakfast for her men, as Lacy called them now, she emptied her stomach several more times.

The last time, Rawley followed her. "You okay, Sunshine?"

Going back in, rinsing her mouth out, and then washing her face at the sink. Lacy replied, "Must be a bug or something."

Rawley felt her forehead. "You don't have a fever. Why don't you go and lay back down, I'll finish up here," he offered.

Casting a grateful glance at Rawley, she went and curled up on the bed, and was out like a light.

Sending the boys off to school, Rawley checked on Lacy before he went to the office. Covering her up, she seemed awfully pale to him, millions of freckles the only color. Maybe he'd get Doc to check on her, later. Closing the door softly to their bedroom, Rawley headed for the marshal's office.

That night, dinner at Liv's was interrupted several times, by Lacy jumping up and running out the back door.

Liv cocked an eyebrow at Doc.

He gave his usual grumpy reply, "Humph." And then he said, "Son, bring Lacy by my office tomorrow, let me check her out."

Rawley nodded, concern showing as he watched Lacy approach the table once again.

Olivia smiled as she went back to get the pie, a sing-song cadence began repeating itself in her mind. *We've got a baby on the way.*

* * *

Pacing to and fro in Doc's office, Rawley thought, *What the hell was taking them so long!*

Doc finally emerged, and not saying a word, he walked over to the washbowl. Water from the pitcher splashed into it. Doc began washing his hands.

Exasperated at Doc's lack of verbal communication, Rawley followed. Turning, the crusty doctor began drying his hands, still not saying a word. The marshal, stood only inches from him, blue eyes trying to bore holes through his skin.

Not receiving any word from Doc, Rawley bent his face closer, making the crusty old coot rear back. "Well?" He demanded. "Is she gonna be all right?"

"Nothing seven months won't cure," came Doc's flippant reply.

"What the hell is that supposed to mean?" Rawley questioned. "She's not gonna die on me, is she? What's she got, Doc?"

Lacy came out, tucking the shirt back into her britches. She kept flicking eyes from one man to the other.

Doc glanced Lacy's way. He said, "You're gonna be a daddy is all, Rawley."

Surprise floated across chiseled features, Rawley straightened. "A da…you mean Lacy's gonna have a baby?"

"No. You two are gonna have a baby."

Rawley glanced at Lacy.

She shrugged her shoulders.

Still stunned, something stupid came out of Rawley's mouth, "But...how?"

Doc rolled his eyes. "Rawley...I swear. Sometimes I don't know 'bout you. If you hain't figured it out by now, you never will." Doc held two fingers up, so close to the tall lawman's eyes, they almost crossed. "It takes two to make a baby, or had you forgotten all that? Or was you two jus' having too much fun under the covers to realize it was bound to turn into a baby, one of these days." Doc grumpily replied, shaking his head.

A tan face turned beet red, making blue eyes, even bluer.

Doc gave his usual harrumph.

Walking over to his medicine cabinet, Doc took a bottle off the shelf and handed it to Lacy. "Young lady, I want you to take some of this tonic, it will help settle your stomach, the sickness will pass in a few more weeks. Now you go home and get some rest."

Turning, Doc's finger pointed and waggled at the big lawman. He threatened, "And you let her rest, you understand me, son?"

Starring at the finger, Rawley's face abruptly broke into a wide grin. "Yes...sir!" He said, saluting the crusty old coot.

Shaking his head, Doc's face smiled, too.

CHAPTER FIFTY THREE

January 1881

Glancing out the kitchen window, a deep azure blue painted the cloudless sky. Dried stalks, left over from her flower garden, peeked through the wind driven snow they'd had a week ago. Lacy smiled, this past Christmas had been the best she'd ever experienced. Rawley had surprised her with a cradle, he and Luke had made. She sighed happily; the baby would be here in another couple of weeks. She and Rawley had called a truce, *sorta,* on picking out names, as neither liked the others choices.

A pain gripped her swollen tummy, scaring her. Lacy doubled over, gripping the sink counter. Straightening and breathing deeply, once the wave had passed, she slowly made her way to the table. Gripping the back of the chair and the edge of the table, she eased herself down. Her mind tumbling, Lacy tried to gather her thoughts on what she was supposed to do now.

Rawley came in the kitchen, rolling his shirt sleeves up. Taking one look at Lacy's surprised and scared face, he squatted next to her. "What is it, Sunshine?"

Her husky voice squeaked. "I don't know...I had this awful pain..." Her body became ridged as another wave gripped her body. Fingers clawed the edge of the table and the chair seat, making her knuckles turn white. "Oww..." she whispered.

"Black brows furrowed over blue eyes. "Sunshine...is it time?"

"I don't know...I think so," Lacy said. Her hand reached out latching onto his thick forearm, as her body dove into another spasm of pain. Her fingers became talons digging, pinching into his arm. When that one had passed, she relaxed her grip, saying, "Please, hurry."

His long frame stood upright. Rawley's hand reached out and lovingly caressed copper curls. "I'll be back as soon as I can. I'll stop by Liv's and send her over...okay?"

Lacy nodded, breathing deeply. "Rawley?" She said abruptly, stopping him in his tracks. "I'm scared."

Spinning on his toes, Rawley came back to the redheaded freckled girl that was now his beautiful wife about to birth their child. "I know honey, so am I," he said. His hand cupped her chin, and watched as those burnt coffee pools filled with moisture. "But, Doc knows what to do," he said, lips brushing hers.

* * *

"It'll still be awhile yet, son, if you've got business to take care of," Doc offered up. "Liv's making fresh coffee, we may need it."

Lacy heard that. Reaching out, she grabbed her husband's shirt in a death grip. She growled at the two men, "He's not leaving...owww," she wailed, as another pain twisted her gut, moving around to her back, lasting longer than the others, leaving her breathless.

Blinking rapidly as the pain finally subsided. Lacy still gripped her husband's shirt, pulling him closer to her. She sent an evil black look first at her husband then at Doc.

"He's not leaving," she squeaked. "You hear me?" Her voice regaining full volume, Lacy crossly yelled at the two men. "He got me this way! He's gonna watch me suff....owww..." her words cut off in mid-yell by another pain, this time stronger than the last.

Hearing commotion coming from the bedroom, Liv picked up the tray with cups of coffee and a glass of cold water for Lacy. She headed toward the bedroom.

Lacy gritted through another pain. "He's gonna see what I'm going through, so this big moose will appreciate me more." Freckled face beet-red, Lacy gave her husband the nastiest look she could muster at the moment. Panting the words out, she said, "You...hear...me Rawley Lovett? You...ain't cutting and...and running!"

Standing in the doorway, holding the tray, grey eyes bounced across the two men's faces that tried so hard not to burst out laughing, and one beet-red freckled face full of venom aimed at Rawley. Liv bit down on her bottom lip, corralling her own smile. But, that didn't hide the gleam of laughter within twinkling eyes.

Slowly untangling his wife's iron grip from his shirt, Rawley gave Doc and Liv a resigned grin. Rawley sighed noisily. Pulling a chair closer to Lacy's bedside, he sat to begin the long wait. He gratefully, accepting the cup of coffee, Liv handed him.

*   *   *

Gently wrapping the tiny bundle in her new blanket, Liv handed their daughter to Lacy and Rawley. Stepping back, she gazed at the couple, who had become like a son and daughter to her, also. Now, they held their own special blue ribbon prize. Liv glanced at Doc, standing at the foot of the bed, and she smiled. Picking up his bag, Doc motioned to Liv. Holding open the door for her, they walked into the living room. Doc softly closed the door behind him and gingerly collapsed in the winged backed chair, dropping the bag to the floor by the rock fireplace.

Placing a hand lightly on his shoulder, Liv said, "I'm going back to the house. Tell Rawley I'll gather the boys after school and they can stay at my place for a few days."

Squeezing the hand on his shoulder, Doc just gave a tired nod. She brushed a kiss across the grey stubble gracing his cheek. He settled deeper into the chair. As Liv threw the heavy cloak over her shoulders opening and closing the door softly, Doc sighed.

* * *

Brushing damp copper curls from a freckled face, Rawley smiled, asking softly as he gazed at his two redheads. "Well...Sunshine, have you picked a name yet, for our daughter?"

Tired, dark eyes settled on blue ones. Lacy witnessed the love shining there. "I'd like to name her after mama," she answered. "Marie."

Thinking about that for a few moments, Rawley then offered up, "How 'bout, we name her, Hanah, after Cotton's sister and Marie after your mama. Hanah Marie Lovett," he said.

Her lips moved silently, trying out the name, then Lacy spoke them out loud. "Hanah Marie Lovett." She smiled and nodded in agreement.

Rawley kissed her deeply.

* * *

Still slumping in the winged back chair, Doc knew he needed to do something about the growing love he felt for Liv, before she gave up on him and shooed him out of her life for good. But if he asked her to marry him, it would mean he'd have to be truthful and tell her about his past. That he is a wanted man back east, running from the law for murder. Doc had covered his tracks well twenty-five years ago, but one of these days it was bound to catch up with him, and he didn't want Liv being in the cross-hairs of what might happen.

When Rawley opened the door, it startled Doc, pulling him out of the past and into the present. He jumped. The lawman closed the door softly.

"Well...?" Doc asked.

"The baby is beginning to nurse and Lacy's drifting off."

Doc harrumphed.

Rawley led the way into the kitchen. Doc rose stiffly and followed him. Reaching for two glasses in the cabinet, he set them on the counter. Walking back to the sideboard in the dining area, Rawley picked up a decanter and walked back into the kitchen where Doc waited. Generous amounts of amber liquid splashed into the glasses. He handed one to the crusty old coot.

Taking a sip, and swallowing, Doc said, "Looks like ya got another redhead, son."

Rawley just gave a tired nod.

"Wouldn't surprise me none, if she turns out to be another firebrand, with lots of freckles and venom, just like her mama."

Focusing tired eyes on the crusty bachelor, Rawley said, "Aww...c' mon, Doc. Don't say that...I can barely handle the adult version, as it is."

Doc chuckled.

Rawley grinned.

Two glasses clinked in mid-air.

Juliette Douglas and Bearhead Publishing thank you for reading *Freckled Venom: Copperhead Strikes*, Juliette Douglas' second great western novel. Now that Juliette Douglas has continued to make her characters stay your best friends, we invite you to be on the lookout for the third book to this great series: *Freckled Venom: Skeletons.*

Need a teaser for this fantastic read? Okay, we aim ta please:

Big Joe Kannon had his plan in place now. His boys had become pretty restless because of the long wait. But, he'd kept them busy gathering supplies and a wagon to haul their cargo. A wagon would slow their progress down, some, but he thought they'd make it across the border alright. He'd had his boys cut limbs and tie them to the back of the wagon. The brush would drag along the ground erasing the wheel tracks as they moved. The schoolhouse was out of town a ways, setting on a little knoll, with trees and brushy ground cover behind it. Perfect, as long as one of his boys didn't fire off a round. Kannon had warned his boys numerous times, no gun play.

This was gonna be his biggest payout, yet. Taking all the kids from the schoolhouse. It'd be a handful, but they had guns and rope and bandanas to shove in the kids' mouths. *It was payback time.*

Kannon ground out in his gravelly voice, "Time to move...boys. Git them mules hitched ta the wagon and saddle up," he said. "We's gonna capture us a passel of kids."

* * *

Giggling and laughing at their freedom, Ben and Hanah tore through the underbrush on their way to the river to spend the afternoon skipping stones across the rippling, sun-drenched waters.

An arm suddenly caught Hanah around her waist as a hand clapped over her mouth, stifling her surprise. Glancing around, she saw the same thing had happened to Ben. He struggled against the arms holding him in the air. Hanah did, too. She heard a gruff voice say, "Back to tha schoolhouse boys...we gotta collect the rest of them kids."

* * *

Beth Shemwell's toe tapped impatiently against the planked flooring as she glared across the faces of her students. Ruler slapping angrily against her hand, Beth sent a frosty look toward Cotton. "Where's your sister, Howard?" She asked.

Not flinching a lick, Cotton returned her frosty look. No one except Miz Shemwell called him Howard. He hated that and was beginning to hate her, too. Miz Shemwell had turned going to school from fun into sheer living hell. And he hated her for that, because he liked school. He gave a shrug for his answer.

Beth sighed inwardly. She'd had it with Hanah Marie Lovett. She remained the culprit behind Ben's rapscallion ways. Turning her son from a nice sweet boy into a hoodlum. Today, was the last straw. Tomorrow, she'd pay a visit to Adam Brinkhoff, the lawyer in town, and file for divorce. She would resign this position, take her son and move back to civilization. But, first, before she did all that, Beth would give Rawley and Lacy Lovett a piece of her mind.

Refocusing on her students, Beth opened her mouth to say something, when the back door of the schoolhouse shattered, tearing itself off the frame and settling with a soft whump against the floor. Six woolly mammoths entered, pistols drawn, holding a bead on her and her students. Girls screamed, trying to get out the front door. A tall lanky, stinky, lecherous man, with a sickening smile, quickly blocked this exit, his pistol aimed at them. The girls scrambled to the center of the room, still screaming.

"I want quiet," a gravelly voice bellowed. He pointed his pistol at the girls. "I mean it," he said. Abruptly, the screams ended, but it didn't cut out the soft whimpering sounds.

Beth tried to say something, but the words stuck in her throat, cutting off her air supply.

Cotton's eyes narrowed. He remembered overhearing a conversation between his mom and dad about Big Joe Kannon and the reason his dad thought they were in town. Cotton hadn't liked what he'd heard, then; he liked it even less now. His eyes flicked toward Chad and Thad. The three of them were the oldest in the school, Dobie Litchfield was next in age at twelve. It would be up to them to do something about their current situation. He was about to gain their attention when he heard boards crack. His head swiveled toward the sound. Two more men had walked through the fractured doorway, one holding a squirming Hanah and the other, Ben. Cotton's lips turned into a hard thin line, marking his otherwise pleasant heart-shaped face.

The men suddenly dropped the two kids. They landed with a thump, arms and legs tangling with each other. After a few moments of struggle, Hanah and Ben were able to pick their limbs out of each other's way. Scrambling up, they both ran to Cotton. He wrapped protective arms around them.

Beth's mouth dropped when her son ran past her to the safety of Howard's arms. That made her angry. Reaching behind her, she picked the pointer stick out of the chalk tray under the blackboard. Beth aimed it at the man closest to her. *Thwack!* It cracked against his cheek leaving a welt. Big Joe whirled, facing the schoolmarm. "That wuss the wrong thang ta do...sister," his gravelly voice told her. His pistol waggled at her gut.

Eyes wide, they flicked from the muzzle back to the man's angry face. Beth backed up, saying disgustedly, "You're nothing but a pack of wild animals."

"You sit...sister," Big Joe said. "And not a peep outta

ya...or I'll kill ya where ya stand." Beth obeyed, plopping into her chair.

Kannon looked around. "Wheat...you and Jake tie 'er up...and gag 'er good."

His eyes gazed over the frightened and still whimpering girls, the boys standing silently glaring at him. Absentmindedly, he began totaling up the money he'd make off of this haul. Fifty to a hundred per kid, except that bright red-head with the freckles standing next to the white-haired boy. Now, that one, Kannon figured, he could get at least two hundred for her.

They needed to get out of there. Waggling his weapon at the kids, his gravelly voice ordered, "Ya'll kids line up, now. Boys, git that rope and tie 'em together in a string."

The whimpers grew louder as Kannon's men began shoving the girls into a line, then the boys. Cotton's eyes caught Thad, Chad and Dobie's. He nodded.

Bedlam ensued. Thad and Chad jumped over the desks, toppling them in the process. Arms stretched, they attacked the men closest to them. Dropping them to their knees, the string of girls went down with them, ending in a tangle of rope, legs and arms. The girls screamed again. More desks overturned, clattering to the floor. Boots scuffled against the wood, umphs and grunts mingled with the swirling stench of week old elk carcasses in the heat of summer. Dobie and Cotton dove after the tall, lanky one, knocking his feet out from under him. He yelled as they both pounced on him, their fists clenched, landing blows. As he stayed hunkered down beside a desk, brown eyes wild with fear, Ben Hudson didn't know what to do. Ned Buntline never said anything about stuff like this.

Kannon pushed and stepped over the squirming bodies in the middle of the aisle. His muzzle barrel found the sides of Thad and Chad's heads, rendering them unconscious. They slumped into a pile. That same barrel found the side of Cotton's and Dobie's heads. They, too landed in a pile, unconscious.

Hanah became a miniature red tornado, yelling, "You don't hurt my brother!" She plowed and pushed through the bodies in the aisle. Scrabbling up the side of Big Joe Kannon, her teeth latched on to his ear. Fingers like talons, clawed into his ratty coat. She hung on.

"Ooowwwweee...git 'er offen me!" Kannon yelled. Whirling, he tried to shake off the little she-devil. Lenny jumped up. His pistol barrel landed across the top of Hanah's head. She slid unconscious to the floor with a thump.

Kannon's hand gingerly touched his ear. It was throbbing and hurt like hell. Pulling his hand away, he found it blood drenched. Looking down at the little firebrand, he realized he'd seen squirrels scramble into trees, but he'd never had a human crawl up him like this kid did, latching onto his ear like a steel trap. He heaved in air. The situation was not going according to his plan. He didn't expect the kids to fight back. He hauled in more air.

Beth sat tied securely to her chair, a stinky rag stuffed into her mouth. Bewilderment and fear, then anger, kept flicking across brown eyes. She couldn't believe what was transpiring in her classroom. *Animals...*she thought. *Dirty, rotten animals, even the children.* This escapade further reaffirmed her belief that the sooner she took her son, and went back to where people were civilized, the better off they would be.

Kannon heaved in more air. "Awright...boys," he began. "We got them troublemakers under control. Tie 'em up and start herding them to the wagon."

Whimpers mingled with the quiet sound of boots and high-top shoes scuffling and rising. Weapons prodded the children and they funneled out the back door toward the brush. Two of his men carried the four unconscious kids. Kannon, the last one out the door, cut a look at the schoolmarm, trussed up like a hog. Brushing dirt-crusted fingers across a hat as ratty as the buffalo hide he wore, he said, "Have a good day, m'am."

Beth Shemwell burst into tears.

So does Big Joe Kannon make off with the children of White River? Will he have his hands full with Hanah Marie Lovett?

The only way to find out the answer to these questions, and many more, is to continue reading about the characters you've come to know and love in this book. Check the Bearhead Publishing website often, www.bearheadpublishing.com for updates on when *Freckled Venom: Skeltons* will be released. Or let us know if you'd like to pre-order one of the first 100 numbered copies. We'll be happy to oblige!

CPSIA information can be obtained at www.ICGtesting.com
Printed in the USA
LVOW06s0141261113

362783LV00001B/3/P